ANGRY DRAGON

ANGRY DRAGON

The third of three fact-based police procedural
novels of tremulous political intrigue
set in present day
Hong Kong
and
the People's Republic of China.

George H. Stollwerck

To order additional copies of this book, contact:
Xlibris Corporation
1-888-795-4274
www.Xlibris.com
Orders@Xlibris.com
36802

SUGGESTED LIBRARY CROSS REFERENCING

[1. People's Republic of China—Fiction. 2. Hong Kong—Fiction. 3. Hong Kong Special Administrative Region—Fiction. 4. Macau Special Administrative Region—Fiction. 5. Hong Kong Police—Fiction. 6. People's Liberation Army—Fiction. 7. Forensic Pathologist—Fact. 8. 2008 Olympic Summer Games—Fact. 9. Military weaponry—Fiction. 10. Forensic Science—Fact. 11. PRC President Hu Jintao—Fact. 12. Mystery and Detective stories—Fiction. 13. Federal Bureau of Investigation—Fiction. 14. Pacific Rim Terrorism—Fact. 15. Interpol—Fiction.] Title.

OTHER PUBLISHED WORKS BY THE AUTHOR

FICTION NOVELS

Angry Dragon—*2007*
Project 119—*2006*
Hongse Spider—*2005*
The Battlefields of Pax Americana*!*—*2004*
Terrorism: America's Incurable Disease*!*—*2003*
The Vanishing Hero*!*—*2002*
Nine lives Minus One*!*—*2001*

TRAVELOGUES OF ASIA—PUBLISHED IN THE PRINT MEDIA

Hong Kong
China
Macau
Singapore
Malaysia
Bangkok
Seoul, South Korea

MY APPRECIATION:

I would like to express my appreciation to the Federal Bureau of Investigation, Interpol, and the Hong Kong Police department whose websites and public information officers were most helpful in the writing of this book.

Consultants
Optical Systems
Stuart B. Adams, O.D.

World Historian
Captain Russell Juckett, U.S. Army (Ret)

Computer Technology
Heather McCormick, Attorney-At-Law

Business Advisor
Ms. Eleanor Poppe

Medical Consultant
Thomas J. Powers, M.D.

CHINESE PROPER NAMES

Traditional Chinese Sequence
Family name comes first,
followed by the given name.
(I.E: Hung David)

Westernized Sequence
Given name come first,
followed by the family name.
(I.E: David Hung)

It is not unusual for
an individual who wishes to westernize
his or her proper name, to select
a nom de guerre which
the western tongue finds easier
to pronounce.
(I.E.)
Traditional name: Leung Kwok-hung.
Westernized name: Harry Ling

SPELLING OF CHINESE NAMES

*C*hinese *citizens from the northern part of the People's Republic of China, especially those involved in the upper-levels of the communist party and government, generally speak Mandarin Chinese, either as a native language or as an acquired second language. On the other hand, most Chinese immigrants, legal and illegal, that find their way to Hong Kong are almost always from the southern part of China, where Cantonese, among other dialects, is spoken, written and read.*

The pinyin system introduced in 1979 of converting Chinese to a system westerners are more familiar with, has been used throughout this book for personal and geographical names, as well for people, places and things in the People's Republic of China.

Despite the fact that the Wade-Giles system is used in Taiwan, Pinyin is considered by the Academic community to be the superior system. Pinyin definitely is the easier to learn, as it is pronounced more or less how it appears in print. This is not to say that English speakers who are untrained in other languages will not find that Pinyin has its occasional deviations:

Pinyin	English	Example	Pronunciation
C	TS	CANG	TSANG
Q	CH'	QIAO	CH'IAO
X	SS	XI	SHE
Z	DZ	ZANG	DZANG
ZH	DJ	ZHONG	DJONG

In English words such as 'vanity,' the 'i' is often pronounced.

For continuity I have elected to use the literal transliteration of Hong Kong names in the context of the South Chinese Cantonese dialect.

Transliteration example:

Hong Kong; A Special Administrative Region of the People's Republic of China (PRC) located to the east of the Pearl River (Chu Chiang) estuary on the south coast of China. Wade-Giles: t'e-pieh hsing-cheng-ch'ǔ; Pinyin: tebie xingshengqu).

TIME ZONES

*W*riters *of any genre, whose narrative covers both Asia and the United States, must eventually tackle the ten-thousand-pound 'gorilla' of time continuity.*

The unavoidable fact is that Hong Kong, Beijing, and Singapore are all located in Singapore's SST time zone, or as designated in this novel, the Hong Kong (HKT) time zone while most novels by other writers sold in the United States, if they address the matter at all, generally use EST or the Eastern Standard Time zone.

The reality is that New York City is located in the EST time zone, twelve (-12) hours behind Hong Kong. That means that if it is 7:00 p.m. local time on Sunday, the 6th of February 2006 in New York City (EST), it will already be 7:00 a.m. HKT time on Tuesday, the 7th of February 2006, in Hong Kong. The February 6, 2006 date is the constant established by UTC or GMT time, which at the times showed above, would actually be MIDNIGHT.

Hong Kong does not observe daylight savings time. Time differences with some other major cities include: Chicago—13 hours; London—7 hours (minus 8 during DST); Los Angeles—15 hours; and Sydney + 2 hours.

As the majority of this book's scenes occur in Asia, I have elected to default to the day/date continuity of Hong Kong referred herein as 'HKT' so it will be unnecessary for the reader to keep a calendar in hand to calculate the time difference between Hong Kong, Beijing and New York City.

Enjoy the read. Thanks again for purchasing another one of my books.

George H. Stollwerck

BACK STORY

*W*ith *the publishing of each new novel, our office receives dozens of e-mails from readers, suggesting how our books could be made more interesting to the reader.*

One of the most frequent suggestions that we receive is that we provide a back story or backgrounder in future books that will give the reader a deeper insight into what Hong Kong, the most vibrant and interesting city in the world, is really like beneath the surface, where competing writers chose not to go, due to their lack of personal boots-on-the-ground knowledge. Or in the belief that readers of international police procedurals have little interest in Hong Kong's infrastructure and the trial and realities of life its citizens must deal with on a day-to-day basis.

We thank readers who have taken the time and effort to bring this suggestion to our attention. We think it is an excellent idea, and thus have incorporated it in Angry Dragon, my seventh novel; my third featuring former NYPD homicide detective Augustus Fox, who continues his thinking man's crime fighting against the almost overwhelming dynamics of Hong Kong, and its administrator, the People's Republic of China.

At the back of this book you will find backgrounders on the Hong Kong Police Department, Hong Kong's triads and tongs, and basic forensic science. Enjoy.

CAST OF CHARACTERS

People's Republic of China—the PRC
Hu Jintao: PRC President.
Wen Ziabao: PRC Premier.

Hong Kong—Special Administrative Region
David 'Davis' Tsang: HKSAR Chief Executive.
Rafael Hui: Chief Secretary.
Henry Tang: Financial Secretary
Wong Yan-long: Secretary for Justice.

Hong Kong Police Force
Lee Ming Kwai: Commissioner of Police.
Tang King Shing: Deputy Commissioner—Operations
Fung Siu Yuen (Gordon) Deputy Commissioner—Management
John Russell: Assistant Chief of HKP (Personnel.)
Edward Augustus Fox: Chief Inspector (Crimes Against Persons.)
Mimi Yin: Inspector (Street Crimes.)
Ho Pham: Inspector (Homicide.)
Chen Ko: Inspector (Counter-Terrorism and Hijacking.)
Zhou Ming: Bodyguard and driver for Chief Inspector Fox.
Elizabeth Stewart: Fox's Administrative Assistant.
Xueguang Laoxi: Inspector, HKP Crime Lab Manager.
Du Ming: HKP Homicide Squad Lieutenant.
David Kan: HKP Homicide Detective.
Lu Dong, M.D.: HKP Assistant Medical Examiner.
Elizabeth Guan, M.D.: HKP Assistant Medical Examiner.
Dang Lao, M.D.: HKP Assistant Medical Examiner.

Betty Fang, HKP Assistant to the Medical Examiner.
Guan Xueguang, Constable Recruit.
Johnny Yang, Traffic Constable.
Chow Yung Su, Traffic Constable.
Lau Lai, Tourist police Constable.

Political Dissident

Leung 'Long Hair' Kwok-hung: Leader of Dissident Faction.

Others

Alicia Ho, M.D.: Chief Inspector Fox's roommate.
Edward Pham: Mandarin Oriental Hotel, General Manager.
Jenny Woo, Mandarin Oriental Hotel, Guest Services Manager.
Chang 'Blue Eyes' Ching: 426 'Red Pole' Leader of the 14K triad.
Chung Shan: 415 'White Paper Fan' of the 14K triad.
Sinclair Leymon, Angry Dragon, Interpol Supervising case agent.
Hans Hapwanegg, Interpol field agent.
Gustav Hapwanegg, Interpol field agent.
David Chow, Senior FBI Legate, U.S. Consulate General, Hong Kong.

28 September 2007, Saturday, 12:45 a.m. (HKT)
The Boathouse Restaurant Bar
86-8 Stanley Main Street
Stanley—Hong Kong Island

The young woman had gone out tonight to be with friends who were attending a going-away party. The party had begun about ten that evening and was still going strong at an hour past midnight.

The Boathouse Bar is a legend along the Stanley strip, one of the fancier locales that tended to attract its fair share of expats and well-heeled recreational boaters fresh in off of the waters where they had been testing their meddle against the idiosyncrasies of the South China Sea.

Although the high season of the Boathouse is in June when the Dragon Boat Races are held; here in late September, those at the bar, eating fish and seafood in the dining area, or clumsily attempting to shake their inebriated derrières on the micro-sized dance floor, were spilling out of the front and rear doors onto Stanley's main street, an occurrence that soon would attract the attention of a cruising Hong Kong police car.

———

She admitted to herself that she was drunk. She knew she had a drinking problem but mostly blamed it upon her heritage. Everyone in her family drank, and not just socially either. Her biological mother had once exclaimed that the entire family was genetically programmed to end up as sots. So why fight it? she thought.

As the evening progressed she had been flitting from table to table, flirting up a storm with any single guy she met, or even married ones if the wifey dear or girlfriend was in the *loo*. She knew her height, coloring, accent, and ample bodice were extraordinarily attracting to men of any marital status, and her personal motto was 'Use it or lose it.'

She ended up sitting at a table with three young Asian guys she knew only by their first name and employer. The cocktails she had been tossing down all night, called a Number Ten Martini, Grey Goose Vodka from the freezer with a pimento-stuffed olive in a chilled glass, were progressively slipping her into that deep fugue state that in her case was always alcohol's end destination. She knew she needed to get out of the club, hail a cab, and get home to her apartment.

Even though she by nature had a very aggressive sexual appetite, the liquor seems to have made her numb, even down there. But perhaps just one more drink, she thought. Then I'll haul my inebriated ass out of here and go home.

She asks for one more drink. One of the young men stands up and works his way up to the four-deep bar to get it for her. Now that someone is getting her a drink, she returned her toes under the table to the crotch of the guy directly opposite her she'd been making a project for a good half hour.

But then the other two guys at the table declare they are all partied out. One of them calls to a passing waitress, "*Mei dan M'goi*," (bill, please), they split their hefty bar tab, and say "*Joy Gin*"(goodbye), explaining "We are going to get our American classic Camaro out of the club's parking lot and head up to the northern end of Hong Kong Island to call it a night."

Impulsively the woman decides to ask for a ride home. She explains she lives in an apartment in the Wan Chai district. "May I catch a ride with you since you are headed in the direction of the Wan Chai district, anyway?" She gave them her address.

The classic Camaro apparently belongs to the guy she has been romancing with her toes.

As she chugs down the drink that was just delivered to her, the three men exchange a knowing look between them before the driver tells her they will be glad to give her a lift home.

The valet fetches the tricked-out Camaro and is rewarded with a miserly tip for his trouble. They all pile in with the woman grabbing the shotgun position as they head north on Stanley Village Road. The road will morph into Carmel Road before they arrive at her place in the Wan Chai district.

Twenty minutes later the car and its four occupants pulls up on Triangle Street in the front of her five-story walk-up. No elevator, thank you, not for the bargain rent the landlord is charging her because of her self-espoused connections. The drive home has returned some of her party spirit so she decides to ask the three men up to her walk-up apartment for a cold beer before they continue on their way home. After some hesitance they agree, but say it can only be one, because they have to work a shift the following day, Sunday.

As with most all leased or rented Hong Kong living spaces, her apartment is small, less than six hundred square feet with a cubbyhole bathroom. However it is a little above average for a single occupant apartment in the expensive Wan Chai district. When they finish the long climb up to her apartment, the cold beer is welcome.

After handing out the cold Tsingtao beers, she goes into her cubbyhole bathroom, pulls the privacy curtain and removes all her party clothes. They are replaced with a pair of bright white short shorts and an aqua blue t-shirt she pulls over her head without bothering to put on a bra.

Returning to her company she flops herself down in a low worn-cloth couch. She is exhausted, sweaty, and her hair, normally hair sprayed in place, is stringy. She notices that her t-shirt is clinging to and highlighting her nipples which are engorged from the strenuous climb up the five flights of stairs. She smells herself. She stinks from the dance floor, the cigarette smoke, and the sweaty bodies of the men she has invited up to share a nightcap.

The woman is thirsty and chugs her beer. Then asks one of the men who are sitting on the floor leaning again the apartment walls, she has already forgotten their names, to get her another beer. The guy she had been diddling with her toes for the past hour or so responds while concealing a look of mild distain.

The humidity, primarily due to Hong Kong's ubiquitous evening *woo*, or fog, is so high that her window air conditioner has fallen far behind the temperature curve. They all just sit there sweating, sipping their brews.

She permits herself to close her eyes and enjoy the deadening of her senses brought on by all the alcohol she has consumed that night.

Suddenly, she finds herself pinned to the couch by her intended romantic interest of the evening. As he restrains her upper torso the others grab her flailing wrists and using plastic wire ties that have materialized from under their party shirts, tie her wrists together in back of her, and stuff a rough cotton handkerchief in her mouth.

She is a big girl and fights using her feet to kick anything in her range, butting with her head and attempts to scream through the gag.

The man she had been interested in urges her to relax, "You know you want this, no sense fighting and bruising yourself. You've been begging for it all night."

Collectively they manage to lift her and place her lengthwise on the couch. They tie one of her ankles to the front leg of the couch and the other; using her bra one of them has obtained from the bathroom, over the back to a rear couch leg.

One of them holds her head against the seat cushions while another tears her t-shirt and short shorts off then unzips his shorts and mounts her plunging himself deep into her moist vagina even though she is twisting and turning and bucking with her butt in an attempt to unseat her attacker.

Momentarily she does manage to dislodge her first assailant but when he gets up off the floor, he hits her with a closed fist twice in her jaw.

While she is groggy from the blows, he climbs back on to pump his hips a few times before he ejaculates. In her subconscious, she thinks, *"The asshole can't even maintain an erection."*

The other two follow their leader who now is masturbating as he watches his drinking buddies sexually assault her. It takes no longer for them to finish their business than it did him. After the last guy spews his sperm, gets off and zips up his pants, the first guy returns to stand over her body and pumps his come all over her *Xiong*, her breasts.

The first man, once he has finished wiping himself down with a piece of her clothing, rips the telephone cord out of the wall socket then slaps the woman's face to get her attention before he says, "Look, we haven't tied you up that securely. You'll be able to work yourself loose in a few minutes. We are leaving now, you bitch in heat. Everyone who saw us leave the Boathouse together will testify you were begging for this for the past hour, you and your educated toes, sweetheart."

"However, just to keep you honest, I'm going to wait just outside your door listening for any movement or sound. If I hear nothing after ten minutes, I'll leave and you can do what you want. But if you cause us any problem on this remember that we are untouchable. If you know the crowd at the Boathouse tonight, you'll realize that, darling."

"If I hear of you going to the cops then we'll all come back for another late night visit. And you won't be getting off as easy as you are tonight. Now if you understand, nod your head once." When she did, he repeated, "Remember what I have said. If you go to the cops, I'll know it immediately. You'll pay for it with those looks of yours that you employ so effectively."

The three men, giggling, waved at her as they left the apartment leaving her door wide open as they began the five-floor descent to their car.

The woman forces herself to count slowly to six hundred before she began to struggle with her bonds. When she finally gets loose, there is nothing she wants to do more than take a hot shower for as long as the hot water was available. However, she'd been raped once before when she was in college and knows the drill. She isn't hysterical and knows exactly what she has to do to get justice for this infamy.

She carefully pokes through her belongings until she comes up with a handful of new plastic Zip-lock sandwich bags, a couple of tampons, a dozen Q-tips and a small apple paring knife she briefly sanitizes by holding the flame of a disposable cigarette lighter under the blade until begins to get pink. The paring knife will be used to recover scrapings of the men's skin from under her fingernails.

Then she picks some dressings from a box of sterile ABD bandages she keeps in case she cuts herself while preparing her meals, and gathers the digital camera she'd bought to take close-ups of flowers last year.

Disciplining herself she spends the next twenty minutes using each of the materials she had collected in the method she observed during her previous rape investigation. Only after she finishes, bags everything, and writes her name, date, and time on each bag does she finally reward herself for her diligence and step into a hot shower.

When the limited hot water is gone she dries herself off and orders her brain to record the faces of her attackers before she falls into a deep sleep. She doesn't have to work tomorrow so she plans on sleeping all day long, getting up only to pee.

None of the guilty parties involved in the sexual assault knew that the vengeful monster of payback would soon be dropping to see each of them to collect its due.

1

02 October 2007, Wednesday, 9:00 a.m. (HKT)
Arsenal Street—Hong Kong Police Headquarters
Arsenal Street and Harcourt Road
Wan Chai District—Hong Kong Island

They came for Chung Shan a little before 9:00 a.m. on Wednesday morning.

———

Chung had spent a sleepless night attempting to sleep on a damp floor in a cell deep under what he assumed was the Hong Kong Police headquarters building. He had been literally snatched off Wan Street yesterday afternoon in the Mongkok District by a four-man Asian team dressed in camouflaged coveralls and no insignia. His faithful bodyguard had been repeatedly 'tased' into submission by one of the masked men until he was writhing like an epileptic and had lost control of his body functions. Initially Chung had felt pity then disgust for his faithful retainer who lay helplessly in the offal-filled gutter.

Chung tried to put two and two together and wondered if the assaulters were one of Hong Kong's infamous police SWAT teams. Infamous, because to the best of his knowledge, any criminal ending up in the hands of one of the dreaded special Weapons units had never been seen alive again. Yes, you could say Chung, his family name, was a bit nervous as to his future prospects. As hard as he had tried to maintain control over his body functions, he failed and pissed his pants in inescapable fear.

He had been roughly searched, then thrown in the backseat on the floor of the black Dáimler-Benz sedan its windows except for the windscreen heavily-tinted which effectively prevented anyone from viewing the vehicle's occupants.

His pockets had been emptied, his watch and jewelry taken from him, his arms manacled behind his back, hobbled with leg irons, blindfolded, gagged, and a six-foot-long dog collar and chain snapped around his neck. The heathens showed no regard for the fine US$2,000 suit and US$500 custom made alligators shoes he had put on that morning.

After getting over his surprise that he had been kidnapped off the streets of Mongkok, acknowledged triad territory, Chung Shan began to silently pray to his god that his captors were cops—not rival triad members.

The heavy car had pulled away from the curb, his kidnapping and the car's tire-spinning departure studiously being ignored by all the hundreds of passersby's on Wan Street at that hour. The two men in the back seat rested their feet none-too-gently on his back, kicking him if he made any movement.

No one said anything to him that would enlighten him as to the identity of the four large men in the car. His captors didn't talk among themselves, apparently following a prearranged plan.

———

The prisoner estimated it had taken a little more than a half hour for the car to arrive at its destination. Two of the car's doors, apparently the front pair, were opened and then slammed shut. The two thugs who had until that moment had their feet on the back of his expensive suit coat opened their doors and dragged him out of the car using the dog chain.

Chung was roughly yanked to his feet and given a push. Then led blindfolded into a building where he was forced to take baby steps due to the leg irons. He sensed being shoved into an elevator, which after the doors slid closed, seemed to abruptly fall uncontrollably causing him to lose his balance and fall to the floor. Wherever he was, he sensed he was somewhere deep underground.

He heard a guttural curse in Cantonese insulting his ancestors, then was yanked to his feet and propelled forward to where his blindfolded eyes couldn't tell him. But he then heard a noise that had the effect of calming him slightly. The clanging and slamming of heavy steel doors informed him that his assailants were likely cops.

He involuntarily let out a sigh and thanked his gods it wasn't a 426 Red Pole execution squad from one of the 14K's rivals. After all the cops had to follow some rules and regulations even though since the takeover of Hong Kong by the People's Republic of China in June of 1997, a criminal could expect fewer and fewer safeguards on his or her personal safety when in the police custody. The since-cast-out English had at least been civil in prisoner treatment assuming the prisoner didn't sass the jailers.

Chung was dragged blindfolded along a concrete floor, then permitted to regain his footing before he was yanked to a halt and spun around ninety degrees. He heard a heavy steel door being unlocked, which they passed through, and then it was relocked. There his handler had yanked on the dog chain stopping him in-place.

He was once again searched, and the manacles, blindfold and gag were removed, but the legs irons remained. He was fingerprinted, photographed, and the inside of his mouth swabbed with a cotton swab that one of his captors removed from capped glass vial, returning it there after obtaining the DNA sample.

Chung found himself being led further into the jail complex before being roughly shoved into stinking cell occupied currently by nothing but a shit bucket. The shove had thrown him to the floor. With a lot of self-control he forced himself not to yell out knowing any protest by him would cause him to lose face, and due to the hatred all honest cops had for triad members, could well bring physical harm to him.

He got to his feet and dusted himself off. But as he opened his mouth to ask for a lawyer, a couple of pieces of hardtack were thrown into the cell behind him and the heavy steel door was slammed shut with not even a fair-thee-well.

There was nowhere for Chung to sit so he was forced to assume a coolie squat sitting on the heels of his fancy shoes. No furniture, not even a bunk, no blanket. He made a brief assessment of his surroundings and noted that the moist, stinking cell was about six feet square, eight feet high with a single recessed light bulb in the ceiling. There were no windows except for the spy hole in the door that was currently shuttered. At least the shit bucket appeared to have been recently cleaned.

But of course this was Hong Kong. After the cell lights were extinguished the cockroaches and the rats would make their appearance. With his shod feet restrained he couldn't even do a very good job of defending himself against their eventual onslaught. He damn sure wasn't going to try to grab the visitors in his hands, the uncallused hands his mother told him one day would make him famous as a concert pianist.

A half-inch metal pipe protruded out of the concrete wall less than a quarter inch in diameter, about forty-two inches off the concrete floor. Water dripped from it before draining down onto the sloping concrete floor and into a rusty drain. Apparently that was to be his water supply. They had provided some rudimentary food if you could consider the hardtack that, so he assumed no one would be coming to collect him for interrogation that evening.

Chung forced himself to squat in a corner and pretend to munch on the hardtack promising himself that he would stay awake tonight. Considering his occupation this obviously wasn't the first time he had been locked up. But this was the first time he had been snatched off the street without due process and incarcerated in a police prison at a currently unknown location. Not to mention being denied a phone call to one of the highly paid lawyers the 14K triad kept on retainer. Not to mention he had effectively been put on a forced diet of bread-and-water.

Now that Chung had began to gather his senses he permitted himself to admit that he was astonished that the cops had dared to kidnap a high-ranking member of the 14K triad such as himself off a city street ignoring the unofficial established protocol that required going through one the triad's lawyers.

The protocol had been put in-place last year in 2006 when the *gweilo*, Chief Inspector of HPD—Augustus Fox, had targeted three of the gang's facilities for police raids. When the triad guards had resisted it had cost Chung the lives of a couple dozen of the expendable street soldiers.

The raids had been the police response when the 14K's 426 Red Pole at that time, Chang "Blue Eyes' Ching, had been so brazen as to kidnap, torture and eventually kill one of Chief Inspector Fox's people on the spur of the moment without any regard for the potential consequences.

There were over 350,000 14K members in Hong Kong currently. Such an insult to the 14K could have resulted in citywide blood bath and gang warfare. Something that neither the leadership of the 14K triad nor the puppet administration of what now was called the Hong Kong Special Administrative Region, under the control of the People's Republic of China, wanted.

Hong Kong is all about making money, be it legal or illegally. That is still what Hong Kong is all about even if the PRC had been in limited control over the former colony's day-to-day activities since June of 1997.

Fortunately the special administrative region's politicians were weak. Their future prosperity and support from Beijing depended on maintaining a continued favorable business climate in Hong Kong. But Hong Kong citizens were built out of stronger stuff; they wouldn't permit the cops to let the triads run unfettered.

After all, the PRC hated the triads more than the HKSAR administrators did. The gangs interfered with the orderly administration of the financial star in the PRC's financial crown, Hong Kong, which in part had been responsible for Beijing being selected as the site of the 2008 Summer Olympics.

———

Asian experts in the know were surprised that Beijing had gotten the nod as the site for the 2008 games. As soon as the award became final, city officials had promptly issued a shocking new policy despite 2006 being the Year of the Dog.

If you believe what the China's official Media was saying in 2006, almost 69,000 Beijing residents died of rabies in 2005. Not the type thing to inspire foreign tourists to visit.

Beijing had instituted the "One dog per household" policy, apparently thinking it modern chic that the name of the new rabies policy sounding like their relatively successful "One child per household" policy announced in the 1970's which has been credited with preventing the addition of 400 million citizens to the present day 1.3 billion population of China.

The "One dog per household" policy outright prohibited dogs that were defined as 'large' or were more than thirteen inches in height. Beijing citizens, under threat of arrest and fines for non-compliance, were forced to take any dogs they kept in the family household over the one that was allowed, plus any large dog, to city police stations who actually had been assigned weekly kill quotas.

The campaign was intended to stamp out rabies before the beginning of the 2008 Games. Rabies continues to be of epidemic proportions in China largely because unlike America, less than 3% of the nation's billions of dogs receive vaccinations against rabies.

This was cited by the politburo as one of the direct causes of the rabies epidemic in the PRC and the unusually high number of deaths in Beijing. Rabies almost always results in death to humans after they have developed symptoms.

Beijing had received the nod to host the Summer Games which had 'green lighted' the PRC politburo's Project 119. That politburo scheme had the targeted goal of sweeping the vast majority if not all of the event medals at the Summer Olympic Games.

———

To avoid any potential of bloodshed, and maintaining an attractive tourist environment, HKSAR politicians agreed that under most circumstances the Hong Kong police would notify the triad's designated lawyer before serving an arrest warrant on any of the 14K's high-ranking members. The low-rank soldiers were fair game, no advance phone call required. *That protocol has worked effectively for the past ten months*, Chung thought, *at least until now.*

But something obviously had changed. Or some HPD cowboy had either not gotten the word or had chosen to ignore the protocol. There was no other reason Chung figured that could account for his being humiliated and locked down in this filthy gaol.

Unless, he mentally corrected himself, unless someone had found out about his ambitious plans and feelers he had put out to al-Qaeda to form an alliance with the 14K. An alliance that would further both their agenda's during the 2008 Summer Games in Beijing.

Chung shuttered with the thought that his contact might have been discovered.

There is nothing that the People's Republic of China, who were Hong Kong's masters, hated more than triads, criminals in general, and terrorists. At least terrorist groups that the PRC hadn't sponsored *themselves.*

The 14K is the most powerful of all the world's triads. Nearly all of its power and wealth comes from its being the king pin of the world's drug trade, a lofty position bought with the blood of literally thousands of the 14K's soldiers. The 14K controls production, marketing, and shipping of the heroin out of Southeast Asia to drug markets in Europe and North America. The 14K also controls drug markets throughout Asia.

This included their control of the Hong Kong fishing fleet that regularly rendezvous with Thai ships a hundred miles out in the South China Sea to trans-load hundredweights of heroin, cocaine, crack, morphine, date rape drugs, all in bulk.

Through an alliance forged with the Italian Mafia the 14K triad had established itself as major power broker in all illicit drug sales in the organized crime drug trade. The American Drug Enforcement Agency, supported by its own statistics, admits that the 14K is the largest supplier of heroin, a full eighty percentile, in New York City.

The police were powerless to stop the 14K in their control of the worldwide drug trade. Decriminalizing heroin might injure the triad's back but the gang's interests are so diverse today, experts have little doubt that the criminal core of the triad would survive.

Of course all this ruminating, thought Chung, didn't answer the question why Mrs. Chung's favorite son Shan ended up here today?

It was then that the single ceiling light in the cell had been extinguished. Shortly thereafter the screeching and scurrying sounds of the gaol's long-time residents began.

———

It had been a long night for Chung. He had drifted off to sleep numerous times only to be jarred back to consciousness when some creature or his imagination brushed against one of his custom-tailored pant legs like his father's old cat had done with his tail so many times when he had been a toddler in China. Except the cat had just wanted attention. In his imagination, tonight's visitors wanted fresh meat—his meat.

Chung was overjoyed when morning came and the light in his cell came on once again.

About 9 a.m. two plainclothes dicks and a uniformed cop had come to collect him. Without a word, conveying their wishes instead with slaps to his face, they once again manacled his hands behind him, attached the handcuffs to a heavy chain around his waist, leaving the ankle hobbles in place. The blindfold was reapplied and this time taped in place least he try to sneak a glimpse under the bottom of the blindfold.

Chung took it as a compliment that the cops considered him so dangerous that they reapplied the dog collar and chain around his neck. He was shoved and yanked by it through what seemed to be a rat's maze of passageways, through metal doors, and in and out of elevators. Finally, he sensed they had arrived at an enclosed structure of some type. From the echo, perhaps it was a garage.

There was a heated discussion in Cantonese between the members of this latest team of cops about which vehicle they should use to transport him.

One of the detectives that Chung thought had been addressed as Detective Chen Yu, said, "We supposed to follow procedure and use a prison van to transport him."

"Sure," came the surly response from his partner, apparently a senior partner that Chen had previously addressed politely as Ho Tang. "Yes, but we've been told to take him to the old place which is only a mile away, not the five miles south through rush hour traffic to Stanley."

Ho continued, "We can use the Lieutenant's unmarked Mercedes to run the mook over to the 'Vic,' dump him off, get this bullshit transportation detail over and get back to working our caseload. It'll take at least thirty minutes to get one of the prison transport vans over here from the garage. Look at this scumbag—he isn't anymore Public Enemy Number One than I am. Look, he even pissed his pants."

Detective Chen wouldn't let it go and asserted, "He isn't? If he isn't a triad big shot then why is he wearing a suit and shoes that represent more than a year's salary for us? If we take the unmarked car we'll have to put him on his belly behind the front seat. One of us will have to sit back there with him and it isn't going to be me."

"If you insist on using the Lieutenant's car, let's get it in gear. I need to get back and do some real police work which does not include chauffeuring some over-dressed triad gangsta around town."

The uniformed cop, Guan Xueguang, who felt he had had gotten unfairly rooked into this detail anyhow, decided no one wanted his opinion so he wisely decided to keep his mouth closed.

After the argument was over and the decision had been made, Chung heard a car door being yanked open. He was thrown into what he assumed was the backseat of a large sedan. An assumption he made after rubbing his face against what had to be a metal containment cage between the rear and fronts seats. He could hear the creaking of gun belt leather so he figured it was a uniformed cop that got into the rear seat and placed his boots on Chung's back as he lay on the floor.

The chain around his neck remained. When he was loaded inside and the rear door slammed, it sounded like they had wedged the free end of the chain between the rear door and doorframe so Chung was unable to move more than a few inches in any *direction.*

After a minute both front doors were opened and the car sagged as the two detectives got in and slammed their doors. After the car's engine was started, Chung heard what sounded like an overhead door being raised, then they must have pulled out into the morning sun because he suddenly sensed radiated heat coming in through the vehicle's windows.

Senior detective Ho used the car's radio to call in their assignment to Dispatch. "This is a special transportation unit 318 of the political affairs squad transporting one Asian male to the 'Vic.'" The response from Central Dispatch, in Cantonese, promptly came back over the radio. "10-4, 318. Please report in when you have discharged your current assignment and are heading back to HQ." Ho answered, "Roger that, Dispatch." And hung up the microphone.

The unmarked car pulled into traffic on Arsenal Street. With a few moments to think Chung replayed the two cop's conversation over in his mind. The 'Stanley' that Officer Ho had mentioned obviously was Stanley Prison at the south end of Hong Kong Island on Tung Tau Wan Road.

Chung, much like the average triad criminal in Hong Kong society, thought crime did pay. So they are often surprised when he or she eventually arrived at a destination they never anticipated, behind bars in the seventy-year-old detention center on the Stanley peninsula.

Built before World War Two, this high-security prison, since Victoria Prison officially closed in March of 2006, now houses the former colony's most vicious murderers, gangsters, serial rapists and drug dealers. Inmates incarcerated at Stanley have little chance of escaping because like the America's Alcatraz in San Francisco, it is surrounded by a harbour filled with hungry sharks.

Chung was confused about "the other place" the cop had mentioned, the 'Vic.' The only detainment facility operated by the Hong Kong Correctional department within a mile of the Arsenal Street HKP headquarters was the old Victoria Prison.

He shivered when he recalled that Victoria Prison had been designed and built as a hard labor punishment facility. Some claimed it was the worst, the most inhumane prison in Asia.

Some of the elderly convicts who over the years have been released for humanitarian reasons, claimed the miserable cells in Victoria Prison were only four-feet-wide by five-feet-deep.

Each cell had small barred window purposely placed six feet off the floor. Thus it denied the shorter of the prison population, Asians, the ability to get an occasionally glimpse of the outside. Unless they were foolish enough to use their shit buckets as a precarious step up.

Prisoner's hair at all Hong Kong's detention facilities was cropped close to their skulls to deny the ubiquitous lice a proper home. Roaches nibbled on prisoner calluses at night on their hands and feet but supposedly never bit the skin below. After all this forced pedicure attention, most prisoners had baby smooth hands and feet.

The incarceration floors of Victoria Prison were segregated between Asian prisoners and what were referred to as 'white' prisoners. Their prison identification numbers ended with an 'A' if they were of the Asian race, and 'E' if they were judged to be of the white race. The 'E' came from the fact that until 1997 most of the prisoners designated as 'white' were of British heritage.

Mentally shaking his head as the police car thumped through potholes on the way to their destination Chung remembered that there had been a lot of tuberculosis in the Victoria Prison population. He wondered if the disease still lurked in the cells today?

The guards at all prisons and correctional facilities in Hong Kong are heavily bearded Sihks; Punjabi warders wearing tightly wound Turbans and pressed pants, considered by everyone to be the most-trustworthy race of individuals in the former crown colony. There never had been a confirmed report that a Sihk has ever violated the trust placed in him by his employers, or shirked his duty, even to the point of giving their lives.

It was impossible for Chung to forget that discipline and court sentences were administered at Victoria Prison by flogging or a practice called 'topping' which was the hanging of the sentenced individual on Saturdays before the guard's weekly Cricket game began.

Today, the flogging process had gotten more humane. The strokes handed down in decries by the Court or prison administration for offenses perceived against one of the guards for breaking one of the dozens of petty prison rules, was administered in 2007 using a rattan cane applied to the convict's bare buttocks. A far cry from the bygone days when a Cat-of-Nine-Tails was the designated instrument used in the disciplining of prisoners.

Chung knew that the HKSAR claimed that Victoria Prison had been officially closed as a detention facility in March of 2006. But it wouldn't surprise him to find that a remote portion of the prison was still used to house high-value prisoners like himself. Those high-ranking prisoners that were frequently transported to and from the HKP Headquarters for the purposes of on-going interrogation.

After all, the driving distance and convenience of using Victoria to warehouse high-value prisoners versus the long drive south to Stanley in Hong Kong Island's constant gridlock traffic was an efficiency move. Hong Kong if nothing else was a very efficient society.

The Hong Kong police were just following the lead of the Americans who had secret CIA prisons all over the world including the ball-buster Guantánamo in Cuba.

A hopped-up, jacked-up white Land Rover SUV with brush guards and heavily tinted windows had been waiting parked behind a driverless delivery truck on Lochhart Road just off and perpendicular to Arsenal Street, when the black unmarked Mercedes pulled out of the police headquarters garage and turned right.

Behind the Land Rover the second half of the triad team was in a green one-ton Toyota pickup truck. First the SUV then the green pickup pulled out to follow the police car. The Land Rover was careful to maintain approximately four car lengths behind the cops driving the unmarked Merc.

Like cops everywhere, the detective's egos prevented them from even considering that the bad guys might be brazen enough to follow them especially on streets adjacent to police headquarters.

The SUV and the pickup followed the unmarked car. It first turned right, south, on Arsenal before again turning right, westbound, at the stop sign onto Queensway. A scanner under the Land Rover's dashboard reported the conversation between Central Dispatch and the officers in the car ahead of them.

The more experienced of the triad soldiers, Wie-Cao, spoke in guttural Cantonese, "It's them, I know it."

His partner, Yin-Lu, a smaller and younger man of Northern Chinese descent asked, "How do you know, Wie? I don't see Chung Shan in the car. There are two plain clothes coppers in front and a uniform copper in back, but no Shan."

Wie corrected the younger man, "You just heard the cops tell Dispatch they were transporting a prisoner. He has to be lying on the floor in the back seat. Now cut the bullshit and use your radio to let the women Lei Jie and Kan A Que in the pickup know we are ready to implement the attack."

Both men checked one more time to make sure their Uzi machine pistols were loaded and that their pockets were filled with extra magazines.

Ahead of Wie and Yin, Detectives Chen and Ho were bored by the transportation detail and were discussing the China's chances of sweeping the upcoming 2008 Summer Games in Beijing.

Chen stated his opinion, "I think the PRC has to sweep all the medals because it is trying to induce foreign industry to move to China, and that would impress the foreigners. If the Chinese athletes don't win all the medals some Beijing party officials are going to be sweeping streets in 2009."

Ho, of habit, was a little more negative primarily because he knew it messed with Chen's head, which was his favorite pursuit other than hassling triad members. He told Chen, "Except for the swimming and gymnastics sports, Chinese athletes don't have superiority over the American athletes. So those Beijing officials you are talking about better get their brooms ready for their new job."

Both the detectives continued to rag on each other about which country was going to take the most medals at the Olympic Summer Games and weren't paying the attention they should have, either to their surroundings or situational awareness, cop talk for paying attention to what is going on around you.

The big black Mercedes continued down Queensway in the slow lane. The police car came to a stop for the red light at Cotton Tree Drive next to the Bank of China Tower.

As the detectives continued their verbal jousting, a green Toyota truck cut out of line behind them and raced up alongside of the police car. With screech of tires the pickup swerved in front of them almost clipping the Merc's left front fender as the smaller vehicle dynamited its brakes.

All the driver of the police car saw was the piercing glare of the pickup's brake lights as he instinctively stomped on the heavy car's brakes causing it to slide to a halt just kissing the bumper of the truck that had cut in front of them.

Detectives Chen Yu and Ho had no time to reflect on the near collision as suddenly they became aware of the screaming engine of a white Land Rover as it pulled up on the left side of their car and jammed on its brakes effectively blocking the unmarked police car against the curb.

As the detectives in the Merc's front seat were attempting to collect their wits, Guan Xueguang, the uniform in the rear seat with the prisoner who had not been distracted by the bantering in the front seat, yelled, "*Watch Out! Down-Down-down! Gun-Gun-Gun!*" as the ugly snot of a Uzi machine gun poked out of the open passenger window of the Land Rover.

Detectives Chen and Ho tried their best to crawl under the dashboard in the front seat while in the back seat Officer Guan threw himself on top of Chung.

The air was filled with shots and the sound of breaking glass as the shooter's nine mm bullets—there were at least three Uzi's firing now—poured into the car. The shooter's plan called for changing magazines and continuing to pour lead into the Mercedes. By now, all the four men in the police car had been deafened. The hot incoming slugs were igniting small fires in the car's upholstery and dashboard.

Throughout all the madness the prisoner remained strangely quiet and didn't make any movement. Guan thought the first volley might have gotten Chung as he thought he felt warm blood seeping into his uniform tunic.

None of the cops had an opportunity to return fire. They were far too busy just trying to stay alive. Suddenly the rear door to the police opened and pair of large hands dragged both Officer Guan and the prisoner out onto the street surface and around to the rear of the Mercedes. The car's engine remarkably continued to run despite the fact the body now resembled the final scene from a Bonnie and Clyde gangster movie.

The mysterious stranger with no apparent concern for his own well being, ran back to the front seat of the police car with the intention of assisting the two detectives in getting out of the car. He came to a halt when he saw that the plainclothes officer's clothing was saturated with blood and gore. Both detective's skulls were in pieces held together only by pieces of skin, tissue, and sinew.

When the stranger finally did rip the driver's door open, blood flowed freely over the doorsill and down to pool on the pavement.

The triad shooters in the Land Rover and the Toyota pickup knew police backup would soon arrive at the scene. Thereby interrupting what the 426 Red Pole had assured them was a simple mission to rescue or assassinate the 14K's elder, Chung Shan.

The shooters were returning to their stalled vehicles intending to flee the scene when they began aware of the tall, dangerous-looking *gweilo* in shirtsleeves who had been dragging people out of the smoking Mercedes that just now was beginning to burn.

The triad street thugs once again returned to emptying their machine pistols at the unmarked police car hoping to hit the interloper. This forced the shooters to multi-task, shoot and start the car, a skill none of them was even remotely qualified for.

When they did finally get their cars running, in their haste to escape, both the white SUV and green pickup truck sideswiped an on-coming white van placarded with the Red Crescent logo on both sides of the box, the Asian equivalent of the Red Cross.

The glancing impact caused the van to ricochet across the two traffic lanes into the eastbound lanes of Queensway where it wrapped its entire front end around a utility telephone. The violent collision effectively disabled the van.

The discovery of the disabled Red Crescent van at the scene would open the books on one of Hong Kong's most bizarre, most grotesque crimes ever to come to the attention of the police department since the People's Republic of China took over the day-to-day administration of the former crown colony in June of 1997.

———

02 October 2007, Wednesday, 9:34 a.m. (HKT)
The Good Samaritan
Intersection of Cotton Tree Drive and Queensway
Central District—Adjacent to the Bank of China Tower.

A stranger with his driver coincidently had been passing through the intersection on the way back to his office when they had spotted the shootout in progress. Both men had put their own lives at risk by coming to the aid of the police officers who were under attack.

The man had returned a final time to the front of the demolished Mercedes to check on the condition of the two detectives. But once again he realized his intention to rescue them was a futile cause after seeing the carnage in the vehicle's front seat.

Returning to the rear of the car the stranger found a very frightened uniformed police officer sticking the trembling barrel of a huge Webley service pistol in his face.

The uniformed cop, Guan Xueguang, had enough sense to have used his handcuffs to manacle the already-restrained prisoner to the unmarked car's bumper support. He was standing but continued to shake from his first near brush with death. In a nearly hysterical voiced, Guan yelled, "Get hands up, Long Nose!" both in Cantonese and thickly accented English. "Get hands up now, *Gweilo*, or I shoot!"

As commanded the stranger raised open hands to shoulder level and stood very still, recognizing that the frightened young cop was only a nanosecond away from pulling the trigger.

Suddenly, in his own ear, Guan heard a gruff demand in Cantonese, "No, officer, it is you who will place your weapon on the asphalt. Then kick it back toward me with your heel of your left foot. And do it now!"

Now terrified, certain that the gangsters had returned and were going to execute him, Guan carefully placed his weapon on the hot asphalt, shot both of his hands in the air as high he could get them, and with the edge of his heel kicked the gun backwards towards the sound of the authoritative voice.

Guan noticed the Good Samaritan was lowering his hands as the voice behind him instructed the young officer, "Keep you hands in the air and slowly turn around to face me, officer."

Despite the fact that he was terrified, the tone in the voice behind him convinced Guan that he'd better do what was he had been ordered to do regardless of the potpourri of potential dire consequences running through his head if he didn't.

The uniformed officer slowly turned around all the while keeping his eyes tightly closed certain he would momentarily be the recipient of a fatal bullet. After thirty seconds without feeling the anticipated ballistic impact Guan forced himself to open his eyes and there standing in front of him was a huge Chinese man in a dark civilian suit with a stub nose .38 caliber snub nose pistol extended in his left hand, holding a Hong Kong sergeant's shield in the other.

"The sergeant said, "Officer Guan, is it?" He had caught the man's name off his uniform nameplate. "If you ever intend to go anywhere in the HKP department it probably isn't very good political sense to be pointing a weapon at one of the department's living legends, Chief Inspector Augustus Fox, even if you think he is a long-nose barbarian," the literal translation of the Cantonese word *Gweilo*.

Despite the seriousness of the situation with two dead coppers in the smoking wreck of the police car, and a furious and unrepentant prisoner struggling to work his wrist out of the handcuff that Guan had applied before bracing the Caucasian Samaritan, Guan started to laugh nervously. He realized how close he just came to ending his career.

Inspector Fox gave him an order, "Get control of yourself, officer. Run over to my car, the white Mercedes that Sergeant Zhou Ming so excellently parked half on, half off the sideway in front of the noodle shop on the opposite side of the street. While the good Sergeant goes back to trying to direct traffic around this goat fornication, you get on the radio and request that Dispatch get an ambulance, a traffic supervisor, backup units, and homicide detectives rolling to the scene here immediately."

"You might also suggest that a detective from the political affairs squad would also be a welcome addition to this party. Tell Dispatch to make the callout code three and tell them that police officers are on the scene and have taken enemy fire. We have casualties of the Force and soon might have some more unless backup gets their ass here quickly."

"Tell dispatch that the second unit out the garage should be SWAT. It wouldn't be unusual for that hit team to make another run at us."

"Also inform them that Chief Inspector Fox suggests they get one of the Gazelle traffic helicopters up over this location as a pair of eyes-in-the-sky certainly will be needed to figure out how to divert traffic away from this location. This neighborhood is going to be locked down solidly for the remainder of the morning. Now, do you have all that, Officer Guan?"

Guan answer, "Yes Sir, I think so." He turned to run across the street to the Inspector's car when Sergeant Zhou yelled after him, "After you've made that call, go over and see if you can render assistance to the driver of the white Red Crescent van. He hit the utility pole pretty hard and may need emergency medical care."

"Yes, Sir, I understand, Sir." Guan answered. Still mainlining adrenaline he began to run towards the opposite side of the street until he realized he had forgotten to retrieve his pistol from where he had only moments earlier laid it down on the asphalt.

He darted back embarrassed to where the sergeant was standing over his discarded pistol. Which gave the inspector an opportunity to make an additional instruction to Guan, "See if we are lucky enough to have any off-duty HKP volunteer reserve officers in that crowd. If there is, get them to assist with crowd control. Once you get someone in place and you think he'll be reliable, get back over here in case the shooters make another run at us."

The Sergeant added, "Something tells me this at this isn't over yet. Those triad shooters can't go back to their Red Pole and tell him they got the two cops but allowed a couple of 'suits' to run the four of them off. My guess is that the Red Pole told them either to rescue this mook from custody, kill him, or don't bother to come back. That is a hell of an incentive for the shooters to come back and finish the job."

Guan took off across the street to see if there were any off-duty reserve cops in the crowd that had now swollen in size. As there are 5,449 reserve community-action cops in the HKP department and most of them live on Hong Kong Island itself, that wouldn't be too optimistic a hope in the situation. Even if the reserve was out of uniform and as usual, unarmed.

Reserve officers for decades have been the go-to option for the HPD in times of needed crowd control, containment of civil disobedience, and community relations.

Fox checked Chung Shan's cuffs to make they were secure but weren't cutting off the man's circulation. Then he squatted down and pulled his stub nose Chiefs Special out of his ankle holster and settled in to wait for backup's arrival or the shooters to return to finish their job. Unfortunately it turned out to be the latter of the two possibilities.

———

02 October 2007, Wednesday, 9:49 a.m. (HKT)
The shooters return.
Intersection of Cotton Tree Drive and Queensway
Central District—Adjacent to the Bank of China Tower

All four shooters suddenly reappeared at the intersection on Cotton Tree Drive driving the same two vehicles but now down the sidewalk with no regard for pedestrians who were diving into the street to get out of their way.

As the shooters pulled to a stop a hundred yards from the disabled unmarked black Mercedes a triad shooter from each car hopped out and scurried into the crowd. They obviously would attempt to flank the cops and the prisoner.

Fox thought, *Christ all mighty. Here I am with a nervous uniformed rookie constable who probably is too frightened to shoot straight. Ming and myself only have our lightweight, off-duty weapons and not even a spare speed-loader for either gun between us.*

We are less than a mile from Arsenal HQ but no backup has arrived yet although I just heard their sirens beginning to 'spool up'. They certainly are taking their sweet damn time getting here.

What with the gridlocked traffic this shootout has caused, backup will be at least another five minutes getting here even if they, like the shooters, use the sidewalks. Between the constable, not counting his spare magazines, Ming and myself, we only have seventeen rounds of ammo between us. We are going to have to make that paltry amount last until the cavalry arrives.

Guan Xueguiang, his uniform, face and hands blood spattered from the earlier blow-back from the front seat of the Mercedes, returned back at the disabled police car, gasping heavily from his run, with his weapon in his hand, mumbling "There is no one there. I don't know where they went, Boss."

Fox glanced at the young man, and said, "Guan, you position yourself to protect the prisoner, and let no one, repeat, no one get to him. Save your last bullets in case they make a rush on your position or if Ming or I go down. All Ming and I have are our five-shot, off-duty weapons which probably would be more effective if we threw them at the shooters."

"Remember, Guan, no one gets to the prisoner without first going through you. As long as he is in HKP custody, he is our responsibility to protect. Whatever you do, don't allow these assholes to take you prisoner. Whatever you have to do here to stay alive no matter how painful it is far better than what you can expect from the Red Pole who sent these shooters if they take you prisoner. Now do I have to explain what this means to you in greater detail, constable?"

"No, Sir," Guan answered nearly inaudibly as he took up position in front of where the prisoner was handcuffed to the bumper support. If Guan hadn't been wearing a police uniform a passer-bye might have mistaken the youthful cop for a high school student.

"Okay," Fox said, patting the scared young officer on the shoulder.

Just then, Ming slid to a stop at the rear of the disabled Mercedes in the best baseball slide Fox had ever seen. Fox looked at the Sergeant and commented sarcastically, "What a shame, looks like you'll need a new set of slacks there."

Ming, ignoring his boss's sarcasm, reported, "Guan found two police reserves in the crowd. They'll try to keep everyone away for the scene here until backup arrives. As they are both in suits perhaps the crowd will think they are detectives and give them some slack. I told them to give us as much notice as they can if they see the shooters attempt to flank us."

"There only four shooters and so it pretty much will two-on-one if they all attempt to rush us. Now aren't you glad that our wise leaders have forced you to stay current in your shooting qualification every month, Chief?" Ming asked with equal sarcasm, both men grinning despite the potentially deadly situation they were in.

Suddenly, a large Asian male broke from the crowd and charged the bullet-riddled police car firing his Uzi in short bursts, changing clips, and firing again. He was backed up by covering fire from the shooters that had remained with the triad vehicles that also were pouring round after round into Fox and Ming's positions.

The lumbering Chinese man was an obvious professional; he was squeezing off perfect three-round bursts rather than wasting ammunition with full automatic fire. Huge rips appeared in the metal of the police car. The remaining window glass exploded out of its frames.

Ming and Fox cautiously poked their heads over the rear fenders of the police car and slowly squeezed the triggers of their pistols both putting two slugs in the shooter before he crumbled less than twenty feet away missing a good chunk of his face.

Sergeant Ming heard a shout from the crowd, which he correctly assumed, was one of the two reserves keeping an eye out for a flanking action on their position. Ming spun around to address the new threat. He saw one of the female shooters was charging the police car as fast as she could run. She'd was nearly to their position firing her Uzi and changing clips as she came.

Ming extended his hands in a two-handed grip and fired at the charging woman three times *bam-bam-bam* missing her with all three of his shots. Just then a small Asian man also appeared from the crowd and raced for the police car firing a close-quarters-equalizer, a 12-gauge shotgun, at Officer Guan and his prisoner.

All Ming could do was concentrate on the woman who apparently now had run out of ammunition. She cursed, threw the smoking weapon to the grass, and pulled a dagger out of her boot. The Sergeant didn't have time to warn Fox about the shotgun-totting man who was running at the car and now was within twenty feet of the kneeling Chief Inspector.

But as the on-coming gunman attempted to slide to a stop he slipped on the broken window glass and blood-soaked grass and swore as his shotgun jammed.

Returning his concentration back to his own more immediate problems, Ming knew he was going to have to take a cut from the woman to get beyond the knife. He sprung to his feet just as he felt the sharp blade plunge through the meaty tissue of his left forearm.

Despite the pain the sergeant dug his feet into the grass like a lineman he was once the East Asian Senior High School Championship football team.

Ming jammed the stiffened fingers on his right hand into the woman's face. They sunk into the woman's eye sockets up to the third knuckle until the fingertips came into contact with the rear of the woman's optical sockets.

Gelatin-like optical fluid first squirted then gushed like a waterfall from her punctured eyeballs to run down over the rear of Ming's hand, wrist and forearm as she screamed like she was in hell. Which was a fair assessment of her situation considering she'd spend the remainder of her life as a blind prisoner in a Hong Kong maximum-security prison.

In the meantime Fox had spotted the man with the shotgun as the shooter stood in the open desperately attempting to clear his jammed shotgun.

The Inspector fired his final three rounds that with the two-inch barrel were only accurate to within seven feet at best. The bullets sailed over the mook's head just as the shooter got his shotgun operating again and returned to laying down buckshot on Fox's position.

Having no other option Fox came to his feet. He ran at the man as fast as he could, actually throwing his empty pistol into the face of his attacker. Then he stopped right in front of the man, pivoted, brought his right leg up to his chest and kicked the man viciously in the genitals. The shooter screamed in agony and rage and started to fall backwards as Fox, regaining his balance, pivoting once again on his left foot and slammed a full extension kick into the man's face crushing his nose and optical bones.

Seeing no other threat in the immediate vicinity, and to ensure that his opponent would no longer be a threat to Ming's or his safety Fox used the heel of his right hand, callused from countless hand trusts into sand boxes in Karate classes to jam what was left on the man's nose into his brain with a powerful thrust. The man screamed once more before landing on his back where he lay unmoving.

———————

Both Ming and Fox their hands bloody with gore from defending themselves returned their attention to Constable Guan and his prisoner.

Faithful to what Fox has ordered him to do when the shootout had resumed, Guan, with massive holes in his back from the shotgun and many smaller entry wounds from the Uzi, lay on top of the prisoner.

The rounds had passed through Guan's muscular young body and into the prisoner. But neither man's wounds were bleeding. Their hearts had stopped. When the heart pumps no more, bleeding stops.

Constable Guan although a rookie, had died a hero, Fox and Ming thought simultaneously as with one mind. *A real hero who had taken his oath to heart. He had kept one of the shooters off their backs.*

The sirens slowly spooled down in crescendo as the backup and aid cars pulled up at the bloody killing field. Fox and Zhou—both longtime cops—were proud to have had a chance to know Guan, the man, even momentarily. Because in today's self-centered, selfish and ambition-driven world, a hero is a rare find.

Both men being very careful they weren't observed performing an ancient Chinese custom by spitting a blob of phlegm onto the dead body of the prisoner that had cost Guan his life. Then both men walked over to report in to the department's rolling command post.

There was bloodstains and broken glass all over the grass and more on the pavement. And remnants of blast-separated body parts that had not been there a half hour before. Good cops had given their lives today for a scumbag triad gangsta. Fox thought, *I am damn well going to find out why*.

2

03 October 2006, Thursday, 10:30 a.m. (HKT)
Hong Kong Police Headquarters
Arsenal and Harcourt Road
Admiralty district—Hong Kong Island

After yesterday's shootout and the four deaths that resulted, Sergeant Zhou Ming and I were tied up at HKP headquarters into the early evening hours. 'Officer involved shootings' require endless report writing.

Before returning to the office we had stopped by the emergency room at Matilda hospital to get the deep laceration in Ming's left forearm disinfected and stitched up. The doctor said it had been a clean cut and that the wound while painful should heal without complications.

———

Following completion of the paperwork, we had been ordered to make ourselves available for interrogations by the CAC, Commission Against Corruption, Hong Kong's version of what other police departments often refer contemptuously to as the Internal Affairs Unit or Rat Squad.

Then we had been questioned by our armchair superiors who probably wouldn't have known which end of a gun to point.

———

The Commission On Corruption was formed in 1994 to deal with police and civilian official corruption. Its formation had became necessary because Hong Kong had become industrialized so quickly and experienced such massive influxes in its population that the get-rich-quick refugee mentality had resulted in a spectacular growth of official corruption especially on the Hong Kong Police.

The commission has far ranging powers including arrest. For a police officer of any rank to be indicted by the Commission can best be compared to stepping off the curb in front of a moving bus.

By the 1980's because of the efforts of the CAC, Hong Kong formerly known as one of the most corrupt places in Asia was today one of the straightest and most transparent.

———

Ming and I finally left the Arsenal Road Headquarters at 8 p.m. By the time Ming dropped me off at my condo in the Peak District, or what more commonly is known as the Peak, it was 8:30 p.m.

Because of the late hour I told him to not pick me for work the following morning, Thursday, until 10:30 a.m. I told him the same order applied to him. Whenever Ming gets home late because of work his wife has occasionally bolted the front door and refused to make him a late dinner. I figured perhaps a few hours off the following morning would mollify her, but probably not. The woman was well known to Zhou Ming's many friends in the police department as a certified battleaxe.

I walked into the condo, tossed my briefcase on a chair, and locked the entryway door behind me. The gunshot residue and blood-spattered clothing got tossed on the floor before I went into the master bathroom to take a long, hot shower.

Losing four men today made me for question for the 500th time my sanity in choosing to remain in the law enforcement profession.

———

The Peak condo I was renting belonged to my roommate and girlfriend, Dr. Alicia Ho, M.D. who is temporarily living in the city of Taiyunan outside Beijing in the People's Republic of China.

The Peak is fairly touristy. Attractions located here include *Ripley's Believe It Or Not! Odditorium*; *Madame Tussaud's*; the *Peak Explorer Motion Simulator*; the *Peak Tower*; and children's favorite, the *Marché*, a restaurant of several floors arranged like a market so you can pick and choose the type food that will tickle your taste buds on that particular day.

The reason that kids love the *Marché* is because of its animal chairs, vibrant-colored wall murals, and an area that permits parents to take in luscious views of the harbor while the kids play their hearts out on the playground equipment.

If tacky tourist souvenirs are yours or your kid's interests across the street you'll find the *Peak Galleria* that will fit the bill with Mao caps, pigged-tailed Chinese hats, ceramic Buddha's, half-size chopsticks made of slivery pine wood—you get the idea.

Since the upper terminus of the Peak tram is a significant distance below the actual top of the Peak, the fit can enjoy an uphill climb through several parks by following carefully manicured trails to reach the true summit.

At my age I find the downward route that takes you to the Central district following the Old Peak Road to be enjoyable if I don't try to do it anymore often than once every springtime.

To access the Old Peak Road, which is just a grand name for a trail, you turn to your left once you leave the Peak Tower and follow the zigzag path downhill. It weaves through thick jungle and past some grand old colonial mansions.

Weekend warriors must to take extreme caution. The colonial trail soon morphs into one of Hong Kong's steepest residential streets—not recommended for the orthopedically challenged.

———

Over the past eighteen months Alicia and I have grown very attached to the penthouse condo. It was our favorite spot for downtime, an admittedly rare commodity in both of our lines of work.

The place always has been Alicia's favorite place because her well-to-do parents had spared no expense in furnishing it to her exacting specifications. The good doctor's tastes run a bit 'western' in that she prefers hard-to-locate pieces like King Gorghelli secretaries, Belgian Walnut inlaid sideboards, Monica Empire Style Inlaid China cabinets, and generally as much Louis XV and Chippendale-style furnishings as she could stuff into the place.

When I moved in with her, I gave away or otherwise dispensed with the furnishings from my old Sheung Wan apartment. We often joke that when she eventually throws me out, I will be back on the street without a bed, chair, or any furniture.

When she playfully threatens me with eviction from time to time, I always launch into my patented spiel explaining to her just how many young, hot, well-to-do women in Hong Kong are just waiting for the day that happens and I once again become available on the 'singles' market. This always receives a roll of her eyes followed by a contemptuous, very unladylike snort.

I now regret that we'd made such a joking matter out of our short time together. I miss her and look forward anxiously to the day she returns to Hong Kong. Although in reality I know our previous plans of getting married someday may now be a fantasy. I am finding it difficult to accept that may be the case.

Too much water may have passed under that bridge in the past year. I sense the Alicia I talked with only occasionally by phone now isn't the same lover I've been intimate with for the past two years.

When asked, I continue to pass Alicia off to acquaintances as my girlfriend in absentia. Perhaps that is a defensive mechanism of mine to avoid having to put into words the incident that had interrupted our torrid relationship last year.

We lived together until late last year when Alicia first learned that her mother was near death from a frightening, debilitating illness. At the same time, coincidentally, her father, a medical doctor who lives with her in the family home in Taiyunan, a Chinese city with a population of three million, began a slow slip into dementia when her mother suddenly became gravely ill from cancer.

After the funeral all the wraps had come off the family's medical history. Alicia had discovered she could be genetically predisposed to cancer, a fact her family had selfishly kept secret from her until the death of her mother.

A little background; Alicia is a contradiction in appearance. At work, on the street, or in public, the good doctor displays a dragon lady image, very conservative, very professional, and a hard-ass attitude that would inspire a casual observer to make the erroneous assumption that she could be a dominatrix in her personal life.

In reality Alicia has never flaunted the fact that she is a member of Mensa, the International Organization for Geniuses, membership only offered to the top 2% of the population with the highest IQ's. By all measurements of intellectual intelligence she is the smartest person I've ever known.

Due to her position as the head of emergency medicine at Matilda Hospital and the board of director's stuffy and archaic view towards professional women practicing medicine there, Alicia always strived to display a haughty, attractive, but sexless exterior to everyone including her fellow medical professionals.

I had experienced her black widow persona firsthand the first two times I'd had occasion to encounter her on my several work-related involuntary visits to the Matilda Hospital's emergency room last year. Obviously something about those first impressions of her had intrigued me. I had pursued a relationship with her for months before she finally bought into my proposal that we become a monogamous 'item.'

Alicia is an excellent actor primarily due to her college background in traditional Chinese live theater where she bragged she had played both male and female parts. And she is still acting—her true personality in private tends to lean more towards that of a courtesan rather than a dominatrix.

She is a well-proportioned, five-foot-tall woman weighing almost 110 pounds, which she keeps firmed-up through thrice-weekly workouts in the resident's gym. Her dark brown hair never seen in public in anything but a prim and proper bun reaches down to her trim waist.

Her dark eyes sparkle like diamonds in an expensive crystal chandelier except on those rare instances when she gets shrieking, object throwing, obscenity sprouting, angry. Unlike the majority of Hong Kong women her complexion is flawless and her skin alabaster in color.

She is drop-dead beautiful at least in the mind's eye of this *gweilo*. In the vernacular of today's Hong Kong indigenous American-aping college crowd Alicia is 'way cool.' Her personal scent of choice, off-duty of course, is 'Nasty Girl,' the current in-fashion perfume preference of well-to-do Hong Kong divas.

Alicia had come to Hong Kong as a refugee from the People's Republic of China fourteen year ago, having escaped with a boatload of other upper-middle-class Chinese teenage girls who had personal ambitions far larger than their parent's plans for their future. Which mainly consisted of arranged marriages to bolster the family's position in the State.

When her parents had discovered that she had fled China they were furious for about a month. But they soon came to respect her determination to make something of herself. Shortly thereafter, her father contacted a friend of his, a high official in the Beijing government, and through that contact had made arrangements for issuance of both Hong Kong 'student' and 'working' visas for her. They also had paid her tuition through ten years of pre-med and medical school at the University of Hong Kong.

Since her mother's death last year, Alicia has been living just outside Taiyunan in her parent's home. She runs her father's medical practice, "At least for the time being" as she tells me on those rare moments lately that she has felt like communicating with me.

———

As Ming and I walked into our third floor office a few minutes before 11 a.m. my staff was already cloistered in the conference room waiting to hear the details on the previous day's shootout.

After Wednesday's blood bath I had decided that I should to put forth a little extra effort in my dress so the employees of the police department would continue to believe the 'hardman, nothing-bothers-me' persona I had cultivated here over the last ten years.

Despite the tragedy of losing three cops and what it meant to me personally, I couldn't permit the tragedy to become an excuse to get slovenly or deviate from my commitment to project a high self-image for my co-workers, peers, and bosses.

I learned early in my career as a highly visible NYPD first-grade detective that clothes indeed do make the man, especially on the occasional T.V. news spot, as well as directly impacting how the public perceives you.

Today as usual I was well turned out and felt I looked at least seven years younger than my actual age of 47.

Despite reaching middle age I certainly don't fit into the categories that an article in the People's Republic of China's PRC mouthpiece, the *Xinhua News Agency*, had published in late 2006 stating that 60 million of its citizens were obese, and more than 160 million had high blood pressure.

Today I had selected a perfectly-tailored, elegant expat 'uniform' consisting of a blue Giorgio Armani blazer with gray Oxford slacks, a pale yellow Robert Taylor silk opened-necked shirt, soft gray kid-leather Gucci loafers, and a $3,950 (US) Cartier 'Roadster' watch with matching crocodile band.

Even though the two of detectives killed in yesterday's ambush were from the clandestine political affairs unit that reports directly to the chief of police, or the commissioner of police as the position is known in Hong Kong, any cop shooting or in fact any homicide is handled by my department.

The uniformed cop who was killed had been assigned to the Traffic Department. The assassination of the dead triad mook Chung Shan was being somewhat jadedly classified as what in police work is referred to as a crime against NHI, or No Human Involved.

My department would be responsible for bringing the shooters to justice in Chung's assassination. There is no doubt that the case would continue to be of a major interest to the political affairs unit. But it was my people that were tasked with solving the homicides.

Except for the grunt-level detectives such as those that had been killed, political affairs cops generally all have PhD's with graduate degrees in political science. For that reason they are not considered by the average copper to be *real* cops.

And although Inspector Ho Pham's squad, Homicide, would be directly involved in the investigation of the massacre, nothing was going to keep my other people from attending this morning's meeting. Of course with three of the four shooters known and in fact dead, the homicide detectives would be primarily attempting to ascertain the motive behind the unusual, unprovoked attack. And more importantly whether the triad's intent had been to break Chung out or simply to assassinate him.

———

03 October 2006, Thursday, 11:00 a.m. (HKT)
Arsenal Street HKP Headquarters
Arsenal and Harcourt Road
Admiralty district—Hong Kong Island

If you know anything about cops you know that our humor occasionally can be very dark. Two things of the many things that most of us are especially accomplished at is drinking and gossiping, not necessarily in that order.

The crimes against person's department, which I manage as it's chief inspector, includes Homicide, Street Crimes, and Anti-Terrorism/Anti-Hijacking squads. The head of each of those squads or units, a Lieutenant, reports to a designated Inspector in my office. The lieutenant and his sergeant run the day-to-day activities of his or her organization with their most important and non-negotiable standing order being, "Always keep the Boss advised of everything that goes on!"

When I walked into the conference room Thursday morning I noticed the inspectors had already beat me to the refreshments and now were either sitting or holding up a wall.

The first person my eyes fell on was my newest staff member Inspector Yin. She had filled the empty slot on my staff when her predecessor

Inspector Silvia Guan had been murdered in the line of duty in October of 2006.

Mimi Yin is a Eurasian from the City-State of Singapore. She prefers to use of the western style for her name, Mimi Yin; given name first, followed by her family name.

Mimi has outstanding skills in getting people to tell her secrets they swore to themselves they'd never reveal to anyone. She also possesses the most subtle and diplomatic skills in my department. She is polite to a fault until you get her mad. Then she discards her nice girl persona and morphs into a street person that most prudent persons would cross the street to avoid encountering.

She is 32 years-of-age and has an associates degree in police science. The woman is a nine-year veteran of HKP, seven of those years as a detective in the Domestic Violence Unit. This month would be her first anniversary of heading up the Street Crimes Unit.

Through no fault of her own she is a hard-looking woman. Her face in her youth had suffered from an untreated outbreak of acne. She is street-smart, stands 5 feet, 4-inches tall flat-footed, has a martial arts background and is very athletic in build.

Mimi prefers traditional western suits, as do most of the female detectives in the HKP. On the job, she is never one to wear exotic shoes, over-the-top earrings, or flashy jewelry.

Inspector Yin's black straight hair hangs down to a very trim waist; she has the darkest eyes in the city. They are magnified the prescription glasses she has to wear, as do many Asians due to vitamin deficiencies in the only basic food their parents could afford to put on the table when they were growing up. Like most female cops on the department Yin is a woman no one ever refers to as a 'girl' to her face—at least not more than once.

Today she had chosen a navy blue pant suit with a matching oversize blazer (to conceal her weapon), sensible flat shoes, a pair of simple sterling silver droplet earrings, and wore a facsimile of her gold HKP inspector's badge made into a brooch on her left jacket lapel.

Mimi is among the deadliest officers on my staff, the criteria for earning that designation being the 'demonstrated use of deadly force.' She has been forced in years past into unavoidable confrontations with armed spousal abusers and had to shoot the men to protect the lives of the victims whose major injuries she had been investigating. The department judged all of them to be 'good, justifiable, and unavoidable shoots.'

Ho Pham, the inspector who supervises Lieutenant Du and his Homicide squad by self-admission is gay. His life partner has the bad *joss*, or the bad luck, to have contracted pancreatic cancer. At 35-years-of-age and being blessed with a physique like the Governor of California somehow I have to believe that no one has ever dissed Ho's sexual preference to his face. His posture tends to remind me of James Dean albeit black-haired, and he never stands upright when he can slouch against a wall or in a doorway.

Pham is a seven-year veteran of the department and tends to dress the part of a cowboy and occasionally has been mistaken for a triad wannabe. He wears tight black jeans held up by a four-inch wide piece of black leather with a large imitation gold-plated rodeo belt buckle. Today his outfit was augmented with a black cowboy shirt with pearl buttons worn with short sleeves to display his awesome biceps. Rumor has it that he carries two SIG Sauer .357 pistols; left-ejecting in his left hand, and right-ejecting for his right hand, concealed in the waistband behind his back under an extra-large unbuttoned denim jacket when he is out on Hong Kong's mean streets.

His face is the unfortunate result of a glancing blow from a slow-moving tram when some years ago he heroically jumped onto a rail track to rescue a little girl that her father had discarded, apparently having no further use for the child. The injuries Pham suffered when the train passed over their bodies resulted in his face today appearing as if it has been put together out of a grab bag of parts from many faces. But due to the officer shielding the little girl forcing her to lay motionless while the train passed over their bodies, the little girl had emerged unscathed.

Ho Pham occasionally jokes about his face saying that if the French divorcee's face transplant that was all over the newspapers back in January of last year is successful; he is going to apply to be their next patient.

What only his co-workers and I know is that when Ho had been a street cop he had grown to appreciate his face because it scared the bejesus out of all the triad thugs. His street name at that time was *Tahn Cheng Pham*, or 'One-Way Pham.' The triad wannabes who thought they knew the story behind the nickname explained that once Pham took you in for questioning you never were seen again. The gangsters literally would take off running in the opposite direction when they saw him sauntering towards them on the street.

The last inspector in my small but unique squad is Chen Ho who is in-charge of Anti-Terrorism and Hijacking crimes. Inspector Ho is a dark, squatty Japanese man with humongous shoulders, upper arms, and vice-like hands. Chen, despite the inbred hate all Chinese have for persons of

Japanese heritage owing to the years that Japan ruthlessly occupied Hong Kong during WWII, has stuck to his guns and risen through the ranks from ordinary tourist constable to his current position on my staff.

While Chen still encounters occasional distrust and lack of cooperation from the citizenry, in my book he is one of the few really superior cops on the department having a native IQ of close to 160 and is the best operations planner on my staff.

Chen normally wears navy blue suits, wraparound sunglasses and is partial to black leather wingtips. Chen, as is Pham, is a committed weightlifter. The arms of Chen's suits bulge noticeably in the upper arms and shoulders, a fact that isn't lost on the criminals he has occasion to confront on the street.

He keeps his mustache clipped military neat and always carries a briefcase. Inside that briefcase if you can believe what a few busy bodies in the community claim is an H&K. Heckler and Koch, MP-5 sub-machine gun. I don't want to know about it if he does.

And of course I'd never correct these well-meaning citizens by telling them that the weapon is a 9-mm Uzi, not a HK. The inspector's shoulder-length black hair today was swept back in a pony tail, and he appeared to be extremely unhappy as he sat at the conference table playing with a set of matte-black handcuffs.

Last but not least is my primary administrative assistant, Elizabeth (never Liz she had informed me when I hired her) Stewart. She is an aggressive, 6 foot, 2 inch-tall expat Aussie. Although not a sworn police officer she often is able to give the team insights that we otherwise would have missed in a particular criminal or political situation.

She also supervises the office's clerical staff, keeps me honest on my expense accounts, sees I meet the deadlines of the burdensome administrative reports I am responsible for, and protects us when she is able from the overbearing and nit-picking upper administration micromanagement that hinders the efficiency and effectiveness of most modern police departments.

I had asked Elizabeth who appeared to be in one of her contemplative moods this week to forward the phones to one of her assistants and join the meeting to take notes and enjoy the team interaction.

Rumor in the department is that Elizabeth is a committed social butterfly. If one puts any value on what a few of the jealous Chinese female cops claim. And they tattle, as if I had any interest, that away from the office she wears clothes that shock. She has an excellent tan and today was wearing a vivid green silk outfit with tan mules, bright red lipstick and a pair of large gold hoop earrings.

As far as department confidentiality is concerned I knew that Elizabeth could be counted on to carry any embarrassing fact about one of us with her to the grave before revealing it. She has earned the trust of our entire team.

———

Zhou Ming walked in with a cup of coffee and helped himself to two of the remaining calorie-packed pastries. Elizabeth was in-charge of ensuring the pastries appeared in our office every morning a meeting was scheduled, courtesy of the police department. Unknown to the HKP bean counters she cleverly accounts for cost of them under the cost center for 'Durable Meeting Supplies.'

When everyone had pulled up a chair, a wall, or sat on the floor I arranged my notes preparatory to beginning. I planned on filling the staff in on the firefight that Zhou and I had stumbled into yesterday when he was driving me back to the Arsenal Street head shed HQ from a 'mandatory appearance' meeting. I had been invited to appear at the LegCo, the Legislative Council building, at the request of the HKSAR Chief Executive Donald Tsang's office.

———

Tsang was first appointed acting *Baidu*, or acting chief executive of the China's Hong Kong Special Administrative Region, on March 18, 2005 replaced the aging Tung Chee Hwa who had resigned citing poor health.

With his trademark burgundy and gray bowtie with matching handkerchief pointing from the breast pocket of a three-piece suit, David Tsang has a reputation as a natty dresser, a smooth operator, and a successful track record as a 38-year Hong Kong civil servant veteran.

Only a fool would not be aware that Tsang had been selected for the chief executive position by Beijing. But for public consumption his temporary appointment had come from the 800-member HKSAR electing committee. As expected the committee also promoted him to permanent chief executive at the end of his predecessor's remaining second term in July of 2007.

———

The reason for my requested, read *demanded*, attendance at yesterday's legislative council meeting at the LegCo was that a few of the HKSAR legislators wanted my department to evaluate yet-another proposal to install additional hi-speed cameras in the high crime areas of Hong Kong Island. It seemed tourist complaints had been increasing even though the city's crime rate overall was holding steady in all categories except pick pockets at Happy Valley racetrack.

Happy Valley may be Hong Kong's favorite local attraction. The racetrack is open ten months a year, closed July and August, and is the second largest racing venue in Hong Kong eclipsed only by the Sha Tin racetrack that is located in the New Territories.

Happy Valley opened in 1846 and except for a period during the Japanese occupation of Hong Kong during World War Two has been in operation and the traditional home of horse racing in the former crown colony ever since. As such it draws its share of pickpockets.

———

Someone I hadn't expected to be in this morning's impromptu meeting stood leaning against the room's back wall with his usual sardonic look on his face, Assistant Chief of Personnel John Russell.

Actually I should have expected Russell to turn up here or just be waiting for me in my office. After all as personnel chief in the department Russell is directly responsible for keeping the top police administrator informed of progress on all high-visibility cases, so he could in turn keep HKSAR Chief Executive Donald Tsang's office up to speed on all matters that have the potential to become shit magnets for the Media.

It was assumed that Tsang then kept the People's Republic of China's politburo in Beijing up to speed on media-sensitive matters in its newest SAR, as of June of 1997, Hong Kong.

Assistant Chief Russell was a long-time holdover from the days of the British Royal Hong Kong Police. It was said that the assistant chief of personnel knew where too many bodies were buried for the police commissioner to even consider replacing him.

The police department's personnel head was a big man at over six feet and 375 pounds, an Australian ex-pat with ruddy face who had come to adopt the disgusting Chinese habit of spitting whenever and wherever he chose. It is rumored throughout the department that Russell has an out-of-control drinking habit. But during working hours he apparently was capable of a keeping it under control.

Russell seems to favor gunboat-size brogans and inappropriately gaudy clothing. His reputation is one of micromanaging and excelling as a skilled political manipulator.

During the first eight years of my employment here in Hong Kong Russell had never been anything but fair with me. In fact he had shielded me from a few of my then-supervisor's attempts to discipline me, even threatening to fire me, without cause.

To qualify that statement, at the time I had been hired back in 1997 and for the next eight years until the onset of the 2005 serial homicides, I had not been aware that Russell was a charter member of the small covert group of police administrators who had sold their first loyalty to China, a traitorous secret hidden by Hong Kong police department brass for the past ten years.

Until October in 2005, I had no idea that the man that I had considered my mentor, who I openly sharing my concerns and problems with, eventually would turn out to be my worst and most deadly enemy in the department in fact in all of Hong Kong.

After my men and I had solved several serial murders that year, murders which had been committed by Detective Martin Chen on the orders of Chief Inspector Deng Shan, Russell had promoted me for my team's work in solving the high visibility cases.

But it was Russell's accompanying comments that convinced me of his covert involvement in the plot when he had ordered me to destroy Deng Shan's confession. Deng at the time was incarcerated in Victoria Prison pending trial. However, before he could be brought in front of the docket where no doubt he would have produced the names of his fellow conspirators, he had been found dead under suspicious circumstances. He'd allegedly hung himself in his cell despite being under a 24/7 suicide watch.

Since that time, I've been hiding my revulsion of Russell. Waiting until someday he inadvertently screws up and I can bring him to justice as being ultimately responsible for those 2005 homicides. One of which included indirect responsibility for the torture and murder of my then-girlfriend Peng Lige and the death of our unborn child.

Today, working with Russell, I was demonstrating to myself the effectiveness of the mental wall I'd erected between reality and what I must do in order to one day have the opportunity to take the big Australian down. I looked forward to the day when I could administer a figurative *coup de grace* to the treasonous double agent.

At the moment in 2005 when I first learned of Russell's complicity, only quick thinking on my part had prevented the certain deaths of my men and myself. Admittedly prostituting myself, I had agreed to unconditionally and irrevocably stand behind a number of fabrications of the facts. They specifically sought to conceal who actually was behind the *Hongse Spider* plot. The fabrications came directly from Russell and the police department's highest level of administration.

————

"Okay," I began, glancing at my gold Cartier Roadster watch to see it was nearly 11:15 a.m., "let's gets started, people."

As soon as the muted discussions among the inspectors and Elizabeth had ceased I welcomed the presence of Assistant Chief Russell who still hadn't made any comment or acknowledged my presence in any manner.

I made a point to nod at Inspector Ho Pham; and his lieutenant and my former partner, Lieutenant Du Ming, both of Homicide, onto whose plate the investigation of the cop killings and the Chung's assassination would fall.

"Yesterday," I began, indicting by gesture of my left hand to my driver Zhou Ming that he should feel free to jump in if I missed something pertinent, "a few minutes past 9:30 a.m., Ming and I were returning to HQ from a meeting at the LegCo building. We were in my Mercedes, both of us in the front seat. Ming was driving."

"We had turned eastbound off Jackson Road as we left the LegCo and were continuing in that direction on Queensway in the Central district. We were approaching the stop light at the intersection of Queensway and Cotton Tree Drive, at the Bank of China Tower building, when we observed that a white Land Rover and green pickup truck had a black westbound unmarked Mercedes police car jammed into the curb and was shooting into it."

"Due to the traffic conditions on Queensway at all hours these days, Ming had to pull the car onto the sidewalk to enable us to respond as backup to the situational emergency. I directed Sergeant Ming to set up some type of perimeter and traffic control to prevent any motor vehicle fatality accidents as I dodged the traffic and ran across Queensway traffic to provide back up to the cops in the unmarked car. The car by this time was being turned into Swiss cheese by the shooters."

I continued, "After the recent administration directives that supervisory staff were not to carry any supporting firearms or equipment in our assigned vehicle's trunks, with exception of the light-weight weapons we were permitted to carry on our persons, all Ming and I had to provide support to the police officers who were under fire were our off-duty .38 caliber Smith and Wesson Chief's Specials which have a five-shot capacity."

"Neither of us had spare ammo, again in keeping with the directive from the department's administrative head shed."

At that point Chief Russell push himself off the wall and interrupted. "Chief Inspector, I assume you are aware that the directive you so sarcastically are referring to was deemed necessary by the commissioner's office since some wannabe *boohowdoys*, triad foot soldiers, have been brazenly breaking into a police cars right here in the HQ parking lot and stealing weapons and other costly police equipment we don't want the triads we get their hands on. Understand?" He growled.

I dropped my head momentarily to take a deep, calming breath before looking at Russell at the rear of the room, and said, "Yes, Sir. You are right. I had forgotten that was the reason behind that directive. Thank you for clarifying that and correcting me."

Pretending I didn't hear my staff silently chuckling among themselves I resumed with my report. "As I approached the unmarked car it was filling with smoke and starting to burn; some of the window glass was shattered and all the tires were flat."

"I looked into its front seat and observed that the two PAU, political affairs unit, detectives I know as Chen Yu and his partner Ho Tang had been riddled with bullets and could not have survived their wounds even if an aid car has been immediately available to provide emergency trauma treatment and transport to a hospital."

"I was trying to sneak and peek into the rear of the unmarked car but the vehicle now was under constant fire from at least four weapons, all of them Uzi's or other fast-firing automatic pistols."

"I spotted two men firing from behind the protection of the white Land Rover and what appeared to be two women firing in three-shot bursts from behind the body of the green pickup."

"There was a brief lull in the incoming fire as the shooters moved forward to take up improved positions for their assault. That lull gave me a second to pop up and take a look in the rear seat. What I saw was a lot of blood spatter, apparently thrown into the rear seat by the near continuous impact of the shooter's 9-mm slugs into the cop's bodies in the front seat."

"There was a rookie HKP constable later identified as Guan Xueguang lying on top of a civilian-clothed, manacled and chain-hobbled prisoner in the foot well behind the front seat. I cracked open the left side rear door which at that time was partially out of sight of the shooters and dragged the cop, then the prisoner out of the car and around to the rear of what was left of the police car."

"Constable Guan at that time showed good sense in taking a second pair of handcuffs and manacling the prisoner, later determined to be Chung Shan, a high-level member of the 14K triad, to the rear frame of the car."

"Sergeant Zhou had rejoined me at my position after locating a couple of police reserves in the growing crowd of on-lookers who agreed to take over crowd control until backup arrived," I explained.

"I sent Constable Guan across Queensway to get on our car's command frequency to request immediate backup and other assistance. Secondly, Constable Guan was directed to check on the welfare of the occupants of a white Red Crescent van that later had been forced into a utility pole by the shooter's cars sometime during the altercation."

Taking a breath, I continued, "After completing his assignment Guan dodged his way back across the four lanes of grid-locked traffic to rejoin us and resume his duty of protecting the prisoner. Guan muttered something to me as he resumed custodial control of the prisoner, something to the effect that 'No one was there!'"

I didn't mention the fact that Guan had pulled his gun on me in his confusion over who I was. The dead deserve the benefit of the doubt.

"The shooters upon seeing the sergeant and I appear on the scene jumped in their cars and fled. But they soon returned to finish the job they had began."

"The shooters improved their firing positions by taking advantage of the crowd when they returned. The hailstorm of incoming bullets resumed once again."

Looking over at Ming I saw him nod as he remembered the gunfight we'd both be extremely lucky to walk away from. I continued, "It was about then that three of the shooters decided we were defenseless and decided to rush us. There were two men and a woman—their tradecraft suggested they all were professionals."

I continued, "The first man who left the protection of the crowd to charge us we later found out was a mook named Wie Cao who we were fortunate to take down with our revolvers."

"The last two shooters, a man Yin Lu and a woman Lei Jie from their identification, Ming and I dealt with using hand-to-hand combat. The 14K must be getting pretty sloppy if they are letting their shooters go out carrying ID. It more or less led responsibility for the attack back to the 14K."

"When we were checking the bodies to make certain they were no longer a factor relative to our safety, Ming reported seeing the remaining woman shooter get into the green pickup and take off at a high rate of speed down the sidewalk adjacent to Cotton Tree Drive. The grid-locked traffic prevented any travel on the road itself. A minute after that backup arrived on-scene."

I gestured to Sergeant Zhou Ming and said, "You know the part about Constable Guan and the prisoner better than I because at that point I had to go and report in to the responding backup commander. Ming, why don't you fill us in on that." I took my seat.

Ming shyly stood up to address the group. He wasn't much of a talker except to me in unguarded moments. To say he is a large man would be an understatement. He had been my driver since I made chief inspector going on several years ago and we owe each other. Several times over the past two years we have saved one another's life in armed confrontations.

My driver is about 50 years-of-age with a dark complexion, married with no kids, stands an even 6-feet tall and weighs in at about 255 pounds. He is a natural athlete and played with distinction with a local Hong Kong championship soccer team when in high school.

Ming began, "There isn't much to say about this. The Inspector had ordered the kid to protect the prisoner at all costs and the kid did that. The constable ended up taking number of shotgun rounds and 9-mm rounds in his back, doing his duty—anyone of them fatal in itself. The 9-mm rounds had continued through the officer's body into the prisoner. Both were dead. The kid's body was really torn up by the shotgun slugs. He did a damn fine job." Finished and seeing no one had any questions, Ming sat down.

Then I gave out assignments. I told Ho Pham, the Homicide inspector to have Lieutenant Du get detectives over to the political affairs unit and pry out of them why Chung had been picked up in a warrantless street snatch in the first place.

I also wanted to know which administrator had ordered the PAU boss to execute the apprehension, rarely used since 2006 when Inspector Guan of my squad has been murdered.

If Du couldn't find out at his level then he would escalate it first to Ho Pham, and if that didn't work, to me and I'd go to the commissioner's office to get the reason for SWAT picking up Chung.

At that time Russell pushed himself off the wall and interrupted once again. "Fox, get this written up and on my desk by 2:00 p.m. today. The commissioner's office is already on my phone demanding an accounting on how three of *his* men got slaughtered in broad daylight."

"And get with the triad intelligence unit and find out what this Chung character knew what made him so important that the 14K would risk committing the unforgivable sin of killing a cop, or in this case, three cops. They had to know that is going to bring heat down on them, disrupt their normal street scams, and send them at least temporarily to the mattresses. All to either break Chung out of custody or kill him to stop him from talking to us. Must have been very damn important to spend that much political capital to ice one man," he concluded.

With that the assistant chief walked out of the room. As soon as he left the room, Elizabeth got up and went over to a telephone to make a call in a guarded voice. After a minute, she hung up and turned back to the room. "Yup, the security guard at the metal detector says Russell just got on the elevator and punched for the button for the fifth floor—commissioner's country."

While Elizabeth had been on the phone checking her illicit sources, everyone else had refreshed their coffee and green tea and snagged another pastry before returning to their seats.

I never had dared to embarrass Elizabeth by asking her how she got all the cops in the Arsenal Street HQ complex to do her bidding especially when they knew if they got caught it would mean the loss of their jobs. I guess I was afraid of what her answer might be. Someday I would regret that I hadn't had the courage to have gone ahead and asked her anyway.

3

03 October 2006, Thursday, 12:00 noon (HKT)
HKP Headquarters—CAP's Conference room
Arsenal and Harcourt Road
Admiralty district—Hong Kong Island

When we returned to our seats at the conference table after devouring what was left of Elizabeth's pastries, I dropped the bombshell. "However, there is a back story to yesterday," which immediately got their attention. They all knew since I had made a point of not mentioning it when Russell was in the room, then there was a distinct possibility that what I had to tell them had such impact and the longest legs, that it was not inconceivable that police corruption at the top, perhaps even internationally, could be involved.

This crew of outlaws I have, they thirst for out-of-the-boundaries cases like these. They had already risked their careers in 2005 by putting a HKP chief inspector and several detectives into Victoria Prison. I wondered, do we all have a death wish driving us to rejoin the forbidden hunt?

I began, "Remember the Red Crescent van I told you about that the shooters had forced into a utility pole yesterday at the gun fight? Well, when officer Guan returned, running back across four lanes of Queensway traffic to rejoin Ming and myself, he had said, "No one was there?" At the time I was to busy trying to save Ming's and my own life. Thus I hadn't taken the time at that point in the firefight to quiz Guan to find out which 'No one' he was referring to."

"Well Guan, bless his departed soul, was correct. There was no one in the van when the medics checked it for casualties. Apparently the occupants of the van had fled the scene after discovering the van was not drivable."

"The medics followed procedure and reported the empty vehicle to the crime scene commander. He, in turn, had Traffic toss it as a suspicious circumstance. What the Traffic unit found resulted in them dragging me over to look into the van's cargo box."

"First of all, we all felt that the inside of the van's box, especially the floor appeared to be too high, or it had too little headroom as compared to the outside height dimensions of the truck," I explained.

"Add to that the fact that there was a commercial vehicle air conditioner running on its highest setting concealed inside the cargo box. But for all the frigid air that was being generated, the temperature inside the box was hot as hell."

Searching back in my memory to ensure I was accurately reciting the facts, I continued, "One of the SWAT guys grabbed a crowbar off their truck and began poking around until he found a concealed trapdoor in the floor of the van's cargo box. When he pried it open, frigid air and a very pungent smell of decomposing body parts assaulted our noses. The smell was so foul that everyone but the SWAT guy crawled out of the cargo box and barfed at the curb."

"We noticed that the supply line from the air conditioner was piped directly down through the van box floor and into this concealed area. Without any visible point of exhaust venting, we assumed that that method of piping had the effect of super-chilling the hidden compartment, perhaps to prevent the putrid decomposition smell from leaking to the outside environment where it eventually would have been noticed."

"Everyone backed away from the truck at that point. We strung the crime scene tape fifty feet away from all sides of the truck except where we were obstructed by the side of the adjacent building. Then the crime scene commander called out the fire department's biohazard team."

"Now, I have heard of draconian body part harvesting operations before. In fact there is variation of it in Pakistan. Its poorest citizens, when they need money for basic medical care, food, or medicine, go to a specified hospital and a surgeon removes one of their kidneys."

"For giving up the healthy kidney they are told they will receive payment that in U.S. funds would be $2,500. But after the hospital charges them for the surgical supplies and whatever they need during their recovery they only net about half of that amount."

Dredging my memory for further details I continued with the gruesome recitation, "The surgeon who does the harvesting turns right around and sells the kidney to a transplantation service that deals in body parts. He receives the equivalent in U.S. funds of $6,000 to $12,000 unless the purchaser is from China where the black market is up to $72,000 per healthy kidney."

"I recently read in USA-Today that frequently an entire Pakistani family has been each forced to sell one of their kidneys when it becomes critically necessary to obtain money for the family's survival. I know, it sounds barbaric, doesn't it."

"The Medical Examiner tells me the body parts we found in the ice chests likely were harvested post mortem in a illegal harvesting location. Possibly without either the permission or knowledge of the corpse's relatives or loved ones. They found a lot of highly-transplantable tissue, bones, organs and even the corneas from eyes, all of which I am told are hot items on both the legal and illegal body part transplantation market."

Grabbing a refill on my coffee, which served to start a stampede to the urn and the crumbs of the pastries, I continued, "When the biohazard team arrived we moved the crime scene tape another fifty feet away from the van effectively closing down Queensway. That sent the ranking Traffic officer on the scene into the ozone, literally. Despite a commendable effort on the part of the biohazard squad leader to explain to him why it was necessary, and therefore, nonnegotiable."

"Cutting to the chase here," I continued, "the medics that are embedded in the biohazard team determined that the harvested body parts in the refrigerated compartment hadn't been cleaned yet, or what is referred in the medical field as being 'processed.'"

"That is a chemical cleaning process that must be accomplished before the parts can be certified as sterile of contaminates and disease before being sold to a tissue bank for transplantation."

"As the medic advised us that the parts were not being handled in accordance and in the approved manner specified in the transplantation protocol we are going to assume that we have just stumbled on a outlaw body part harvesting operation."

"The crime scene commander called medical examiner Dr. Lu Dong, M.D. to the scene. After a brief inspection of the macabre scene Dr. Dong told us that the parts appeared to have been harvested from deceased bodies in the past six hours. Making a quick tally he estimated that what was in the hidden compartment was worth well over US$500,000 on the world transplantation black market. The doc suggested we look for a illegal human bone and tissue harvesting 'chop shop.'"

"Okay, "I concluded, "this hasn't been released to the Media yet but I have no idea how long we can sit on it. You know how the Chinese feel about their ancestors and handling of the bodies of their deceased relatives so we need to get on top of this *yesterday*."

Turning to our newest Inspector, I queried, "Mini?"

"Yes, Boss," she replied.

I spoke to the woman having absolute faith in her ability and willingness to accomplish the unusual assignment I was handing her despite the admittedly limited timeframe I able to give her to produce it.

"Mimi, none of us know anything about this type of crime. I want you to go to the ME's office or anywhere else you need to go and by 9 a.m. tomorrow morning put together a educational briefing on what we are dealing with here."

"Do not share this information with anyone but the ME's. They are already aware of the incident today and know if they ever leak to the Media they'll find themselves occupying one of their own body bags. Any questions?"

She replied, "No, Boss, sounds pretty exciting though."

When I heard that, I raised my head from my notes and looked her directly in the eyes. "If you think that this is exciting, Mimi, I can see why there still isn't a Mr. Mimi."

The rest of the team broke up in laughter as the new kid's face turned pink. We shoved our chairs back and returned to the full afternoon of traditional crime fighting we still had ahead of us.

Very soon we would come to discover that this latest atrocity was anything but a laughing matter.

————

03 October 2007, Same day, 6 p.m. (HKT)
Interpol calls
The Penthouse Condo—Peak District
Hong Kong Island

After a steady steam of adrenaline-junkie cops sticking their heads in my office all afternoon, and having to repeat yesterday's massacre account ad infinitum, the remainder of my day was relatively non-productive.

At 5:30 p.m. I walked into the conference room where Zhou Ming was studying for the Lieutenant's exam, at his wife's insistence he told me, and said, "Let's roll."

By the time Zhou rounded up the car and we crept our way through rush hour traffic, it was 6 p.m. when we pulled up in front of my condo. I told Ming to pick me up at 8:30 a.m. the next morning. Before I got out, I once again thanked him for having my back at the shootout yesterday. Then headed into my building as he drove away.

The lobby of our building seemed eerily deserted when I walked through it to catch one of the two elevators that went to the penthouse. Not even the doorman was in attendance.

Once inside the condo door I went directly to the bedroom, changed into kitchen clothes, and headed there to prepare my dinner. I felt that I needed to keep my mind occupied with mundane chores. So I decided on Asian Noodle Soup. What with preparation and cooking time, that would keep my mind occupied for an hour, long enough to unwind from the day's activities.

A fledging gourmet cook, I keep the kitchen's cupboards well stocked, more so than before Alicia had moved to her family's place in Taiyunan. Feeling I was pretty well stocked up but not wanting to be interrupted while I was creating what at my entry-level ability would be considered a culinary masterpiece, I opened and closed cupboard doors, pulling out what I needed, checking each off a mental inventory until I was certain that all the necessary ingredients were on hand.

Gathering all the ingredients to within easy reach between the butcher block and counter, I started building my dinner. I combined some fat-free, low sodium chicken broth, one garlic clove, freshly peeled ginger root, and soy sauce in a large stockpot; and then put the pot on the glass stove top, to bring it to a simmer.

I added a half-pound of pork tenderloin, covered the pot again and let it simmer until I could insert a thermometer into the thick part of the pork and get a reading of exactly 155 degrees, which took about twenty minutes.

At that point I removed the pork from the pot and stuck it in the preheated oven to maintain the pork at its current temperature. Then in went peeled carrots, sliced diagonally and about an eighth of an inch thick. I replaced the cover on the pot after venting it slightly, and allowed the pot to simmer another few minutes.

Once that had been accomplished, I added the green portion of half-inch sliced bok choy, sliced shiitake mushrooms, some frozen corn, diagonally sliced scallions, and fresh chopped cilantro. The pot had to simmer another five minutes until the vegetables would be tender.

At the same time I had been separately cooking Yakisoba stir fry noodles according to the package's direction. When they were ready, I drained them.

Measuring out just the right amount of chili garlic sauce, I added it to the soup; then seasoned everything to my personal taste with kosher salt and restaurant-grade pepper.

Then I thinly sliced the pork that had been kept warm in the oven. I ladled a healthy portion of the soup into an Augustus-sized bowl, including pork slices and noodles in the proper portion, the remainder of which I would package as a leftover in the Sub-Zero stainless-steel refrigerator following dinner.

Pouring a small glass of Chardonnay and grabbing a soupspoon from a drawer, I carried it and my dinner into the living room, setting both on the T.V. table alongside my black special-order Lazy-Boy recliner. Then flipped on the Star-TV channel evening news program, all ready in progress, and sat down to enjoy my creation.

About 7:30 p.m. while watching a week-old edition of *America's Most Wanted*, my phone rang. When I answered it, *Wai*, I heard a series of clips and clacks that indicated a scrambler device was attached to the telephone set on the other end. I said *"Wai,"* or 'hello' into the headset again, this time including my name.

Out of the ozone came a disembodied voice, the typical vocal aberration generated by an electronic voice masking frequency scrambler. The voice instructed me "Call Angry Dragon," which was repeated twice before the connection was broken.

————

I need to give you a little background here before continuing. As you know the Hong Kong police department's commissioner reports to David Tsang, the HKSAR chief executive. Tsang in turn owes his job to the boys on the communist politburo in Beijing.

Therefore, I am reasonably certain that you have figured out by now that important intelligence information or exchange of almost any level of security classification that has the even the slightest possibility of reflecting unfavorably on the Peoples Republic of China, will never be distributed downward through Hong Kong police communication channels. That has been the situation ever since June of 1997 when Hong Kong officially became one of the PRC's special administrative regions.

Occasionally I find it necessary for me to reach out beyond HKP traditional channels when there was a threat to America, or American interests, of which I am still a citizen. Especially since I would have as much chance of obtaining in-house support from the Hong Kong police to expose and deal with a anti-American plot as the proverbial life expectancy of a snowball in hell.

An excellent example of a situation like this is when I discovered a plot by the Chinese to smuggle a nuclear warhead-tipped missile from North Korea into the PRC through Hong Kong last year, 2006.

Communist Chinese officials had paid North Korea millions for the illegal purchase. It was their intent to covertly ship it through the former crown colony's lax custom's procedures in Hong Kong to the Chinese port of Guangzhou. Using a rogue merchant vessel to transport it out Victoria Harbour and up the Pearl River into Mainland China.

Despite the threat to nuclear proliferation not to mention the threat to America's west coast cities, I could expect no assistance from Beijing's puppet, Hong Kong's chief executive or anyone in my own department.

The Hong Kong Police owe their first allegiance to the department's commissioner, who in turn owes his loyalty to HKSAR's chief executive, and he to the People's Republic of China.

But despite all the roadblocks that stood in my way I couldn't just let the communists in the PRC politburo take ownership of a nuclear-tipped missile thereby upsetting the world balance of power. That would permit China to step up on the world stage to confront America's MAD, mutually assured destruction, capability which for decades has kept all the world's nuclear-capable countries in check.

So I committed what admittedly was a covert treasonous act against my employer and the HKSAR, and by extension the PRC, by covertly arranging to meet David Chow, the Hong Kong U.S. Consulate's Senior FBI Legate out in Hong Kong's New Territories to enlist his assistance.

The bad news is that after a two-hour discussion in the back of a small noodle shop in the town of Lok Ma Chau, just a short distance from Hong Kong's northern border crossing into the PRC at Lo Wu, Chow and I decided that political protocol prevented the Federal Bureau of Investigation from getting involved solely on the word of an expat American who technically was committing treason by even bringing the world peace-threatening matter to Chow's attention in the first place.

The good news was that David Chow eventually came up with a plan to kill two birds with a single stone. He would request the covert services of Interpol, which would conceal my having any knowledge of the situation. The international police agency would interdict the weapon in-route and thereby prevent the weapon from being added to the Chinese communist's Armageddon capability. Interpol would employ a mercenary action team to prevent the weapon from ever reaching the People's Republic of China.

Realizing that this likely wasn't the last time this type of politically sensitive situation would come up, arrangements were by Chow and Interpol at the request of the FBI, to provide me with a hi-tech classified satellite cell phone. This would permit me to have a limited conversation directly with the designated Interpol case agent, code named Angry Dragon.

FBI Special Agent, or in State Department-speak, Consulate General Legate Chow, instructed me the special phone was only for use in the remote instance that I again came across knowledge of any plan in the future that threatened the safety and security of the United States. And in an instance where I found myself unable to address the threat from within the framework of the Hong Kong police department for political reasons. Chow suggested that we refer to any action Interpol might subsequently be willing to undertake based on the information I provided as "Plan B."

The arrangement the FBI and Interpol set up was to provide me with the clandestine cell phone on U.S. soil to shield me from the potential of any trumped up charges of treason by the People's Liberation army, or PLA, which have an adequate if limited presence in Hong Kong.

Because the PLA had an intelligence presence in Hong Kong, I knew they occasionally kept me under surveillance as a matter of form, my being a citizen of America which essentially equates to being an enemy of China, and with my working in a sensitive position in police agency in what legally is a Chinese city.

I had already been scheduled to travel to the United States to represent Hong Kong, thus the PRC, by attending an urgent intelligence briefing concerning a previously unknown al Qaeda terrorist threat to the 2008 Olympic Summer Games in Beijing.

I was ordered by the office of the HKP commissioner of police to attend the briefing solely because the FBI had refused to let any PRC intelligence operatives into the U. S. to attend the briefing.

The FBI painted them all with a broad brush claiming that a PRC operative, even if escorted to and from Quantico, the FBI Academy, and the U.S. point of entry, constituted a threat to the national security of the United States. So I was strictly an errand boy, assimilating the briefings intelligence, and then repeating what had been revealed to the PRC intelligence directorate once I returned to Hong Kong.

The handover of the high-tech satellite device was to be made by the Interpol agent. As the FBI as explained it to me, the normally avoided one-on-one contact was so I would know what the agent looked like in the extremely remote chance that at a future date a situation arose that was so critical that he would be forced to approach me directly in Hong Kong.

The transfer of the instrument would take place immediately following the end of the last day of the FBI briefing. During the controlled confusion as the attendees were rushing around to finish their packing. Turning in their visitor credentials so they could get their rental cars released from FBI's high-security academy parking lot and begin the drive back to the airport to catch a shuttle to New York City.

If one of the visitors wandered away briefly it wasn't likely to trigger a facility alert, which I knew from experience from my training there over several decades ago, would have been announced by sirens, bellowing loudspeakers, and the call-out of armed Marines.

———

The FBI Academy resides on a 385-acre secure facility in Quantico, Virginia, in the middle of a 4,000-acre USMC base.

The main street at the academy is appropriately known as 'Hoover Road.' It is reached by turning off Highway I-95 onto a two-lane road, which is exactly one-mile from the facility. The FBI likes to be exact. The access road into the FBI academy is guarded by U.S. Marines. They wear fatigue uniforms and are armed with automatic pistols and loaded M-16A assault rifles, modified to return to their fully automatic capability in lieu of the three-shot maximum burst now available on traditional U.S. Army M-16's.

Identification and prior written approval to enter the academy grounds is required. Those special agents not on permanent assignment to the academy, along with all visitors of any type, must display the 'visitors badges' issued by the Marines at all times.

The FBI facility is bordered by woodlands and literally surrounded by Marine personnel, equipment, weapons, and brick and mortar buildings. Unless you are a staff instructor, or enrolled in an academy class, an escort is required on the campus. Visitors notice that the FBI academy and its new companion, the DEA academy, have an austere, college-like feeling. The grassy lawns and stands of trees that surround the facility do not suppress that feeling.

The FBI Academy has both indoor and outdoor shooting ranges, and a new state-of-the-art forensics center that it and the U.S. Drug Enforcement Agency fund and share. There is a cluster of three concrete and brick hi-rise buildings, each ornamented by ground-to-roof pillars, connected to each other and the class facilities by glassed-in breezeways known to staff and students alike as 'gerbil tubes.'

The three high-rise buildings are residential student dormitories named 'Jefferson, Madison, and Washington.' Madison and Washington are traditional residential adult living environments divided into two-person rooms, with two sharing a common bathroom/shower.

Jefferson has single-occupancy rooms and is generally reserved for higher-ranking visitors. Each room contains a bed, TV, desk, chairs, nightstand, lamps, dresser, Internet access, motel-sized refrigerator and a bathroom with shower.

The dormitories are all within easy walking distance of the classrooms, pool, gym, dining hall, and conference halls in the various buildings. Military visitors often comment that the overall complex appears to have been purposely arranged in a tight, defensible geometrical pattern. Woodlands bordering the athletic fields and Hogan's alley, a self-contained, fully functional village used to train agents in crime scene scenarios, are rigorously pruned back and held in check for obvious security reasons.

To the north behind the red-and-white striped water tower, the forest continues down to a lake that is reserved for use by the military and academy personnel and their families. It was behind the striped water tower on the last day of the extended briefing that I made the pre-arranged contact with the covert Interpol agent, Angry Dragon, and took possession of the clandestine satellite cell phone.

Angry Dragon turned out to be a large 6-foot-tall, dark-skinned, athletic man. He was wearing an expensive dark blue suit and nontasseled back loafers with a white shirt open at the throat. His face and neck seemed inappropriate as compared to his elegant custom-made suit, which I recognized as likely being the work of one of the master tailors whose shops proliferate Nathan Road on the Kowloon peninsula in Hong Kong.

His neck and face bore old scars that identified the man as a person accustomed to dealing out and being on the receiving end of violence. It was obvious from his scars that at one time he had fancied himself an accomplished knife fighter. His eyes were a penetrating icy blue, his gene pool probably French, and he had enormous hands.

After the exchange, he took his leave first. As he rapidly walked off I had observed that he walked with a slight favoring of his right leg no doubt owed to one of the man's physical confrontations in the past.

———

I went into the condo's master bedroom clothes closet and retrieved the satellite cell phone from the bottom of a basket of dirty laundry. From memory, I dialed a number. The phone only rang once. Angry Dragon answered the phone almost immediately.

He began to speak before I had an opportunity to say anything. You see, when making a surreptitious phone call in Hong Kong, time is of the essence. The listeners are PRC security organizations. Which essentially means the People's Republic of China. And the paranoid PRC army listens to everyone in Hong Kong.

This includes the Hong Kong police department if the caller or recipient of the call is conducting an unscheduled contact with another police agency. Even if that agency is the international policing organization Interpol.

"Chief Inspector Fox, I need all the pertinent details you have on the body parts case your people began to work on yesterday. But remember the sixty-second rule. Now, talk!"

Noting the exact time carefully on my watch, I summarized all the information I currently had on the body parts discovery into a sound bite of slightly less than sixty seconds. Angry Dragon's call would be bounced off a number of Hong Kong cell towers and communications satellites over the Hong Kong Special Administrative Region, before reaching the Interpol agent to disguise both the caller and call recipient's physical location.

Sixty seconds is maximum amount of time that the FBI tells me one could use a phone in Hong Kong without its physical location being triangulated by the PRC secret police. Their sophisticated antennae are located atop the Chinese People's Liberation Army Force building located at the corner of Edinburgh Place and Murray Road in the Admiralty district on Hong Kong Island.

If this evening's telephonic contacts between Angry Dragon and myself were triangulated and traced back to me, by tomorrow I would find myself either in Stanley Prison, or worse, forcibly shanghaied into the PRC, likely to never to be heard from again. It would be like I never existed as far at the paranoid communist officials in Beijing's internal security organizations were concerned.

I finished my spiel with about five seconds to spare, which Angry Dragon consumed by his response. "Fox, you need to absolutely keep me in the loop on this. It has serious international implications." Then the spook cut the connection.

I sat back in my recliner and finished off the glass of chardonnay. Then I policed up my dinner bowl and utensils and carried everything into the kitchen remembering to follow Alicia's instructions about always rinsing everything off before putting it in the dishwasher.

Returning to the living room I shut the TV off and began to give serious thought to the phone call I had just completed. How had Angry Dragon, I didn't know his real identity, have known about the Red Crescent van with the hidden compartment and its load of body parts?

Only my staff, a tight-lipped police Medical Examiner, a couple of supervisory-level traffic cops, and the fire department's biohazard team even knew about the discovery. And I would bet my life that my people were not the source that leaked the information, no matter how hard someone above them may have pushed.

And how could a single discovery of a stash of smuggled body parts less than forty-eight hours ago have reached the ears of Interpol so quickly? What was Interpol's interest in what basically was a local investigation?

Why would Interpol of all organizations be investigating a black market illegal bone-and-tissue harvesting investigation in Hong Kong?

The Interpol organization's operating charter did not permit it to maintain any 'operations' personnel.

Anytime the shadowy organization found itself in need of deniable covert field action teams, say like when they had played a valuable role in what I refer to as the option "B" operation which Interpol had utilized last year to steal and dispose of the highly radioactive shipping container containing a damaged nuclear missile and warhead, they contracted the job out.

Interpol regularly contracted with Arhat Thais, meaning they are honest Thai cops who occasionally took on covert contract jobs from the worldwide police agency. Internally, the Thai team proudly thought of itself as the Naja Siamensis, which in Thai means 'Spitting cobra snake, which never lets go once it has sunk its deadly fangs into a victim.' The team's unofficial theme song from the days of the Green Berets in Vietnam was 'The Ride of the Valkyries.'

Arhat teams welcome the covert mercenary assignments. It provides their families with a few of the nicer things available in the notorious expensive shops of Bangkok. And for the officers themselves, it provides needed temporarily relief from having to enforce some of Bangkok's archaic laws such as the one requiring elephants working at construction projects inside Bangkok's city limits at night to have a red tail light affixed to their swishing tails.

Interpol paid their contract action teams well and promptly in the country's local currency which in the Thai's case was the Baht. In addition, Interpol picked up all their related expenses.

I didn't have enough information to come to any conclusion about why the international investigative agency would be interested in our black market harvesting case. I promised myself to push Angry Dragon for more details when we next communicated. Until then I decided to put the matter back up on my mental shelf until I did have enough information to come to an educated assessment.

It was almost ten by now, and I was headed for bed when the phone rang once more. This time it was Alicia calling from her father's home in Taiyunan.

I have to be very careful when talking with Alicia on these rare occasions when she calls as she is hypersensitive to any comment I might make that could conceivably be misconstrued as being critical of her. She hadn't yet permitted me to initiate calls to her saying it was because her hours were unpredictable what with caring for her father and running the clinic. I understood that her sensitivity was the actual reason behind her wishes on that matter.

She had left our home in Hong Kong suddenly without notice when she heard her mother was near death from inoperable cancer. When Alicia arrived in Taiyunan she learned that her mother had already passed on.

Then, when talking with the Oncology doctor at the hospital where her mother had passed on, she learned her family had been keeping two secrets from her.

One was that her mother's cancer was hereditary. Her mother and her mother's mother had died from the same disease meaning that Alicia also could be genetically programmed to get the disease.

I could understand her fear. My wife had died tragically in 1996 of undetected pancreatic cancer back in New York City. Although we'd had no children, I could now admit to myself that my loss and my inability to deal with it had been one of my reasons for applying for early retirement from NYPD before I was even offered this Hong Kong job.

The trauma of my wife's death had driven me to drinking on duty and picking fights with my superiors. If the offer from the Hong Kong police hadn't come along a year later, I knew I soon would have been forcibly retired from the NYPD on Stress Disability.

Secondly, Alicia's father had been slipping into dementia for some time but with her mother's death, she learned that fact had also been kept from her because her parents felt Alicia was a sensitive child and therefore couldn't handle the knowledge.

When she had called to inform me of this last year, she had been understandably hysterical and had screamed at me over the phone, "I have to have a blood screen, a test, either the BRCA1 or BRCA2, or both, I don't know at this stage. I'm not a gynecologist. The test is designed to determine the presence of positive markers for a bad, mutated gene in a woman whose family has a history of breast cancer."

She had continued, "The screen is to determine whether the female off-spring or sibling also has the mutated gene. The test results will give the woman an opportunity to begin prophylactic treatment which sometimes can include removal of both breasts to avoid the cancer."

She ended up slamming the phone down the phone on me that night, after accusing me of being insensitive when I suggested she return to our home in Hong Kong and we would fight the disease together.

Didn't he know, she had wondered from her father's home in China, *she just couldn't pack her bag and return to Hong Kong as Augustus was suggesting when her father needed her? Someone had to care for his senility and keep his medical practice operating, and there was the matter of burying her mother. Why didn't he understand?*

And things had gone from bad to worse when the results of her tests came back 'positive.' That required that she start making decisions immediately about what surgical procedures she was willing to undergo in an attempt to save her own life.

When I had asked, Alicia refused to permit me to come to Taiyunan, sarcastically saying, "Augustus, you of all people, Mr. Self Sufficient, certainly wouldn't understand what I am going through."

That was nearly a year ago and she still was being secretive with me whenever she called. She had finally told me earlier this year that she had gone ahead with the recommend prophylactic surgeries and was slowly recovering, although she admitted that she continued to put in full shifts at the clinic five days a week so her father's practice wouldn't lose its patient base. I sensed there was something else that was going on in Alicia's life that she wasn't telling me but I knew better than to push her for an explanation.

Tonight she sounded tired but upbeat, amusing me with stories about her day, including all the cranky patients she had to deal with. Especially those that spat on the floor from the time they walked into the small clinic waiting room until they left, a centuries old habit of the Chinese. She said she had put up with the spitting today as long as she could until one 85-year-old geezer had spat a huge glob onto one of her freshly polished white buck shoes. She said she couldn't help herself and momentarily went crazy. She spat back hitting one of the dirty lenses of the old codger's coke bottle-thick glasses. She and I had a good laugh about that.

Then abruptly, before I could ask a meaningful question about her health, her future plans, or when I could come to Taiyunan to spend some time with her, she said "Good bye," and hung up on me.

The confusing telephone conversation with Alicia followed me to bed that night. I lay on the set of expensive linens Alicia had bought home only last year before she left for Taiyunan; Sferra brand, a manufacturer of high-end Italian-made linens worldwide, their latest offering, the Burano Luce edition if you please, rich peach in color, a 1,020 thread-count with a silken scroll you could scarcely see. One of only eight sets of this model made in 2006, purchased for her by her mother before her death at a cost of $15,000. We also have a set in light lavender.

Sleep came to me slowly as it had every night since Alicia left Hong Kong. When it did finally sneak in the back door of my mind, it was troubled.

Life is like spending the time reading a novel only to find that someone has torn off the last chapter. But in our case, I planned on continuing to push her to give our relationship a chance, even if I had to write that final chapter myself.

4

04 October 2007, Friday, 9 a.m. (HKT)
Arsenal Street Police Headquarters
Crimes Against Persons Department
Wan Chai District—Hong Kong Island

Mimi Yin was sitting in my office when I arrived Friday morning. She looked tired, very tired, and I assumed that she had been up most of the night putting together her summary on the illegal body part harvesting industry.

The woman looked beat, had stains and wrinkles in her blue pants suit, a smudge on the sleeve of her matching blazer, and the slightest hint of body odor about her if one had a discriminating nose. She had put her hair up in a bun on top of her head but I was reasonably certain she was wearing the same outfit she'd had on yesterday. I almost felt a little embarrassed walking in on the woman dressed like I'd stepped out of GQ, Gentleman's Quarterly magazine.

This being Friday, unofficial casual day in the department, I had worn pair of gray slacks, a blue blazer, a yellow silk open-necked shirt, and a pair of fawn-colored Gucci loafers without socks. My gold Rolex Oyster Perpetual Day-Date watch was on my left wrist, and the rubber pale-yellow band honoring Cops Who Have Gone before Us celebrating the sacrifices of the NYPD police officers who had died trying to rescue citizens from the crumbling World Trade Towers in New York on September 11th, on my right.

Burying my discomfort knowing I'd just embarrass Mimi more if I made a point of the unintended disparity in dress, I said, "Good morning, Mimi. Whatchagot?"

When she handed me her report I said, "Let's go to the conference room. Please tell the other guys I'd like them to be there also."

As Mimi walked out of the room, I removed my coat and weapon, shoving the latter into my desk drawer and locking it. I briefly glanced at the pink Please Call slips Elizabeth had neatly centered in the middle of my desk but decided there was nothing there that that was so urgent it couldn't wait.

On top of the stack dated "8 a.m." this morning, written in her trademark vivid purple ink was a note from Elizabeth informing me that one of our two junior Administrative Assistants would be answering the office phone temporarily as she had gone over to Records to dig out some information that one of the inspectors needed for a status report.

The note stated that she also intended to return a piece of evidence to the HKP Property Room. Elizabeth occasionally did this to avoid the necessity of an inspector having to leave an investigation-in-progress to go physically stand in the oft-time lengthy 'Return Evidence' line, just to maintain the department's chain-of-evidence protocol.

This was the third time this week she had gone to Police Records, which was unusual. However, not anymore so than anything else that happened in my department where I put the emphasis on catching the bad guys, not following the department's mostly archaic rules to the letter like some blind savant.

Although doing record searches and returning evidence to the Property Room didn't fall anywhere in her job description I had no problem with Elizabeth showing initiative and helping out the inspectors to permit them to devote more time to their criminal investigations.

Although Elizabeth's presence in Records, therefore in criminal and personnel files, is a clear violation of police department protocol because Elizabeth isn't a sworn police officer, I figured the Records department supervisors over there didn't have a problem with her presence in the restricted area or one of them would have been on the phone chewing on my ear about it.

And relative to her occasional visits to the Property Room, I didn't even want to go there. I refused to think of all the potential grief that could cause me if my superiors discovered that deviation from department regulations.

———

After Ho Pham, Chen Ho and I poured our coffee, Mimi's was green tea, we all sat down along the large rectangle-shaped oak table. As Friday wasn't a scheduled meeting day in our office Elizabeth hadn't ordered in pastries which was probably best at least for my waistline. With Alicia up in Taiyunan for nearly a year now I do my own cooking. Add in the fact that due to my ever-increasing administrative workload my physical exercise level has been noticeably reduced.

Mimi took a dainty sip from her china teacup before opening her pink report portfolio. She'd been using the pink folder ever since the women in the department had participated en masse in a 5K walk for the Cure of Breast Cancer earlier in the year.

Inspector Yin began detailing a summary of what she had found out in the past twenty-four hours about the illicit, not to mention gruesome, body part harvesting industry.

Apparently the illegal practice of harvesting bones and tissue and other body parts for resale had only a couple of years ago came to the attention of the law enforcement in the West. When the indignities to the body of the host Alistair Cooke of the celebrated and long-running Masterpiece Theatre became known.

The famous old man's death in March of 2004 and the facts about what had happened to the old gentlemen's corpse brought the entire sordid practice out from under a rock and placed it center stage under law enforcement's spotlight.

In a secret backroom of a New York City funeral home the remains of the 95-year-old award-winning commentator had been dissected and 'parted out' like a valuable car in a chop shop. After the criminals removed the salable parts of the famous persona's body, they cremated the remainder so the authorities would have no evidence that anything untoward had occurred.

Luckily or unluckily, depending on your point of view, Cooke's daughter had been contacted by the NYPD Major Case Squad, the TV cop show that is featured on the American NBC and USA networks called *Law and Order—Criminal Intent*. The detective in Major Case had informed the woman that her father's body had suffered gross indignities no human should ever have happen to them, before or after death. Mimi reported as an aside that in his lifetime the Queen of England had knighted Sir Alistair Cooke.

Callous NYPD detectives had told her that her father's body was one of more than 1,000 such cases attributed to a ghoulish ring of multimillion-dollar illegal human bone—and tissue-harvesting operations in 2004. The discovery had the entire medical ethics community, organ donor agencies, and body part transplantation industry worldwide, under the microscope.

The Captain in-charge of New York's Major Case squad told the daughter that tissue and bone had been surgically removed from her father's body without her or anyone in her family's consent.

Then the products had been sold to companies that apparently don't ask too many questions, who clean and prepare the material for resale to the surgical transplant industry. Who often didn't complete the due diligence required to verify the source of the specimen.

The NYPD cops went on to tell the woman that the person who surgically removed the bones and tissue had also falsified her father's death certificate by reducing his age at time of death, and changing the cause of death to something that would not be of undue concern to a transplant surgeon making the decision about the body part's suitability.

In other words, to explain using a hypothetical situation, a person's bones and tissue who had died of complications brought on by AIDS certainly wouldn't be marketable, but by reducing the deceased's age and changing the cause of death to heart failure from old age, the body part became very marketable and in fact highly sought after. This despite the fact the transplant recipient of the bone or tissue would eventually contract AIDS from the contaminated body part. Not to mention the risk of exposure to the transplant team.

Despite the fact that her father didn't have any communicable or disease that would have made the bone or tissue unacceptable for transplantation, the detectives and the daughter were livid. People who were so ill that they needed a transplant were the victims of this scam as well as the transplant team who had the accepted the tissue.

This was especially worrisome when you understand that more than a million transplants are performed each year with tissue and related products that repair injured knees, spinal columns, defective heart valves, or are used to replace badly burned skin.

Transplant teams are supposed to acquire these replacement parts legally from tissue banks. The banks must document the body part's journey from the donor source to the tissue bank, and certify the part to be free of communicable disease, accompanied by a notarized copy of the medical examiner's death certificate.

The processing of bones and body tissue by a legitimate tissue bank requires high-tech procedures performed by a medical professional, licensed to do business in that jurisdiction. Screening, procuring, storing and cleansing the tissue are all extremely expensive procedures.

The American Medical Association estimates that the legitimate transplantation of body parts from cadavers to be a multi-billion dollar industry with an ever-increasing growth rate.

New York city authorities reported that illegal body part harvesting operations were crude beyond imagination. Unlicensed and under-trained medical personnel plunder corpses and sell body parts to organizations that are known to be lax in their verification of the source and certification of replacement parts, which are subsequently offered for sale to transplantation surgeons.

University of Hong Kong Medical School experts estimate that some disgraced Hong Kong Board-trained surgeons, who live on the wild side or whose drug use has cost them their license to practice medicine in the past, remove skin, bones and other body parts from up to 2,000 corpses annually in the HKSAR all without next-of-kin approval or knowledge.

To give us an example, Mimi used the following hypothetical case. In this instance, the femur bones—the thighbone—had been harvested from a deceased. That particular bone is in high demand. A harvested femur sells on the black market for between US$3,000 and $4,550 each.

A tibia—lower leg bone—sells for between US$390 and $600 a copy. Individual veins and arteries and there are literally miles of these, depending on their diameter, condition and length, can demand between US$900 and $3,500 each. An adult's circulation system is made up of about 60,000 miles of arteries, veins and capillaries. Add it all up and you'll see that a individual harvested body on the black market can generate as much as US$250,000—very big business indeed.

In the hypothetical case, depending on the family's wishes, the illegally harvested body may still have to be transported to another funeral home for embalming and burial. So the ghouls would remove the bones from the legs of the corpse, replacing them with a couple two-foot-long, one-inch-in-diameter piece of PVC pipe with PVC elbows used at the hips to hide the fact that the body's femurs had been illegally harvested.

Illegal body part harvesters are only interested in bones, ligaments, tendons, skin, corneas, heart valves, and blood vessels. They have zero interest in the organ donor industry that uses hearts, lungs or kidneys, because the retrieval process must be immediate because of the need to keep oxygen and blood flowing to the organ.

Since this past Wednesday when we came to realize a criminal operation such as this was actively operating somewhere in Hong Kong, Mimi had asked the New York cops what things her squad should look for, things that would be required to support the atrocious crime.

Mimi told us that there were two things that NYPD Major Case had told her would be required to make an illegal harvesting operation such as that cost effective.

First was an operating suite. Preferably located in an existing funeral home, kept separate from the public side of the business. To maintain the salability of the harvested parts the room would have to have a refrigerated walk-in freezer and optimally, a crematorium hidden away in the facility.

The existence of such a facility would be known only to a handful of individuals. Included in that very short list would be the overall head or leader of the racket, possibly a foreigner whose job permitted him to come and go at will in Hong Kong. And of course the medical professionals who actually operated the facility.

Secondly, and actually the more important of the two: You could meet the first requirement and the scheme would essentially be worthless without assistance from Customs or law enforcement. Someone willing for a price to turn a blind eye and overlook the transshipment of the product out of Hong Kong.

That would require a method to physically get the harvested body parts out of Hong Kong. After they had been cleansed and prepared in the outlaw tissue banks, probably by one of the former crown colony's firms that continue to operate under the law's radar. The parts and tissue couldn't be offered for sale to legitimate transplantation medical facilities in Europe and the United States until the parts arrived at a out-of-country facility, say in France, whose credentials and reputation were currently beyond question.

The Chinese are the world's biggest gossipers. Because of that fact attempting to operate the operation from donor source to recipient solely within the Hong Kong Special Administrative Region would be both foolhardy and impossible.

Mimi's assumption was that the bodies being plundered were either illegal immigrants from China, or the destitute and homeless here in Hong Kong, neither of which could afford to go to the police to report a missing relative.

So now we knew what our investigation had to accomplish to solve the case, put a stop to the illegal practice, and put some very bad people in prison. First we'd go after the operating theatre. Our paid confidential informants that no police department in the world can effectively operate without should be able to get us some leads on possible facilities that fit the profile for such a facility.

Identifying, isolating and exposing the cutting facility ought to flush out the crooked official or officials that were taking bribes to permit the practice to flourish, and turning a blind eye to getting the product out of Hong Kong. Oh, Boy, I thought, here we go again.

But perhaps the product was being smuggled out of Hong Kong under the cover of a legitimate operation, right under our noses. Wouldn't that be a genuine *whodunit*?

Regardless we had to get on top of the situation before the Media learned of its existence. I assigned continuation of the illegal body part harvesting investigation to Mimi Yin. It would be her street informants that should be able to turn up the location of the covert operating room if we promised them 'thirty pieces of silver'—but not the silver Tyrian shekels that Judas Iscariot got for betraying Jesus—as a performance incentive.

Next, Ho Pham reported that Homicide Lieutenant Du Ming, my old partner, had rousted his triad informants yesterday and had uncovered a potential reason why Chung Shan seemed to be so valuable to someone in the HKSAR chief executive's office. And subsequently so important to the leadership of the 14K triad that they would risk the certain wrath of the Hong Kong police department by slaughtering three of its sworn police officers just to break one of their gang members out of police custody.

Reading from the Ming's notes, Pham said that the information Lt. Du had purchased from his confidential informants, CI's, or snitches, is that the internal security directorate in the People's Republic of China, the PRC, had stumbled upon the 14K triad's '432'—the Straw Sandal—in a roundup of Falun Gong religious dissidents in Beijing last month.

Author's Interjection: A 432, or Straw Sandal, is at the same level in the triad hierarchy as the 426 rank of Red Pole; and the 415 rank of White Paper Fan. However, they serve different functions. The Straw Sandal functions as a triad messenger. Someone needs a cease-and-desist ultimatum note delivered? The 432 will deliver the note despite the risk to his or her personal safety by doing so. The 432 holds primary responsibility for organizing branch meetings and gang confrontations.

Should the reader be interested, please refer to the overview at the rear of this book for an insight into triad/tong hierarchy, history and operations, both in Hong Kong and in the United States today.

————

Under torture by the People's Republic of China's interrogators who are not restricted by democratic niceties such as individual human rights, the 432 had given up the information that a certain 14K '415' or triad administrative officer, Mr. Chung Shan, had received a visit from two high-ranking members of al-Qaeda in late July of this year.

The covert meeting was reportedly held at an obscure 14K business office located in Hong Kong's lawless Mongkok district. Chung supposedly was in negotiations for a proposed combined operation that would include members of both groups.

According to the babbling 432, the prearranged visit by the two Arabs was to discuss a major joint operation between the two criminal organizations during the upcoming Olympic Summer Games in Beijing in 2008.

The 432 also revealed that al-Qaeda planners came to the bargaining table with knowledge of two things.

First, was that the internal security directorate of the Peoples' Republic of China had been charged with the nonnegotiable mission of ensuring that the three-week schedule of the Summer Games in Beijing would be totally without any criminal incident that would reflect poorly on the potential of PRC emerging as a world super power.

Secondly, it was common knowledge among intelligence agencies around the world that Chinese triads hate the PRC communists; and they, the triads, for ideological and business reasons.

Communism requires a high-controlled social environment for it to work and prosper. But the triad's many schemes and rackets could not operate in a highly controlled environment. That specifically was the reason that the triads left the PRC decades ago and set up shop in Hong Kong which figuratively enjoys a democratic government.

————

China was speeding billons to induce the world community to come to Beijing in 2008. To see just how modern the country is, how skilled their people have become, how superior their infrastructure is as compared to that of the West, and how law bidding China's 1.3 billion citizens are.

The PRC could never fulfill the politburo's goal of becoming a superpower by 2010 without hundreds of billions of foreign investment dollars in their country. The funding was desperately needed to modernize China's industries and rural infrastructure to bring the entire country out of the agriculture age where 'As goes farming, so goes China's economy.'

Should criminals succeed in pulling off carefully planned and timed vicious attacks on the spectators attending the 2008 Summer Games, the politburo would have no option other than to turn loose their military to quell the violence.

That action in itself would cause hundreds of thousands of Olympic visitors to flee the country. They would return home with the thought firmly planted in their minds that China will never be anything but a backward nation of over 1.3 billion farmers.

In any case, such violence would prove to the world's tourists that the PRC certainly wasn't capable of handling the awesome responsibility of donning the mantle as a world super power, not now, not ever.

That slamming of the door on China's future would drive the PRC and its people even deeper into communism, preventing the country from achieving democracy, creating an environment that would be an increased threat to world peace.

And, of course, vis-à-vis, the World Trade Center towers in New York City in 2001, al-Qaeda would have proved again that their fanatics were capable of attacking 'Crusaders and infidels' anyplace and at anytime, no matter the magnitude of the security forces allied to protect them from the 'faithful.'

————

Once the captive had given up this intelligence, the PRC internal security organs had immediately alerted the politburo, which had notified the China's President Hu Jintao. He in turn had sent a personal envoy on a military flight directly to Hong Kong to demand an immediate meeting with Donald Tsang, the HKSAR's chief executive.

The message delivered to Tsang by Hu Jintao's personal envoy was simple. "Have your police pickup Chung Shan and deliver him to an appropriate location such as the Victoria Prison." Victoria Prison was specified because it had become impossible to economically operate and thus had been closed by the Hong Kong's Prison and Correctional Department earlier in the year.

A half dozen of China's most effective interrogators were being flown in commercial that afternoon aboard China Air and would take over custody and questioning of the prisoner from the Hong Kong police.

The last part of the instruction to Tsang was that it was imperative that Chung was delivered to the PRC interrogators in good shape, literally without a hair mussed on his treasonous head. The prisoner must be heavily guarded to prevent the 14K from attempting to silence him through assassination. The triad would have little doubt that eventually Chung would give up the triad's secrets to ruthless PRC interrogators.

In fact the envoy reported to Tsang that Hu Jintao actually favored the second alternative, as the how and why for the planned attack was not as important as making certain it never happened.

After PRC President Hu Jintao's personal envoy had met with Tsang, he had been driven back Kai Tak to catch a military flight back to Beijing. Kai Tak was the old closed Hong Kong airport, but currently still in use by the PRC Liberation Army to ferry people and equipment in-and-out of Hong Kong as needed. Before the envoy had left his office, Donald Tsang's administrative assistant had placed a call to Hong Kong's commissioner of police and demanded that he present himself at Tsang's office within the hour.

When the commissioner arrived with hat in hand as he served at Donald Tsang's convenience, the chief executive lost no time in relaying China's president's specific instructions regarding the action to be taken in regards to Chung Shan, the 14K's 415, in the next twenty-four hours.

The only additional information that Pham added to his report was something he'd gotten from Lt. Du Ming just before the meeting began. It was concerning a body that patrol officers found in Mongkok yesterday afternoon, that of a Ms. Kan a Que. She had been the surviving the female triad shooter who had panicked and used the green pickup to desert her colleagues during the firefight.

The 14K never leave loose ends lying around for the police to pickup, manipulate, and interrogate. And true to form they had wasted no time in eliminating the last potential witness who could have provided probative testimony that would have resulted in the conviction of triad's leaders for Chung's assassination in a Hong Kong Court of Law.

I thanked Ho Pham and asked him to please pass on to Lieutenant Ming my appreciation for digging out the triad's motivation behind the unusual public shootout that took the lives of three of our family members.

Turning to Chen Ho, I asked, "What did your anti-terror/anti-hijacking squad find out about the van, Ho?"

"Well, Boss, I had one of the mechanics from the police garage go over to the impound yard where the white 2002 Toyota van now empty of the body remains was towed and secured by the BioHazard team. The van's license plates turned out to be phony and all visible vehicle identification numbers had all been obliterated with acid."

"But there are about a dozen other locations on the vehicle where manufacturers emboss the VIN number that aren't so accessible or even well known to the average person. The mechanic was able to obtain a readable VIN from about six of the other locations on the van. We ran the records from the date the van had been first been sold, to the last year it had been legally registered. Here is where it gets suspicious," Ho grinned.

"It seems that particular van is registered to a front organization located in Lyon, France. I plan to get with the David Chow, Senior FBI Legate at the U.S. Consulate over on Garden Road in Central district, to see if they have access to the U.S. Central Intelligence Agency's computer base," Ho said.

Continuing, the inspector said, "If the CIA can't find out who runs the French front organization the van is registered to, then it doesn't exist, or so I'm told. The only problem is that what with approvals and such we could be looking at a couple weeks until they can work us into the computer's schedule. But if it is okay with you, Boss, I'll drop a dime and call 2523-9011 for an appointment. Then with my hat in hand, I'll head over there to ask the Hoover boys for their help.

Shaking my head, I replied, "Sure, go ahead Ho, but no agitating the animals when you are over there. We are fortunate those guys still do favors for us from time to time after you go over there and claim you don't speak English, then rag them when they try to communicate with you in their terrible Cantonese. I know that amuses you but let's get a little esprit de corps going here. We are mostly on the same side, you know."

"Sure, Boss, sure," Ho said insincerely as he continued with his report. "Okay, here is where it gets real interesting. Hong Kong Customs impounded that same van a couple of years ago at the Shenzhen border when it was caught being used to circumvent the *Sun Yee Mun* accords."

————

Sun Yee Mun is Cantonese which when translated literally means a new immigrant from the People's Republic of China. Only 150 Chinese are permitted to emigrate from China to Hong Kong each day, or a total of 54,750 a year.

Naturally the demand is much higher than the 150 limit permitted daily. This has given birth of virtual cash bonanza for smugglers who use vehicles like the van to move ten illegals at a time across the border into the Hong Kong Special Administrative Region, each paying up to US$10,000 a head.

Even though the PRC border guards don't pay much attention to this, the Hong Kong Customs inspectors do. When they discover a shipment of persons attempting to be smuggled into the HKSAR, they not only deport the cargo back across the border but they also impound every asset of value the smuggler has in his or her possession, such as the van.

————

Ho continued, "Boss, I went over to Customs and got a copy of their report. A physical inventory of the van revealed the same hidden compartment we found a couple of days ago. The Toyota van was dark blue at that time so it has since been repainted. And the Red Crescent logo is a phony. I called the Red Crescent managing director here in Hong Kong. She told me that they never use Toyotas because of some warranty matter that came up with Japan in the 1990's."

Grinning again, the man being a practical joker without equal in our department, he said "Then I pulled that particular HKP impound lot's records covering the past three years and guess what I found?"

Ho looked around the room at Ho Pham, Mini Yin and myself, his patented idiotic grin still had plastered on his face.

Finally losing my patience I said, "Ho, unless you are planning on quitting your day job to become a standup comedian, I suggest you stow it and continue your report."

With a fake hurt look on his face, Ho turned to me and said, "Okay, Boss. What is interesting here is that a van with those VIN numbers was checked out of the impound yard three months ago by a mechanic wearing a regulation police coverall. The paperwork he submitted said he was to deliver it to the Forensics lab for their evaluation, to see if it could be converted into a Crime Scene van seeing as they always are getting stolen even though the techs claim they never leave their keys in the ignition."

"Trouble is," Ho said, sitting down, still looking like the cat that ate the canary, said, "it never reached the lab, and it was not seen again until two days ago. Which was when the van crashed at the crime scene during the triad hit. And its occupants fled the scene leaving us with a box full of decomposing human body parts."

After giving what Ho had told us some thought, I complimented him on doing a good job in a very limited timeframe. And since he had proven his expertise, he was to please follow up on to who the van's current legal owners were, front company or not.

Now we all were up to date on where we stood in the shooting, the illegal part body harvesting operation, and attempting to trace the legal and registered owner of the van the body parts had been discovered in. With nothing else to discuss at this point, and with each of them having their assignments, I asked them to get back to me when they obtained additional information, or need me to get involved if they ran into an impregnable brick wall of bureaucracy.

Then I headed back for my office, they to their respective offices situated off the detective's bullpen, to answer our respective pink Please Call slips before heading to lunch.

————

It was after 5 p.m. Each of the inspectors had stopped by my office to wish me a good weekend. When I had first taken over the department, I'd felt guilty about going home when I knew my inspectors still were burning the midnight oil to bring their open caseloads to acceptable conclusions.

But then I had thought back to the many hours I routinely spent at my job. That caused me to come to accept the wisdom behind the saying, 'Those of who manage, also serve.' And frankly I haven't thought much about it since.

Fact was with the cop killings, the mysterious theft of white Toyota van previous impounded in a smuggling seizure, and then the gruesome body part harvesting operation apparently going on right here in our own city, we had three high-priority open cases.

If we didn't solve all three of these cases them in a timely manner, I was sure the commissioner, other politicians, or the Media wouldn't hesitate to ring my chimes. That grief I didn't need.

When I got to a stopping point in my backlog of paperwork, I paged Zhou Ming to take me home. It was after 6 p.m.

As we pulled out of the Arsenal Street HQ on the way to my condo, I asked him Zhou to stop by the Peak Café Bar. I had to pick up an order of take-out food I'd earlier ordered by phone.

————

The Peak Café Bar formerly was located where you would think a restaurant with that name should be, at the top of Victoria Peak. However when it had came time for the owners of the world-famous eatery to renew their lease on the government-owned property, they discovered that Hong Kong's usual political connivery was still alive and well even under Beijing's handpicked Hong Kong chief executive, Donald Tsang.

The Peak Café, the existing lessee, had been forced out of its lease by another restaurant group, which evidently had deeper pockets, or *Meiguo*—money, and more *Guanxi*—connections.

However there is a centuries-old saying among Asians. It went something like this, 'Forego the immediate tendency to seek revenge, for getting even is a much more satisfying objective.'

The evicted owner of the Peak Café owner had simply packed up his successful marketing formula and equipment and moved lock, stock, and barrel to 9-13 Shelley Street in the Midlevels district, half way down Victoria Peak on Hong Kong Island.

The owner of the Peak Café had also taken the business of his restaurant's loyal customers with him, much to the chagrin of the new restaurant, the Peak Lookout. The owner of which had assumed the *meiguo* he had put out in bribes to obtain the lease on the valuable piece of government real estate would guarantee immediate over-the-top profitability for years to come.

The owner of the relocated Peak Café had a good laugh about putting one over on not only certain government individuals with sticky fingers but also the desirable location's new tenant who had willfully conspired to cause financial harm to the owner of the long-established restaurant group.

The management of the relocated Peak Café has tightened up their menu a bit; a move most of his customers felt was long overdue. But they still offer a wonderful selection of Thai, Indian and Western dishes, including, believe it or not, pizza. And based on their frequent standing-room-only bookings the last laugh had indeed been on the connivers.

————

While Zhou Ming patiently waited in front of the restaurant, I hopped out and went in to pick up my to-go meal of Thai-style tom yam and roast chicken. Stopping on the way out to thank the owner for accepting my carry out order, a practice that simply was no longer done by long-established restaurants the caliber of the Peak Café.

When he delivered me to the front entrance of my condo building, Zhou verified once again that I had no plans of going into the office this weekend. This meant he got an entire weekend off, something his wife complained happened much too infrequently.

As Ming drove off, juggling the fragrant-smelling take-out boxes, my briefcase, and keys, I stopped and checked the building's residential mailbox. Again the old adage proved true. Anytime my hands are full I can count on our mailbox being full of mail.

Somehow I managed to cram the mail into my pockets so I had at least a couple fingers free, then stepped into one of the waiting elevators, which whisked me up to the penthouse.

I managed to unlock each of the three locks on the condo's front door, enter the penthouse, close and lock it the entry door behind me, all without dropping everything. Perhaps I missed my calling to be an Olympic juggler.

Tossing the mail onto the seat of my recliner, I set my briefcase alongside it on the carpet, and walked the take-out down onto the kitchen. Then it was off to the master bedroom where I changed into a pair of old sweats and slippers for a much anticipated undisturbed evening of unwinding and mindless TV entertainment.

Remembering my verbal commitment to Angry Dragon, or whatever the hell his real name was, I dug the satellite cell phone out of the laundry basket, sat down on the edge of the bed and punched in the international number from memory.

Before I left the office a half hours earlier, I had mentally taken what my people had told me this morning, edited it into a rough format, one I could communicate in sixty seconds or less of conversation, necessary if one is to defeat the antennas of PRC eaves-droppers.

The Interpol agent answered on the first ring. I gave him an update on the illegal body part harvesting case in a burst of hopefully understandable sentences. I finished my spiel and observed the minute timer indicator on my Rolex creeping past fifty seconds. Angry Dragon thanked me like I was one of his lackeys.

In the remaining five seconds we had left he again instructed me, "Call me the instant you have any lead your department is pursuing that you feel will eventually expose who is behind this illegal practice." Then the connection was terminated.

Unhappy at being treated like some servant, I petulantly tossed the phone back into the laundry basket. Which reminded me I had several loads of laundry to do before my dinner date tomorrow evening with the gorgeous Jenny Woo.

Returning to my recliner still littered with unopened mail; I stacked it on the adjacent TV table before going to the kitchen to retrieve my takeout meal. I plunked myself down and grabbed the remote tuning in to the Star TV evening news show already in progress.

Then I attacked the take-out cartons, tearing the plastic envelopes from the plastic utensils, and spreading the paper napkins on my lap before digging into the delicious Thai food that the Peak Café touted was MSG free, cooked in 100% vegetable oil.

I would soon wish I would of had the omnipresence at that time to know what would happen in the early morning hours that would once again would bring a reign of homicidal terror back to the mean streets in Hong Kong.

5

05 October 2007, Saturday, 2:00 a.m. (HKT)
The Wharney Residential Hotel—Rear lot taxi stand
Lockhart Road, between Fenwick and Luard Streets
Wan Chai district—Hong Kong Island

The lights in hotel's rear parking lot in this section of the Wan Chai district, what with the drug dealing that ran rampant throughout the area, were lucky to be burning at all. The few lamps that were unbroken and their lenses clean enough, did provide some faint light.

To the pair of rage-filled eyes that watched the comings and goings of the occasional taxis into and out of the hotel's rear lot taxi stand station, there appeared to be impenetrable darkness pooling everywhere except under the few functioning lampposts. The watcher remembered the old Jimmy Durante television show on American television, actually didn't remember their original airing, but had seen some old reruns of them on the Cinema channel before moving to Hong Kong.

Durante had a patented sign-off shtick that began, "Goodnight Mrs. Calabash, whereever you may be." The famous comedian would be seen walking away into the darkness under about five street lamps spaced at twenty-foot intervals. As Durante arrived in the puddle of light beneath each one he would pause and look back over his shoulder like he was looking for someone. It was supposedly a tribute to his deceased sister. He would turn back after pausing and continue on to the next pool of light. Real tear jerker stuff.

The watcher spotted a taxicab approaching the stand and pull to a stop. Then stepped back further into the darkness but not so far to prevent positive identification of the twenty-something young man dressed in civilian clothes who was returning home having just gotten off the evening 'swing' shift.

The young man climbed out of the taxi's rear seat and stepped up to the driver's window. He engaged in a little good-natured negotiating with the driver before paying his fare. As the taxi pulled out of the parking lot to look for another fare, the young man sighed and began to walk out of the puddle of dim light provided by the remaining parking lot lights that were working, towards the darkness at the rear of the hotel.

The dilapidated hotel's rear entrance had formerly been intended for servant's use some decades previously. But now it was used almost exclusively by the tenants who like the great majority of persons in Hong Kong, taxied to and from their places of employment.

As he approached the rear entrance the young man noticed that the light over the doorway was out. Shuffling his feet around in front of the door he felt shards of glass underneath the soles of his shoes. Apparently vandalism was alive and well in Hong Kong.

The man felt around for the old brass door handle and upon finding it attempted to insert his key. For some reason the key wouldn't slip into the old lock. It was so dark he couldn't see what was obstructing its entry. He switched hands and tried again to slip the key into the old brass lockset. He tugged on the handle briefly but the door would only yield about a quarter of an inch.

He switched hands once again and tried inserting the key and jiggling it but it still wouldn't slide into lock. He'd never had any trouble with the rear lock before and was surprised that his well-worn key didn't work. He tugged on the door handle again and even tried pounding on the door. But he knew the closest apartment was two stories above the rear entrance. Due to the slope of the lot the hotel sat on, the builder back in 1935 had to locate the rear entrance to the building at its second basement level.

If the building super had locked this door for whatever reason, the young man would have to walk all the way around the building to the front entrance, not something he looked forward to at this hour of the morning, particularly in this neighborhood.

For only about the thousandth time he wished his employer would permit he and his coworkers to wear their weapons home following these late night shifts. However the powers-that-be were worried one of them would stop in a bar on their way home and get into a shootout with some wannabe gangster.

Well, the distance wasn't going to get any shorter he rationalized before turning around to begin the three minute walk around the building to its front entrance.

But suddenly, startled, he stopped. Twenty feet in front of him backlit by the dim glow of the parking lot lights stood an apparition wearing all black, as tall if not taller than him.

The figure initially said nothing, just stood there, unwaveringly pointing the barrel of what looked like a small caliber Ruger semi-automatic target pistol fitted with a crude sound suppressor directly at his face.

Automatically, the young man as he had been trained raised his arms to his shoulders and in Cantonese said, forcing himself to remain calm, "Okay, let's relax now, just relax. I don't have much money on me but you are welcome to what I have. You can have this leather jacket. It is worth at least fifty American dollars. You are welcome to it. And you can have this watch and my diamond stud earring. Please, don't shoot me, please!"

As the man began to negotiate for his life the shooter interrupted. "Step exactly two steps closer to me, no more. If you try to rush me, I'll kill you, you can bet your life on it."

As the young man forced his feet to step forward, his bravado fled and he began to shake uncontrollably.

Then the shooter asked, "Do you know who I am, maggot?"

The man shook his head frantically *"Poo shih!"* Cantonese for 'No.'

"All right. Take exactly one more step closer to me, no more. I know all about the martial arts training you've had. I'm not stupid or as helpless as you once thought, maggot. You are going to get one more chance. If you can't recognize me from there then you'll die without knowing who sent you to meet your maker. Okay, last chance, asshole. Do you know who I am now? Have you figured out why I am here tonight, Maggot?"

Realizing his life depended on his powers of observation and hoping the gunman would let him go if he could come up with the identification demanded, the man squinted as hard as he could until a sudden and awful realization hit him nearly stopping his heart, causing him to foul himself.

With the knowledge that he now knew the identity of the stranger, he began to beg tearfully in earnest. "I'm really sorry. And I'll find somehow to make this all up to you, for what we did, for what we said. But please, please, please. It wasn't my idea. You know that. I had to go along, you know. We had to stick together . . . please don't kill me!"

The word 'me' was no sooner out of his mouth than the young man sensed his head explode in a blinding flash of white light much brighter than the sun, as two soft nose copper slugs impacted his forehead exactly one inch over his eyebrows, spaced one inch apart.

When the young man crumpled to the pavement the shooter moved up to him and put two more copper slugs into his genital area causing his lower abdomen to burst like an over-ripe watermelon. The shooter had modified the bullets into a dum-dum configuration using a double-edged surgical steel razor blade.

Satisfied that the man was dead and his secret knowledge was now trapped in the pieces of his shredded brain where it was incapable of causing the shooter further concern, the weapon went back under the long jacket and down behind a waist belt.

The shooter bent down and used latex-gloved fingers to collect the four ejected brass shell casings. They went into a jacket pocket for dumping that morning in a watery Victoria Harbour grave, never again to see the light of day.

To delay the process of identification of the body when it was found, the man's wallet was dug out of his hip pocket, plucked clean of all its identification but leaving the money before being carelessly tossed back onto chest of the dead man. The ID would join the brass into the Harbour.

Turning on a boot heel the shooter walked confidently across the sparsely lit parking lot which connected with Jaffe Road on its west end. Once there the shooter turned right and continued three blocks east before arriving at the Century Hotel on Stewart Road.

A red-topped taxi seeing the shooter's hand summons, stopped, and the driver opened the cab's rear door without leaving the car. The shooter slipped into the dimly lit rear seat of the cab and gave a destination address as the driver pulled out into Steward Road.

––––––

05 October 2006, Saturday, 8 p.m. (HKT)
Grissini's Restaurant—Grand Hyatt Hotel
#1 Harbour Road—Wan Chai district
Hong Kong Island

We arrived at Grissini's about 8 p.m. It is one of the top five restaurants in Kong Hong today. As a perk of my being a midlevel commander on the HKP, we were shown immediately to a table.

Tonight I had worn tan slacks, a blue cashmere blazer, an open yellow silk shirt, and a pair of highly shined oxblood Bally leather loafers.

My date was Jenny Woo, a 5 foot, 10 inch tall, 35-year-old Eurasian who is the customer relations director of the Mandarin Oriental Hotel located at #5 Connaught Road in the Central district of Hong Kong Island. My friend, Mr. Edward Pham, general manager of that esteemed accommodation, had introduced Ms. Woo to me in February of this year in an attempt at match making.

For the evening, Jenny had selected a snug black velvet pants suit, strappy black sandals with stiletto heels, and a simple yet elegant triple-strand pearl necklace clasped around her exquisite neck.

Jenny and I had just come from the Mandarin where we'd previously agreed to meet when she got off shift at 7 p.m. We'd enjoyed a glass of champagne at one of our favorite places, the hotel's fabled Chinnery Bar, before hailing a taxi to take us into the Wan Chai district for dinner.

———

The Chinnery Bar oozes traditional British style. Founded as a Gentlemen's club, it only recently began admitting women. It is a relatively small place, very dark. Its few tables and chairs are made of highly polished dark woods with generous use of wrapped red leather.

Most of the lighting in the room came from under the red leather-covered bar and from inside the three tall, built-in liquor display cabinets, the middle topped by a heavy maritime, eight-inch brass-clock hanging on the dark-paneled wall behind the bartender's position.

The eight sturdy bar stools were handmade and likewise done in red leather, dark woods and have a highly polished brass handle on the seat back. A bright metal ashtray stood alongside each of the stools.

Over the access portal that was provided so the head bartender has serving access to the secondary bartender who is responsible for keeping the dining room guests satisfied, are sterling silver cups, assumedly for coffee-type drinks.

Several individually lighted portraits of long deceased scions of the British Empire adorn the dark-panel walls. The bar lighting is supplemented by small spotlights recessed in the dark paneled ceiling.

———

Also located in the hotel is the Mandarin Grill, one of the favorite rendezvous of the local business community. It serves the finest traditional fare in salubrious surroundings for breakfast, lunch, and dinner.

After dinner, one can try the Cohiba Cigar divan for a relaxing cigar. The area is named after the Cuba's most famous export and offers an extensive range of Havana Cigars. There are dark marble floors and sterling silver serving ice buckets of chilled champagne, sterling silver serving dishes and chalices of fresh fruits, sea food, and other delicious snacks on a leather-wrapped, bronze-ornamented, marble-topped serving counter, attended to by tuxedoed waiters.

The high-ceilinged area has 24-inch-thick, light wood panel-wrapped columns, with the tables on a raised dais. Carved and inlayed wood walls, huge windows and brocade chairs, indirect lighting, large potted plants, and goldthread-laced draperies complete the presentation.

———

Jenny and I began dating shortly after we first met. But before we had sex I had a frank conversation with her to explain my situation with Alicia, although the woman now lives outside Beijing. I really had no idea whether she'd ever return to Hong Kong.

Jenny had given the matter some thought overnight, then on our next date surprised me by saying, "Augustus, let's just enjoy ourselves and not worry about tomorrow. If Alicia is living in China she obviously has her own life. It would be selfish of her to not think it is proper for you to be doing the same."

The only ground rule we established between us is that we'd never overnight at my condo, inasmuch as it was owned by Alicia. I felt it was an honorable agreement. We go to Jenny's place whenever we plan on my staying overnight.

Jenny's home phone number and address are on-file in the police department's 'squeeze file,' their term, not mine, which all ranking police officers and detectives must provide for contact in an emergency.

———

This was our first dinner date at Grissini's even though we both like Italian food. One of the reasons was that it was very pricey. Since Jenny and I eat out at least a couple times a week, my personal finances, although the HKP pays me a very respectable salary, encourages moderation with only occasional spending sprees.

Grissini's is one of the finest Italian restaurants in Hong Kong. The restaurant features only the highest-quality lobster, veal and homemade pastas that according to Jenny, "are to die for."

She also tells me that her eye candy girlfriends, most of which are on the lookout for a wealthy man seeking a trophy wife which she knows I am not, tell her the biggest decision one must make when dining at Grissini's is deciding what to order.

For the past week with her typical school girl-like enthusiasm, Jenny has been expounding on the merits of Grissini's even going on at great length about some of their seasonable specials, dishes that incorporate white and black truffles. *No thanks*, I think mentally, *and I hope that she hasn't fabricated the hope in her mind that this is in anyway an engagement dinner. Been there, done that.*

Although the 'toney' restaurant is generally packed with businessmen on expense accounts in the early afternoon, they usually clear out after 6 p.m. making room for the local residents who also enjoy and can afford a fantastic meal from time to time.

I had designated tonight to be a 'spending spree' date so we both ordered the lobster even though I mentally grimaced at the thought of the extra pounds it will load on my 6 foot 4 inch frame that already is fighting a losing battle with middle age.

Over dinner we mostly people-watched as we chatted about our individual days. The terrifically popular Jackie Chan was in attendance accompanied by action star actress Lucy Liu, and what I understand is his normal entourage of friends and retainers from the film industry.

When dinner was over the server came around to suggest something sweet for dessert. I declined but Jenny who never seems to put an extra ounce on her athletic frame had a cup of sweet nut soup. I settled for a glass of eighteen-year-old Macallan Highland Scotch whiskey, considered to be the Rolls Royce of single malts.

It was about 10 p.m. by the time we settled our bill and stepped out of Grissini's front door into an unusual phenomenon this early in the evening. Fog so dense that the streetlights overhead seemed to hover like flying saucers in an old 1950's Alfred Hitchcock movie.

Surprisingly, as we waited for the doorman to summon a taxi for us, the fog felt warm and cool at the same time as it caressed our faces with its light seductive fingers. Or was it simply the effects of the alcohol, I wondered as a red top taxi pulled up.

On the downside the scent of acidic fumes generated by combustion engines were captured within the fog as was the fetid smell of decaying seaweed and dead fish from the saltwater side of the docks.

I opened the taxi's rear door permitting Jenny to slide in, then got in myself before closing and locking the door, something that prudent folks did after nightfall in Hong Kong. In Cantonese, I gave the driver Jenny's address in Wan Chai Gap district, a upscale condo building located just north of Lover's Rock on Bowen Road.

The taxi took us south on Fenwick Street from the Grand Hyatt Hotel to Johnson Road, where he hung a left until we reached Tai Yuen Street. There he turned south again and followed the extension of that street part way up the far eastern side of the Peak, before navigating a sharp hairpin turn which headed us due east once again until we pulled into the parking lot of Jenny's condo.

As usual with streets on Hong Kong Island, the scenic route was also the most direct route even though it had more curves than Hong Kong 1960's Cinemas screen diva Nancy Kwan who starred alongside William Holden in the movie classic The World of Suzy Wong.

The ride had taken nearly fifteen minutes. The taxi fare was HK$34 including the optional HK$1 tip, or the equivalent of four dollars in U.S. dollars.

———

If this seems inordinately inexpensive to you, taxis are plentiful in Hong Kong and thus still are relatively reasonable. Red Top taxis service Hong Kong and Kowloon; Green Top, the New Territories; and Blue Top, Lantau. All will service the new Chek Lap Kok International Airport located on Lantau Island.

Most taxi drivers understand if not speak English. However it is always prudent when traveling in Asia to have your destination written down in Chinese on the back of a hotel business card. And for you scofflaws, the 'everyone must wear a seatbelt' law is strictly enforced in Hong Kong.

———

After paying off the taxi we checked-in with her building's security guard in the lobby before we got on the elevator for the silent ride up Jenny's floor. Of course he was accustomed to my coming and going. But

I've always felt that if you depend on building security for your well-being you'd better not play the big shot and expect to be treated as an exception by violating any of its established procedures and safeguards.

Jenny's condo building is one of the city's most exclusive. The walls are tastefully wallpapered. The lobby floor and hallways are so thickly carpeted you think you will submerge into them like they are quicksand and you will soon sink out of sight.

When we reached her floor, Jenny unlocked the triple locked doors. In Hong Kong, even in doorman-serviced residences, it is prudent to take security precautions.

We walked into a splendid sunken living room with subdued lighting which features a marvelous view of the HK Convention and Exhibition Center in the Wan Chai North district, the Center built on piers over Victoria Harbour.

"Like some thing else to drink?" she asked.

"Sure, I don't have to work tomorrow, why not. I'll have a flute of champagne if you have it, my love."

When she carried the flute in to me Jenny gave me one of her patented come-hither looks and murmured "I'll just go change into something more comfortable. Make yourself comfortable, Augustus."

When she came back from the master bedroom a full fifteen minutes later she wore what to me, the fashion-challenged, appeared to be a see-thru silk 'Michael Kors' shirt, and not much else.

Walking into my personal space, a concept that actually doesn't exist for most Asians, she said, "Handle me, Chief Inspector. I've been waiting for you to quit dawdling around and seduce me. I've been thinking about it all during dinner, especially when I had something sweet in my mouth."

She hooked her leg behind mine, circling my waist with her arms. Unusual for Jenny, tonight she was being the aggressor. I'll never understand women.

"Oh, is that right, love?" I asked. "Please explain to me exactly what it is that you want."

"Oh, you know. I want you to think about me being naked all the time even when you are at work, especially around that sexy Australian slut Elizabeth Stewart. Don't be so naïve to think I don't have my spies in your office, Chief Inspector."

"Now why don't you quit playing the sophisticated act and undress me, Augustus? Don't you Americans ever do anything by impulse? Or say what you are thinking? I mean, what is wrong with just saying, 'Lets fuck' if that is what you want?"

I could feel her body through the thin silk shirt and knew I only had to unbutton it or reach underneath to enjoy how warm, smooth and desirable her skin was.

Jenny was wearing my favorite Hong Kong female scent, 'Nasty Girl,' which seemed to be the perfume of choice despite its ridiculous expense worn by every exotic woman I've had the pleasure to meet in the past three years.

Jenny was touching me, shyly at first then eagerly. She began tugging off my clothes right in the middle of her sunken living room. Despite the fact that what she was doing was clearly visible to the world through the floor-to-ceiling plate glass windows. She was acting like she was in some type of frenzy.

We sunk down on the living room carpet just as she drove a very hot tongue down my throat at the same time she was ripping my jockey shorts from my hips. It was far too late to worry whether I would have any reasonable presentable clothing left to wear home in the taxi in the morning.

She began fondling me, bringing me close to instant ejaculation until I got myself under control. However she was very close to circumventing that control. It seemed as if she was trying to get me to lose myself in her, and wasn't worried whether or not I could find my way back.

She crawled on top of me and rode my cock down into her juicy warmness. I could feel her heart and mine thumping against each other's chests as if it was a battle of the percussion instruments. She reached down and grabbed onto my testicles with the intent of spurring me on, I guess. Her perfume heighten by our sweat would have been smothering had I not occasionally turned my head to the side for a gasp of air.

She was demanding I climax first; something this spoiled woman never had done before. She drew me deeper into her vagina as if she wanted to swallow me with her *yindao*, or genitals. When I tried to get greedy with my hands in an attempt to bring her to climax, she thrust them roughly away from her clitoris and nipples, sending me a message via ESP that there would be time enough for that.

I fought my way out from under her. Then crawled onto her sweaty body, pinning her. I began using my tongue to stir up little quivers, little fires, and with my hands, I fought to keep her educated fingers away from my anus to prevent myself from getting aroused with too much, too soon.

I worked my face down her silken belly, which was difficult while still fighting to restrain her wrists to prevent her from reaching the body orifice on me she sought.

I wanted to taste her deeply, her shoulders, breasts, her trim waist, her bikini-shaved pubic area, and finally her womanhood. I slid my tongue into her and she went wild, screaming. I feverently hoped the walls in the condos were sound proof so the Hong Kong domestic violence cops wouldn't soon be kicking the door down thinking Jenny was being forcibly raped.

When she did come, she came like the Lone Ranger's horse, Silver, in an all out gallop. Her body turning alternately hot and then chilly as the pleasure smothered her. I gave her all I had in me, inserting my tongue as deep as it would go, and using it to massage the inside of her vagina until I began to fear my head might be swallowed up in one of her convulsions.

Finally, I had to get out of there so I could breathe. I pushed myself up on my trembling arms, and once again implored, "Jenny!" She frenzied hands grabbed at me all over my body, unable to get a firm hold due to the sweat on my skin. Then she screamed again as she once again climaxed.

Jenny continued to hold me in a death grip as close as two bodies can get and my mind began to blur. I said her name once more, before I lost all control and managed to insert myself inside her vagina barely in time as I emptied myself of sperm that I didn't know I had even produced yet.

Whatever I had thought I had gotten myself into before, I'd just fallen into the big leagues. Of course, that problem had a solution.

6

07 October 2006, Monday, 8 a.m. (HKT)
HKP Arsenal Street Headquarters
Crimes Against Persons Department
Wan Chai district—Hong Kong Island

Zhou Ming got me to the office on Monday morning by 8 a.m. so I could attack my in-box and return any urgent Please Call phone messages before the staff meeting.

I had dressed positively for what I hoped would be a productive week. I'd selected a yellow Giorgio Armani blazer, black Oxxford slacks, royal blue Robert Taylor open-necked silk shirt, dark blue kid-leather Gucci loafers, and a Rolex gold-and-stainless steel Sub-Mariner Day/Date watch with a blue bezel and faceplate.

Elizabeth was already sitting at her desk with one of her typical smug looks on her face. She indicated to me with a sideways movement of her eyes that I had an early visitor.

It turned out to be Inspector Ho Pham. He was slumped in one of the two visitor's chairs in front of my desk looking dejected and embarrassed. I took one look at him and closed my door before sitting down beside him. His expression hinted at depression, which seemed out of place on a man who was one of, if not the most, together cops in the entire department.

We sat like that for about minute before Ho began to speak. He started right off like we had been discussing what he was going to talk about for minutes now—kind of jumped into the middle of whatever thoughts were streaming through his head at the time.

"Boss," he began. "I know I don't have to mince words with you. You have been very open and accepting of all of us, just as long as the job gets done. You know I am gay and that my life partner John Wong, the man I live with, has been sick."

"He has had to give up his concert performing and stopped even going to practices at the *Ko Shan Theatre* in the Hung Hom district. That's home to the Hong Kong Coliseum which he worships."

"I wanted to speak with you before this morning's staff meeting because I know that a lot of what is on the department's plate this week rests solely on the shoulders of myself and the Homicide squad. That is what I need to talk with you about. I need some time off, perhaps an entire month, because John has taken a turn for the worse. These may be the last days of his life. And I must, I mean, I want to be able to spend this quality time with him in case things don't work out for us."

Ho was starring into my eyes imploring me to give him what possibly could be the last time he would have with his lover. I knew it wasn't AIDS or HIV. Ho Pham loved life. He came to work each day so enthused I often felt jealous of the commitment and enjoyment he got from doing his job.

He clearly understood the non-negotiable difference between surviving as a person, and being willing to make whatever hard decisions were required to ensure he would never engage in unprotected activities that could jeopardize his life. Ho and John had a monogamous relationship, I assume wore protection, and never strayed outside the marital bed, or whatever the gay community refers to it as.

So I had to ask, "Ho, you know that you can take off whatever time you need. Do you feel that you can tell me what the problem is and why this particular time is so important to you and John?"

Ho chucked, and said, "I assume you have enough faith in me to know this isn't about any sexually transmitted disease, Boss?"

"Yes, Ho, of course you can assume that. That never crossed my mind. And who am I to be critical of you and John for your sexual preferences? You are the best case-closer in this department. And if it is within my authority I want to do what I can for you to make whatever you and John are going through a little easier on you both."

"Thanks Boss. John has pancreatic cancer. What with all the crappy stories and off-colored jokes that circulate about us among you straights; you never seem to stop and realize that we gay men can get ill from traditional diseases just like you do."

Ho continued, "Even the Oncologist, when he found out about John's sickness months ago, seemed surprised it wasn't AIDS. Believe it or not,

Boss, gay men don't catch AIDS any more often than you straights catch gonorrhea or STD's from your wife, girlfriend, or one-night stands."

"How far has the cancer gone, Ho," I asked?

"Well," Ho replied, "John has been on chemotherapy using the drugs Gemzar and Taxotere. I think it is the Taxotere that has made him lose his hair. But doctors have told us that in 80% of the cases it grows back in about six months."

"Taxotere is a semi-synthetic drug, Boss. Before scientists learned how to synthesize it in the lab, it had to be made totally from the needles of a yew tree. Now they synthesize it in the lab using only a small portion of extract from the yew tree."

He hung his head briefly, expelling a deep sigh. I could tell explaining this to me was hard for him. Ho raised his head back to look into my eyes to judge my sincerity I expect, then continued. "The recipe, the cocktail, however you want to refer to it, is nothing but a combination of poisons that is supposed to kill the cancer."

"And initially it seemed like it was helping John. He appeared to be getting better. Although from all the literature I've read you never get completely cured of the cancer, you just go into remission. But he even went back to practicing his concert scores on the piano for a couple hours each afternoon like he did before he got sick. The cocktails appeared to be shrinking the tumors in his pancreas."

"We were so excited with his treatment's apparent success we began looking for a apartment closer to the Coliseum so he wouldn't have to take a taxi so far just to attend practices," Ho said. You could see from the far away look in his eyes, how being able to do that for John would be important to the homicide inspector.

Shaking his head, Ho paused before explaining further. "But when John got the results of his latest CAT scan, it almost killed both of us. The cancer had spread everywhere, the stomach, liver, lungs, and even is beginning to encroach on his brain."

"Bottom line is that the cancer doctor told John he only has a short time to live. Perhaps not even a month. What I need the time off for is that John has always wanted to see the Cantonese Opera, *Xiqu*, in person."

"We've been putting it off for years, almost ever since we've been together, because most of the time the troupe is on the road, mostly far away from Asia. But this week they are performing in Singapore. I want to take him to see it while he can still enjoy it before he gets too racked with pain."

"Boss, I wouldn't ask if I absolutely didn't need to do this, have to do this. I know that with the three cops murdered, because feces runs down hill, Donald Tsang is going to be all over the commissioner, and rest assured, his puppet will be all over you. But I have to do this, please."

Glancing at my watch and seeing it 9 a.m., time for our staff meeting to start, I looked Ho in the eye and said, "Take whatever time you need, Ho Pham. I assume you already have Du Ming up to speed on everything your squad is working on?"

Ho stood up, and nodded his head. We shook hands. I gripped his hand in my and said, "Please feel free to call me, Ho, here or at home if I can be of any help."

"Please give me a call once a week or so and let me know how much additional time you'll need, but don't rush back. There is nothing more important than John right now and I want you to do what you need to. Du is a good man, as you know. Hell, he was my partner once and I can't count the number of times he saved my *gweilo* butt."

Ho turned and walked out looking like a load had been lifted off his broad shoulders. I grabbed my case folders and portfolio, observed that Elizabeth had already left her desk and headed for the conference room to supervise the coffee, tea and pastry detail, and get first dibs on both, I suspected. I hurried down the hall.

———

07 October 2007, Monday, 9 a.m. (HKT)
Crimes Against Person's Conference Room
Arsenal Street Police Headquarters
Hong Kong Island

When I walked into the meeting room, its width bisected by the oak conference table, Mimi Yin; Lt. Du Ming—sitting in for Ho Pham; Chen Ho; and Elizabeth, who was prepared to take notes; and Zhou Ming, were waiting for me.

I grab a cub of Joe, glanced at but didn't weaken and take one of the scrumptious-looking pieces of pastry after the little bird on my shoulder reminded me that I had gained ten pounds in the past two months.

I purposely tossed my thick manila case folders on the table surface making a noise loud enough to make Chen Ho lookup and stop playing with his handcuffs. Then I sat down.

First things first, "Good morning, everyone. Inspector Ho Pham had an emergency and is taking a little time off. Lieutenant Du Ming will be sitting in for him until his return. Please fill in all your people about Ming's temporary assignment because Homicide has a lot on its plate. We can't afford to let anything fall through the cracks on this cop assassination case, or the cops killed during the triad hit the other day."

When I said that, I saw Ming's eyes momentarily lift away from the file he was familiarizing himself with, shake his head, and return to his reading. I decided whatever was bothering Du Ming would have to wait. I wanted to get started.

"Chen Ho," I began, "anything new on the white van?"

"Just what I've passed on already, Boss. Oh, and I sent my guys and gals around to all the police garages in Hong Kong. Even had them stop by the PRC motor pools at Fort Stanley, and at the CPLAFHK—Chinese People's Liberation Army Forces Hong Kong—building on Tim Wa Avenue."

———

The CPLAFHK building, formerly known prior to June of 1997 as the Prince of Wales Building, like another Hong Kong building, the Jardine House (The House of a Thousand Arseholes), has its own sobriquet as it often is compared quite favorable to an upturned gin bottle.

The building formerly was the mooring home of the HMS Tamar that was used as a floating naval base until the Japanese scuttled it in World War Two. Now as the names suggests, it is one of the two base postings for the PRC army in Hong Kong.

———

Inspector Chen Ho continued where he had left off. "Had them show around the likeness that the HKP sketch artist worked up with the supervisor and mechanics on-duty at impound garage the day the van was stolen. Everyone had the same story. 'Had my head under some vehicle's hood. Hong Kong Police have crap for police cars. All the time, broke. All crap. And my personal favorite, 'Never see anything, Detective.' I think all these civil service mechanics get on their cell phones when we come around and agree on some bullshit story just to pull our chains."

"What I did turn up by thumbing back through some of our unsolved homicides is that an individual fitting that description was found floating off Fenwick Pier one day after the van theft from the impound yard, two .22 caliber holes behind his left ear. Classic western style execution. I don't think it was a triad hit."

"There didn't seem to be any message being sent by this killing so the triad shooters wouldn't have wasted their bullets. This guy was just a ballsy vehicle thief at best. Someone important didn't want to leave him around and take a chance he would spill the beans to one of his drinking buddies or a whore."

"It would have been much simpler to use the traditional triad method and use a hatchet, meat cleaver or machete." Chen Ho sighed.

Chen waited for questions and hearing none, returned to his seat and immediately took a bite out of his apple turnover.

"Ok, Mimi, we've heard your excellent report Friday on the basics of how this body-parts-for-money scheme operates. Now what are you and your lieutenant doing to run down the chop shop where they are doing the illegal harvesting?"

"Well, Boss," she began. "I have pulled everyone from the squad onto day shift until we find this butcher shop. Two of my detectives, the two with the most engineering acumen, I have going through the city building department reviewing the layout drawings that all businesses must be on-file in order to obtain an operating license."

"The process has gotten more complicated since the HKSAR tightened up the permit process. This is because the building department and mayor's office is finally attempting to shut down some of the unlicensed operations in Hong Kong, especially those in the Mongkok district."

"We are looking for funeral parlors or mortuaries, perhaps even located in an abandoned building. Somewhere they could build a covert level-3 surgical facility without creating a lot of attention. Such a facility, according to my guys, would have to have fairly strong built-in biohazard provisions because they couldn't just drop the offal down the drain, or put it out in plastic bags and set it out at the curb for the weekly garbage pickup. So the facility likely will have a on-site crematorium."

Inspector Yin continued, "Next, I made arrangements with the HK Health Department to use their helicopter. My detectives at the moment are up in the chopper are taking a close look at the larger funeral parlors that have plans on-file at the building department to see if any of them appear to have been expanded or modified, off the books."

"The remainder of the squad is out in taxis doing drive-bys of each of the facilities where the 'chopper detectives' find visible evidence of a off-the-book modification."

Elizabeth interrupted, "Mimi, why are you using taxi cabs instead of the squad's own unmarked cars?"

Mimi turned to Elizabeth, and said, "Because, Elizabeth, a person would have to be an idiot to not make one of our unmarked cars the second time it drove by their place of business. Ho Pham once told me that it is suspected that several of the police mechanics who are deep in debt to loan sharks have sold lists of all the department's unmarked car's license plates, make, model and color to the criminal element just to get an extra week or two grace period before some thug visits them at home to break their legs for late payment of loans."

Mimi turned back to addressing the rest of the group. "Our detectives are having to spend a considerable amount of time pulling surveillance, observing any mortuaries or parlors we suspect to get enough information to prepare a affidavit for a search warrant. Therefore we are forced to spend a lot in those neighborhoods, both on foot and by car. Catching a separate taxi each time to perform a tight surveillance gives us a better chance of not getting made by the suspect facility's employees."

"If one or more of these facilities have an illegal parts harvesting operation residing in their facility, you can bet they have lookouts posted to alert them to any undue police interest."

Mimi looked down at her notes before adding, "Wednesday, when an accident forced it into a utility pole, the white van was observed driving east on Queensway before turning south on Cotton Tree Drive. Therefore we are concentrating our resources right now in the Central, Midlevels and Sheung Wan districts. Now anyone have any questions?"

Without rising to my feet, I complimented Mimi on her squad's having a good plan before I called on Lt. Du Ming for Homicide.

Ming lay back in his armchair and sighed deeply before sitting up and speaking. Ming was never much of a talker but he had been a lieutenant for over a year now and out of necessity had overcome his basic shyness and improved on his platform skills.

"As you probably heard on the news, my squad, working in conjunction with the political affairs unit and SWAT, raided 14K's Mongkok headquarters at midnight Saturday night."

"This is the same building that the Boss, our teams, and SWAT raided back on 10 October of 2006 when Inspector Silvia Guan was kidnapped by Chang "Blue Eyes" Ching, 14K's Red Pole. Just before the Boss was forced to blow the man's head off with his .50AE caliber IMI-manufactured (Israeli) seven-shot Desert Eagle."

———

Yes, I admit the huge six-pound automatic handgun is a bit James Bond for everyday police-use in Hong Kong. As such, I don't carry it routinely. However I have found that as a special-use weapon it extremely effective in triad confrontations such as a raid situation. No one can even begin to imagine just how much damage a fifty-caliber bullet normally used only in the largest tripod-supported machine guns can do to the human body.

———

Everyone in the room had stopped munching and sipping their hot drinks when Ming made his statement in memory of, and respect for, our former co-worker. Inspector Silvia Guan had made the fatal mistake of getting over confident when conducting a rolling surveillance on "Blue Eyes" Ching, in October of last year.

After the 24-hour waiting period that goes into effect in the event of a missing officer as proscribed by department procedures, we had raided the Mongkok HQ of the 14K triad hoping Guan was either being held captive at that location, or we could find evidence or obtain the location she was being held from of a cooperative triad solder.

The bottom line was that the raid did not turn up Silvia. Nor any evidence as to her whereabouts. We were unsuccessful in forcing her location out of any of the triad members. They were more afraid of their own leaders than anything we could have done to them during the time they were on a 48-hour hold at Victoria Prison.

I had the misfortune to kill Chang "Blue Eyes" Ching in self-defense. Two older police officers about to retire had been brutally killed. Run down when five mid-level triad leaders escaped in a Fotomat van, which had been staged behind a tarp, painted to match the exterior of the rear walls of the building.

Silvia Guan's remains eventually were discovered inside a compacted vehicle when we had raided a triad scrap yard out in the new Territories.

———

"The intent of our mission on Saturday night," Du Ming continued, "was to arrest anyone we could in the dragnet. We planned to transport the prisoners to the basement interrogation center here in this building."

"Our goal," the large homicide lieutenant clarified, "was to cull out the highest ranking triad officials possible. Even if realistically we know that the vast majority of Hong Kong's 300,000 members of the 14K triads are merely 49's, foot soldiers."

"But we felt that as a department we had to take some over-the-top action. Even though it would clearly violate the protocols the Legislative politicians drew up last year. The 14K had killed three cops, three members of our family, and although the killers had also been killed in the attack, when you take the life of a cop in Hong Kong the scales are never going to be balanced equally."

Scowling, Du Ming stated, "When the 14K made the mistake of torturing and killing Inspector Guan last year, several dozen 14K triad members paid the ultimate price, some department critics claim in retribution, when we raided three of their Hong Kong hideouts and the deceased foot soldiers resisted arrest."

"Early Sunday morning, as the warrant-less confinement 'hold' clock was already ticking, we began to process anyone brought in for questioning through the holding cell process; including fingerprinting and photographing them."

"We arranged to surreptitious obtain a DNA sample from each individual which really was a snap as we merely walked behind them picking up discarded cigarette butts. They all smoke like chimneys. Then the specialists interrogated them; fluttered them on the polygraph; and cross-referenced the interrogation product to assign a reliability value to what they had been telling us."

Referring briefly to his notes, Du carried on, "We then fed them and told them they could get a few hours sleep. Then we hit them again in the middle of their naps. All of this occurred within the permissible warrant-less hold period 48-hours."

Du Ming chuckled, "And naturally while all this is going on, we sent their attorneys on wild goose chases down to Stanley Prison, or one of the other thirteen Hong Kong correctional department holding tanks, while the interrogators attempted to work their magic."

"Our goal although admittedly unrealistic was to snag a 432, the Straw Sandal; a 415, the White Paper Fan, the administrative officer; or the 426, the Red Pole, the triad enforcer and branch leader. It would have been nice to hook the 438, the Assistant Mountain Lord, if we had the opportunity.

But Du admitted, chuckling, "We certainly had no aspirations relative to stumbling upon the 489, the top guy, the Dragon Head. If he is smart he never sets foot in the Mongkok headquarters."

"This is how Saturday night's raid went down," Du recited.

Lt. Ming after a period of reflection continued, "Even at that late hour there were a handful of triad wannabes 49's standing sloppy guard all around the building."

Ming added, "However, all of the command staff on the raid, the political affairs Lieutenant, the SWAT commander, and myself, decided we couldn't delay the confrontation any longer. All the adrenalin that the entire takedown team had built up over the preparation for the raid would soon peak and begin its enviable plummet into the depth of despair and depression. It never fails—just the downside of the human 'fight or flee' syndrome."

I nodded to myself remembering that memorable day a year ago.

"When we did give the 'Go' order," Lieutenant Du Ming said, "I think we woke up everyone inside a one-mile radius of the 14K headquarters. The foggy night air was pierced with screaming sirens and our French-style whooping horns which peak at well over 150 decibels, nearly deafening to someone not prepared for the onslaught of noise."

Again chuckling at the thought of tens of thousand of the criminally-inclined residents of the Mongkok district falling off their sleeping cots onto the filthy floors of their living hutches shortly after midnight upon being rudely yanked out of their slumber at hearing all the audio emergency equipment being turned on at once, Lieutenant Du Ming prodded on.

"The SWAT commander, the priggish political affairs boss and I, for reasons of self preservation, frankly didn't want to get run over by the hard-charging, adrenaline-driven stampede of 150 trigger-happy uniformed cops and SWAT officers that suddenly appeared at the warehouse's front door."

"So we waited until those gentlemen had executed an classic 'entry by force' into the building with their battering rams and C-4 'door-opener' shaped charges."

"The handful of 49s, the foot soldiers at the bottom of the triad hierarchy who a few seconds earlier had been walking a sloppy guard duty, decided that since the raid obviously was in retaliation for a triple cop killing, discretion was the better part of valor. They almost popped their shoulders out of joint when they raised their hands apparently attempting to grab a passing cloud."

"As soon as the 49s raised their hands, they started to dump their weapons on the concrete where they were standing. Not one of them looked like he was weighing the decision whether to run back inside, stand his ground and fight, or surrender."

Ming continued, "Within thirty seconds we had two armed cops with automatic weapons at every exit of the warehouse, and snipers on the roofs of the buildings surrounding the warehouse. There were additional police officers stationed underground at every entrance into the tunnels which run under these old warehouses."

———

Author's note: Firearms are banned in Hong Kong for everyone but the police and the PRC Army. While it was well known that the triad maintains a wide range of illicit firearms in their warehouses, the homeboys only carry an excellent selection of homicidal cutlery.

The tunnels had been constructed by the triads in the 1800's as a way to transport the massive crops of opium that the British, at one time, traded to the Chinese as barter for goods such as silk, spices, gold, and precious stones.

———

Du Ming paused for a moment to look over at me. "Boss, the next time the corner office upstairs tells you that the 14K leadership is some type of brain trust, I want you to tell them this."

Then he expanded on his comment, "All of us remember that on our last raid on that warehouse, two old cops almost ready for retirement had been posted in the back of the 14K triad's headquarters. There were no visible truck doors in the wall of the building back there so the commander of patrol figured a couple old cops with AK-47's could hold the position."

"Yes," I spoke up, interrupting Ming, "I should have taken another look at the rear of the warehouse before we went in but the intelligence officers that checked out the back of the building, missed the tarp."

I mumbled, still deep in thought, "The 14K cleverly had an artist paint the outside of a hanging tarp to resemble the rest of the wall on the rear of the warehouse. And behind the tarp was either an authentic or replica knockoff of a Fotomat van. That was the 14K leadership's fallback position if the place was raided and we successfully overran the triad's 49s who had been assigned to defend the facility with their lives."

"Bottom line," I said, "is that the fleeing Fotomat van filled with panicked triad officers blasted through the camouflaged tarp running the two old cops down killing them instantly. Although we had a chopper courtesy of the PRC army hovering overhead, the van escaped because no one but the 14K apparently had ever wondered how difficult it would be to identify a fleeing Fotomat van in a city where there are dozens of them on city streets all hours of the day and night."

Turning back to Du Ming who was patiently waiting for me to finish, I apologized, "Ming, sorry about the interruption. Just had to get that off my chest. It was something I had should have verified. My not doing so may have cost those brave men their lives."

"Okay," Ming took over again, "I had a bet with the SWAT commander that those feeble-minded dopes would pull the same trick, just waiting for us dumb cops to raid their headquarters again so they could kill some more of us."

"The SWAT commander thought I was being a little—no, not a little, a lot paranoid but he agreed with my plan to have a big surprise in place for the scumbags in case I was correct. After all, as the Boss has always told me, 'Fool me once and it is the doer's fault—but fool me twice and it's my fault!'"

"So," Ming chuckled again, apparently getting real self satisfaction out of his plan to fool the triad if they again tried to use the Fotomat van to escape, "it was dark, so we had one of the department's lowboys surreptitiously transport a BEAR to the rear of the warehouse loaded with SWAT and a full load-out of automatic weapons. And about fifteen minutes after our guys breached the warehouse's front door, those idiots tried the same trick they had used last year on us and nearly got blown away for their arrogance."

———

Author's Note: After a wave of increased violent criminal behavior in Hong Kong in 2005, Beijing's puppet, the Chief Executive of the SAR's Legislative Council had appealed to the People's Republic of China to make some mechanized muscle available to our police department. We needed the muscle desperately to balance the scales of the sophisticated arms, munitions, and motorized equipment the triad had access to due to the depth of their pockets. Their money come from the proceeds of their extortion, protection, hijacking, kidnapping, counterfeiting, vehicle theft, cargo theft, murder-for-hire, smuggling, pirating, weapon's sales, and the other dozen or so rackets the gangsters committed in any given week.

When China took over administration of Hong Kong in June of 1997, the SAR had been compelled to either dismantle her military self-defense force or turn all heavy equipment over to the People's Liberation Army.

The PRC had a heyday with what its commanders called 'rearranging assets.' A few outspoken members of the HKP nearing retirement called it 'robbing.' The PRC 'disappeared' the former crown colony's modern light tanks, personnel carriers, military vessels and equipment.

When the citizens of Hong Kong protested the PRC grudgingly replacing the purloined equipment, if they did at all, with worn out mostly Russian cast-off equipment that the People's Liberation Army had been intending to scrap, anyway.

Today the PLA, which to be honest has acted in a relatively civilized manner since 1997, garrisons their commanders at the Chinese People's Liberation Army Force building, located at corner of Edinburgh Place and Tim Wa avenues in the Admiralty district on Hong Kong Island. Two to three thousand PLA troops and a substantial amount of light armor also is garrisoned at Fort Stanley located on the most southern tip of Hong Kong Island.

Beijing's puppet, Donald Tsang, the SAR's chief executive, and the commissioner of police who had submitted the request, assumed the PRC would might turn over to the Hong Kong police a few worn-out, rubber-tracked or wheeled tanks and personnel carriers, if in fact they responded to the request at all.

Both men assumed that the use of that equipment would be permitted only on a case-to-case basis, that basis to be determined by the PLA commanding general who maintains offices at the Tim Wa Avenue complex.

However, Beijing's decision had surprised both men. Communist party officials in Beijing charged with the smooth transition of Hong Kong into China's day-to-day economy, knew that the citizens of Hong Kong still felt betrayed that China had not permitted them to elect all sixty members of the SAR's Executive Council by democratic vote.

The party leaders knew that this sensitive situation would further antagonize the citizens of Hong Kong if they observed PRC tanks clacking along and crumbling the surface of the SAR's concrete streets.

———

For those whose plans haven't yet included visiting Hong Kong yet, you may find this interesting. Although the relative mild heat of Hong Kong's summer, 75 to 85 degrees F max, isn't the primarily factor prohibiting its use, asphalt is rarely utilized for the construction of weight-bearing roadways in Asia. Concrete has more bridging ability and roadbeds in Asia almost always are poorly prepared and compacted prior to paving. Concrete although more expensive, lasts longer, and longer is good in humid Asia.

———

In this case the buck, as the sign on President Harry Truman's desk said, would most certainly stop with the PLA commander who had just two days ago approved the use of one of their helicopters to backup the Hong Kong police in the Mongkok confrontation with the 14K triad. The People's Liberation Army was doing their best to not have the citizens of Hong Kong view the PLA in the role of an occupying force, much as the Americans were attempting currently in the cities of Iraq.

When Donald Tsang was summoned to Beijing to learn the party's decision, he discovered that the decision-makers in the PRC in order to downplay the presence of the PLA in Hong Kong, had decided instead to allocate US$1,000,000 to the SAR to purchase a SWAT-type civilian vehicle that the citizens would see as just another weapon in their police department's inventory rather than anything that was an extension of the People's Liberation Army.

Chief Executive Tsang was told that the rules for engagement of the new equipment would be entirely under his and the HKP police commissioner's authority. And further, that in the situation where the new equipment was ever used in a manner that brought discredit on their mother country, both men would suffer China's perdition.

Thus, it was in the Peoples' Republic of China's self-interest that the funds to purchase for two of the BEARS and necessary supporting equipment become available to the Hong Kong's Special Administrative Region.

Before the ink was dry on the funds transfer into the police department's capital budget, the commissioner had his assistant chief of transportation place a order for two copies of what American law enforcement were calling the BEAR.

The BEAR is a 15-ton armored vehicle manufactured by the firm of Lenco Armored Vehicles at their factory in Pittsburg, Massachusetts, the state ably represented in Congress by neophyte-swimmer, Senator Edward Kennedy.

The designers of the BEAR were inspired by the 1999 shootings at Columbine High School in Littleton Colorado; the September 11, 2001 terrorist attacks in NYC; terrorist attacks by the 2004 bombing of trains in Madrid, Spain; chemical attacks on the subways in Great Britain; and the Chechen attacks on a school house and movie theater in 2004, both which had taken many lives in Vladikavkaz, Russia.

All of those terrorist acts forced police officers into dangerous situations beyond their ability to protect themselves from bullets, explosives and other deadly weapons.

The BEAR stands twelve feet tall and with all support equipment costs roughly US$500,000 a copy. BEAR stands for 'Ballistic Engineered Armored-Response vehicle.' Aside from the sheer intimidation the diesel-powered monster brings to a confrontation, it can ram vehicles, or smash through concrete walls. It is capable of stopping armor-piercing ammunition, can detect explosives, deadly gases and radiation.

When used in a SWAT capacity, the BEAR can carry fifteen fully equipped tactical officers into the threat environment of a confrontational situation, and can be used to extract up to thirty hostages to safety.

———

As the rest of us sipped our coffee or tea, and munched on pastries, Lieutenant Du Ming continued his report on the results of his dragnet of 14K triad members.

"We didn't catch any big fish in our dragnet which considering the lack of depth in their hierarchy wasn't a complete surprise. The University of Hong Kong's school of business could learn some valuable lessons from the triads. What other entity or organization can operate with less than a couple of dozen management types to direct, follow-up on, and discipline 300,000 front line employees?"

"Most traditional organizations have at least seven layers of supervision between the lowest rank employee and the CEO, the average of span of control for those individuals being twenty to twenty-five-to-one. The 14K triad controls 300,000 members just here in Hong Kong, with only five levels of supervision."

Ming continued, now warming to the triad subject of which he was the acknowledged expert in our organization, "If nothing else the triad enjoys a significant cost avoidance from having to pay these two additional levels of supervisors and at the same time, reduces the number of knowledgeable persons who know at least a portion of the overall operation of the criminal conspiracy who can be arrested, interrogated, turned, and through blackmail, by threats of a life prison sentence or other forms of coercion, be forced to roll over on their 432, 426, or 415, even though it would eventually result in a horrible death sentence for them."

With a sigh, Ming returned to his accounting of this past weekend's raid of the triad's Mongkok headquarters.

"We culled the group that was going to spend their next couple of days being held in lockup for investigation. We elected to give special handling to five senior soldiers who normally perform supervisory functions over the cutlery-carrying street wannabes, the 49's. All of the individuals we selected were comprised of those who so bravely sought to save their collective butts in 2006 by attempting to escape in the replica Fotomat truck."

Ming reflected, "To prevent this already long meeting from going past lunch, let me summarize. We are confident that the only thing these first-level street supervisors knew was that the 426, or Red Pole, issued an immediate command when it was learned that Chung Shan, the 415 or White Paper Fan, the triad's senior administrative officer had been snatched off the street by the HKP Political Affairs squad backed by SWAT."

"The order for the non-procedural snatch came from the HKP commissioner's office who was acting on the orders of Donald Tsang. I assume Tsang got his orders from Beijing."

Consulting his notes, Ming resumed, "When the 14K learned Chung was in our custody, they put together a squad of fully deniable shooters. Their assignment was to either seize Chung from our custody, or to assassinate him before he could talk and reveal details about his meeting with the fundamentalist al-Qaeda representatives earlier this year."

Du added, "The 14K hit squad was following the uniformed police officer and two political affairs detectives in the black unmarked Mercedes transporting Chung Shan to Victoria Prison, where he would be more or less inaccessible to the triad or its killers. When the hit team correctly guessed the HKP's destination, they immediately executed their mission."

"Until Ho Pham gets back from his family emergency and assumes command once again, I intend to work with the political affairs unit and SWAT to continue to make warrant-less pickups of triad members off the street in hopes of getting lucky. But don't get your hopes up. I'm sure the ranking officers of the 14K have gone into hiding. They know that killing three cops negates any previous agreements or protocols the desk cops in administration might have made."

Ming continued, "And they know we'll continue with to shakeup their operations around the clock until the triad boss decides the 14K has lost enough money and makes the decision to cut their loses by turning the person over to us who ordered the hit."

Du Ming looked around the room as if silently asking with his eyes if there were any questions? When no one spoke up, I thanked him for his excellent report. He began to sit down until he apparently remembered something he'd forgot to cover and came back to his feet.

Taking a deep breath, Du looked down at a note he fished out of his jacket pocket, and said, "Last, but certainly not least. We had another cop killed early Saturday morning."

"He was Johnny Yang, five years of service, a patrol officer just off the evening shift. He was apparently was headed to the studio apartment he maintained at the Wharney Residential Hotel on Lockhart Road in the Wan Chai district."

"Yang's body was discovered by other building resident who was also returning home after working the second shift at his place of employment. That resident, a Mr. Ho Wong, had just been dropped off by a taxi at the rear parking lot stand about 3 a.m."

"Ho says he was walking up to the rear security door of the hotel and admitted wasn't too alert after a hard night of washing dishes for minimum wage at a local restaurant. He was headed for the entrance he usually uses when he tripped over Patrolman Yang in the near darkness. Wong says he recognized the man on the pavement as a neighbor of his who he knew to be a Hong Kong cop."

"Mr. Wong, not knowing that Yang was dead, picked himself up off the pavement. But upon suddenly becoming aware of a nauseating coppery smell, he panicked. He says he tried to yank the rear security door open to take refuge inside but was unable to as the lock wouldn't accept his key."

"Wong then ran around to the front of old hotel and used the main entrance to enter the building. After he was safe and sound in his apartment, he felt guilty he hadn't offered to help his neighbor who he assumed may have just been intoxicated, and used his cell phone to call 911."

"Patrol responded a few minutes after 3:20 a.m. and found Yang non-responsive, apparently from gunshot wounds. When the aid car arrived he was transported to the Matilda hospital emergency room where he was pronounced dead at 4 a.m. A body temp taken of his liver was nearly normal which showed the victim had been dead less than an hour."

"Robbery does not appear to have been the motive. Yang's wallet was found laying on his chest with a modest amount of money in it, but his warrant card and other ID had been stripped from it. He was wearing a leather jacket that looked to be the real thing. And he was still wearing a HK$100 knockoff Rolex watch and a poor quality half-carat diamond stud in his left ear. Looks like someone was sending a message that whatever this was, it wasn't a garden variety mugging for cash."

"About 6 a.m. that morning the hospital transported the body to the Medical Examiner's office. When the morgue assistant was doing a routine fingerprint analysis, he discovered the victim was a police officer. The duty ME immediately jumped Yang's body to the head of the autopsy queue. By noon on Saturday, October 5th, the preliminary autopsy report had been messengered to the duty commander at Arsenal Street. He alerted Homicide."

Ming explained, "Homicide and the crime lab both dispatched teams back to the site of the apparent homicide. There wasn't much evidence to find at the scene with exception of the fact that someone apparently had used a wooden match to jam the lockset to prevent its accepting the insertion of a key. Our detectives knocked on every resident's door in the building and finally located someone that said they had used that door shortly after midnight and the lock had been working fine."

"So, Homicide's supposition is that the wooden match was stuck in the lockset after midnight, but before 2 a.m. Saturday morning, when Yang arrived in the taxi."

"The criminalists reported that a half-dozen golf ball-sized stones were laying on the pavement next to the rear entrance. That led them to believe that the security light over the rear door had been purposely broken."

"The crime lab says the stones were not indigenous to the area so the shooter apparently brought them with him to accomplish the task of eliminating as much illumination as possible. Remember, this victim was a trained cop. The shooter would have been stupid to permit him any advantage."

Du Ming reported, "There was no brass discovered at the scene which means the shooter either was careful enough to police up his expended casings or used a revolver."

"And the preliminary autopsy report, which is all we have until the toxicology report comes back, reveals Yang was shot four times with a .22 caliber-longs. If we can go by the six grooves and landings, and right-hand twist, it's a Ruger semi-automatic target pistol. Twice in the forehead and the last two in the groin. Apparently the shooter isn't a stranger to handguns."

"The only on-scene observation of the body was that Yang had dirt on both knees of his pants. No defensive wounds. Perhaps he thought his assailant wouldn't shoot. Otherwise his clothing was immaculate with exception of his own blood. So he either was made to go to his knees to beg for his life or did it on his own accord. And, supporting the first assumption, they found dried salt on his cheeks."

Elizabeth stopped taking notes long enough to say, "What does that tell us, Lieutenant Ming?"

I decided to answer that. "What it tells us, Elizabeth, is that Yang was crying just before he died. Which would support the theory that he had been begging for his life. Understand?"

Always one who had to have the last comment, Elizabeth quipped, "Seems like a lot of work to go to extract payback on a cop who gave you a spending ticket if you ask me." Then she resumed taking notes.

We all had long ago realized that Elizabeth despite possessing near genus—level intelligence could make extremely inappropriate comments at times. But we overlook it because of her other strengths. And, of course no one *was* asking her.

Ming said, "We've put the cop killing on the top of our assignment sheet. But I want to keep a couple of teams assigned to continuing to pick up triad members in hopes someone will break, rollover and give up his boss. Once again, question?" There were none so he sat down.

────

With everyone having assignments I adjourned the meeting and returned to my office to enter everything that had been presented into the computerized Rapid Start case management system. Years ago, I had finagled a copy of the software out of the system's prime user, the FBI.

The brass up on the commissioner's floor expected the Rapid Start case files to be brought up to date within four hours of the conclusion to any police department status or operational meetings. It was an extremely efficient case management tool. Frankly, I didn't know how the Hong Kong police department under the British had managed for so many years without it.

All I knew at the moment that three, now four cop killings, meant things for the HKP and my department specifically had gone from bad to about as terrible as it gets. Little did I know at the time that things would get much worse before they improved.

7

10 October 2007, Thursday, 7:30 p.m. (HKT)
Fox's Penthouse Condo
Peak district
Hong Kong Island

I arrived home about 5:30 p.m. I'd spent the past three days monitoring the squad's progress in running down clues on the body part harvesting racket; the deaths of the three cops killed when transporting the 14K White Paper Fan 415 to Victoria Prison; and following-up on the yet-unsolved murder of young police officer Johnny Yang that occurred early Saturday morning, the fifth of October.

Inspector Yin had a raid planned for around midnight tonight on a funeral parlor she and her team felt was suspicious. An adrenaline junky I normally would have gone along on the raid strictly as an observer.

However after giving it some thought I decided that as a woman Mimi might take my being there in any capacity as a lack of confidence in her. So I had suppressed my basic urge to get involved. Instead, I'd only mentioned to her in passing that I was just a phone call away if her team ran into something they hadn't planned on.

Looking forward to a relaxing evening, I had just flopped down and kicked up my feet in my recliner after having returned the clandestine satellite cell phone to its hiding place in my dirty laundry basket. My conversation with Angry Dragon had made him aware of my intention to continue to poke the police department's nose into the black market body part harvesting operation. Although I hadn't mentioned it to him, I was fast tiring of the 'Me Tarzan, you Boy' relationship the Interpol agent seemed to expect of me.

I flipped on the TV and tuned into the nightly local news. Naturally, that is when my home phone rang. I put the TV on mute before picking up the receiver. Although fighting my agitation at being interrupted on what I had planned to be a relaxing night, I was pleasantly surprised to find Alicia on the other end of the line. I could tell she was upset. Still, I thought, two calls from Alicia in less than a week, frankly amazing.

While Alicia's calls were infrequent and sometimes confusing, I still enjoy hearing for her. After all, we lived together as lovers for the better part of a year before her mother's death.

———

There is an old saying that Trouble Comes In Threes. That certainly had proved true in Alicia's case. She had just buried her mother. And hired care providers at the Taiyunan home for her father. Thinking she had everything under control she was shocked when she found out she was genetically predisposed to cancer.

Her parents, in belief their daughter should be free to live what life was available to her without fear, had concealed the fact that her grandmother, great-grandmother, and great-great-great-grandmother had all died of cancer in their late thirties.

When Alicia's tests returned, they had revealed she tested positive for the mutated gene that almost always results in cancer. An Oncologist told her she had an 87 percent chance of developing breast cancer, and up to a 60 percent chance of developing ovarian cancer.

Even though her specialty was emergency medicine, not gynecology, Alicia knew that women with the mutated gene have to immediately take drastic prophylactic steps if they want to avoid the certainty of being stricken by possibly three forms of cancer. She shuttered as she thought about what those 'drastic steps' consisted of.

First she'd have to have a full mastectomy. According to what she'd shared with me, that reduced her chances of getting breast cancer by 90 percent. Next on the schedule she had committed to was the removal of her ovaries thereby reducing her risk of contracting ovarian cancer by 96 percent.

She had thought for a few minutes before making up her mind to have her uterus removed as well, even though there is no firm evidence that her genetic mutation was linked to uterine cancer. What Alicia did know is that developing cancer once she had completed the surgeries would be extremely rare.

Of course, she hadn't had to take those drastic steps. Not unless she'd wanted to live long enough to see her child grow old enough to begin to attend school. Or wanted to live long enough to host her grandchild's first birthday party.

She had been pregnant when she left Hong Kong. That had been the secret she had been hiding from me ever since she'd left for Taiyunan last year. She still couldn't explain to me why she had held off telling me about being pregnant.

When I asked why she had stumbled through an explanation saying it had something to do with my wife dying from undiagnosed pancreatic cancer in 1996. I had been on the NYPD at the time. The shock of my loss had resulted in a temporary emotional breakdown and turn to alcoholism when I had difficulty accepting the situation.

And then there had been the murder of my previous lover in 2005 here in Hong Kong, who unknown to me at the time had also been carrying a child of ours.

Alicia's rationalization for not telling me she was bearing our child was that when she left our home in Hong Kong without notice, essentially undecided as to whether she would ever return, I would end up hating her for denying me a second opportunity to have a child. And she, on top of everything else that was going to hell in her life, didn't think she could handle the additional burden of having to explain her deceitfulness to me.

On the last day of July this year, she had relented. She had called and informed me in a businesslike tone that she had given birth to our son on Christmas Day, 2006. He was a fine healthy child who had my eyes and nose, and that she had named Augustus, Jr.

But she admitted to me at the time that she hadn't yet figured out how she as going to deal with this complicated situation. After all, an unwed mother in the People's Republic of China, professional woman or not, was officially an embarrassment to the State. Alicia begged for me to continue to be patient until she felt she could deal with me coming to visit my son and her in Taiyunan later in the year.

So for the past four months I've forced myself to remain patient. To be fair about it, she has kept a steady stream of photos of my son's progressive development in the pipeline to me.

But I figured I shouldn't share the news that I was a father with coworkers and friends who knew about Alicia's leaving Hong Kong in case Alicia decided to never permit me to see our son.

I had checked with the American Consulate and found out I had no legal grounds on which to demand that she produce the child. The reason was because she had retained her Chinese citizenship all the while she had attended the University of Hong Kong medical school, and later, when we lived together in her penthouse condo in Hong Kong's Peak district.

————

Tonight's phone call started out with a tirade directed at me because she hadn't yet been able to pass the test for a Chinese driver's license. Apparently because I was a cop, I was the one responsible for her not being able to pass the test. So she was venting, at me.

Although I wasn't going to tell her, and thus provide more fuel for her argument, I have heard that the test is an absolute monster. Only a handful of U.S. diplomats posted in China have been able to pass it. In fact, my friend David Chow, the Hong Kong U.S. Consulate's Senior FBI Legate, had been laughing his socks off when he shared the fact with me that no U.S. diplomat in our Chengdu consulate had yet managed to pass it.

After the Chinese police had stopped several of the Chengdu diplomats and discovered that their drivers were operating the vehicles without a valid Chinese driver's license, traditional International Driver's Licenses not being accepted in the PRC, they cited their drivers for illegal driving. The diplomats had been forced to call a taxi to get them and their drivers back to the U.S. Consulate. The Chinese authorities impounded the cars which cost the Consulate US$ 5,000 each to get out of hock.

After that the Chengdu diplomats were forced to leave their fancy black Mercedes embassy cars parked in the Consulate garage. Instead, they had to take one of the decrepit taxi cabs known for their filthiness and tendency to break down at the worst possible times, the only for-hire cabs available in that town.

————

She was already yelling in my ear when she began our telephone conversation. "You cannot believe it, Augustus. You cops are all the same. The questions on this test are ridiculous and show what little regard you hold the average citizen in."

I tried to interrupt her in an attempt to explain, "I am a Chief Inspector, not a cop, and probably couldn't pass the damn Chinese test myself. So why are you taking this out on me?"

But that didn't slow her down one iota. She continued to vent her complaints with the Chinese drivers test.

"Ok, Augustus, you answer this question, Mr. Mr. Smart Ass policeman. Lets say you are driving down the highway in China. And in your rearview mirror you spot flames coming from your gas cap. Now, do you (a) Strip off your cotton clothing and use it to smother the flames, (b) Toss water on the blaze, (c) Dig out the carbon-dioxide fire extinguisher every car in China is required to carry, and spray it on the flames, or (d) Call the China's AAA auto club."

I gave that some thought, secretly glad she had given me an easy question and replied, "It would be answer "C" of course, Alicia."

I was totally unprepared for her unladylike response that used every word I remembered existing in her obscenity repertoire. After she exhausted all the terms I knew she had she possessed before she moved back to Taiyunan, plus a few more, she howled like a wounded banshee, "Wrong, Mr. Policeman, the correct answer is "A."

Ops, I should have guessed that. The Chinese have always tended to prefer using the most basic of remedies, first.

––––––

Let me describe what I know of this test to you readers while Alicia continues to vent in my ear. It is a multiple-choice, 100-question test of vague mechanical facts, oxcart etiquette, and last of all, rules of the road. It is a must for anyone who intends to operate a vehicle in the world's third-largest country.

Get more than 10 questions wrong on the computerized test, and the screen lights up with a weepy yellow emoticon and the sorrowful message, "It is sorry that you do not pass."

Incidentally, I was at a Consulate party a month ago and heard some wag that obviously had never taken the test, state in a whiny voice, "It can't be that difficult, Ole Chap, I mean 95% of the Chinese pass the test on their first try, and some of them are illiterate."

––––––

By now Alicia had calmed down a little, but had gone on to her second question: "When driving on the road and encountering a cattle-drawn cart, a motor vehicle should . . ."

In frustration, I blurted out, "Alicia, how would I know the answer to that? We don't have ox-carts in Hong Kong as you well know."

That set her off again. "Well, if you don't know the answer then how could I know? I'm much younger than you (first time in the history of our relationship she had every brought that up) so you should be wiser."

"Ok, Alicia, what is the answer to that question?"

"Blow the Horn with as little sound as possible.'"

I said, "Christ almighty, Alicia. Why are you wasting your money on this call if all you want to talk about is the arcane questions on the Chinese driving test?"

"Just one more, Augustus, and then I tell you something you'll find exciting. Okay?"

"Ok, Alicia, give me your final question."

"What should a driver do when he needs to spit while driving?"

"Ah, come on, Alicia, how would I know that?"

"Augustus, I said that was your last question. But only if you answer it, otherwise I'll keep this up."

"No, no, I'll answer it Alicia. Err, how about hold off spitting until he gets to his destination?"

"No, Augustus, you can't even answer the simple ones. The answer is 'Spit into a piece of waste paper, then put it into a garbage can.'"

"Ok, Alicia," deciding I had to come up with some recommendation for her or she was going to continue to drive me nuts with this foolishness, "You may find this unusual coming from me, but why not slip a couple hundred yuán into the hand of the test proctor."

"Oh, Augustus, you are so smart. That is exactly what I finally did. But she put the money in her pocket and still gave me a failing grade."

Now, I could understand her frustration. I mean if you give someone a bribe, they ought to respond quid-pro-quo, right?

"Ok, Doctor, how is my son?"

She changed her tone of voice to cooing, "Oh, he is growing so fast. Augustus Jr. is trying to walk already. The nanny says he holds on to her fingers but his little legs aren't strong enough yet. Luckily he had a well-padded rump because he falls on it a lot."

"When am I going to be able to come up and see him? I've waited four months since you told me about him. Sure, you have sent me plenty of great pictures of him but I'd like to meet him first hand so he will get to know me as 'daddy' before he continues to grow into his formative years."

"I need more time, Augustus. I've told you that. Be patient. I still am trying to learn to be a mommy. And you know I am devastated because I can't breast feed him. Don't you understand that the mastectomy took the most basic privilege of being a mother away from me? I need more time, maybe next month you can come up, but in any case, before the holidays. You can spend the Christmas holidays with Augustus Jr. and I. Get to know your son. Would you like that?"

"You know I would. Okay, what is the other thing you want to tell me? The thing you said I would find interesting."

"Certainly, Augustus, but first I have to ask you something. Are you dating? Have you slept with anyone? Is it serious? Have you brought anyone home to our condo, darling?"

I gave that a few nanoseconds thought, before answering. I certainly didn't want to start lying to the mother of my child at this point in our relationship. "The answer to that is yes, yes, and no, no," I replied.

"Well, good, Augustus, you need a woman to keep you balanced, but please be honest enough to tell me if the latter changes, Ok?"

"You'll be the first to know, Alicia. Now, fess up, we've been on the telephone tonight for nearly a half hour and you still haven't told me your secret."

Alicia sighed, and said, "It isn't a secret, Augustus. I just didn't know how to tell you. Okay, here it is. As you might guess, all the surgery seems to have made me feel less like a woman, like my womanhood has been stolen from me. Do you understand that?"

"Yes, I think I can, it would be like a male discovering he had testicular cancer which forced him to have his testicles surgically removed to save his life, I guess."

After a brief pause, Alicia continued with her story, "Well, last month I was feeling pretty down. Even Junior's crying was getting on my nerves. So I decide I needed something to perk me up. I've met a woman acupuncturist here who also does body art. I had her give me a nipple tattoo on one of my reconstructed breasts, and a cute little heart on the other. What do you think about that? I wanted to make myself realize every time I was naked and looked into a mirror that my breasts could be beautiful again after my mastectomy."

I guess that floored me, I was expecting almost anything other than nipple tattoos. But I couldn't let her know that I was shocked, so I said, "Sounds just beautiful, sweetheart. I can't wait to see them in person. Like when I hope you'll permit me to visit you and Jr. in Taiyunan for Christmas." *Nice save, Fox*, I thought to myself.

Then Alicia said she had to go put Jr. to bed, so we said "Good night," and wished each other a nice weekend. We both told the other "I love you" before hanging up the phone.

———

I watched the late news before retiring for the night. While I hoped for a restful sleep, I knew I'd be up a number of times during the night to urinate. Apparently this is not unusual in men my age according to the Urologist I'd been forced to see. I had become concerned about incontinency when I returned from attending a terrorism seminar in the United States in September of 2006.

He had given me literature to read that made me aware that as men age, at about 45 and older, they begin to experience difficulty urinating on-demand. Coupled with that, we get the urge to get up multiple times a night to relieve ourselves. Trouble was, as I have since experienced, sometimes you stand over the toilet, preferably with the seat up, and find yourself unable to go.

Or worse, when you do go, your stream splits in two or shoots off at a tangent, meaning cleaning up the bathroom floor before you return to bed. And while I was 46 at the time, now 47, and still feel that I have the body of a person in their late 30's.

Unfortunately my PSA—Prostrate-Specific Antigen test—had been high enough that the doctor recommended a biopsy to rule in-or-out prostrate cancer. When the test results came back, I felt like celebrating. At that time it indicated that I didn't have cancer.

What the doctor said I did have was a condition called BPH, or Benign Prostatic Hyperplasia. Since being diagnosed a year ago, I have been taking the prescription medications, Flomax and Avodart. But in my case, I still have to get up multiple times a night.

The last time I'd had an appointment with the doctor to explain my concerns, he told me that it was just a normal part of aging. That if I quit taking the medications the number of my nocturnal trips to the bathroom would increase.

Thinking about what Alicia had shared with me tonight, and mentally reviewing the cases that were on my plate at work, I didn't manage to get asleep until after eleven p.m.

But my sleep would soon be interrupted. The unthinkable had happened.

8

11 October 2007, Friday, 12:01 a.m. (HKT)
Five Ram Chinese Funeral Parlor
Rear of 123 Hennessy Road—Wan Chai district
Hong Kong Island

As the SWAT cops blasted the funeral parlor's heavy doors off it's hinges, the two primary detectives who had requested the assignment of being the first through the vertical coffin, cop talk for the door, nervously entered the reception area with weapons at the ready.

Both hated their uncomfortable bullet-resistant vests. The vests were only capable of protecting the wearer against small caliber handgun fire. However, Inspector Yin had insisted they were to be worn by everyone who was participating in tonight's raid.

The primary detectives, after clearing the immediate area in their field of vision, were followed by four more detectives assigned the task of completing the search of the first floor for occupants, unfriendly or otherwise.

Only when the four backup cops returned from their search of the first floor premises and gave the "All clear" signal did the two primary detectives begin to edge their way up the main staircase. The silence, excepting the shuffling and murmuring of the cops signifying that a particular room was clear, would be described by any observer experienced in police armed confrontations as deafening.

When the two cops reached the second floor they observed boxes stacked in alcoves on at either side of the landing, and directly in front of them, a padlocked double door.

The detectives had come prepared to deal with entry into a padlocked room. The male cop carried a pair of commercial bolt cutters in a harness on his back.

Both cops held their positions crouched at the top of the staircase for almost five minutes to permit their hearing to recover from the loud, violent breeching of the parlor's main entrance door. But the frenzied announcements of the backup team declaring various areas on the first floor "All clear" continued as the two strained their ears attempting to hear even the faintest movement from anywhere on the second floor.

When they were reasonably certain that no visible overt threat was waiting for them on the second floor, the female detective straightened up and moved to take up a covering position on the left side of the landing, assuming a Weaver stance with her weapon as she had been taught in the academy years earlier.

As soon as his partner was in position, the male detective switched his pistol to his left hand and noiselessly pulled the commercial bolt cutters from the improvised harness on his back with his right.

Rotating his body until he faced the door with his left side facing the door, his left hand pointing his weapon down at the floor and with the bolt cutters in his right, the detective cautiously and as silently as possible side-stepped his way up to the double door until he was close enough to cut the padlock.

But before the tool made any contact with the padlock, both detectives took another five minutes listening for unexplained sounds before going to the next level, breeching the padlocked door. The muted sounds the backup team was making downstairs filtered up to the second floor landing, making it difficult for the detectives to decide which sounds came from the first floor, and which came from the floor they were on.

Finally, the two detectives gave up in frustration. There was no way they could decide which sounds were coming from where. So with a hand motion to the woman, the male detective slowly extended the jaws of the bolt cutters until it came into physical contact with the padlock.

Inside a nanosecond an electrical charge arced between the padlock and the jaws of the bolt cutters and shot through concealed wires to the alcoves.

There were two horrific explosions.

———

The concussion from the blasts struck both detectives before they could even scream. The blasts originated in the alcoves at either side of the padlocked door. The second floor landing became blindingly bright then smothering dark as a hailstorm of hundreds of steel projectiles shredded both detectives.

The bolt cutters shot through the space where the landing's railing had been only a second before, and fell towards the first floor, bouncing off the chest of a backup detective who fortunately was protected by his inspector's insistence that all the raiders wear their vests tonight.

As bloody pieces from the shredded bodies of the primary detectives began to rain down on the stunned cops on the first floor, an extreme corner of the second floor landing collapsed from the force of the explosions but left the spiral stairway up to the second floor still accessible.

The explosion deafened the four men and Inspector Yin who had remained on the first floor. After they had instinctively sought cover upon hearing the explosions, they had been frozen in place, utterly transfixed by what had happened on the floor above them.

Each of the cops on the main floor experienced a momentary sense of survivor's syndrome. Whenever someone is killed, his or her partner experiences a wave of sickly exhilaration of happiness that any normal individual feels when another person is killed because it spared him or her. Shrinks call it survivor's guilt.

One of the surviving younger detectives on the main floor of the funeral parlor began to scream uncontrollably. Deafened by the explosions, he could not hear his own screaming. The acrid smoke from the bombs had caused him to gag convulsively and he wasn't able to get his breath.

Then the screaming cop felt someone grab his shoulders. He struggled and cursed but seemingly was powerless to avoid being literally dragged across the now bloody carpet of the parlor's reception area, through the demolished main door and out in the relative fresh air outside.

The first thing he remembered seeing after he had been carefully placed on his back on the damp sidewalk was that he was encircled by a circle of concerned cops. Including the person who had dragged him to safety, Inspector Yin.

He made a final frantic effort to free himself from the hands that held him immobile as he saw the medics from the aid units running over towards him with aluminum stretchers in one hand and their first-responder emergency car kits in the other.

———

11 October 2007, Friday, 1:00 a.m. (HKT)
Five Ram Chinese Funeral Parlor
Rear of 123 Hennessy Road—Wan Chai district
Hong Kong Island

I told the sleepy cop driving the district patrol car who was transporting me to drop me off a block from the crime scene.

Call me perverse but I find something exciting about a crime scene in the middle of the night. This one was glaringly lit by the magnetic pulsating blue rooftop gumballs of the detective squad, red-and-blue flashers of the marked black-and-white Land Rovers, and the yellow rooftops strobes of the Crime Scene team's white stretch vans. I got out of the car and the patrolman drove off to find a parking spot closer to the scene.

The streets at an hour after midnight were nearly pitch dark. It was obvious to me that the city's maintenance crews apparently hadn't spent too many hours replacing burnout and broken streetlights along this section Hennessey Road.

I knew enough to be exceedingly aware of my surroundings at this hour and in this neighborhood. I walked down the median in the center of the street to where the emergency vehicles were parked haphazardly, forcing the occasional vehicle out at this god forsaken hour to either come to a stop or attempt to drive over the median into the opposite lane to get through.

My experience told me to take a moment to look around and acclimate myself to the crime scene. Then I walked up the mist-slick sidewalk to the poorly lit entrance of the funeral parlor to where a guy in a bad suit but a pleasant look on his face was holding the required In-and-Out crime scene clipboard. He held a regulation police five-cell flashlight he'd apparently borrowed from one of the dozen or so on-scene patrol officers.

Based on the 'flash briefing' I received from Inspector Yin when she called me at my condo about twenty minutes ago, I assumed the man was one of the alleged "just-in-the-neighborhood" guys she told me about. This one she obviously had assigned as crime scene control officer. He was a thick, round man with thin brown hair that at his age should have been turning gray. The combination of sparseness and the unnatural darkness of the brown pigment gave his hair a dirty look.

He had a weather-beaten face, the face of a hunter, fisherman, homeless person, long-time smoker, or just possibly the hard face of a long-time cop. He was probably an investigator based on the fact that he worn the almost obligatory rumpled suit, had an distinct odor of smoke on his clothing, and a stain on his fingers that indicated he was a chain-smoker who hadn't yet discovered that smoking causes cancer.

The man who I would later learn was Hans Harwanegg asked me in the worse example I've ever heard a Aussie attempting to massacre the English language, "And you are who, Yank?"

I should know better than to smart off to these international police types. But this after all is my town. Where did he get off asking me to identify myself?

"I'm your goddamn worst nightmare if you don't let me into the crime scene," I responded quite pleasantly.

The friendly smile abruptly vanished. Then pointedly through clenched teeth my new friend said, "I'd like to see your ID before you sign in. Even then I might not let you pass." It was easy to see that I had just managed to enroll a new member into the Augustus Fox fan club.

My response, you know me, never step into a shallow hole if you can dig yourself in deeper, was, "If I show you my ID then I'll have to kill you."

Now my new friend and I were getting along fabulously. He growled, "Seriously, if you don't show it to me, it'll be me, Yank, who will have to kill you."

Just when things were about to get interesting, Inspector Mimi Yin poked her head out of the doorway of the funeral parlor, saw me about to change the oil on this Interpol dipstick, and yelled down to him, "It's okay. That's Chief Inspector Augustus Fox. I'd suggest you permit him to pass unless you are amenable to a transfer to Adak, Alaska, once you are relieved for cause for being rude to a HKP commanding officer."

The only reason I was giving the Aussie a hard time anyway was because his body English shouted that he was long overdue for a rigorous attitude readjustment. That, and because I always try to slip by without signing into as many crime scene logs as possible as usually I am there because of my professional curiosity rather than duty. A management tool that Tom Peters, the author of *The Five-Minute Manager* calls Management by Walking Around.

And the fewer crime scene logs a Boss signs walking around overseeing his investigators, the fewer times said Boss gets sued if anything, for whatever reason, goes to hell in a proverbial handbag.

This was my city after all. Not only do Inspector Mimi Yin and her detectives report to me but the Hong Kong Crime Lab Criminalists on the scene work for one of my peers, not Interpol.

I could see the Aussie wasn't going to budge no matter how many threats he received—perhaps he fancied that he would enjoy working in Alaska—so I grabbed the clipboard and purposely scrawled a rough approximation of my signature across three columns of the written log. Now let's see how he is going to explain that in a Court of Law.

My new fan reluctantly stepped aside to let me pass. I walked up the handicapped ramp to the main entrance into the Five Ram Chinese funeral parlor. It is a large two-story building built on a 'flag' lot behind the Alliance Francaise, a library located at 123 Hennessy Road in Wan Chai district on Hong Kong Island.

Mimi meet me at the door, gave me a pair of latex gloves and white paper booties, both which I slipped on before she waved me past the uniformed Hong Kong patrol officer charged with preventing people like me from contaminating crime scenes. We walked into a bloodbath that can only be described as an abattoir, a slaughterhouse.

According to the on-site briefing update Mimi gave me at that point, this was one of several Chinese funeral parlors that her team, after protracted aerial and street-level surveillance, suspected could be involved in the illegal Body-Parts-for-Harvesting operation.

She said her team had sat surveillance on this funeral parlor and observed multiple white vans come and go all day long. They only had stopped long enough to discharge or deliver a white plastic refrigerated chest before hurriedly driving away from the location. The surveillance also revealed that the funeral parlor's employees, who came and went, appeared to be acting very furtively like they had something to hide.

I was frankly surprised that she had gotten a search warrant because normally an affidavit that lame would have been tossed out, totally inadequate to get a search warrant authorized by one of Hong Kong's notoriously liberal magistrates.

Mimi looked at me with those big brown eyes. I could clearly read the message in them. *Don't be such a candy ass, boss. I am smarter than that.*

Her team, receiving information that this parlor had a second floor that reportedly was kept locked even during daytime hours, had caused Yin to send a illegal black bag expert into the place after midnight, night before last, for a little illegal sneak-and-peek after all the employees had gone home. But her expert had decided she could not get into the mysterious second floor room without leaving evidence that the padlock had been picked.

With the information she had from her surveillance operation, augmented by some of the opinions of her sneak-and-peek expert, and by fudging a few facts, Inspector Yin had gone to one of the few tame judges our department has access to in HK and obtained a 'No knock' search warrant for the building. The pretense used in the affidavit stated that the detectives thought there was a white slave operating from behind its locked second floor doors.

At 12:01 a.m., Mimi's detectives had used a battering ram to knock the parlor's front door off its hinges. After a cursory check of the first floor for any hostiles, two of the detectives had carefully worked their way up the spiral staircase to the second floor where shortly all hell would break loose.

As soon as one of the detectives had pulled a pair of heavy-duty bolt lock cutters from a jury-rigged harness on his back, and reached over to the door to begin cutting the heavy padlock off the second floor entrance doors, two things happened in a nanosecond.

First, what appeared to have been two booby traps, each set in the dark alcoves to either side of the padlocked door on the second floor, suddenly exploded. The blasts and steel projectiles from the bombs dismembered Mimi's detectives propelling body parts and the steel bolt cutters through the second floor's wooden hand railing to fall to the first floor.

Secondly, seemingly out of nowhere, two white males holding badges and ID wallets over their head in one hand, and cocked and locked 9 mm SIG Sauer semi-automatics outfitted with infrared sighting devices in the other, charged into the middle of the first floor fray, shouting, "*Stop-stop-stop, Interpol officers, stop now or we will shoot.*"

––––––

While her Lieutenant called for aid cars for her fallen officers, Mimi had her surviving detectives disarm the men alleging to be Interpol officers. They looked enough alike to be brothers, which it turned out they were. They claimed their names backed up by their ID were Hans and Gustav Harwanegg from Perth, a city in southwest Australia near the Indian Ocean.

After taking more than ten minutes to inspect the identification the two men had in their possession, noting they had no temporary accommodation permits or gun permits issued by the HKP, the Inspector separated the two men and questioned them separately, out of the hearing of the other.

She'd specifically asked each the question, "What is Interpol doing sticking their nose in our local Hong Kong Police investigation? And if you were in the area on legitimate police business, what is the 'color' of the day?"

The older of the two Aussies had replied, "We were in the neighborhood looking for a international terrorist's address when we observed what appeared to be a triad raid taking place. We just jumped in to stop it."

Inspector Yin didn't believe the agent's story because even Interpol isn't stupid enough to stick their noses in a triad retaliatory raid.

———

Author's note: "Color of the day." This is a means of verifying whether an alleged police officer had the right to be where he is, regardless of department affiliation. The practice was established a decade earlier by law enforcement agencies through the world after too many officers became unknowingly involved in shootouts with other undercover cops.

When a outside police agency enters a jurisdiction other than their own, they must check in with the police administrator of that jurisdiction who will inform them of the color code for the day. It is to be zealously used anytime the visitors will be working out of their primary area of responsibility, off their home turf. The procedure works about 95% of the time. It was the remaining 5% that results in unnecessary cop shootings, usually at the hands of overeager cops who foolishly make a conscious decision to ignore the procedure.

———

In the current situation, both men when questioned separately knew that the official HKP color was Emperor Red for the day immediately following the hour of midnight. Still, Mimi didn't want them mucking up the crime scene. So she had used her on-scene authority to give each man a special assignment; one to maintain the In-and-Out log recording visitors to the crime scene, and the other to search the rear alley of the building for any evidence that might explain what had happened at the scene a few minutes earlier.

Mimi then had waited outside in the near darkness outside the funeral parlor under a broken-out streetlight to guide the aid cars to the scene.

While she was waiting she had dropped a nickel with her cell phone to my condo which she knew was located less than four miles away. Her call subsequently resulted in me being transported to the scene by one of the district's sector cars.

———

My first thought after Mimi had called before jumping into a cold shower to wake up was, *Not another cop killing!* Going to dead cop's funerals was starting to become a regular occurrence in this department. Cop killing was beginning to be an epidemic.

———

After applying a dab of Vicks Vaporub under our noses, Mimi and I gingerly made our way into the funeral parlor's huge foyer being very careful where we placed our feet. The foyer had a wall-to-wall blood-red rug on its floor and red velvet embossed fleur-de-lis wallpaper, which looked suspiciously like some I'd seen in the social rooms of the Mustang Ranch in my younger days on visits to Las Vegas.

To the left was a sweeping spiral stairway constructed of dark teak and carpeted with an expensive reddish-orange handwoven oriental runner that provided access to the second floor.

As we stood there looking up at a six-foot shattered crystal chandelier my nose despite the Vaporub was assaulted by an overwhelming nauseating smell. Body parts lay at our feet; blood not yet coagulated enough to stop oozing from under the second floor hand railing, fell to the floor below; the wallpapered walls and stark white ceiling of the foyer appeared to be have been smitten with pox, small holes the size of double-aught buckshot; and the familiar odor of partially burned cordite.

The night-shift criminalists whose crime lab is located just a handful of blocks away at the Arsenal Street Police headquarters had arrived on scene promptly. Since all of the parlor's lights that may have been functioning prior to the booby traps exploding were no longer operational, the Crime Scene Unit (CSU) had set up three batteries of generator-driven, portable klieg lights; two sets downstairs, and the third on the second floor landing.

Lying at our feet were the gory body parts of a Chinese woman in her early thirties who looked like she had kept fit using the police gym. Hard to judge from what was left, but I shot-gunned her stats as in the mid-thirties, about 5 foot 5 inches and 120 pounds.

Mimi informed me the woman had been the lead detective. She'd been wearing what appeared to be a stylish brown suit with a nondescript jacket and a short skirt, now insultingly in death hiked well above her bloody thighs displaying a pair of red silk thong panties, and thighs that were no longer connected to her lower legs. She looked like a Raggedy Anne doll that had viciously been torn limb from limb.

The woman had a wedding ring on her left hand, and not-surprisingly, her holster no longer contained her weapon. Her arms no longer were connected to what I was sure had been well-manicured hands.

Before her heart had stopped, and before it had congealed, blood had seeped out of her severed body parts. The woman's head was missing. The blood before congealing had began to form halos. Her body parts appeared to have been shredded by flying objects intercepted enroute to achieving ballistic-speed.

A few feet away lay the body of the woman's partner, also very dead. He also was Chinese, perhaps 5 foot 8 inches tall, of stocky built, about 170 pounds. He had been nearing middle age and appeared to have dressed more appropriately for a raid in blue jeans and a blue dungaree shirt. His upper torso seemed hunched over as if trying to get enough leverage to get the bolt cutters to cut through the hasp on the heavy padlock when the booby traps had exploded.

His injuries included a missing leg. The leg that was still attached was minus its foot. His buttocks and genitals had been shredded into a virtual sieve. His back had been laid open all the way to his neck exposing the spine. His head was still in place but his ears, the hair on the rear of his skull, and the muscles on top of his shoulder blades had all been stripped by the blast from the perforated corpse.

Mimi leaned over and quietly told me, "There is something upstairs I need to show you. I am well aware that since I am a relative rookie and a woman, there is going to be a lot of hindsight criticism of this raid. Perhaps enough that you may even have to take my squad away from me, 'Pluto' me, or reassign me to deskwork. But I want you to see everything on your own so you can draw your own conclusions, Chief Inspector."

We carefully worked our way up the staircase stepping around anything that would be considered evidence—blood, skin, imbedded projectiles from the bomb, and bits of clothing, congealing blood, and body parts. At the second floor landing Mimi led me across the badly scarred floor, now minus its carpet, first to one alcove then the other. It seemed obvious that the booby trap devices had been planted in the two alcoves.

The booby traps had been directional or shaped charges. Both had been aimed to obliterate anyone attempting to access the room where Mimi suspected that the illegal body part harvesting was taking place. The door itself was steel, painted red and had stenciled on its surface in eight-inch-high black Cantonese and English letters, NO SMOKING.

The padlock that had been on the door before the male detective had attempted to cut it off was missing. The room had not yet been entered either by the cops or criminalists on the scene. The explosions appeared to have been triggered by an electrical charge arcing metal-to-metal, padlock to bolt cutter jaws, before the male detective could cut the padlock or turn the now heavily pitted chrome door lever. The door's surface was covered with little depressions or pocks marks made when projectiles had ricocheted after failing to piece its thick steel facing.

I noticed a heavy cardboard box in one of the alcoves that apparently had been left behind when the explosive devices had been placed. Because the mine had been directional, and set to blast outward to cover the door entrance and the second floor landing, the box was still relatively intact. Inside the box were two unarmed explosive devices I recognized from my military days.

The heavy cardboard box was stenciled in six-inch-high black ink, in English: "**PROPERTY OF U.S. ARMY—CLAYMORE MINES (4)**."

Printed below that in black four-inch-high letters was the warning; "**CLAYMORE: 650 GRAMS OF EXPLOSIVE AND 700 STEEL BALLS. BALLS DISPERSE BALLISTICALLY IN A 60-DEGREE ARC CREATING A KILL ZONE UP TO 2 METERS IN HEIGHT. FOR MAXIMUM EFFECTIVITY PLACE MINES ON 25-METER CENTERS TO ENSURE OVERLAP. EFFECTIVE INSIDE 50-METERS**."

Directly below that in red two-inch-high letters were the instructions: "**FIRE ONLY THROUGH THE USE OF A HAND 'CLACKER' OR TRIP WIRE DEVICE PLACED BY A CERTIFIED DEMOLITIONS EXPERT. MAKE CERTAIN TO READ INSTRUCTIONS BEFORE USING. THIS PERSONNEL MINE IS DIRECTIONAL IN THE EXTREME. PLACE DEVICE AS EMBOSSED, "*THIS SIDE TOWARD ENEMY.*"**

Well, now we knew what had killed the two detectives even though we had no idea of where the killers had obtained the weapons. But I'd be lying if I said that man-killers such as this were not available on the lucrative Hong Kong black market that traffics in weapons, because they were. Expensively, but yes, they were.

I turned to Inspector Yin who still looked a little shell-shocked. A natural reaction as she'd had lost two of her people. And on the first opportunity she'd had to lead her team into an actual armed confrontation since she taken over the job as inspector a year ago.

She was realistically clairvoyant in her awareness that there would indeed be a lot of hindsight day-after quarterbacking, a lot of it because she was a woman. And most of it would be coming from armchair police commanders who likely had never been under fire themselves.

Thinking she had earned the right to open the door of the mysterious room and hopefully discover what she hoped would be a clandestine body part harvesting operation, I stepped out of the way and motioned her toward the buckshot-pocked steel door.

She stood in front of the door for a few seconds, I imagine praying to whatever god she worshipped that what was behind the door would be the surgical suite she and her team had suspected was located in the room.

Then taking a deep breath—actually, I also took one because we both had a lot of political capital invested in what lie behind the door as I believe in supporting my people even if they occasionally happen to be wrong in their decisions—she twisted the handle and bravely stepped into the dark room using her flashlight to illuminate what it contained.

The room was filled with small wooden workbenches. Gaily colored crepe paper lay in bundled rolls on some of the tables; other contained cardboard barrels labeled in Cantonese, CAUTION: BLACK POWDER—EXPLOSIVE; and others supported vertical wooden racks that were filled with hollow cardboard tubes of various diameters and lengths.

There was a red ten-pound ABC fire extinguisher hung on every wall and support column, and a sign every five feet saying in Cantonese, NO SMOKING! If it was necessary to keep people who worked here aware of the seriousness of that non-negotiable regulation, the ambient air bore the nostril-irritating smell of black powder.

There were no surgical facilities, no stainless steel autopsy tables, no stink of decomposing flesh, and no evidence of any cutting, slicing, or dicing instruments.

The inspector's flashlight beam revealed one of the many quasi-legal fireworks factories that continue to exist on Hong Kong Island somehow avoiding the inspections of the HKSAR's elite fire department. We had been had, set-up, screwed—whatever you want to call it.

All the coming and going of trucks similar to the one that had been abandoned after it had crashed at the shootout scene this week, the people coming and going to the funeral parlor acting furtively, everything, staged. A set-up designed to draw our forces in by encouraging us to raid the place. It was obvious that our intense surveillance of the funeral parlor and its employees had not gone unnoticed by the criminals involved. They had set a trap for us. We had walked into it.

The nagging thought that had been bothering me ever since I arrived on-scene was that something here was very wrong! I now knew my first priority had to be determining why those Interpol thugs had coincidently been in the area; and specifically why they had violated all establish law enforcement protocol by butting into Inspector Yin's raid, thereby putting her and her team of detectives at extreme risk.

Turning back to Inspector Yin whose discovery of the fireworks factory instead of the surgical suite she'd anticipated had drained her face of color, I instructed, "I want those two self-acclaimed Interpol agents disarmed, detained, and transported to the Arsenal Street headquarters and held in the interrogation cells."

"The fact that they have not showed us written HKP acknowledgement or approval of their presence in Hong Kong, and they don't have HKP-issued gun permits, when taken altogether are felonies. That is the basis on which we'll hold then pending orders from higher authority to do otherwise."

"Make certain they are not permitted any telephone privileges. As far as I am concerned, they can sit there and rot until they can come up with a satisfactory—no, make that a believable—explanation of how they became involved in this thing. Understand, Mimi?"

The opportunity to extract a little payback to these two intruders who had barged into her carefully scripted operation filtered into her voice as she assertively replied, "Yes, Sir. I'll take care of advising our two friends of their new status, personally."

———

Later than day word came down from the commissioner's office that the Australian Consulate, located in the Harbour Center complex, 25 Harbour

Road in the Wan Chai district, had received an anonymous phone call that two of its citizens were being detained on criminal charges. The Consulate demanded and the police commissioner ordered that the two brothers be released immediately.

My countering argument that they were being held for operating in Hong Kong without the our department's knowledge or approval, and that they were in possession of firearms for which they possessed no HKP permits, fell on deaf ears and we had to kick them loose just before 5 p.m. that day.

Our case was imploding in on itself like the fizzling core of a hydrogen bomb. But good cops had given their lives in service of the citizens of Hong Kong. I was going to make certain those deaths were avenged.

9

12 October 2007, Saturday, 1:30 a.m. (HKT)
The Propaganda Club
#1 Hollywood Road—Central district
Hong Kong Island

About 1:30 a.m. Chow Yung Su, a young Chinese male about thirty walked out of the Propaganda Club which is located in the Central district, Hong Kong Island. He turned east to head for the Central Rail station to catch the Tung Chung MTR line home to his apartment in Mongkok. He was about 5 foot 7 inches tall, weight approximately 160 pounds, and appeared to be in good physical condition. In less than fifteen minutes he would be dead.

The Propaganda is the only openly gay disco in Hong Kong and as such makes welcome both gays and lesbians. The staff is surly, the cover fees humongous, and the music is close to being monotonous. Still it reputedly is one of the places that tourists shouldn't 'miss' on a Saturday night regardless of their sexual orientation.

Chow was dressed foppishly in an off-the-rack dark brown silk suit, a yellow ruffled shirt, tan Gucci loafers and an expensive Corum steel GMT classic watch. Pausing only to light up an American Marlboro cigarette he set off with a self-confident step as he walked west from #1 Hollywood Road. His strut was so over-the-top it would be easy for someone unfamiliar with the man to assume he had just be awarded some "Best of . . . contest," perhaps even had been recently been knighted by the Queen of England.

As Chow walked through the evening mist he felt some guilt for ending up in the gay nightclub that night. But he seemed unable to control his urges ever since his private physician had broken the news to him last month that he was HIV positive.

He knew it only would take a matter of days for his doctor to notify his employer of his positive HIV status in accordance with Hong Kong health department regulations. Although he had not yet been called in to speak with his employer's physician, he was certain the results he had been dreading for almost a year now had already been 'two-hole punched' and placed in his employee personnel file.

The proverbial shoe was about to drop. There was no doubt about that. When it did he knew that, if not drummed out of his current employment all together, he would at least be reassigned to a job where he would have no public contact.

Since Chow had received the career-ending news a month before, he sensed himself steadily losing control of his personal life. He started going out with his buddies to all the hot clubs in Hong Kong, gay or straight, and usually went home with a man or woman depending on what the club had to offer that particular night.

He took his personal death warrant, the HIV soon to be AIDS, out on everyone he slept with refusing to use a condom and never, ever, breathing a word that he had a high-communicable, sexually-transmitted disease.

While he had no idea which of his homosexual partners in the past had infected him, he was committed to taking as many people with him as possible. He was mad, horrendously mad. How could this happen to him?

Chow was exercising slightly more situational awareness than normal tonight after the killing last week of his sometime drinking buddy, Johnny Yang. Yang had been shot to death at the rear of his subsistence-level residential hotel last weekend. Yang had been an acquaintance that enjoyed acting the role of player as much as Chow and his other drinking buddies.

Although he wasn't armed, Chow wasn't particularly worried about his own safety tonight. He, like most of the citizens of Hong Kong, assumed Yang's death was just been another of the dozen or so 'wrong place-wrong time' killings that happen on the mean streets of Hong Kong every month.

According to what Chow had read in the papers, the cops had yet to come up with the shooter let alone a motive for the shooting. The local newspapers had tried to float a story that it was a triad hit. Chow knew that was just hogwash created out of thin air to sell papers.

He had started to hang out with a couple of bi-sexual toughs he met in nightclubs. Their modus operandi was to use date rape drugs to dope young women and men, and then force them to engage in unprotected group sex.

When his conscience made a rare appearance, Chow told himself that he was going to eventually die anyway. What were they going to do with him, put him in jail? What a joke.

As he walked east on Hollywood Road which was nearly deserted at this hour, lost in his thoughts of self-justified revenge and self-pity, he didn't notice a black for-hire four-door Toyota sedan slowly cruise by him, first east on Hollywood Road, then turn around and creep by him the other direction.

A set of angry eyes followed Chow's progress along the road from the driver's seat of the Toyota. Finally it pulled over to the curb a block ahead of him in an area where a high percentage of streetlights were burned out or broken out west of Aberdeen Street.

When Chow's walking brought him past the car the driver had stepped out, quietly closing the door, leaving the engine running, the exhaust propelling a cloud of steam into the humid night air, and began to follow him. Trained to maintain his situation awareness Chow became aware of the individual's presence almost immediately.

He moved closer to the building abutting the sidewalk, turned his back to the wall, faced the intruder, and assumed a defensive Karate position as he had been taught to do at the academy a couple years ago.

Upon his doing this, the person following him had come to an abrupt halt about twelve feet away from him. In the darkness Chow couldn't make out the features of the stranger only that the person was tall and was wearing dark clothing with a 'hoodie' over the head. The sinister figure had a right hand buried in a jacket pocket.

"What do you want?" Chow demanded in Cantonese. "I have little money. You don't know what you are dealing with here, I warn you. Come one more step closer to me and you are going to get busted up very much, then dragged to the closest police station. No aid car for you, criminal. So you better got out of here, now!"

The stranger just stood there waiting for the young man to decide whether to fight or flee.

When the young dandy did neither, the dark-clothed figure pulled a long black target pistol with what appeared to be a small black can clamped onto its barrel from a jacket pocket with the right hand, concealing it from the view of motorists driving past by holding it against a trouser leg. Then using the left hand the stranger slowly reached up and pushed back the hood of the jacket.

The first words out of the stranger's mouth were, "Do you recognize me, scum?"

The young man, now beginning to fear for his life, shook his head frantically wondering why one the motorists that passed by every few minutes traveling Hollywood Road hadn't seen the confrontation and stopped to offer assistance.

"No, why would I know you? From where do I know you? You have the wrong man. Believe me, you won't get away with this. I am . . ." Chow sputtered.

"Shut up, tough guy," the stranger replied. "Next word out of your mouth, unless it is an answer to a question I've asked you, buys you an immediate kneecapping, right here, right now. Do you understand the ground rules here, asshole?"

As the shooter said that, both hands were brought into play to steady the gun. Chow's initial impression was that the weapon was a .22 or .32 caliber pistol equipped with a crude silencer. It appeared that the stranger had received training in shooting from the Weaver stance, left foot slightly forward, a good two-handed grip on the revolver with isometric tension in the arms.

The young man nodded he understood the ground rules with his head like one of those little bobbing Buddha heads you see in the back of taxis in Mexico City. Chow continued to hold his hands out in front of him as if he thought he was Superman and his hands would ward off bullets.

The shooter cautiously advanced two paces closer to the cowering young man and demanded, "Do you recognize me now, big shot?"

Suddenly like the blinding morning sun raising over the mountains after a dark night, realization came to the young man causing him to void his bladder down the inside of his silk pant legs. He began to quiver and his entire body began to shake uncontrollably. Then his nerve abruptly deserted him and he fell to his knees as if asking for supplication.

"Please, please," he knelt in his urine, begging. "It wasn't my idea, it was theirs. I was only along for the ride. If I had tried to interfere or not participate they would have become alarmed that I might report it and become a witness. And they would have killed me on the spot. You know that. Please, give me a break."

Babbling, Chow continued, "I'm just thirty years old. I have a family of three sisters that my paycheck is putting through college. My parents are both infirm and I pay for caregivers to take care of them during the day when my sisters are at school. Can't you understand? I couldn't do anything. Please . . ."

No sooner had that last plea passed the young man's lips than the shooter's finger twitched on the trigger. A blinding white flame about four inches long appeared to leap from the gun's silencer. Followed by a *Phut-Phut* sound amplified by the canyon-like effect of the buildings abutting both sides of Hollywood Road. Two entrance holes spaced less than an inch apart and approximately one inch above his bushy eyebrows, appeared on his Chow's forehead.

The shooter stepped up to the dying man who now lay in his own urine and feces, kicked open his legs, and fired two more silenced shots *Phut-Phut* into Chow's groin area. The shooter kicked the body one more time to ensure that any sign of life had fled with Chow's soul.

The shooter pulled the jacket's hood back up. Then pulled a small flashlight from a jacket pocket, and after checking to make sure there was no traffic coming flashed its beam about the dirty sidewalk until the four brass cartridge casings the gun had ejected were located.

Holding the smoking gun in one hand, the shooter bent over to retrieve the expended brass with the other. Then stuck the brass into a large clear quart-size plastic baggie. Crouched over the body, the shooter took a knee and used latex gloved fingers to poke around in the dead man's jacket until locating the victim's wallet.

The shooter didn't want there to be any question that the shooting was not part of a botched armed robbery or mugging gone bad. The wallet with any money still in it would be found on the victim. If not, the body wouldn't send the desired message to authorities and the Media.

But Chow's ID cards, credit cards, anything with the man's name on it, had to be removed from the wallet to cause the cops a few hours delay in learning the victim's identity.

The shooter needed the additional time to develop a believable alibi and take care of a number of nit-picky details before having to report back to work on Monday, two days hence. A lot of things would have to be staged in a very short time.

While the killing and the man's begging had been very satisfying, the shooter's fear of being caught had intensified. More time for the escape and stage setting would be good.

As the gloved fingers worked to pry out the driver's license, resident cards, credit card, and any other cards bearing the victim's name, the shooter became impatient at having to spend so much time at the crime scene, almost three minutes now, a direct violation of what cops call the 'three-minute rule.'

The rushed attempt to extract the cards out past the sharp edge of the plastic window and out of the wallet caused the latex finger on the glove of the shooter's right hand index finger to tear. Due to the shooter's increasing frustration and the poor lighting, the rupture in the glove went unnoticed.

Finally the I.D. cards came free. They followed the shells into the plastic baggie. Then the shooter snapped the gloves off without taking time to inspect them and also stuffed them into the baggie. A handkerchief that the shooter would discard immediately upon leaving scene was used to close the baggie's zip-lock seal then returned to a jacket pocket.

Standing up, noticing that the body was completely obscured by the adjacent building's shadow, the shooter turned and retraced the earlier steps towards the idling Toyota with no more haste than a ordinary citizen out for a early morning stroll.

Getting in the car after patting the pocket in which rested the baggie with the brass, ID cards, and used gloves to make sure it was secure, the shooter looked into the car's rearview mirror to make sure no traffic was coming before pulling way from the curb in a law biding manner.

Continuing to drive at slightly below the limit the shooter followed Hollywood Road east before turning south off on Old Bailey Street. Then pulled the car into the dark visitor's parking area of the infamous, now-shuttered Victoria Prison.

After parking the car exactly between the parking lot's yellow lines, the shooter after looking around to make certain there was no one watching got out of the stolen car and locked it before walking a few hundred feet to a taxi stand at the front of the Victoria Prison police station. Although the building was occupied, it looked like a tomb at this hour of the morning.

When the shooter had been in prep school, stealing their parent's vehicles had been all the rage. Knowing how to jimmy doors and hot wire cars, along with becoming an accomplished shot using a handgun and winning at least brown belt status in Karate, all were mandatory rights-of-passage into the school's outlaw clique.

———

Within five minutes a red top taxi trolling for business spotted a potential fare standing in front of the police station, pulled over and the shooter got in. The driver dropped his flag. The base figure of HK$15 appeared on the meter as the car pulled away from the curb headed for the address his fare had given him.

The cab driver didn't give the lateness of the hour nor his passenger a second thought. All the cabbie cared about was the HK$1.40 that was added to the meter's digital display for every additional 200 meters the taxi traveled. Anyway, it didn't pay to be curious in the early morning hours in Hong Kong. What Hong Kong taxi drivers knew that being curious often got you dead.

————

12 October 2007, Saturday, 3:30 a.m. (HKT)
Four blocks east of the Propaganda Club
#1 Hollywood Road—Central district
Hong Kong Island

When the crime lab vans pulled up to the scene, the officers from the two first responding patrol units had already fenced off the area with crime scene tape.

————

One of the differences that American tourists find unusual in Hong Kong is contrary to what they are used to seeing on TV crime shows in America—black letters on yellow Mylar tape, repeating "Police Line—Do Not Cross."

In Hong Kong, crime scene tape is white Mylar with the words "Police Line" and "Do Not Cross" in both English and Cantonese. The warnings alternate between being blue or purple in color, alternating straight or slanting division lines. Why, you ask? The answer is because that is how it has always been done in a police department that was established by the British more than a 150 years ago.

————

Young medics from the aid car were attempting to resuscitate the victim. First thing the senior Criminalist on-scene did was gently elbow one of the medics out of the way long enough for her to check the pulse of the man lying on the sidewalk. As she expected there was none.

However the inviolate rule in Hong Kong is that at all vehicle accident and violent crime scenes, only the Medical Examiner, his assistants or a licensed physician currently providing care to the individual can pronounce a victim dead. Thus the body would be transported code-three to the emergency room of the closest public hospital.

After the aid car nosily departed with its passenger, crime scene investigators in their light blue coveralls, white latex gloves, and bulky crime scene turnout kits were ready to being their search for evidence. However, dispatch had advised the senior Criminalist to await the arrival of Lieutenant Du Ming, Acting Head of Hong Kong's homicide squad.

Lieutenant Du after only a year in his present job was becoming very conscious of the importance of politics in Homicide investigations. He had rapidly come to realize that the on-scene commander's role was not only to solve the crime, but also to prevent the case from becoming a Media free-for-all, or in the parlance of the police community, a cluster fuck.

Du Ming knew how much Media interest is generated by late night killings especially in the rare instance that there was even a remote possibility that the victim was a cop. Thus he had left word with the night duty team of homicide detectives that he wanted to be called out on any homicide where the victim could even conceivably be a cop.

Since tonight's body was found under similar circumstances as the yet-unsolved Johnny Yang homicide last weekend, the lieutenant was notified at his home and picked up ten minutes later by a sector car and transported to the crime scene.

Du had arrived at the Hollywood Road scene twenty minutes later only to discover the victim had already been transported to a hospital.

Over the external loud speakers of the patrol cars, Du could hear sharp, unhurried authoritative voices, speaking in English, Cantonese, and occasionally Mandarin. As usual, the on-scene police walkie-talkies and the police dispatcher's transmissions were stepping on one another over the various radio nets.

After a moment to mentally catalog the crime scene and visually identify who had arrived at the crime scene thus far, Du gathered the street cops in their winter blue uniforms and responding Criminalists in their lighter blue coveralls, together. The cops had been the first-responders to the scene. Arriving shortly after the cops were four members of the graveyard shift Criminalist team.

The immediate area where the body was found would be classified as primary-class crime scene, or where the crime actually happened. The primary designation was opposed to that of a secondary crime scene, a location where a body or something else had been dumped, which didn't appear to apply here at the Hollywood Road scene.

As most persons know, blood in the artificial light of night appears almost black but retains its distinctive sheen.

The weather at the crime scene that night was pretty much typical of Hong Kong this time of year, which is to say that the temperature was about 63 degrees Fahrenheit and humidity about 73 percent. On the average, most days begin with a couple hours of a light rain or mist. The remainder of the day, the sun is normally out until nightfall.

After dusk, the penetrating mist off Victoria Harbour starts to roll in. Since the crime scene was only six blocks southwest of the harbour there was a brisk fragrant breeze out of the north, blowing in off the water.

Before things got totally chaotic at the scene Lieutenant Ming needed to ensure that the physical dimensions established by the first responders, the circular area established by the white strip of crime scene tape, was large enough to be encompassing but small enough to be securable. Everything inside the tape would have to be dusted, photographed, sampled, videoed, gathered or vacuumed up.

Chief Inspector Fox, Du Ming's partner before he had been promoted and Du had taken over Fox's former job of running the Homicide squad, now reported to Inspector Ho Pham who was on family leave this week. Ming had learned from Fox that a supervisor's responsibility at crime scenes was to provide oversight and guidance to the forensic team.

That meant the Lieutenant's function this morning was to ensure that the young police department Criminalists had a plan to ensure that everything inside the white crime tape would be gathered up, bagged, and tagged if there was even a remote possibility of it being probative evidence.

As the ranking police supervisor currently overseeing the crime scene, Du quickly established a single route using bright yellow stick flags that everyone regardless of rank or authority had to use to access and egress the taped-off crime scene.

When the next patrol car showed up at the scene, he assigned that young, English-speaking police officer who obviously was fresh out of the police academy to guard the crime scene and maintain the In-And-Out crime scene sign-in log which documents the name and badge number of all persons coming and going.

The young cop's job included enforcing the crime scene 'No Smoking' rule which in Du's fifteen years on the job he'd found was nearly impossible to enforce, most Chinese smoking like an oil-fired furnaces.

Working with the department's CSI criminalists, the Lieutenant assisted them in dividing and then sub-dividing the scene into zones. Then a grid pattern was established using a carpenter's yellow chalked string to delineate the various zones. Each zone would be visually and microscopically searched, not once but twice.

Du had already decided that surveying the area beyond the confines of the white crime scene tape was a fool's errand. It was obvious that everything that had happened at the crime scene had occurred inside the area now fenced off with tape.

However before they would be released to return to patrol, the two patrol officers were detailed to make a list of all vehicle license plates within a two-block radius of the crime scene.

Du got on his handy-talkie radio and requested that Dispatch detail four more patrol officers to report to the scene, chopped to his authority.

When they arrived Du ordered two of them to obtain the owner's names and addresses of all businesses within a block of the scene. Deciding there was no requirement for a Lieutenant of police to be reasonable in his orders, Du instructed the address-takers to make a list of persons who normally worked within a block either direction on the Hollywood Road scene. The cops walked away into the darkness, mumbling to themselves.

As it wasn't even daylight yet, Du figured there would be no benefit to be gained by calling additional homicide detectives out of their warm beds to begin to interview the merchants and individuals, the names of which the canvassing officers should be obtaining from disgruntle citizens they were now dragging from their night of slumber.

As with any well-managed crime scene, criminalists were following the inviolate procedure of prioritizing their sampling. First, the on-scene CSI supervisor and his or her team processed the scene for transient evidence such as odoriferous smells. They document their impression of the scent for future follow-up.

Second, the technicians searched for conditional evidence such as the disposition and condition of any body parts found at the scene, as well as noting the ambient lighting conditions present at the time of the alleged crime.

Third, they evaluated in-place and document pattern evidence such as the dispersion of broken glass; blood spatter, or burn marks.

Fourth, attention was given to transfer evidence which primarily consists of fiber and hair. Convictions sometimes hinge on these microscopic findings.

Last, but certainly not least, was the collection and identification of any items found at the crime scene that appeared to belong to the victim but sometimes seems to find its way into the possession of bystanders who never admit to being at the scene before the cops arrived.

All evidence once collected goes first to the Evidence Control Unit (EDU). They in turn log it in and assign it for analysis to the applicable specialty forensic unit at the central HKP Arsenal Street crime laboratory.

The victim once pronounced dead at the hospital would go to the medical examiner who would attempt to determine the identity of the victim, or at the least the body's race, sex, approximate age, and COD, the cause of death.

———

Hong Kong's excellent forensic system had come into its own when immediately following the return of the former crown colony to the PRC in 1997, the outgoing British Royal Hong Kong Police Department administrators had convinced the newly sworn-in HKSAR legislative council to adopt a modified version of the British Empire's 'Plain View Doctrine' at crime scenes.

That meant ratifying the law to make it the first responder's number one responsibility to first see to the safety and security of any potential victims. The doctrine went on to state that in that capacity, the first responder could search the premises for victims but also could collect any apparent evidence that lay in 'plain sight.' Especially if there was any possibility, no matter how slight, that subsequent events at the crime scene might cause deterioration, damage, loss, or even theft of the evidence by a third party.

While this doctrine appeared pretty straight forward, what it was covertly attempting to do was by-pass the historically ultra-liberal courts of Hong Kong that forbid any collection of evidence without a warrant except under highly-arguable circumstances. That legal tool was a blow to the bad guys especially in triad killings where the triad Loaban or boss would routinely dispatch a shaggy peroxide-haired, tattooed, 'satiny coat,' a young Chinese wannabe triad member to the crime scene immediately following a homicide that the gang committed, to steal, remove, or otherwise destroy any damning evidence.

———

The Hollywood Road crime scene had the unpleasant bloody-steak, coppery smell of sudden death intertwined with the odor of decomposing flesh and cordite. That stench overrode its usual environmental perfume of rotting garbage, leaky engine oil, ill-tuned gasoline and diesel engine exhaust, and the tart and oily smell of the South China Sea.

Lieutenant Du noticed that one of the young Chinese police officers looked like he was going to throw up from the stench. He quickly escorted the young man outside the tape so that the crime scene would not be contaminated when his stomach and sinus cavities rebelled.

To teach the young officer a valuable lesson, Du ordered the young Chinese police officer who by now had finished his barfing, to walk the scene and do nothing but pickup and 'bag' as evidence, stray body parts, and every little piece of paper or discarded offal that the citizens of Hong Kong thoughtless littered the landscape of their beautiful city.

If the young Chinese was going to stay in the law enforcement business he needed to learn to control his emotions and basic bodily urges. Or he might as well hang his uniform and gun belt up and find another line of work.

Due to the hour, there were no on-lookers at the crime scene to provide eyewitness accounts concerning the circumstances of the shooting.

An enterprising young patrol officer tiring of standing around unable to smoke started flagging down the taxis that trolled Hollywood Road for fares at this time of the pre-dawn morning.

The cop politely took down any information the cab drivers provided, then used his department cell phone to call the cabbie's dispatcher to confirm he or she had even been in the area of the crime scene after midnight.

The problem with this commendable extra effort by the young ambitious officer was that Hong Kong taxi drivers are notorious for operating off the cuff—screwing their dispatcher and the cab's owner out of fares was a way of life for them. Unless the passenger insisted on paying for his fare with a credit card, or demanded a receipt for the fare paid, the dispatcher likely never even knew the taxi had a fare. The likelihood of the driver calling a cash fare and destination in to his company dispatcher was slim and none.

As the police criminalists continued working the grisly scene in the chilly early morning hours, the word came down from the hospital that one of the male nurses had recognized the shooting victim as a cop he knew from pickup basketball games in his neighborhood.

That information justified Du Ming's formally taking over the crime scene although he knew he'd get static for doing so from the HKP crime lab boss, Inspector Xueguang Laoxi. But since Laoxi and Fox were fast friends, Du he knew the Chief Inspector would easily make the complaint go away.

The Medical Examiner upon learning the victim was cop had wasted no time sending an investigator up to the hospital with a fingerprint kit. Because rigor had already set in, the emergency room physician acquiesced to removing the corpse's fingers to permit them to be inked and rolled on the five-finger and palm print FP cards.

The ME investigator had hurried back to his office to run the fingerprints through AFIS. That was the Automatic Fingerprint Identification System computer that-then Lieutenant Fox had managed to pry out of the hands of the American FBI on a grant in early 2003. AFIS reviewed its database of millions of prints and kicked out a 'hit' less than twenty minutes later.

The politically aware investigator had then insisted on waking up someone from the police department personnel office to have the suspect victim's 'paper' fingerprint cards pulled from his employment file to double check the identification.

As soon at the investigator did a manual visual scan of the paper fingerprint card he had called the duty Medical Examiner to inform them that the HKP had another cop killing on their hands.

As soon as Lieutenant Du had been advised of the identity of tonight's victim, he had used his cell phone to notify me at home.

———

Later that morning the HKP crime lab using the superglue method turned up a partial fingerprint on the inside of the victim's wallet. It wasn't a complete enough print to run through AFIS but when a potential suspect was identified and brought in for questioning it would only take a few seconds to rule-in or rule-out whether it belonged to the suspect after a brief comparison under a microscope.

The fingerprint analyst had told his boss that he thought the partial was probably a thumb, or index finger, or possibly even a fragment of a palm.

The analyst reported to Laoxi, "The partial is a tented arch, but it's smudged. If the shooter is in the single-print database, which is highly unlikely, then I might be able to get a match. But better tell Chief Inspector Fox not to get his hopes up."

Until then the partial fingerprint would be stored on the secure hard drive of the Crime Lab to be available for recall when a viable suspect was developed.

———

Author's Note: Superglue, or Cyanoacrylate, is an excellent method of revealing nearly invisible fingerprints. Superglue is heated using a chemistry spirit lamp inside an enclosed container, which produces a violet haze or fume. All fingerprints have fatty matter that will absorb some of the fumes when the superglue method is employed.

It takes about an hour to run the process. Then the intensified print is photographed with a digital camera. The digital image is entered into a computer. Adobe PhotoShop is used to sharpen the contrast of every ridge and whorl. The enhanced print is printed onto a transparent sheet and 99% of the time the resulting reproduction is impeccable.

———

12 October 2007, Saturday, 8:00 a.m. (HKT)
HKP Medical Examiner's Autopsy Suite
Arsenal Street Police Headquarters
Wan Chai district—Hong Kong Island

When Du Ming had called me at home around 4:00 a.m., there had been nothing I could do that Du Ming hadn't already done at the Hollywood Road crime scene.

However, Du told me that the ME's investigator had ordered the surgical-removal of the fingers of the decedent for printing. A hand-pull of the actual fingerprint cards in the department's personnel files, and a 'hit' by AFIS, had identified the victim as another dead cop.

Du Ming had been up all night. Therefore he made the decision to assign David Kan, a young ambitious detective who had left medical school a couple of years ago to fulfill his life-long wish of getting into homicide, to cover the autopsy.

I thought Ming's choice of David Kan was an excellent decision. I became familiar with Detective Kan in 2005 when my live-in girlfriend at the time, Peng Lige, had been tortured and killed on the orders of a now-deceased crooked cop. I had been forbidden to attend her autopsy for obvious procedural reasons. Kan had gone in my place and frankly had come back with a better insight into what had happened than I would have been able in my traumatized condition.

So I had no problem with Kan being my department's representative at the autopsy of what we now knew to be another dead cop.

Still, I thought it politically prudent and case management desirable for me to accompanying Kan to this morning's post mortem strictly as an observer. Everyone in the department was outraged. They were more than a little afraid. With this death, a total of seven cops in the past ten days had been killed. Would they be next?

Three cops had been killed in the triad assassination of Chung Shan, on 02 October, the 14K's White Paper Fan on Queensway in the Central district; Officer Johnny Yang apparently was the victim of a revenge killing in the Wan Chai district on 05 October; the two officers who had been blown to smithereens by a booby trap on the Five Ram raid on 11 October; and this, the killing of a cop named Chow Yung Su who had been killed on Hollywood Street this morning, 12 October, in the Central district—all on Hong Kong Island.

———

Checking my watch and seeing it was just turning 5:00 a.m. I called the duty medical examiner and advised him that the dead body of a cop was being brought in and I wanted it posted first thing that morning.

The duty ME told me they had already been advised by the hospital that the body would be transported to the autopsy suite a little after 6 a.m. that morning. They promised to photograph it, x-ray it, draw toxicology and other blood work, and have it cleaned up and 'on the table' before 8:00 a.m.

He had already called Dr. Lu Dong, M.D., his boss, at home and advised him that there would be a dead cop to autopsy as soon as the ME office officially opened for business, 8:00 a.m. Lu Dong as usual instructed the duty ME assistant to schedule him to do the autopsy since it involved the death of a cop.

––––––

Before showering and eating a light breakfast, I called dispatch and asked them to call my driver at home and ask him to pick me up no later than 7:30 a.m. that morning.

Ming was there promptly with my car at 7:30 a.m. As usual he had taken the time to stop and pick up the morning English language edition of the *South China Morning Post* enabling me to catch up on the night's news on the way to headquarters.

When we pulled into the HQ complex, I asked Ming to drop me off at the entrance to the Medical Examiner's fiefdom. Thanking him, I popped out of the car taking the half-read paper with me and cleared security before heading for the elevator that required a swipe of my ID though its card reader before it would permit me access down to the 'pit.'

When the slower-than-dirt hydraulics of the elevator reached the autopsy basement, its stainless doors slid open. Standing there patiently waiting for me was Detective David Kan. We exchange greetings and shook hands before heading for the entrance to the autopsy suite.

Police and ME jargon commonly used for the room we were headed for was the 'basement' or 'pit' or 'cutting room.' It was a fair decent-sized room about 80-feet-long and 30-feet-wide. At one time it had been considered the state of the art, but no longer.

Like so many other Hong Kong agencies, the suite needed upkeep and modernization but suffered from a lack of funds. The eight stainless steel tables were old and stained from countless postmortems. Old-fashioned spring-loaded scales and a flexible necked microphone hung over each table. A series of sinks, countertops, X-ray Light boxes, ancient glass-front cabinets and exposed piping lined the walls.

Detective Kan and I stopped and signed the investigator's logbook before heading to the investigator's dressing room. We began removing protective gear from battered metal gym lockers that had been new perhaps back in 1955. It only took a few minutes to complete gowning, gloving, booting, and putting on the surgical cotton facemasks.

As we entered the room through the two-stage airlock, a couple of the pre-doctors wearing pink-colored gowns identifying them as medical students grouped around a far table raised their masked faces momentarily to stare at us before returning to their grisly task.

Stretched out on the table in front of the students was the ivory-colored, nude body of a teenage girl, her neck positioned firmly by the black, hard rubber head block. A single bank of overhead blue-white fluorescent fixtures illuminated her body. The lurid scene was made worse by the gurgling noise of blood-reddish fluid swirling down the gutters to the drain at the foot of the table.

At the other end of the room Dr. Lu Dong, M.D. was hovering over the body of a male victim. Standing across the table from Dr. Dong was his assistant Betty Fang.

The body had two small pencil-sized entrance wounds in the forehead. We would soon learn when Fang pulled the body up onto its left shoulder that there were two much larger exit and reentry wounds in the soft tissue of the buttocks.

Looking up, Dr. Dong acknowledged both Kan and myself with a nod. Dong and I were ten-year professional acquaintances. Both of us admitted to the other when we were certain that we were alone, the autopsy microphones were shut off, and under the noise of the water that was draining the corpse's blood away, that Hong Kong has been going to the dogs since the Communists reassumed control back in June of 1997.

Dr. Dong was familiar with Detective Kan from the days when he had been a medical student and his studies had brought him to the autopsy suite to learn the intricacies of performing post mortems, also known as autopsies. It was my impression that the Doctor and the detective shared a student/mentor relationship. I told both that I was along strictly in a observer capacity this morning. David Kan was the detective-of-record.

Dong turned to David Kan and asked, "Ready to start, Detective?"

Kan indicated that it was and pulled a spiral notebook from under his gown to record his observations. Betty Fang moved a stainless steel dead-leg Mayo cart bearing the tools of the trade over until she could reach it from memory whenever Dr. Dong requested an instrument.

Dr. Dong began by pulling down the flexible microphone and thumping it with his index finger to make certain it was turned on. Then he spoke the date, time, victim's name, case number, his name, and the names of myself, his assistant and Detective Kan into the microphone. And began his spiel reciting his findings in a monotone into the microphone, "The decedent is a well-nourished Asian male . . ."

The doctor picked up a scalpel and made a 'Y' incision running down from each shoulder, meeting at the middle of the body at the bottom of the ribs and then continuing as a single incision to the pubic bone.

Dong and his assistant peeled the skin and muscle away in three flaps. Dr. Dong gestured to Ms. Fang who picked up a set of what any homeowner would recognize as a pair of red handled, black rubber grip pruning shears and proceeded to cut, called breaking, the ribs open exposing the lungs and heart.

Then Fang assisted the doctor in tying and cutting of the carotid arteries and colon; then the cutting the trachea larynx before lifting out the entire viscera, heart, lungs, stomach, appendix, liver, kidneys, spleen, and intestine.

Before any further action could take place a calibrated bottle attached to a suction hose was used to extract abdominal fluid from the stomach. The fluid dark red-black and consisting mostly of blood was removed and measured in the bottle. If the collected fluid measured more than a liter it could indicate that the victim had received one or more blood transfusions in the hospital emergency room. The normal blood volume for the entire body is five liters.

Not altogether unexpected, Dong reached a pair of forceps into the lower abdominal cavity and picked out two unrecognizable lumps of what appeared to be bullets and dropped them into a stainless steel emesis basin.

I figured they were the two slugs that the shooter had fired into Chow Yung Su's groin. They were mangled because they had exited through the bowels, femoral arteries and buttocks, before impacting the pavement underneath and ricocheting back in the lower stomach cavity.

Detective Kan held out a plastic evidence container and the doctor's forceps dropped the lumps of metal into it. Kan was careful to affix the seal and initial and date it, per procedure.

The Doctor used a needle and heavy catgut thread to temporarily sew shut the eviscerated body, known inside doors of autopsy suites the world over as the 'canoe.'

Once all the visual observations had been noted and the pathologist had an opportunity to examine each one by cutting sections for examination under a microscope, they all would be returned to the canoe and Dr Dong would close the body up a final time using a baseball stitch.

While the doctor was tied up with the organ inspection process, Betty Fang used a scalpel on the skull to make a circular cut to permit the stripping of the skin and flesh which permitted her to pull the face flap down to the corpse's chin. Using a rotary bone saw she removed the skullcap. Setting the saw aside on a second Mayo stand, she gently removed the shattered brain and placed it into a stainless steel pan that Dr. Dong held in his hands.

Dr. Dong flipped an optical magnifying lens down on his glasses and peered into the now empty cranial cavity. Uttering a grunt of satisfaction at finding what he expected, Dong used a pair of forceps to pick out what appeared to be two small caliber slugs which had played 'Ring-around-the-rosy, Pockets-full-of-posies,' once they entered the cranial cavity thereby thoroughly shredding the victim's brain.

Being very careful not to mar the surface of the two slugs Dong dropped each into a second plastic bag stamped with the large red letters 'EVIDENCE' that Detective Kan handed him. The doctor sealed the container, placed the seal across the cap and initialed it, including the time and date and case number.

Detective Kan and the doctor both signed each other's Chain-of-Evidence forms for all four slugs. As Kan returned his neatly folded forms under the drape of the gown into his pocket, Dr. Dong remarked, "They look like .22 caliber long rifle slugs to me, Detective. And if I remember the details of the autopsy I did on Officer Johnny Yang last weekend, the slugs that killed him looked very similar to these. Incidentally I found all four of those slugs in the identical same locations as the ones I've just removed from officer Chow Yung Su here."

It was critical that we obtain a ballistics comparison of all eight slugs. I told Kan I would hold the fort here for the remainder of the autopsy. He was to get today's recovered slugs up to the crime lab for an immediate ballistic analysis.

After Kan departed, Dr. Dong's spiel continued, "It appears from preliminary indications that the decedent died of a massive insult to the brain. However, even without the injury to the brain, he would have died in less than a minute from massive blood loss caused by the severing of the right femoral artery in the groin . . ."

There was one unusual finding during the remainder of the autopsy on Officer Chow Yung Su. Dr. Dong ran a preliminary HIV panel and it indicated that the officer was HIV positive. Dr. Dong said further tests would either confirm or rule-out that finding, but if he had to lay money on it right now, he'd go with the victim being in the early stages of AIDS.

10

12 October 2007, Saturday, 2:00 p.m. (HKT)
Crimes Against Persons Department
Arsenal Street Police Headquarters
Wan Chai district—Hong Kong Island

About 2:00 p.m. that afternoon, back fresh from the crime lab, Detective Kan raced into my office almost bowling over Elizabeth who had just been returning to her desk after having dropping off some expense accounts for my approval and signature.

I could tell the ambitious young detective was barely able to contain his excitement as I took my time to carefully read what the ballistic examiner had written.

"Shit," I thought, tossing the report back on my desk. The slugs from the two cop killings were not only the same caliber but they also had been fired from the same gun.

It was obvious that we may potentially have a serial cop killer on the streets, one that apparently had inside access to the shift schedules of HKP patrol cops and perhaps even their personnel files.

———

The definition of 'serial killer' varies between jurisdictions, departments, agencies, and prosecuting attorneys. This is the most widely accepted criteria:

1. A serial killer is someone who usually kills more than five people, but may be as few as three.

2. A serial killer usually slays over a longer period of time than say a 'spree killer.' Sometimes even months and years, allowing a so-called 'cooling-off' period between each murder.

3. A serial killer's victims are usually of the same type; prostitutes, hitchhikers, postal employees, what have you, but always easily categorized.

4. Most serial murders are committed by strangulation, suffocation, or stabbing. The mold is occasional broken if a perpetrator prefers using a gun to avoid having to touch his victims.

5. In the United States, most serial murderers are low-esteem males and females. America, Europe, and Russia being the fertile ground that historically have given birth to these monsters, which average twenty-to-thirty years of age. Which just happens to describe one quarter of the Hong Kong's population.

6. Serial and mass murderers do not select their victims randomly.

———

Thus far, the only evidence we had was the partial fingerprint found on Officer Chow's wallet recovered at the Hollywood Road crime scene early that morning.

I said the expletive a second time just for good measure. That made Kan and everyone within earshot aware of how concerned that possibility made me. A serial cop killer! That was all I needed. On 'top' of the body part harvesting investigation. On 'top' of trying to figure out how the thieves were getting the vans out of the police impound yards. On 'top' of having to solve the homicides of a half-dozen cops in the past two weeks.

———

12 October 2007, Saturday, 10:00 p.m. (HKT)
Jenny Woo's Condo
Bowen Road, just north of Lover's Rock
Wan Chai Gap district—Hong Kong Island

Jenny Woo had rang me up from the guest relations office at the Mandarin Oriental Hotel late Saturday afternoon following Chow Yung Su's morning autopsy and Detective Kan's revelation that we soon may have a serial cop killer on our hands. I decided I would to take her up on her offer. I needed to take the rest of the weekend off for some quality time away from the office.

So I was a sucker for her offer to cook dinner for me that night at her place. Not to mention her whispered promises to provide suitable sexual incentives if I would agree to bring over some Coconut Rum, and take her to the horse races out at the Wan Chai Gap's infamous Happy Valley Sports Grounds on Sunday. Not only did I readily agree to her terms but also offered to create a concoction before dinner tonight called a Malibu Scream based on my own secret recipe. So the negotiation was concluded.

About noon, after the autopsy, I couldn't see any sense in getting Mrs. Zhou Ming's panties in a bunch by keeping her husband away from home any longer on a weekend. Ming half-heartedly argued with me when I told him to go home. But as he walked out of the office I heard him expel a sign of relief. Now he would be able to pacify his tyrant wife by being at home to work on her endless Honey Do lists.

I took the time to bring the HKP computer's Rapid Start case management tool up to date. At 6:00 p.m. I had the dispatcher call a red top cab on the department's priority line. It promptly appeared outside the HQ security barrier, and the gate called me.

I locked everything up before telling the administrative assistant who had the weekend duty that I was leaving, and that if needed, she could reach me on the number in the 'Squeeze File,' the emergency contact locater that every detective and all ranks above must keep current per department policy.

I climbed in the red top cab and gave him my home address. When we arrived, I asked if he would be willing to wait out front for me while I showered, changed clothes and packed a small overnight bag. He said had no problem with waiting as long as he could do so on the meter.

After showering I put on a pair of fashionably-worn blue jeans, a blue chambray shirt, darker blue tie, and tweed jacket with leather patches with fit in with the casual look I was striving for, topping it all off by wearing my Rolex Submariner watch with the blue bezel and tan kid leather Bally loafers. I'd wear the same outfit to Happy Valley on Sunday, naturally over fresh underclothes.

Into my overnight bag went a pack of condoms, fresh underwear, my off-duty chief's special pistol, a box of twenty cartridges, my toothbrush, razor and other necessities. After checking the answering machine to make sure no one essential was waiting for a call back from me before Monday, I picked up a number of items I had bagged and walked out of the condo engaging the security locks and rode the elevator down to the waiting red top.

It only took fifteen minutes to get through the labyrinth of streets to Jenny's. I paid the driver off with a nice tip, walked into the building, stopped to check in with the building's armed security officer, and rode up the lift up to Ms. Woo's fashionable abode.

When she opened the door, I was shocked. I turned around and looked over my shoulder me to see if there was another reason for Jenny's outfit of choice for our planned evening of debauchery. Discovering no one behind me, I assumed I was the lucky recipient of this exotic sight. I tried valiantly to regain my composure as she leaned across the threshold to embrace me.

Still being in a state of confusion over Jenny's appearance, I nearly dropped the heavy paper bag I was carrying in my left hand. It contained among other things a bottle of vintage champagne I had added to the bag as I ran out the door to catch the taxi. In my other hand was my overnight kit.

Although it seemed quite a lot of work for her to go to just for the evening-in we had planned, Jenny had her long hair on top of her head and was wearing her little black fuck-me dress.

The dress was cut high on her thighs and low over her breasts and as a trained investigator who has been taught the finer arts of observation, I was certain she was wearing nothing underneath. As with every time I'd dated Jenny, she wore extreme seductive-looking footwear; a pair of strappy black sandals with five-inch stiletto heels.

For jewelry she wore diamond and gold teardrop earrings. Around her sensuous neck, another diamond, this one I estimated at three carats or better on a gold chain.

———

Jenny was one of Hong Kong's women who had elected to undergo breast augmentation the moment the U.S. American Food and Drug Administration in November of 2006 lifted their fourteen-year ban on silicone breast implants after deciding they were "reasonably safe."

After hearing that the American firm, Allergan, Inc., had began selling the implants again to plastic surgeons, Jenny took vacation from the Oriental Mandarin Hotel, hopped on a plane to Singapore and had the surgery performed.

When she had returned and showed me the results I had asked her if she had been aware that the FDA was still saying that women would have to undergo repeated, costly MRI exams to check for broken, oozing implants, and understand that there are other irreversible side effects?

What I didn't say that perhaps I should have was that I'd read in the *South China Morning Post* that Dr. Sidney Wolfe, a consumer activist and longtime opponent, called silicone implants "The most defective, medical device the American FDA has ever approved."

Jenny would have just sush-sushed me saying I wouldn't understand. It seems women have been telling me that quite a lot lately.

————

Being armless due to the bags I was carrying I was unable to return Jenny's ritual hugs, however was an active participant in the welcoming kisses and once again listened intently to her X-rated promises for the evening. Finally I recovered sensual control over my body parts enough to walk into her kitchen that deserves no less than a four-page spread in Architectural Digest and set down the heavy bag down on the butcher block.

Desiring that my jacket and tie remain unwrinkled for our excursion tomorrow out to Happy Valley racetrack, I hung the garments up in her hallway closet before walking my overnight kit into the master bedroom's bath.

Returning to the kitchen I observed that Jenny had already set out some chilled drink glasses. I knew where to get ice if I needed it. I set about preparing our Malibu Scream cocktails after ripping open the bag to remove the bottles I had taken from my condo's liquor cabinet. The grocery contents of the bag went either into her refrigerator or onto a convenient place on the wide, gleaming, white Corian kitchen counter.

I poured seven parts of Malibu Coconut Run into a sterling silver shaker she provided and then added one part of Stoli unflavored Vodka, one part of Hiram Walker Triple Sec, and two ounces of lime juice.

Then doing my best James Bond impersonation, I shook (not stirred) the shaker before straining the contents into two chilled cocktails glasse garnishing both with a lime wedge.

We retired to the heavily-carpeted, sunken living room and plopped ourselves down on a love seat to stare silently out at the magnificent lights of Hong Kong visible through her floor-to-ceiling plate glass windows.

We remained like that for about twenty minutes each lost in our own thoughts. Then she handed her empty glass to me asking that I make another for her while she started dinner. I made two more, one for her and a second for myself, before offering to assist her in the dinner preparations. She politely refused so I returned to the love seat and reveled in viewing the panoramic vista of the city that I consider to be the most exciting in the world.

About every twenty minutes she would walk in and hand me an empty glass and I'd do the refill duties. If we didn't get some substance in us soon I feared I was going to be become tipsy which would be completely unacceptable. I intended to ensure Jenny made good on the sexual incentives she had promised earlier.

Dinner when it came was outstanding. Despite the fact that I consider my being borne an American to be a fickle finger of fate, Jenny had decided to make Oysters Rockefeller as an appetizer, duck à L' orange as the entrée, and peach flambé for dessert.

It was about 11 p.m. when we finished dinner. We weren't quite stuffed but we were close. Jenny insisted to just leaving everything for the morning that couldn't be safety accommodated in her dishwasher.

After busing up the table we retired once again to the love seat in the living room, this time with generous glasses of Rémy Martin cognac. We kicked our shoes off and Jenny laid her head on my shoulder.

———

After about an hour of foreplay we headed for her bedroom.

It certainly didn't take long to undress Jenny. I'd been correct at the front door earlier when I surmised that the only clothing she had on was the little black dress and hooker heels.

We had decided enough of the Malibu Screams and cognac and switched to French champagne before coming to bed. Ever a woman cognizant of the importance of presentation she, at some earlier moment when I was otherwise occupied, had placed a sterling silver three-legged ice bucket adjacent to her king-sized bed.

Distracted, but as soon as she had finished undressing me, I slid the bottle of Champagne into the bucket's icy embrace.

———

When we finally came up for air the clock on her nightstand read 1:30 a.m. We had made fiercely primal love for more than an hour. Reaching out to grasp our flutes which now stood in rings of condensation on the bed stand, we drained them before falling to sleep in each other's arms.

For me, making love with Jenny was an eyeopener. True, we'd sex just last weekend. But sex with Jenny always made me feel that the previous event had been a long time ago. She seems to reinvent the experience every time and make me feel like the current situation was the 'first time' for her.

Although I admit to being a little traditional and old fashioned, I am always willing to consider all the physical possibilities in the actual act of making love as well considering myself man enough to accept a sincere critique afterward. I am committed to providing my partner with as many organisms as we are able to generate.

Although it may sound a little crude for me to say, Jenny Woo is one hell of a ride. She rode me pretty hard, too.

We must have slept for a couple of hours before getting back to it again. You'd have thought we'd been celibate for months. After I poured the rest of the now-tepid champagne into our flutes, we tried another position. Jenny murmured that she marveled at my stamina and I welcomed her enthusiasm. Just carnally being with the Mandarin Oriental's guest relation's manager made it the best morning I'd had all week.

Sunday morning I was awakened by the warmth of sunlight filtering its way through the gauzy window coverings onto my face. For about the hundredth time in my life, I remembered why an alcoholic who not so many years ago had been saved by the Twelve-step program should never take the first drink. My head felt like a small herd of water buffalo was cantering through my brain. The taste in my mouth left no question as to where the herd had spent the night.

Being careful to not wake Jenny whose face bore a look like she died and gone to heaven, I eased myself out of bed and slunk like a snake into the bathroom. After silently easing the door closed, I relieved myself and brushed my teeth prior to taking a long hot shower to get my head operating on all cylinders again.

After drying myself off with a large fluffy bath towel and deciding that nothing productive could be done with my hair at this hour of the morning, I pulled out a pair of University of Hong Kong athletic shorts and t-shirt I'd brought with me before heading into the kitchen to fix the breakfast I had promised.

I had brought a small cardboard carton of blueberries, a half-full bag of biscuit mix, and small containers of both fresh cottage cheese and nonfat milk with me last night.

Retrieving the milk, cottage cheese and blueberries from the refrigerator, the bananas from a drawer in the crisper, and the bag of biscuit mix from where I had put it last night on the counter, I snooped into her kitchen cupboards until I found a aerosol can of butter-flavored non-stick Pam and the bottle of Maple syrup I've seen on my previous visit last weekend.

I heard Jenny running the shower in the bathroom. So I began cooking our breakfast by pouring a cup of blueberries into a small bowl and covering them with water. Locating a larger bowl, I made a batter out of the biscuit mix, cottage cheese and nonfat milk.

After spraying the inside of a large skillet with the Pam, I placed it on a medium-heat stove setting. Once the skillet had begun to warm, the drained blueberries went into the batter.

Slowly increasing the heat under the skillet, I spooned into four equal portions making sure each pancake had an equal number of berries. As the batter had been prepared dry the cakes would be thick and fluffy.

After a few moments I turned the heat down under the skillet. When the pancakes are thick like this, you have to be careful with the heat, hot at first to set the cake and keep it from spreading, then low so that it will cook through without burning.

By this time Jenny had walked into the kitchen wearing casual jeans, sandals, a yellow Donna Karan pullover, and had her black hair wrapped in a purple terry cloth towel. She had no sooner set the table and taken a seat than I announced that the pancakes were done. I heaped them with sliced bananas and maple syrup, before serving.

———

When we finished breakfast I finished cleaning up after myself, washed and dried the skillet and pans, and rinsed the dishes before putting them in the dishwasher.

It was approaching 11 a.m. In an hour we'd have to call a taxi to deliver us to the Happy Valley to get a good seat before the horse races began. In the meantime, we settled down to spend an hour with the *South China Morning Post* that had just been delivered.

While I was sitting on the love seat catching up on the world's sports, Jenny was sprawled on the floor massacring the rest of the paper. Alicia, my lover, had a habit of making certain that after she had read the newspaper it was in such a mess that there was no way I could put the pages back into the paper's designated sections, nor pages that were supposed to be in those section, in numerical order. From my observations, Jenny employed the same method to organize the newspaper. Must be a girl thing.

When the various sections were returned for me to read I'd invariable find the South Asian Regional want ads in amongst the sports section, which was in amongst the international news section, which was in amongst the entertainment section. I have long decided that once a woman has gotten through with a newspaper it is more useful in the bottom of a parakeet's cage than as the informational tool for which it was intended.

As I sat trying to catch up on the results of the first game of the Baseball's 2007 World Series currently going on between the New York Yankees and Boston Red Sox, Jenny was trying to read me an article about Starbucks growth in China.

As both Jenny and I are Starbucks addicts and also coincidently very small private investors, we find ourselves generally interested in what the mega-coffee house's latest plans are for expansion in Hong Kong and China.

Back in 2004 China had decided as part of its show democracy movement to attract investors to their country by easing limits on foreign ownership of retail ventures. Letting companies take full control of operations that once were required to be joint ventures with a Chinese citizen.

Almost immediately Seattle-based Starbucks had leapt into the breech and bought a Hong Kong firm outright. Starbucks purchased High Grown Investment Group LTD from their Hong Kong partner, H&A Asia Pacific, for an undisclosed sum. At the time, High Grown Group was operating sixty of its own coffeehouses in Asia.

In 2006, Starbucks advised its investors via news release that it was planning to double its current number of 20,000 stores with ambitious plans for opening new stores in Hong Kong, China and elsewhere in Asia.

While some investors were ecstatic and already prematurely counting their profits other customers were reported to be muttering comments like, "They have shops in every block in the world already. Now Starbucks also wants to put one in the middle of those blocks?" Go figure.

———

Twelve o'clock noon rolled around and we quickly dressed. Jenny, apparently feeling her oats from last night, decided on a pair of stone-washed Gucci jeans that had her initials etched in rhinestones on the back pocket, a form-fitting yellow silk 'Michael Kors' shirt, alligator skin high-heel western boots, and a large sterling silver faux rodeo buckle on a three-inch-wide leather belt.

To cover her hair she donned a brilliant white western straw hat and pulled a pair of black kid leather driving gloves over her exquisite long fingers.

The red top taxi she called arrived in twenty minutes. We piled in and the cab headed on the circuitous route mandated by Hong Kong's topography features to Happy Valley racetrack.

From Jenny's condo, the taxi had to travel east on Bowen Road until it intersected Stubbs Road, then left and followed that route until it intersected with Queen's Road East where we turned right and drove until that road intersected with Wong Nai Chung Road. At that point we turned right again and drove for 825 meters until we reached the spectator's entrance, across from the Hong Kong Racing Museum.

———

Inasmuch as I wasn't much of a punter, or gambler, I rarely visit the Happy Valley Sports Ground, a fancy name covering all the various sporting facilities in this area. But on the few occasions I had come to the racetrack, I had enjoyed myself watching all the rich Asians and with the faux posing they do with one another, rather than from achieving any success at the wagering windows.

Happy Valley racetrack is light years different than its American counterparts. Despite what one might think, horse racing, not football, cricket or soccer, is Hong Kong's most popular spectator sport. Since the 1800's horseracing has been the sport that has acted as a melting pot for Hong Kong's diverse cultures.

Night horse racing is enormous in Hong Kong. The busiest night at Happy Valley racetrack is Wednesday night. It is there that punters spend up to HK$30 million on a single race. HK$30 million at the current rate of exchange is US$3.8 million.

———

Jenny and I spent a delightful afternoon at Happy Valley. While I people-watched, Jenny spent her time running to the wagering cage, placing a bet, then running back to her seat to watch the race before beginning the whole process again. Since she was playing with her own money I didn't inquire as to what horses she bet on or how she was faring.

However at the end of the day's scheduled races about 4 p.m., I did notice her slipping what appeared to be a respectable sum of money into her bra for safekeeping.

When the races were over for the day and the crowd began to leave the viewing stands, it was bedlam getting a taxi. We waited almost thirty minutes to catch a red top to head back to her condo. As we both had to work Monday, I asked the cabbie to wait while I walked her into the condo, thanked her for a fantastic weekend, promised I'd call her, kissed her goodbye, and grabbed my overnight kit on the way out of the condo and back to the cab.

The taxi got me home about 5:30 p.m. On Sundays, no matter what, I take a hiatus from everything while I do my laundry, take a brief swipe at cleaning the condo, and catch up on some personal correspondence.

I turned in early that night to get caught up on my sleep. However, that self-imposed time-out only lasted until about 6 a.m. on the following foggy Monday morning when the telephone alongside my bed rang, startling me out of a pleasant dream. It was police Dispatch calling.

———

14 October 2007, Monday, 6:00 a.m. (HKT)
Hong Kong City Hall
Connaught Road at Murray Road
Central district—Hong Kong Island

It was early Monday morning and a few minutes before the commencement of Hong Kong's notorious rush hour. The two motor cops who had the graveyard shift detail to safeguard the City Hall were reading the morning newspapers they had bought from a old blind man. The cops knew the newsstand owner was blind because the man still exhibited blindisms—inappropriate facial movements that blind persons must school themselves against.

The cops were reading the newspapers at the same time they were drinking hours-old coffee, insulting each other when the opportunity presented itself, listening with half a brain to the car's radio dispatching occasional calls to the roving patrol units. They both were struggling to stay awake until they were relived from the duty of standing the police department's most boring assignment.

They wouldn't be stuck parked in front of the City Hall on this asinine assignment if they hadn't popped off to their sergeant during the graveyard shift's roll-call eight hours previously.

City hall is located in an almost zero crime area west of the Chinese People's Liberty Army Forces-Hong Kong building, one block north of the HKSAR Legislative Council building on Statute Square, and directly across the street from the Ritz Carlton Hotel.

Located on a prime real estate east of the Star Ferry Pier, City Hall takes up two city blocks. In the 1960's it was architecturally remodeled to reflect its civic place in Hong Kong's scheme of things. Which means that aesthetics took a back seat to function.

You only have to visit the Hong Kong Museum of History to study photos of its original 1900's French classical design. It contains a theatre, concert hall, and a botanical garden. The immaculate garden was erected in memory of the Hong Kong volunteer force that gave their lives to the man attempting to prevent the Japanese from occupying the crown colony during World War Two.

Back to our two wayward cops that had been assigned to City Hall guard duty as a punitive detail.

It had been a chilly night. Of course the aging Land Rover's heater didn't work. Both men had promised the other that neither of them would ever open their mouths again at roll-call in the future, least they once again be assigned to this shit detail.

The assignment required the officers to literally sit on City hall property. One of the officers was expected to perform an hourly walking tour of the entire perimeter of the slumbering city facility, which extended north to Edinburgh Place; East to Murray Road; South to Connaught Road Central; and west to Hong Kong Island's city bus terminal.

Because this particular duty was reserved for screw-ups who irritated the powers-that-be, the marked patrol unit assigned this god-awful boring duty was never permitted to leave its assigned guard station.

This morning, however, the last time their sergeant had stopped by to make sure that both of them were awake, she had reluctantly given them special permission that every two hours they could drive two blocks away to a 24/7 combination Noodle and Cigarette shop to refill their coffee thermos.

The two cops rationalized that the unusual favor granted by their sergeant didn't indicate the woman was getting soft in her old age, but rather she didn't want the two malcontents to get caught sleeping on-duty by the shift Lieutenant she reported to, who also was known to cruise this sector in the early morning hours.

The sergeant had worked hard, sacrificed more, and even lost a good husband earning her chevrons. And a couple of no-account losers like these two cops would cause her to lose her stripes over her dead body.

Thanks to the benevolence of their sergeant, the black-and-white Land Rover patrol car was returning from a coffee run when the cops observed a white van bearing the Red Crescent logo but displaying no license plates purposely run the Jackson Road at Connaught stoplight directly in front of the guard station where they had been parked all night.

Without stopping the van made a squealing right hand turn on two wheels eastbound on Connaught Road Central and took off at a speed in excess of the posted speed limit.

Without a conscious thought the cop driving had accelerated the bulky Land Rover in pursuit while his partner flipped on the vehicle's flashing lights and French-style siren, startling a flock of pigeons who had been minding their own business picking at food scraps dropped on Hong Kong's pavements by increasing inconsiderate tourists.

It never occurred to either officer that the van was acting suspiciously, seemingly baiting the cops into chasing them, nor that by the simple act of entering into the unauthorized pursuit of a mere traffic violator they were deserting their assigned duty station.

The chase continued only for a few blocks mainly due to the fact that the van's occupants appeared to have little interest in ditching the patrol car. When the patrol car finally pulled the van over to the curb they were almost to the intersection of Connaught Rod Central and Cotton Tree Drive right in the middle of the Admiralty district.

If the officers had been alert they might have recalled that back on 02 October 2007, a Wednesday, an identically placarded van had accidentally been forced into a collision with a utility pole. The occupants of that van had abandoned it and fled. That incident had occurred during assassination of the 14K triad's White Paper Fan, and in the same neighborhood, not a more than a long city block south of their current location.

That incident had been the wakeup call to the Hong Kong police department that there was thriving illegal body part harvesting operation going on under their very noses.

Today's van abruptly pulled over to the curb of the eastbound traffic lanes. The two cops observed the occupants jump from the van, one of them pausing momentarily to empty the clip of what appeared to be a Uzi automatic machine pistol at the police car, forcing the officers to seek cover behind the Land Rover's metal dashboard.

While the cops were occupied doing that, the van's occupants had dashed across the street and out of sight into heavily landscaped Harcourt Road parking lot at the Hong Kong's Far East Finance Centre complex.

Only after the frightened cops had raised their heads from behind the minimal protection of their patrol car's dashboard did a lightbulb switch on in their sleep-deprived memory banks. Suddenly they both recalled that at last night's roll call the Street Crimes squad had issued a stop-and-detain-only Bolo, be on the lookout, for any Red Crescent van whose occupants were acting in a suspicious manner.

The two cops decided that having to call the stop into Dispatch seemed like as good as excuse as any not to undertake the other more dangerous option of chasing the fleeing, armed subjects. Unusually, it took the driver only two tries on the radio to get through to Dispatch.

Both officers were aware that they probably were going to face disciplinary action for deserting their assigned duty station to pursue the now-abandoned white van. But, realizing that because of the Bolo, they knew that withholding critical information from the dispatcher in the current situation was a far more egregious infraction.

The senior officer who was the driver sighed and took a deep breath before keying the microphone and embarking on a detailed explanation of everything they had observed and done since they first encountered the fleeing van.

Dispatch came back up on the ancient eleven-year-old Motorola police radio that the British had installed in all the patrol cars before they were forced to vacate the former crown colony on June 1997 when it had reverted to Communist rule under the People's Republic of China. They were instructed to stay put.

Dispatch told the cops to permit no one to approach the abandoned van, and for Buddha's sake, don't even think about giving chase to the fleeing occupants. While the patrol unit maintained the scene, Dispatch would call higher authority for orders.

———

The call startled me out of what had been a pleasant sleep a little after 6:00 a.m. early Monday morning. The Dispatcher seemed excited which was unusual for a cop in that job. He informed me that a patrol unit acting on my department's Bolo had executed a traffic stop on a van meeting the description.

"Chief Inspector," the Dispatcher reported, "when they got the van pulled over to the curb, its occupants jumped and fled just like they did twelve days ago during the Chung Shan assassination at Queensway and Cotton Tree Drive."

My mind flashed back to the Five Rams Chinese Funeral Parlor scene, and what was left of Mimi's two detectives after the booby traps the body parts thieves had set up before decoying Inspector Yin's team into the building, had exploded on Friday just three days previously.

"Dispatch, now hear me clearly on this." I stated.

"Yes, Sir, Chief Inspector. My ears are open, my pen is poised and the audio tape is running, Sir. What are your orders?"

"Dispatch," I asserted, "since the assassination incident on the October 2nd, two good cops with families have lost their lives in the war these assholes who are stealing body parts have started with this department. It is my intent that those will be the last cop's lives lost. When we arrest these scumbags and their boss, I plan on throwing them or their dead bodies under Stanley Prison."

"Tell those two patrol cops to stay put in their vehicle unless anyone threatening attempts to approach their unit or the abandoned van. I want you to dispatch two more patrol units and a supervisor to that scene. Have them secure the entire intersection with crime scene tape."

"Er, Chief Inspector, Sir," the Dispatcher sighed and took a deep 'Why Me?' breath before saying, "Respectfully, Sir, rush hour is just beginning. Shutting down that intersection is going to put the entire Admiralty financial district into massive gridlock. I don't need to tell you whose headquarters is located just a hundred meters north of that location."

What the dispatcher was alluding to was the fact that the headquarters of the Chinese People's Liberation Army Forces is located at Edinburgh Place and Tim Wa Avenue. Their commander would not be pleased by my audacity to block his troop's access and egress to the complex without clearing it with him first.

"Yes, I know, Dispatch. I am going to catch hell for this from the HKSAR Chief Executive, the commander of the PRC Army, even our own commissioner, but I don't want anyone going near that van until it has been cleared by the bomb squad. I won't have any more cops killed because of secondary concerns about traffic flow."

"I also want you to call Inspector Chen Ho of the Hijacking and Terrorist squad at home. Give him my orders to dispatch two teams of his detectives to the scene and tell them to make certain no one overrides my orders."

"Also call out the Bomb squad and the Biohazard squad. Both are familiar with the case and know what to do. Tell them to go over every inch of that van and rule out booby traps before they attempt to open the doors, understand?"

I continued, "And while I'm certain it will not be necessary remind the biohazard unit that if there are body parts in the van, any disease the donors might have had could be highly-communicable."

The dispatcher repeated my instructions back to me to ensure he got everything as I had ordered.

Thinking I have hopefully covered all the bases, I asked the dispatcher if he had any questions? He responded that he didn't. I knew that as soon as he hung up with me, he planned on listening to the audiotape to make certain. Good man, I thought.

"Okay, nice job, Dispatch. If anyone has any questions patch them through to me at home." Thanking the man, I hung up the phone. Inspector Chen Ho and the specialty squad leaders would get today's crime scene under control.

There was no reason for me to call Zhou Ming out early to take me to the scene. I'd just be a fifth wheel anyway. And seen by the media as just another second-guessing supervisor, especially in my case, a *Gweilo*, who didn't trust his Chinese officers to do the jobs that they had received endless training for.

Having made that decision, I walked into the well-appointed kitchen to fix myself a truly decadent American breakfast of three eggs fried sunnyside up, a rasher of crisp bacon, a well-buttered English muffin, and fresh squeezed orange juice, all of which I would consume before showering. Ming was scheduled to pick me up at 8:30 a.m. this morning. So I'd even have time for the unusual extravagance of watching the morning news on the English language edition of STAR TV before heading downstairs to meet my car and driver.

———

Dispatch passed on my orders to the two cops sitting nervously in their marked Land Rover who were watching the van as if expecting it to grow horns. Occasionally, they had to activate the siren and holler threats over the units PA system when anyone got too close to the vehicle. Prevented by Dispatch and higher authority from having to chase the fleeing armed subjects, caused them both to expel a huge sigh of relief.

So far, no one had called them on the fact that they had improperly left their static guard assignment to follow to a stoplight-running van. They both had too much time in towards their future retirement after twenty years with the police department to get fired at this stage of their careers. Especially for something as stupid as they had done on impulse. They both prayed that in the subsequent confusion everyone would forget that they disobeyed orders.

Shortly, the back up units rolled up to secure the entire intersection with barricades and crime scene tape. That single act resulted in the officer's ears being assaulted with almost unbearable pain caused by hundreds of grid locked motorists taking their frustration out on their vehicle's horns.

Momentarily, the bomb squad arrived on-scene by driving down the sidewalks wearing the heavily armored suits they wear over their Nomex underwear and asbestos boots. They even had brought along one of their remotely controlled robots.

One minute after that, the biohazard unit arrived on scene also via the sidewalk already outfitted in their spooky white biohazard suits and hoods, driving their specialty vehicles that seemed to be from another planet.

The original patrol unit was ordered to secure from the scene by the senior commander. The two cops had just exhaled a sigh of relief when much to the two officer's chagrin, the scene commander told them "You guys had no business abandoning your assignment in the first place to chase a van that had no connection with your City Hall guard assignment."

The commander made like he was leaving as he turned to walk off, instead turning back and dropping the bombshell on them, ordering them to report immediately to their sergeant at the district precinct.

———

The bomb squad made a careful, detailed inspection of the van. After they had declared the vehicle to be booby trap-free, they cut the padlock off the rear doors of the van's cargo box.

The bomb squad supervisor waved the biohazard supervisor over who glanced into the interior of the box before inserting the sensors of some exotic space-age looking instruments into and under the back of the van.

Five minutes later the biohazard Boss stepped back, checked his meters, and shrugged.

Apparently frustrated at having to wait for the biohazard officer who essentially had done nothing but wave a couple ten-thousand-dollar virus-detecting sensors around in the air, the bomb squad chief climbed into the box of the van.

After a few minutes he climbed back out. He announced to his biohazard counterpart that he had discovered the van was outfitted with a refrigerated hidden crawl space. Just like the one that had been abandoned by its occupants on October 2nd at the scene of the triad assassin of Chung Shan and three cops. That particular van had been filled with decomposing body parts.

The biohazard boss and one of his men, both clothed from head-to-toe in impervious Level-4 suits and hoods, awkwardly climbed into the van box and were lost from view for about ten minutes.

When they climb back out they reported that the only thing human in the hidden compartment that had stench of death was a dead Asian male. The body was zipped in a clear biohazard Level-two bag. There are no signs of overt violence on the body although there was a shaved patch on his arm where he apparently had tested his knife, called knife fighter's mange.

The biohazard boss like his bomb squad counterpart, both always notorious for their sick sense of humor, joked that it looked like the guy just went to sleep and forgot to wake up.

The senior scene commander observed protocol by obtaining the concurrence from both supervisors, agreeing with his decision to release the scene. No one could come up with a valid reason to tie up rush hour traffic any longer. All three concurred that in their considered opinions the body should be taken immediately to the ME's for an priority post mortem to rule out any hazard to Hong Kong's citizens or the cops themselves.

It took the entire biohazard squad to drag the dead body out of the concealed hideaway and up onto a stainless steel collapsible cart for transfer into the second heavily bio-shielded vehicle. Procedure required that two of the specialty vehicles be brought to every scene where a biohazard is suspected.

The second truck would transported the body to the ME's office located less than a quarter mile away at the Arsenal Street Police headquarters complex.

As a last step in their procedure, while the rest of their team was loading up the corpse, biohazard personnel inundated the entire van with a strong disinfectant figuring its owner could complain later about the soaked upholstery and flooded compartment in the cargo box.

While the biohazard team was loading up, the bomb squad policed up the scene, finally ripping down the crime scene tape and waving the frustrated motorists on their not-so-merry way.

One of the backup patrol units that had been called to the scene originally would stand-bye to provide traffic control for the tow truck. It would be towing the abandoned van to the police impound yard.

The biohazard squad transported the body in their bio-contamination van to the ME's office. After checking the body in procedurally, the squad supervisor went down to the basement to the cutting floor to buttonhole the duty ME.

After waiting for nearly twenty minutes, he was forced settle for the duty ME scheduling assistant.

The biohazard supervisor suggested that the assigned ME exercise extreme caution when autopsying the body due to the prior history of these criminal's willingness to employ booby-traps to kill cops.

The ME assistant listened to the biohazard supervisor with a half a brain, the other half thinking about his recent affair with his neighbor's wife. He absent-mindedly thanked the cop before picking up a phone to advise the ME he had a corpse for an emergency post mortem.

Human stupidity and lack of attention to detail would cost two persons their lives.

11

14 October 2007, Monday, 1:00 p.m. (HKT)
Autopsy Suite—HKSAR Medical Examiner's Office
Arsenal Street Police Headquarters
Wan Chai district—Hong Kong Island

Betty Fang was unhappy that the ME scheduler had assigned her to assist the rookie Doctor, Dang Lao, over her objections. Oh, sure, she was used to being scheduled to work with other pathologists when Dr. Dong, like today, was catching up on his paperwork. But the other pathologists in the rotation, possibly because she regularly worked for the service's senior doctor, treated her with respect, which is very important to a modern Chinese woman in Hong Kong today.

The biohazard squad of the Hong Kong Police had delivered the body she and Lao were assigned. The cops had passed on a verbal warning to the ME scheduling assistant that this body could have something to do with the body part harvesters that so far had murdered a number of cops to avoid being caught.

Although the body had arrived enclosed in a clear plastic bag that was certified only for Level-2 bio-containment, the biohazard squad supervisor had urged maximum caution when the body was posted.

Betty had brought the cop's recommendation to Dr. Lao's attention. She tried to convince Lao that despite the low-level biohazard plastic bag the body was in, what would it hurt to treat it like it was a Level-4 contamination case and do the autopsy in moonsuits?

Despite being only 5 foot tall, Dr. Lao was a bully who hated cops. He had dismissed the police supervisor's warning as the imagination of a group of overpaid, undereducated cretins who liked to pretend they knew something about the practice of medicine. On Lao's orders the moonsuits she recommended were left in their lockers. Hence, Fang and Dr. Lao were dressed for the autopsy in standard gown, cotton mask, and latex gloves.

Dr. Lao was a pig. He was frequently flatulent. When she had complained of that to the personnel department she had been told, "Come on, Betty, you work in a autopsy room. How bad can an occasional fart be to the overall ambient smell of the place?"

Since graduating from the University of Hong Kong School of Forensic Sciences, five years of dancing with the dead had taught Betty the value of hard work and maintaining a positive outlook. Early on she'd decided that survival as a pathologist's assistant could be ensured by the attitude with which she approached her job.

Betty had been born into a dirt-poor farming family outside Guangzhou in rural China. She was one of thirteen children, and the only girl that had survived the diseases and starvation that eventually killed her five sisters.

In her formative years she had risked her life to attend an illegal missionary school outside their small village. A Catholic nun had taught class. A large cave had served for the school's classroom.

The nun taught all the students that were brave enough to attend all about the importance of maintaining their dreams; setting and following through on achieving goals. She never belittled her student's starry-eyed illusions.

Betty had been taught about the 'goodness of man' and the sanctity of life, something she had yet to see any concrete examples of in her short career.

When Hong Kong reverted to administration by the PRC in June of 1997, China's leadership began to acknowledge the importance to the country's future of increasing the number of professionals in its population.

Betty was one of the children who had been permitted to walk five miles each way a couple times a week to compete in tests for the few scholarships the politburo in Beijing had earmarked for the rural population.

After four long hard years of education she now understood the true nature of the urban slaughterhouse. She now saw, firsthand, the array of violence, casual and otherwise, which members of the species were prepared to visit upon one another on a daily basis. Where was the goodness of man, she wondered?

With a cheerful if noiseless whistle, Betty Fang wheeled the stainless steel autopsy table over to a hose bib and began to hose it down. When the trickle of murky water got too loud, she switched to singing a church hymn. The nun, now long dead, had taught her students to whistle or sing while they worked.

When she finished getting the table clean for the next customer, she took great care as she returned it to its designated operating position. Betty was always careful to not park her cart or one of the mayo stands on the six-inch-wide, bright yellow lines that were painted on the tile floor.

The purpose of the yellow lines were to make everyone who came into the autopsy room aware that in the event the lab's virus detection system sensed an airborne pathogen or virus, room-width panels would drop instantly without warning from above the ceiling. The panels effectively and instantly divided the long room into isolated stand-alone autopsy stations.

The intent was to avoid having everyone in the entire suite become contaminated in the rare instance that a team working at particular station had the bad *joss*, bad luck, to be exposed to an airborne fast-acting virus escaping from a surgically-opened body cavity.

In that case everyone, other than those at the contaminated autopsy station, had to flee the room before all the access doors automatically locked down in exactly ten seconds. The pathologist and assistant at the contaminated workstation were locked in for the duration of the alert.

The autopsy suite's complicated ventilation system immediately modified itself into a set of zones, one for every autopsy station that by now would have been isolated by the impervious emergency wall-to-wall, floor-to-ceiling drop-down panels.

The HVAC unit servicing the contaminated workstation would shut the supply vents into the isolated room and reduced the air pressure flowing into the room to prohibit the virus from forcing it way out through the isolation seals. The contaminated exhaust air would be extracted from the room and automatically routed to a series of biohazard scrubbers.

Despite the fact that it was now several times cleaner than the polluted air Hong Kong citizens normally breath, the contaminated air routed to the scrubbers once scrubbed wouldn't be reintroduced into the facility but instead would be exhausted into the outside ambient air.

———

Returning to the real world, the one that paid her the wages she sent home monthly to her infirm parents in China, she put away the power washer she had used to clean the cart. Dr. Lao motioned her to put a new cassette in the recorder, which was his job, but making her do it for him was all about power. Betty replaced the cassette in the tape recorder and stood on her tiptoes to flick the overhead microphone with her fingernail to make certain it was turned on.

One thing Betty reluctantly had to admit was that once Dr. Lao finished his sexual harassment, his flatulence, and the juvenile comments he got to work and was all business. That made it easier on her because once she got her work done and when the procedure was finished, she could leave the autopsy suite, which was just the way she liked it. She never dawdled on the cutting floor.

The pathologist looked over at her. Betty responded to his visual question by answering, "The body is in drawer 2202-07."

She assisted Dr. Lao as he pushed the transportation cart across the room to the bank of refrigerated storage bins that covered the north wall. He twisted the handle of 2202-07 and eased the drawer outward until the entire body came into view beneath the harsh overhead fluorescent lights.

The body covered with a white sheet was on its back, arms at the side. Once the corpse was drained of blood the body would take on the unnatural purple hue of the overhead lights. This one would be an easy gig for the pathologist. Probably a heart attack, she guessed. What the doctors called a slam-dunk.

The body didn't have any visible cuts, bullet holes, needle marks, or lacerations and all of the body parts were flying in formation. The only unusual finding that Betty had seen while washing the body earlier was an irritated rectum and a mouthful of chipped teeth when she was checking it for foreign objects.

These were the ones that bothered Betty. The bodies that arrived at the ME's office without a mark on them. Perfect in everyway except for the purple hue around the lips. Looking like maybe they were just sleeping there on the cold hard metal. Like they might wake up a while later and go out to Chinese dinner. They were the ones who reminded Betty Fang how fragile and elusive life could be, and how close to the line we all tread daily.

Betty used her foot to jack the transport table up to match the level of the corpse. She began to slide the body tray on its rollers toward her but then stopped. The body's head had somehow become stuck to the storage pallet and was resisting coming along for the ride. If she wasn't careful the skull could get hung up and bang against edge of the table. Betty would never permit that. The body had a right to dignity. Bad enough for the guy to be laying supine here naked where every Tom, Dick, and Chen who passes by can see your sexual organ all shriveled up. No need for that.

"Think I may need a little help here, Doctor," Betty said. Dr. Lao stood for a moment bent over the corpse looking down to see if he could tell what was causing the head to hang up on the storage drawer pallet.

"You ready?" the doctor asked. Betty said she was, and on the count of three, they half lifted, half slid the body off the pallet and onto the cart. Betty wheeled the corpse over to the autopsy station and used the toe of her right foot to lock the wheels.

Doctor Lao pulled the overhead microphone down so it was level with his nose and began his monologue. "Subject is Asian male. About fifty years of age. Black hair, black eyes. Scale says he weighs about ninety-two kilograms. The stomach is distended for reasons unknown at this time. Perhaps an enlarged heart . . ."

Lao circled the table, lifting a limb here, poking this and prodding that. Then he began the routine autopsy process, making the 'Y' cut, cutting back the flesh into three flaps, and used a pair of red-handled, black-rubber-gripped pruning shears to cut the ribs, the spreader bars to crack the chest, scooping the guts out using a steel ladle into a large stainless pan which was filled with a number of smaller pans, and using his gloved fingers to delve around in the body's stomach cavity to make certain he hadn't missed anything.

Lao inspected the large pan that now held the heart, stomach, liver, spleen, intestine, kidneys, and lungs. He carefully removed each organ and weighed it before placing it back in its individual pan for further study.

When Dr. Lao picked up the intestine, he accidentally hit the side of the pan. He thought he heard a couple of metallic 'clink-clinks.'

"Well, what do we have here?" Lao said. He turned to Betty and asked if she had heard the sound. She answered, "Yes, doctor, I did. What do you think it is?"

Reaching over to the Mayo stand Lao picked up a scalpel and began to slit the length of the intestine. Then using his gloved fingers he worked whatever was in there up into a wider part of the intestine so he could get a pair of small forceps into the tube to remove the foreign object.

Dr. Lao used a pair of forceps to poke around in the intestine until he managed to extract two small brown glass vials. He handed both to Betty for her to rinse off.

When she returned them to him Lao flipped down an optical cheater mounted on the frame of his safety glasses and slowly rotated both vials in his hand, inspecting them.

Betty quietly suggested to Lao that he might accidentally drop and break the vials if he continued to manipulate both of them at the same time. The doctor's only response was to angrily shake his head at her and arrogantly continue with what he had been doing.

Black rubber stoppers sealed both vials. Lao held the glass vials up to the light. A very fine white powder filled each of the vials nearly three quarters full. Lao shook it and was amazed at how completely it filled the void. Whatever the stuff was, it floated around inside like one of those clear plastic Christmas paperweights.

Lao stood patiently, openmouthed, waiting for the material to settle back into place, but it didn't. It was like the stuff had some kind of motor that kept it aloft. Very, very weird.

Glancing at her, the pathologist displaying a look of wonderment Betty had never witnessed on his face before, then returned his eyes to the vials where the powder was still roiling around inside like a blizzard of artificial snow.

Betty quietly asked, "What do you have there, doctor?

Lao answered irritably, "Maybe the guy was a mule transporting some new kind of cocaine or heroin."

Timidly, Betty spoke up to remind him, "Doctor, you know procedure says that the vials must be bagged and turned over to the police."

Dr. Lao ignored her and continued to poke around with his free hand in the reddish-dark shimmering mass of remaining tissue, searching for more vials.

While Lao searched for more mystery vials with his right hand, he multi-tasked with his left, pushing on the edges of the stoppers with his thumb. Then, all the while still digging in the fetid mass with his right hand, his left turned one of the vials and worked it from the other side. Then he attempted it once again. Nothing. Damn thing was jammed in there tight as hell. He thumbed it again, and again his thumb failed to dislodge the rubber.

Being careful not to squeeze the glass vial too tightly he grasped the stopper with his thumb and forefinger and gave it a twist. The plug squeaked as it turned. He applied upward pressure and finally the plug began to move. A third of the way out it bound up once more and would move no farther. Frustrated, the pathologist gave it a hard yank.

Now the reluctant stopper came out in a hurry, startling Lao, causing one of the vials to slip from his twitching fingers and fall to the tile floor.

Betty watched the vial, now missing its stopper, bounce several times off the tile floor to a height of at least 30 centimeters, about a foot. Finally it shattered. The contents atomized into the ambient air. The broken shards of glass skidded across the tile. Just then her vision began to waver. She blinked her eyes trying to maintain her focus.

Her head suddenly began to throb as if an animal were trying to claw its way out from inside her skull.

It seemed like the air around her was filled with tiny white particles. She felt like she weighed a thousand pounds, that her legs just couldn't carry the load, that she might lose control her bladder and bowels.

A human acquires a viral infection when the individual inhales an airborne toxin, which in this case was in almost weightless fasting-acting weapons-grade powder form. Contamination is immediate and irreversible, and as in most such cases, fatal within a matter of a minute.

Both Fang and Dr. Lao were wearing cotton surgical masks. As such, they were essentially unprotected against what happened next. If Doctor had been suitably concerned of the potential of risk posed by the dissection this particular body, they would have opted to don moonsuits, or particle filter inhalant protection—which is a goofy-looking gas mask with two purple cylinders jutting from it.

Some countries require post mortem personnel and anyone viewing the autopsy to wear the biohazard devices anytime they are on the service floor or in autopsy rooms with a body. The particle filter mask is capable of protecting the wearer from getting TB, SARS, and Ebola. Ebola is the African virus that dissolves your cells so you essentially melt into a puddle of goo.

The partial filter mask filters 100% of the air. However, the mask that Betty Fang and Dr. Lao were wearing that day today was just a piece of white cloth with an elastic band and metal strip to squeeze fit across your nose. Its filtration rate was quite high, 95%. However it was completely inadequate when dealing with the weaponized fast-acting biohazard toxin that had just been propelled into the air they were breathing. They were being contaminated by the contents of open vial that had shattered on the tile floor of the autopsy suite.

Klaxons began howling as the multitude of biohazard sensors located throughout the large autopsy suite detected the fact that an airborne virus was loose in the lab.

It wasn't until she heard the scream expelled from her mouth that she realized she had collapsed to the floor. "Betty?" she faintly heard Dr. Lao nervously call.

Her chest felt like it was full of water. She listened to the drumming of the heels of her white orthopedic shoes on the hard tiles. She felt her bladder and bowels empty themselves, urine and feces saturating her scrubs and gown. She opened her mouth to apologize for her incontinence but could only manage a wet gargle.

Then she sensed Dr. Lao kneeling at her side. His black eyes were opened comically wide behind the thick lens of his safety glasses.

She watched as a red flower bloomed on his white cotton surgical mask. Watched as it grew from a tiny dot in the middle of the mask before spreading into a crimson daffodil shape as the second vial dropped from his grasp to the floor also shattering, before he fell to the floor beside her.

She sought for a phrase. A prayer perhaps. But nothing came to mind. Only the roaring in her head and the sound of her parent's wails when they were told she was going away for college. That she was forsaking the family farm. Their voices came from a great distance and were getting fainter.

Both of them, doctor and assistant, quietly died within a minute of each other. The last sounds entering their ears and registering on their brains had been the thumps of the airtight panels impacting the floor and the deafening sounds of the wailing klaxons.

The sudden under-pressure in the room seemed to be depriving them of oxygen. They didn't hear the snapping sound from the automatic locking of access doors as their colleagues bolted from the autopsy suite.

What they didn't observe and now never would was what happened in the final moments of a person hit by a fact-acting killer virus. The lectures Betty had faithfully listened to in medical school had said, "Your blood vessels explode. You bleed out, right there on the spot. The look of recognition and awareness on the victim's face is horrible. The horror of suddenly knowing with absolute certainly that your ticket has been punched, that your attendance in this world had expired."

Must be what biologists claimed 44-year-old Steve Irwin felt in that last second before a stingray killed him on 04 September 2006. The single nanosecond when the words, *irritated stingray*, etched themselves in neon on Irwin's mind. And the world was, once and for all, reduced to nothing more than the scrape of the twelve-inch lethal barb forcing its way through his rib cage and abdominal tissue before plunging into his heart.

———

14 October 2007, Monday, 1:35 p.m. (HKT)
Crimes Against Persons Department
Arsenal Street Police Headquarters—Third floor
Wan Chai district—Hong Kong Island

My administrative assistant Elizabeth who seemed to have contacts all over the huge Arsenal Headquarters complex was the first to run in and tell me that the Medical Examiner's office was in contaminated lock-down.

She said that when she'd heard the faint sound of klaxons she had called her contact in the department's security unit. He had violated procedure by informing her that the virus detection system in the autopsy suite had registered the presence of an airborne virus and had automatically gone into lockdown.

The complex security officer had surreptitiously whispered to her that a doctor and his assistant were now locked inside one the now-isolated autopsy workstations. Both were apparently unconscious, lying motionless on the autopsy room floor. Blood was observed seeping through their cotton facemasks.

I reasoned that while dead bodies are the purview of the Medical Examiner's office, a crime might have been committed in the autopsy suite and that was my department's responsibility. So I ran for the elevator. When it reached the first floor, I ran out of it slamming into Lieutenant Du Ming (who also had been informed by Elizabeth, I would wager) and both of us headed at a run across the parking lot to the ME's office.

———

14 October 2007, Monday, 1:55 p.m. (HKT)
HKSAR Medical Examiner's Office
Arsenal Street Police Headquarters
Wan Chai district—Hong Kong Island

When Ming and I reached the main door into the ME's complex, two rent-a-cops attempted to prevent us from entering. I went left and Du Ming went right. The two guards embarrassingly found themselves on their butts and no sign of us except a pair of swinging entrance doors.

When we reached the elevator down to the autopsy suite which is located in the lab's basement we were met by the ME's senior pathologist, my friend Dr. Lu Dong.

As we impatiently suffered through the ride down in what had to be the slowest elevator in the Arsenal Street complex, Dr. Dong briefed us on the situation. He said that fortunately the recording microphones at each autopsy station also automatically route a verbal copy of what the pathologist's had been saying into his overhead microphone at the time of the incident to the ME's master computer.

When the elevator reached the 'cutting' floor as it is called, Dr. Dong told me the lab's biohazard system had extracted the contaminated air and had under-pressured the station involved in the incident. Paramedics and a medical doctor wearing moonsuits, humping their own air supply, with Dr. Dong's permission, had broken the door seals and entered the workstation.

The contaminated autopsy station was now effectively isolated from everything else in the building. In the rare possibility that any virus was still floating around in there, the moonsuits would adequately protect the first responders.

Dong said, "They report that both of my people are dead. It would have been a particularly gruesome death. Both bodies displayed the typical symptoms of inhaling a fast-acting bio-toxin. They likely died within seconds after they collapsed on the floor. And that damn Lao's carelessness and failure to follow procedure certainly is to blame for their deaths."

That got my attention. Dr. Lu Dong was a pretty mellow type guy. I guess you had to be to survive in the autopsy business. But Dong had been vehement when he made his last statement.

The senior pathologist continued, "I've had all three bodies put in body bags and sealed. They have been taken to Decomp, the decomposition room, which was coincidently unoccupied at the moment. After the bodies were transferred to Decomp, the main airlock entrance to that room was sealed by the biohazard specialists."

I asked, "Whose was the pathologist and assistant, Lu?"

"Dr. Dang Lao and Betty Fang."

That came as a shock. Lao hadn't been with the ME department long enough for me to have run into him in my official capacity. But I knew Betty Fang as a hard working person who was a professional colleague of mine.

"Well, what happened?" I asked.

Dong turned back from looking through the heavy plate glass into the empty workstation and faced me head-on. His face was beet red, obviously angry beyond my comprehension.

He furiously said, "As you know, I told you that we have a duplicate of the recording that Lao was making when the sensors picked up on the airborne biohazard. I just finished listening to the recording. And I never have been so disgusted with another physician in my entire life."

The doctor sighed and took a deep breath to compose himself before continuing.

"According to the master tape, they were working on the corpse that the HKP biohazard squad brought in this morning. The body found in an abandoned Red Crescent van. The circumstances of the man's death were not obvious. The first responders were unable to determine COD, cause of death."

"Augustus, because you had a similar abandoned van back on 02 October, I figured it was still a open investigation and therefore scheduled a STAT autopsy to determine if the man died of natural causes or fowl play," Dong explained.

"Apparently after Dr. Lao finished cutting the guy open, breaking his chest, and removing his organs, he discovered something suspicious in the man's intestine. Both Dr. Lao and Betty Fang were heard discussing it on the tape."

"From what I can tell after having listening to the tape three times, Dr. Lao had been inspecting the deceased's organs when he accidentally permitted a part of the intestine to brush against the edge of the stainless steel organ pan. That produced a clinking sound like glass."

"The master recording indicates that Lao incised the intestine and discovered a pair of brown gram-sized vials inside it."

Shaking his head, Dong continued. "At that point the tape documents Betty's admonishment to Dr. Lao recommending that he just bag the vials and turn them over to the police, per procedure."

"However, Dr. Lao is ambitious, and no doubt hoping to gain some recognition from the head ME and the Media I would assume. He started trying to pry the rubber stopper out of one of them."

"As you Americans are fond of saying when you want to cut to the meat of the matter—long story, short—Lao accidentally dropped one of the vials to the floor, shattering it."

Exasperated, the doctor continued. "In doing that, he condemned himself; no great loss, and the best autopsy assistant I've ever had the pleasure of work with, to a very ugly death."

I gave Dr. Dong a chance to compose himself, before I said, "Doctor, the body Dr. Lao and Ms. Fang were autopsying is related to the illegal body apart harvesting case. The fact that the vials came out of his intestine could indicate someone may have forced them down his throat while the man was alive and they found their way into his lower intestine. Or, could have used a long stick like a pool cue to push them part way up into the intestine through his rectum."

"During the Five Ram funeral parlor raid this past Friday, these scumbags ambushed two of my detectives, both family men, and massacred them by converting two Claymore mines into booby traps."

My anger was showing when I continued, "I intend to catch these bastards and put them under Stanley Prison no matter how long it takes. That means that one of Lieutenant Ming's detectives must physically inspect the unidentified body for visual signs of foul play, and photograph all three bodies. I need that to take place before you can complete the post mortem on the unknown male, or begin those on the two deceased employees."

"If it turns out these body robbers purposely left the man in the faux Red Crescent van knowing it would be brought to your office and autopsied, they had to know that the his internal organs would examined, which certainly would have eventually led to the discovery of the vials."

"If these criminals watch American television, specifically the CSI shows, they know that at several times during the post mortem there would be several opportunities for the vials to be opened or broken. That makes the deaths of Dr. Lao and Betty Fang premeditated homicide."

"Now how do I go about getting a detective into the Decomp room to do a visual inspection of the unknown body and photograph them all?"

Dong smiled, and said, "I hoped you'd feel the same way I do about my dead staff members. If it turns out to be homicide, I know Lieutenant Ming's homicide detectives will solve the case and bring these criminals before the docket and hopefully sentenced to be executed at Stanley Prison. Which I will insist on attending."

"That is the reason I had the entrance door of the Decomp room sealed. However, there is back entrance to the room through the body storage area. If Lieutenant Du Ming has a detective small enough to squeeze into one of our moonsuits, I'll accompany him into the Decomp room so that he or she can gather whatever forensic evidence you need. Is that acceptable, Chief Inspector?" Dong asked.

I glanced at Ming and asked, "Du Ming, who do you recommend for the assignment?

"No question, Boss," Ming answered, "its got to be David Kan."

Kan was the homicide bureau's medical student turned cop. He also was smaller in stature than most of the other detectives in the homicide squad that for some reason tended to lean toward the other end of the spectrum, as in large and intimidating.

Kan had been my choice, too, but I never step on the toes of one of my subordinates in their assignment of personnel.

"How soon can you locate Detective Kan and have him report here, Ming?"

"Boss, I'll reach out for him right now. I'll tell him to drop whatever he is doing, and get here as fast as he can. But Boss, you and I need to get back to the office. You know the feces will hit the fan as soon as someone leaks it to the Media."

Turning the pathologist, I asked, "Will you wait for Kan, Dr. Dong?"

In a icy tone of voice not characteristic of him, Dr. Dong replied, "Lieutenant, two of my people have possibly been murdered here. I'll have the moonsuits inspected. And I or one of my associates will be waiting here as long as it takes for Detective Kan to arrive."

———

14 October 2007, Monday, 3:16 p.m. (HKT)
Autopsy Suite—HKSAR Medical Examiner's Office
Arsenal Street Police Headquarters
Wan Chai district—Hong Kong Island

The hastily summoned Detective Kan arrived at the Medical Examiners office and immediately took the elevator down to the autopsy suite. Dr. Dong had thoughtfully left a female assistant waiting by the elevator for the detective's arrival. The woman walked him down to the Level-3 dressing area, put him in a small dressing room and told him to remove all his street clothing except for his shorts.

Kan had just completed that task when the woman returned without knocking her arms full of special-use garments and began assisting the diminutive detective in donning the under garments that guaranteed the Moonsuit that went on over all this paraphernalia would form an airtight seal.

When Kan was all zipped in and sealed into the bulky impervious silver suit, he awkwardly stepped into the dressing room foyer to discover Dr. Dong already suited up, impatiently waiting for him. Kan, brought up to be polite in all situations regardless of how unpleasant, extended his heavily gloved hand to the doctor.

Dong didn't extend his hand to touch Kan's. Instead the older man said something every student has been told from the first day they begin medical school.

"Detective, there are no polite niceties to observe when you are in Level-4. Remember that and you may complete the job Lieutenant Ming has assigned you and return to this room, vertically, get me?"

Kan followed Dr. Dong to the rear of the floor that houses what laboratory scientists three floors above in their comfortable and well-ventilated offices refer to as the 'unclean areas.'

The autopsy floor includes the subterranean exterior loading dock where bodies are delivered; the eight-table autopsy suite; the body storage room; and the room reserved for bodies that arrive in advanced stages of decomposition.

Just because decomposing bodies smell bad doesn't mean they don't deserve as much investigative attention at the ones who had died only hours before.

Kan and the doctor entered the body storage double airlock, and then proceeded through the second stage of the airlock into the body storage room.

The BSR, body storage room, in any Medical Examiner's office, funeral parlor, or mortuary, is a refrigerated facility where unclaimed bodies can be held for up to the ninety days required by statute. It also serves as a warehouse for the autopsied bodies that remain part of active investigations.

Non-medical personnel except policemen are not permitted to visit this room. But if they somehow do secure some higher-up's permission, they must wear a Moonsuit and be escorted at all times.

Unless you are accustomed to visiting the dead, you would find the smell of disinfectant and cavity blood very disconcerting. The BSR is kept very chilly to retard further decomposition of the stored remains. Ultraviolet light fixtures high on a wall burn 24/7 and a bug zapper hissed as it cooked a fly—rudimentary germ control.

Stainless steel gurneys, each bearing a body wrapped in a heavy translucent plastic body bag, are parked there. Red liquid has pooled and frozen inside the plastic. Other bodies are on racks on the walls stacked floor-to-ceiling like bunks on a submarine with each rack holding two bodies. They also are wrapped in murky plastic but not so murky that you couldn't see the nude bodies within.

Bare feet occasionally poke through gaps in the plastic, some with tags wired to a big toe. These are people waiting to be processed or waiting to be claimed by their next of kin. Several pairs of feet of unrestrained feet were so translucent you could see the dim smudge of bones within the flesh. Each is tagged by the current year (07) and the sequence in which they arrived at the morgue. (#07-3201).

If the plastic was cut away you'd see a brown paper bag resting between each body's knees that contained the victim's clothes, bloodied or not, (they are placed in a drying room before they are examined), and a case file clipped to the gurney. Some of the bodies have lain on the racks for so many years waiting to be claimed that all the fluids have drained from the tissue.

Some of the bodies are decorated with triad tattoos and seem to be illustrated lab specimens. If the 'tat' is upside down, it likely was self-inflicted. Typical are weeping Buddha's, the occasional Jesus, crucifixes, the names of their Mothers, wives or girlfriends, and words in Cantonese or one of the other languages spoken in Hong Kong, that loosely translate into English as PAIN, MERCY, GOD, and FORGIVE ME, written like they had been drawn by a child.

The tats do not necessarily have to be religious; the victim could have just been desecrating himself. Mottled levity sets in at the lowest parts of a body indicating where the blood had settled; the bloodless tissue takes on a waxy sheen that seems to highlight any tattoos.

One of the plastic bags had split open and a man's face was visible. Obviously no one that worked down here was going to acknowledge that the person had once been a human being, and therefore unworthy of the time it would take to recover the skull.

The exposed face had hardened with rigor into a distorted mask. One eye was closed but the other drooped open. Apparently the corpse had been a skinny man as the skin was stretched tight over the bony cheeks and the hollows of the eyes were pronounced. The mouth hung open as if he was sleeping. Kan wanted to close it, but he dared not.

He didn't because the detective knew that Dr. Dong would see the movement and criticize him for wasting his time attempting to restore dignity to a soulless slab of flesh and bones. Pathologists are taught that a body is just a body, never a person.

The men reached the far end of the BSR where Dong opened another airlock, then closed it behind them. Both men entered a final air lock, this one into the Decomp room, the final space that makes up the autopsy floor.

From his now-abandoned studies of medicine, Kan knew what to expect beyond the steel door in front of them. But like everything in life, the memory of really bad, bad things seems to dim with time.

As the two men stepped into the smaller room Kan had to admit to himself that he still was shocked by the tremendous assault on his olfactory senses.

The malodorous vapor reeked like a concoction of rotten eggs, vomit, and decomposed flesh. The 'Decomp' room is a small mortuary with a walk-in cooler, double sinks and cabinets, all in stainless steel, and a special Biohazard Level-4 ventilation system that sucks noxious odors and microorganisms out through an exhaust fan for multi-level repetitive scrubbing before being discharged to the outside atmosphere.

Every square centimeter of the Decomp room is painted a non-slip gray acrylic that is nonabsorbent and can withstand scrubbing and bleach. The centerpiece of this special room is a single transportable autopsy table which really is nothing more than a guttered cart frame with casters equipped with swivels wheels that have brakes.

Mounted on top of that is a body tray that rolls on bearings all of which is supposed to eliminate the need for human beings to lift bodies in the modern world, but in reality, doesn't.

The table is plumbed so its gutters drain to a hose, which in turn is attached to a slop sink. Dong and Kan used the rolling table to transport the partially autopsied body remains out of the cooler. The table's drain will not be necessary for this man. There was nothing left to drain. The corpse's body fluids were collected or washed down the drain a few hours previously when Dr. Lao began to autopsy him the first time.

They parked the autopsy table in the middle of the acrylic painted floor. The body had been placed inside an impervious Mylar pouch that looked like a cocoon on top of the shiny steel table.

There are no windows that open in this room with exception of a row of observation windows that have been installed too high for anyone to see through them.

That isn't a design flaw. It was just that the ME at the time the building was being constructed felt that no one needed to look into this room where the dead are bloated and green, covered in maggots, or burned so badly they look like charred wood.

The body already had received its Y incision beginning at the ends of the clavicle, meeting at the sternum, and then continuing down to a small detour around the navel and terminating at the pubis.

If the mystery man's post mortem hadn't been interrupted by the release of the deadly killer virus, the Y incision would have been sewed shut, sutured with what is called a baseball stitch using #7 twine by the pathologist or the assistant.

Now it would be necessary for Dr. Dong to use a scalpel if he decided to open the canoe. It would have appeared that the doctor was opening the seams of a hand-stitched rag doll.

After Kan and the doctor worked the large man out of the murky plastic pouch, Dr. Dong removed the file folder that had been taped to the interior of the bag. The doctor took a minute to glance through the body's autopsy protocol and the initial hand-written notes of the post mortem procedure.

The body belonged to a man almost six feet tall and weighing over 90 kilograms. If they had known his identity, they would have been aware that the man had turned fifty-years-of-age a week previously.

Found repeatedly in Lao's original notes was the words "within normal limits." The corpse's brain, heart, liver, and lungs, in fact all of the organs with exception to the intestine, apparently had appeared to be what they should have been for a healthy middle-aged man.

Then abruptly, the preliminary written notes stopped. Apparently that was when Lao discovered the vials, because his scribbling stops. He apparently was depending on the overhead microphone to continue to document his findings until he satisfied himself as to what he had found.

After Detective Kan had taken photos of the body, they returned the remains of the body to the walk-in cooler. Dr. Dong was impatient to get back to his office. Today had been his 'paper day.' He hadn't planned on doing any procedures until the following day.

Kan decided it wasn't necessary to remove the bodies of Dr. Lao and Betty Fang from the cooler to permit him to obtain the necessary photographs. So he took them where the bodies lay. The photos would serve as documentary proof of the deaths if this turned to be homicide. They would be needed in court to supplement Dr. Dong's testimony as to the manner by which the victims had died.

Dr. Dong understood that Kan had finished with what he had come to do. Both men left the Decomp room, carefully securing the airlock door behind them, and proceeded entered the first airlock back into the BSR, then through a second airlock after standing for the required three minutes under a harsh chemical spray, then a carwash-type centrifugal blower, before stepping back into the long hallway servicing the autopsy suite.

They returned to the biohazard Level-3 dressing room to remove their moonsuits that an attendant immediately began to disinfect for future use. In the Medical Examiner business, that could be at any moment.

Detective Kan thanked Dr. Dong. This time the senior pathologist took his hand before heading down the hall to check on his junior staff to make certain they were doing the jobs they were being paid for.

Kan headed for the 'up' elevator. When the doors finally slid open on the main service floor, he stepped off, relishing the relatively fresh air that he hungrily drew into his lungs.

————

14 October 2007, Monday, 4:35 p.m. (HKT)
Crimes Against Persons Department
Arsenal Street Police Headquarters—Third floor
Wan Chai district—Hong Kong Island

When I arrived back from the ME's office my desktop was covered with pink Please Call slips that Elizabeth had arranged in her concept of what order they should be answered.

I reshuffled them, rearranging them into my order of priority then set the slips aside while I made a call that was long overdue. This body-part harvesting ring had cost the lives of four city employees so far in the criminal's attempt to derail our investigation.

The gang kingpin apparently had mistakenly assumed that this tactic would force my people to shelve our investigations into their crimes. That wasn't going to happen. Not as long as I sat in the Chief Inspector's chair.

Thus far the Interpol agent Angry Dragon had treated the Hong Kong Police department like a lap dog in this investigation. He expected me to provide him with up-to-the minute status reports without the quid-pro-quo of sharing any of his intelligence with us.

While he played his international political game, the bodies of the good cops were continuing to pile up here in Hong Kong. That wasn't how the game of inter-department cooperation was going to be played on my watch.

Since the lucrative body part harvesting scheme was an official HKP investigation, I figured the hell with going along with Angry Dragon's initial request that our communications on this case be kept confidential.

Theoretically Interpol and the Hong Kong Police department were both on the side of law and order. The illegal harvesting of the body parts of the deceased definitely fell into the category of the most egregious of felony crimes.

I wasn't going to be their lap dog any longer. And I wasn't going to make a trip to my condo just to use the satellite cell phone to make a call to the agent's secret phone number that was being answered god knows where on the planet.

This case was different than the one that involved the interdiction of the of the North Korean-manufactured nuclear-tipped rocket. The one they had illegally sold to the People's Republic of China on which Angry Dragon and I had collaborated in 2005.

The current case was about bad guys slaughtering Hong Kong cops and Medical Examiner's personnel. They were making what would be a futile attempt at forcing us to back off and let them continue to operate their billion-dollar scheme.

Using my private line, I dialed the number that Angry Dragon had slipped me while we both had been attending a terrorism seminar at the U.S. FBI Academy at Quantico back in 2004.

Normally he answered the phone within five rings. However, this time the phone continued to ring until a digital answering machine picked up, and said, "In sixty seconds or less, state your name, message, time and date called and the phone subscriber will get back to you."

The message I left for Angry Dragon was short but not particularly sweet.

It went something like this, with the expletives deleted: "Agent, we now have a total of four Hong Kong city employees that have been murdered in this war with the body part cartel. In four hours, I am putting a full court press on these bastards."

"I say four hours because I figure it'll take me that long to get a fifty more detectives and one-hundred more uniforms transferred into my span of control to assisting in running down the names of the owners and silent partners of every Chinese funeral parlor, mortuary and other business that deals with the dead in Hong Kong, every damn one. I'll have patrol cars sitting on every one of these establishments with orders to stop and inspect any van or truck leaving or arriving 24/7."

"Anyone even remotely suspicious is going to get hauled into the cells downstairs and interrogated until we learn who is behind this operation. Once we get the names, I intend to snatch every one of them off the street, or out of their palatial Peak homes, wherever they call home."

"The Commissioner has issued me a written order that states "No consideration regardless of political affiliation or diplomatic immunity is to made or given that would in anyway deter the HKP from bringing the ringleaders to *final justice.*"

"And in case you are unfamiliar with that Hong Kong term, I bring to your attention that China performs more court-ordered executions than all the countries on the planet combined. Cop killers don't get any slack in Hong Kong, believe it."

"I am giving you those four hours to fax me every bit of intelligence in Interpol's or your own personal files on this operation of body robbers. After that, your secret agent man phone goes into harbor and the one-way information highway that you have been enjoying, shuts down permanently. Oh, looking at my watch, I see you now have only three hours and fifty-eight minutes left."

––––––

Wow, it felt good to do that. After I hung up, I called every district's COD, chief of detectives, and asked for the loan of every plainclothes officers they could spare for forty-eight hours. I reminded each of them of the current body count in this war being waged by the cartel against the HKP.

Each of them, a big surprise to me, even the ones who I knew resented the fact that a *Gweilo* had taken one of the few good commands available in the HKP, offered to drop every other active investigation they had going and dispatch their detectives to whatever location I desired.

After all, this was a direct attack on our department's family not to mention being a multiple cop killing. They got my grateful thanks. I filled the COD in on where their men should report, their mission, and my promise to keep each of the district precincts informed as to our progress.

Then I called the police commissioner's office and enlisted his commitment to personally call the head of the city's tax and business license departments. This fiefdom of HKSAR bureaucracy, which governs taxation, is located at city hall.

The commissioner's call to those *Loabans*, bosses of those civil departments, would ensure they all opened their files immediately and without exception to the detectives that would be reporting to their offices within the next two hours.

The commissioner suggested that he be the one to call the precinct commanders. He would order them to assign one out of every three patrol units under their command to sit on every business in their sector that deals with the dead; record and run every license plate of all cars parking in the immediate area to find out for the identity of the funeral parlor's employees; stop and inspect every vehicle capable of concealing purloined body parts, especially refrigerated vehicles; and report back to Lieutenant Du Ming with their findings.

I also called Hong Kong Customs, the Coast Guard, and the Hong Kong harbor patrol. I informed them that the commissioner had 'chopped' my command with authority to demand from them a list of all non-scheduled vessels, planes, helicopters, and commercial junks sixteen meters and larger that currently operated with relative impunity and damn little oversight in Hong Kong. Any vessel regardless of type that conceivably could be used to transport the body parts from a Hong Kong pier out to a mother ship beyond the twelve-mile limit.

The Chinese claim a 100-hundred mile security zone but there was no way I was going to get these officers, who hated taking orders from a *Gweilo* anyway, to throw out a dragnet of that size.

I stayed around the office until exactly 8:35 p.m. returning the most pertinent Please Call slips, discarding the remainder into the round file, especially those from the Media.

Before calling Zhou Ming to drive me home, I used my pin code to remotely access and listen to any messages on my home answering machine. There were none. Apparently Angry Dragon had never seen a pissed off former-NYPD homicide detective.

We stopped on the way home to my condo at the world-famous American (Peking) Restaurant located at 20 Lockhart Road in the Wan Chai district. I picked up a carryout order I had placed by phone before we had left the Arsenal Road HKP headquarters complex.

The American Restaurant is known for its Beijing dishes that are prepared in an almost identical manner in Hong Kong as they are cooked in the Chinese capital's rich culinary heritage. Although Richard Simmons would likely caution you to avoid the place, too much MSG, I loved the decadent delectable Peking dock and minced pigeon in lettuce leaves, my takeout selection for the evening.

Zhou dropped me off at my condo about 9:35 p.m. Then he drove off to yet another late arrival home for which I was certain his less-than-understanding wife would berate him.

I checked my mail and took the elevator to the penthouse. After unlocking the security locks I entered closing the condo entry door and locking it behind me, then stopped at the kitchen to set down the takeout. I went into the master bedroom to hang up the coat from my suit-of-the-day, pulled my tie off and tossed it into the pile to go to the dry clearers.

As I had walked through the living room to the bedroom I had observed that there were no calls waiting on my answering machine. So after removing my shirt, I dug the Interpol satellite phone out of the dirty laundry, replacing it with today's dirty shirt and carried the phone into the kitchen and with a sense of satisfaction, processed it through the compactor.

———

16 October 2007, Wednesday, 9:35 p.m. (HKT)
Crimes Against Persons Department
Arsenal Street Police Headquarters—Third floor
Wan Chai district—Hong Kong Island

The twenty-eight detectives of my Street Crime, Homicide and Anti-terrorism squads packed into our third floor conference room were finishing up on their last run through the computer printouts. The ones they had boldly absconded with from HKSAR tax office over the vocal protests and hollow threats of the office's director.

Every one of the cops—sitting, choosing to stand or because they had no chair, kneeling down on the carpet in the room—was bedraggled. The men unshaven, the women wearing makeup originally applied nearly two days earlier, none of which who had gone home in the past 48-hours. Fast food for the group had been catered in. A unusually subdued Elizabeth swept through the room every hour or so emptying ashtrays and picking up discarded food and beverage containers.

This had been the third and final review of the tax and business files that the fifty on-loan district detectives had carted out of city hall over the protests of the bean counters. I thanked each of them for their efforts, and authorized them to return to their home precincts.

The influx of fifty detectives had, unencumbered by the need to use much finesse, rolled over the bureaucrats at city hall. One of the clerks even had a heart attack from seeing his precious files leaving the building. He had to be ambulanced to the emergency room of Matilda Hospital on Mount Kellet Road.

The dedication and hard work by these men and women had zeroed in on the mostly likely target for our investigation, a large Chinese funeral parlor located on Ice House Street. It was located a block south of the New World Tower that fronted on Duddell street, and north of the Former Government house located on Upper Albert Road in the Central district.

The potpourri of data that free and unfettered access to the tax records provided our investigators, included the names of the owners of the Queen's Road Funeral Parlor, a bit of misrepresentation in the first place because the business was not located on that road.

The business had been purchased three years earlier for HK$3.9 million, about US$500,000, by two Australian surgeons whose licenses to practice had been revoked when the men had previously been charged but not convicted of international drug trafficking.

The files showed that Hong Kong's revenue police at the time had been suspicious that the business had become available in the first place. Files showed that the original Chinese owners who built the facility in 2000 had suddenly and without explanation disappeared one night during a particular vicious Hong Kong typhoon.

Two weeks later, two Australian gentlemen had appeared at the offices of the commercial properties department of the mortgage holder, BOC, or Bank of China. They had offered to take the property off the bank's deceased borrower rolls for the unpaid balance of the loan in French currency, which coincidently they had brought with them in four aluminum Halliburton briefcases.

As hard currency speaks much louder than the rights of the missing owners at the People's Republic of China-controlled Bank of China, the deal was concluded with the stipulation that if the missing owners ever 'surfaced' the deal would become null and void and the bank would refund the purchase price.

Investigative detectives of the HKP bank squad had made a note in their files to the effect that the bank officer overseeing the purchase, in calling the bank's caveat to the purchaser's attention, overhead one of the Australians make the statement, one which the man apparently assumed had gone unheard, to the effect that, "Not very damn likely, unless they can swim with an anchor tied to their ankles."

A review of the HKSAR vehicle title and registration records disclosed that both Australians owned Rolls Royce's with gold accruements, each valued for licensing purposes at HK$1,215,800 each, or US$156,000.

The detectives found that interesting considering that in the past three years the funeral parlor never had reported a annual gross income in excess of the Hong Kong equivalent of US$35,000.

Plainclothes patrolmen in unmarked cars had been sitting on the funeral parlor for the past 24 hours. They reported the two doctor's cars and a few vehicles apparently belonging to their staff were in the parking lot. Unmarked white vans were observed coming and going all day long and continuing into the night.

From their vantage point a block away, the surveillance teams had observed what appeared to be body bags being carried into facility; and lighter but more bulky and boxy, white containers looking something like the large ice chests that boaters and campers use, being loaded back into the vans before they departed.

The officers, their eyes fatigued from looking through their binoculars while at the same time trying to look like confused tourists checking their maps, also noticed that a steady stream of smoke was pouring from the building's smokestack. Since it was generally considered too warm at this time of year for local businesses to turn on their furnaces at night, the smoke was viewed as a fact of interest.

A check with the utility company revealed, after being faxed a copy of a vest-pocket search warrant the detectives were dispensing like they were Halloween candy, that the funeral parlor was drawing a great deal of electricity. The utility also confirmed that there was a large walk-in cooler for body storage maintained on the premise in addition to an electric crematory.

————

17 October 2007, Thursday, 7:00 a.m. (HKT)
Crimes Against Persons Division
Arsenal Street Police Headquarters—Third floor
Wan Chai district—Hong Kong Island

At 6:00 a.m. that morning, Inspector Mimi Yin issued orders pulling the surveillance units off the funeral parlor. She also talked with the Central district police commander by phone and requested that they instruct their sector patrols to stay away from Ice House Street until further notice.

Yin was afraid that the sudden influx of police cars in the area might alert the operators of the funeral parlor that they were under surveillance. Especially if the patrol units were seen to acknowledge the undercover teams in manner as cops on patrol subconsciously do. The district commander being aware that Yin was conducting an investigation of cop killings therefore was willing to turn a deaf ear to the usual objections always voiced by precinct commanders when anyone from the hated headquarters contingent intruded on their turf. This was obviously not the time for inter-department pissing matches.

At 7:00 a.m., now that our target had been identified and researched, I thanked everyone before ordering them to take the day off to get caught up on sleep, eat a decent meal, visit with loved ones, and get caught up on family matters.

Eight of the detectives, the survivors of Mimi's Five Ram raid team, volunteers all, with Mimi as team leader of course and assisted by SWAT, were going to take down the Queen's Road Funeral Parlor tonight, a few minutes after midnight. I felt that she had earned the right to go through the 'vertical coffin,' or the door, first if that was her wish. My going along would only give birth to the misconception that I didn't trust her leadership abilities.

After all the sleepy-eyed detectives had filed out of the office one-by-one, I sat at my desk and gave alerting Angry Dragon about the pending raid some earnest thought. Despite the fact that he hadn't returned my phone call of three days ago, there could be a reasonable explanation for that. Perhaps he had been out of town on assignment and one of his underlings had not relayed my message to him. Sitting there, I could come up with a dozen explanations why I should call and inform him of the raid, and despite my ego, none for not doing so.

After all, he had been invaluable to me and my birth country in seeing that the smuggled nuclear-tipped North Korean missile never reached the People Republic of China where it would have upset the world balance of power and likely would have been used to target American cities.

So, as the Interpol satellite phone was no longer available, I picked up my private office line and dialed the phone number I had for Angry Dragon.

The phone on his end rang about five times before once again the digital answering machine kicked in instructing the caller to leave a message. I left the message that we had located what we felt was the location of the local body part harvesting operation, gave him the name, address, and the fact we'd be raiding it with SWAT a few minutes after midnight tonight, 18 October, Friday.

I didn't have too much concern that any of our cops would be hurt tonight as I was going to follow the procedure I'd learned at the FBI academy many years ago.

The American FBI has both a procedure and a basic operating philosophy for raids. The procedure is that of the FBI's SWAT teams: Isolate—Contain—Negotiate. The philosophy is a bit more detailed but it was the plan I had suggested that Mimi use tonight.

It goes something like this if my memory serves: "Bring overwhelming force to a completely unsuspecting target, a force so overpowering, in a situation so totally controlled, that resistance is useless."

I again felt like an idiot explaining to a digital answering machine that we intended to confiscate all movable machinery and equipment and arrest everyone we found at the location. The occupants would be taken into custody and transported to the HKP's headquarters building.

There, we intended to strenuously interrogate them until one of their number agreed to give up the name of the leader of the operation, and the method by which the body parts were being smuggled out of Hong Kong.

I finished the brief message by saying we already had gotten a magistrate to sign some John Doe warrants, and I planned to use them to go after the leader and the route by which the parts were being smuggled out of Hong Kong as soon the information could be wrung out of the subjects we would be bringing in early tomorrow morning.

Hanging up the phone, I returned to my endless war with Elizabeth, her putting paperwork into, me taking it out and signing it and tossing it into my out-basket, my goal being to end up with an empty in-basket. I even considered locking my office door from the inside but felt that wouldn't be playing fair.

I couldn't have known at that time just how bad tomorrow morning's raid would go and what they'd find once they raided the funeral parlor.

12

18 October 2007, Friday, 2:25 a.m. (HKT)
The Queen's Road Funeral Parlor
Ice House Street—Central district
Hong Kong Island

Lieutenant Du Ming's phone call—Mimi had asked him to go along with SWAT and her team on the funeral parlor raid after she took into consideration that Ming had five unsolved homicides on his plate directly attributable to the war the body part harvesters were waging on my department—woke me out of a restless sleep about 2:25 a.m. with both good and bad news.

Inspector Yin had asked Ming to call because she had her hands full securing the abattoir-like scene that had greeted them when they broke down the door at the funeral parlor fifty-five minutes previously.

Yin was fast running out of patience, having to remind her detectives against inadvertently stepping on evidence as the teams of crime scene criminalists struggled to complete the raising of fingerprints, crime scene photography, sketching layouts, collecting shell casings, and the liberal lay down of Luminol to identify blood sources.

Feeling like a coward I asked for the good news first. Ming responded, saying, "This is the illegal cutting operation that we have been looking night and day for the past two weeks, alright. It is concealed in the basement. There is an old but fully equipped operating room. We found it located on the same floor in the complex as a crematorium and a large walk-in cooler."

"Boss, the raid went down at exactly 1:30 a.m. Whoever remodeled the facility appeared to have a reasonable amount of respect for the dangers involved in working on corpses that arrive without any knowledge of their past medical and disease history. Detective Kan tells us the suite was designed to handle biolevel-3 hazards."

Ming continued, "The surgical suite contains a operating table and a pair of parabolic high-intensity spotlights that provide stark and icy light to the room, not that the patients would be complaining."

"No body parts were found on the premises; the cooler was filthy but empty; the outer skin of the crematory oven was still warm to the touch; and none of the white refrigerated cases the gang has been using to transport the harvested parts were found. Inspector Yin says she thinks that everything portable was removed before the raid."

"Okay," I asked, "what do the creeps you've taken into custody have to say? Have they coughed up the name of the gang's leader or how they are getting the product out of Hong Kong?"

"That's the bad news, Boss," Ming said. "We discovered a total of five males and one female; two Caucasians and four Chinese at the scene. All of them were found in the walk-on cooler. Each had been shot in the back of the skull execution-style with a small caliber semi-automatic pistol. From the shell casings we are assuming it was a .22 caliber. The writing on the ejected brass appears to be French according to Inspector Yin."

Readers, there is no nice way to tell you this, but that caused me to totally *lose it*! "Damn it, I was depending on the raid netting suspects we could bring to headquarters and interrogate none to politely until we pried the identity of who is financing and controlling the operation out of them. Not to mention finding out how they are getting the body parts out of Hong Kong!"

I continued, "When I talked with Dr. Lu Dong, he estimates this gang is probably removing bones, tissue, organs and corneas from over a thousand bodies a year. Even with a certain amount of rejects, they still should be clearing 100 million U.S. dollars from the Hong Kong operation alone."

Still livid, I went on, "I doubt that decision-makers behind the scam are the two defrocked surgeons who own that place."

"Boss," Ming interrupted, "I think we may have to look a little farther than the docs for the people behind this. The two doctors were found along with the four dead Chinese technicians in the storage room. Everyone was dressed in scrubs."

"We broke into their lockers and found their identification, credit cards, cash and some expensive jewelry. Between them, the doctors had an eight ball of cocaine in their lockers. But since their personal effects were there, it doesn't appear that the motive for the killings was robbery."

"There were no signs of forced entry. It looks like the doers had the key to the service door on the north side of the building. The truck drivers probably didn't know what was coming next. All they knew was that they were supposed to hump the harvested product that was ready to transport out of the country out to their waiting vans, and leave the area to meet up with the smuggler."

Lieutenant Ming continued to speculate, "After the transfer was complete, a couple professional shooters must have gone in, rounded up everyone and forced them at gunpoint into the cooler. The shooters must have had orders to eliminate anyone who could give up information, testify against the principles, or disclose the method to authorities by which the product was getting out of the country."

Interrupting, I said, "Ming, that means that someone found out about tonight's raid on the funeral parlor, before the fact," I surmised. "*That* someone knew that if we detained one or more of the suspects at the scene, we haul them to Arsenal Street and subject them to intense interrogation until someone broke. Until someone traded away the possibility of his own incarceration by giving up the names of the higher-ups, and how they were getting the product out of Hong Kong."

"The kingpin must have known that he didn't have time to relocate the entire operation or any of the equipment they need to harvest the bones, tissue, corneas, and such out of the funeral parlor. About all they were able to accomplish before the raid was to remove all the product that was ready to ship, and get it moving out of Hong Kong."

"And," I reasoned, "the Boss had to make certain that none of the operators would survive to be interrogated, and eventually give up his or her identity and the smuggling route."

"So it was purely a business decision, much like their killing of two cops at the funeral parlor and two people from the ME's office, not to mention the dead man who was used as a Trojan Horse to carry the virus spores into the autopsy suite. It was strictly a business decision that led them to execute the six men you found at the scene. A very clean operation. No loose lips, no valuable body parts gone to waste, and now they'll to go to the mattresses until we give up looking for them, or have a bigger crisis on our plates."

Ming reflected, "Boss, you hit the nail on the head. They are cleaning up behind themselves, eliminating anyone who can rat them out. They'll write off the loss of the specialized equipment and facilities we'll seize here at the funeral parlor. Then they'll start up business again in Hong Kong when things have cooled down. I certainly like to catch the *Loaban* of this operation. He must have international connections; have access to a lot of seed money; and be able to reach with impunity into Hong Kong to order the murders of people who get in his operation's way."

"Ming, I think you are right on the *Meiguo*, the money. Unless we get a major break we'll never catch the guy that is running this operation. Maybe we can create our own big break. Oh, and Ming, does Inspector Yin want me down at the scene?"

Ming replied, "No, Boss. You've seen a surgical suite and dead bodies before. What would be the purpose? I plan on leaving a half dozen SWAT guys here when the Criminalists finish up just to make certain no one tries to return and remove any of this expensive equipment before we get a formal impound order for the place. I'll see you back at the office in a few hours." he concluded, as he rang off.

Hanging the phone up, I rolled over and tried to return to sleep. But my mind continued to replay the conversation I'd just had with my homicide lieutenant. *Looking for a silver lining in a very dark cloud*, I thought, *well, at least none of the good guys got killed or injured tonight. Perhaps I could generate a break in this case. God knows that no one was going to hand us one.*

———

18 October 2007, Friday, 9:35 a.m. (HKT)
Crimes Against Persons Department
Arsenal Street Police Headquarters—Third floor
Wan Chai district—Hong Kong Island

The expected bedlam had already started when Zhou Ming dropped me off at the office on Friday morning.

Elizabeth, appearing internally conflicted as she was wont to be as of late, told me Inspector Mimi Yin, Lt. Du Ming, and Inspector Chen Ho had had closeted themselves into our conference room.

After setting my briefcase on my desk, having first to push aside a four-inch high stack of Please Call slips, I sighed and walked down the carpeted hallway to the conference room. I had reached the door and was beginning to turn the knob when Elizabeth slipped in between the door and myself, placing her considerable bodice and well-manicured hands against my chest.

Giving me one of her come hither looks that she apparently if incorrectly assumed projected sincerity, she said, "Boss, they said the meeting was closed to everyone, including you. I think I overhead Mimi saying that they were batting around the question of whether the entire body parts case had gone down the *loo*, the toilet, after the mass execution of the operators at the funeral parlor."

Returning to my office, I was thinking, *Unless we can discover how the gang is getting the dissected product out of Hong Kong, we'll never be able to interdict it and the case will go into the cold case files. We might shut the operation down temporarily until the gang covertly arranges for another surgical suite and the professional staff to operate it. But for the most part, the bodies that now lie on the chilly tables in the ME office have taken their secrets of the operation with them to the grave.*

Unknown to me at the time, the kingpin of the gang was making sure the police never learned how the gang was getting the product out of Hong Kong. He had hired two killers from the Wild West triad of the Macau underworld, as the citizens of Macau have nicknamed the gang, to assassinate the two unlicensed surgeons and their dissecting assistants, and it had been an excellent if expensive investment.

The Macau gang's *Loaban* had instructed his two executioners that as soon as they finished their mission to eliminate all witnesses at the funeral parlor, they were to dump their weapons down a nearby sewer and unobtrusively walk northeast on Ice House Road to Queensway. There a taxi would be waiting to transport them back to the jetfoil pier located at the HK-Macau Ferry terminal, just west of Central.

The triad boss had charged the kingpin an unusually high premium to hire the men to accomplish what was essentially a simple, straightforward assassination killing, something the two men had done dozens of times before for a lot less money. There reason for the premium would soon become evident.

After the jetfoil had pulled away from the Hong Kong side of the HK-Macau ferry terminal, it accelerated up on its foils and made the trip to Macau in fifty-five minutes. The other passengers on the foil had just gotten off their jobs in Hong Kong and were headed for Macau's all-night casinos to seek their fortune.

The two hitters were meet by triad's 426, Red Pole, and a couple of his minions. The two killers were enthusiastically slapped on the back and told what a great job they had done thereby enriching the coffers of their triad.

All of them had piled into the 426's shiny black 2007 Mercedes stretch limo. Liquor was freely passed around as the driver started the car and proceeded towards the exit through the adjacent warehouse complex. Normally it was a three-minute ride to the Avenida da Amizade, the access road that services the People's Republic of China's HK-Macau ferry terminal.

Twenty minutes later the limo, now lighter by the weight of the two men who were currently fish food for Macau harbor's enormous shark population, arrived at the access road. Then the limo turned right for 150 meters before crossing the bridge that led to the triad's covert headquarters on Rua dos Pescadores.

————

18 October 2007, Friday, 10:00 a.m. (HKT)
Seaplane Dock—Fenwick Pier
Wan Chai North district
Hong Kong Island

Cary Erwin, ex-Australian air force pilot, a ex-pat who had fled Sydney in front of a felony Transportation of Heroin indictment some five years previously, entered the Fenwick pier security gate, showed his HKSAR pilot's license, and after opening his black flight case for inspection, closed it and walked down the ramp to the seaplane pier.

It was a beautiful, sunny fall day, this Friday, thanks to a persistent north breeze that had earlier dispersed the morning fog. A bunch of ducks were clamoring, strutting around, and playing chicken with persons walking down the docks to various piers.

Few seaplanes currently operate out of Hong Kong. Thus only a single finger pier was required for those that chose to do their mooring at Fenwick Pier. Obstacles to more of the unique aircraft seeking to do in business in Hong Kong included a harbor that was filthy with floating debris, thousands of ships that were anchored-out in the harbor at any one time which restricted available taxiing and landing lanes, and the onerous rules, regulations, fees, and out-and-out under-the-table kickbacks required by

HKSAR bureaucrats since China had administratively taken Hong Kong back in June of 1997.

A floating seaplane pier is shaped like a "U" with squared off corners. The pilot must have access to every part of the aircraft to complete the checklist that is mandatory before every departure. The aircraft must be parked nose out perpendicular to the longitudinal leg of the finger pier.

Additionally, a portable floating pier is needed to permit the pilot to turn and inspect the propeller. It is swung out of the way by the pilot prior to engine start up and would remain tied off alongside the larger pier for the aircraft's return.

On either side for the aircraft were floating segments of pier that were custom-arranged for the aircraft flown by the pier's lessee. Grimy white rubber bumpers were placed between the pier edges and the floating pontoons of the aircraft to prevent damage to the plane's 'floats' or 'pontoons' from boat wakes, or wave conditions generated by storms.

Erwin and the Bank of China owned the marvelous old bright yellow Beaver floatplane. The aircraft was a real workhorse powered by a single radial engine. She had started her life fifteen year ago flying off Australian waters as a flying ambulance. Vintage Beavers are still preferred for that life-saving function as they are the most reliable seaplanes afloat.

Erwin walked up alongside the moored aircraft and attempted to peek into the rear cargo area. He observed that four white refrigerated ice chests had been loaded into the aircraft. The chests apparently had been delivered to his aircraft when Erwin was still sleeping off his nightly hangover. Erwin had no idea how the person who brought the chests got into the secured facility in the early morning hours, and didn't want to know.

His job was merely to fly the refrigerated chests to a predetermined location on the South China Sea, and while still airborne, locate a motorized red-sailed Chinese junk that would be flying a certain sequence of flags on its mainstay. Erwin would circle the general area around the vessel before landing, looking for floating flotsam and seeking to determine the direction and speed of the prevailing surface wind, the height of the seas, and distance between the swells.

Erwin would never harm to his aircraft regardless of the amount of promised remuneration. He always took the time to ascertain that the landing conditions around the junk were acceptable before he would turn into the wind, land, turn around, and taxi back to the waiting vessel.

The junk captain would launch a fishing skiff. It was twenty-foot-long and eight-feet-wide and had a net roll mounted on the aft end. A couple rough looking types whose job it was to unload his cargo and transport it back to the junk, would man the skiff.

As soon the skiff boat was back tied up securely to the junk, and the chests were being carefully transferred off the skiff up to the vessel's deck, Erwin would be given an a visual signal from the boat's bridge instructing him to depart immediately, something he always did in an expeditious manner not wanting to chance that the coast guard would make a impromptu visit after observing the unusual rendezvous of the plane with the fishing junk.

The one time he had been so foolish as to look back over his shoulder during a take off run, he had observed a cargo net had been lowered from the junk by a small dead-leg crane. The white chests he had delivered were being carefully placed in the net, one-by-one, and raised to the deck of the junk.

———

Today, the aircraft hadn't been out on an earlier tourist picture-taking flight so Erwin would have to go through the entire checklist. If nothing else he was a very careful pilot.

He pulled off the wing covers, necessary due to the corrosive particulates present in the heavy industry-generated smog of Hong Kong. He stowed those in a large lockable white triangle-shaped fiberglass box that he had installed with tie down bolts in the corner of his assigned dock space.

Then he stepped onto the aircraft's floats and drained the water traps on the bottom of the fuel tanks before climbing up on the float's strut to eyeball the gas level verifying that the plane was topped off with fuel.

Erwin climbed back down and stepped off the float before making a circuit around the aircraft to check the flaps, rudder, and all movable flight surfaces on the plane to ensure everything was secure and unimpeded as far as its ability to be manipulated on command.

When he was flying in Australia he had known a pilot who habitually had conducted sloppy or minimal safety checks prior to take off. Eventually, what went around came around, and a loose bolt or wedged flap had resulted in the pilot and his passenger's untimely demise.

Erwin carefully stepped onto the portable floating dock. He pulled the prop around several times by hand to remove pooled oil from the big radial engine. Stepping back off the dock, Erwin unlatched one end of the portable floating dock and using a boathook, pulled the free end of the dock over to him and secured it to the finger dock.

Only then did he pull himself up into the cockpit and strap himself into the left hand pilot's seat. He hit the starter then clicked on the engine switch. The engine turned sluggishly at first, as it hadn't been run since the previous afternoon. Then the radial engine belched exhaust and a lot of noise.

Methodically the pilot checked each of the aircraft's gauges including the magnetos to ensure everything was operating inside the 'green' as specified by the Manufacturer's normal operating range operating manual.

As the engine continued to warm, Erwin yanked one last time on his seat belt and looked around to make certain the area around his pier was clear. He slipped a pair of dark Ray Ban sunglasses onto his aristocratic Australian nose and took one more look around as he set the flaps and trim tabs for takeoff.

He gave the rudder pedals a little kick to make certain they were moveable, and pushed and yanked the yoke forward and back twice to make sure the elevator surfaces were unimpeded.

Straightening in his seat, he took one further look around to make certain he was clear of traffic before advancing the throttle forward, easing the aircraft out of the slip before beginning a fast circle taxing around the immediate harbour until he had built up enough speed for take off. He kept up the high-speed taxi, *slap-slap-slap-slap* across the waves, until he felt that the 112 kilometers airspeed noted on the plane's gauges was enough to get the old bird back into the air.

As the plane's indicted speed across the water continued to increase he gently pulled back the yoke with his fingertips to lift the nose off the water and better sense what the aircraft was doing. Once the Beaver broke the water's surface adhesion and lifted off Erwin continued to hold the yoke in his stomach until he had reached a height equivalent to 2,000 feet. The aircraft was functioning well in the typically humid Asian day.

Erwin came west to a course heading of 285 degrees for five minutes to avoid over-flying Sheung Wan before coming to a heading of 180 degrees directly south over the West Lamma Channel. He held the course for ten minutes as the aircraft continued to fly over the South China Sea, passing over the island of Cheung Chau; a former pirate enclave, home to the Pak Tai temple, Tung Wan beach, and Tin Hau temple, all of which soon passed out of sight under the plane's left wing.

The plane continued on its course for fifteen more minutes, flying over the commonly-used shipping lanes before Erwin spotted the junk's red sails and confirmed the sequence of the maritime flags being flown by the boat.

Erwin began to decrease his altitude gradually as he first flew by the starboard side of the junk, continuing on for five more miles until he had convinced himself there were no Harbour patrol or coast guard boats lurking in the vicinity. And that the surface wind although negligible was out of the south.

He reduced the Beaver's altitude further to just 400 feet and put the heavy plane into a wide, gentle 180-degree turn headed back for the junk, which put the aircraft's nose just to the left of the red sails of his target.

The pilot kept decreasing the plane's elevation until the bird plopped down on a ribbon of choppy sea, bouncing along *slap-slap-slap-slap* while Erwin kept the yoke pulled back into his stomach. When the airplane had slowed to a slow walking pace, he used the power of his engine to deflect the thrust from his propeller against on the vertical tail rudder surface to turn around and taxi back to within fifty meters of the junk. Per established procedure, he continued to hold the Beaver's nose into the wind and the propeller turning over at an idle.

The approaching skiff began to slow as it approached the idling aircraft. One of the men stepped onto the aircraft's starboard pontoon, tied the skiff up fore and aft to the starboard struts using a pair of hemp ropes, and opened the plane's rear cargo compartment door. Then the man carefully began to individually maneuver the chests out of the plane's cargo compartment, transferring them into the waiting arms of the other man in the skiff.

When all four chests had been removed, Erwin was startled to hear a loud mournful blast of the junk's foghorn, certainly was not part of the regular procedure. With his attention distracted he didn't see the skiff man set a lunchbox-sized package into the aircraft's cargo compartment before closing and latching the door.

The man untied the mooring ropes and stepped back into the skiff where both men began tying down the chests before heading back to the junk. Just then the 'leave now' signal came from the junk's bridge

As the junk started its engines, Erwin pushed his craft's throttle forward to the stops and bounced along on the sea's surface with the yoke pulled back into his stomach until the aircraft achieved takeoff speed and broke surface adhesion to begin its climb back up through the humid air of the West Lamma Channel back to the altitude of 2,000 feet. Erwin normally then would make a turn to a heading of 90 degrees for return to Fenwick Pier on the north side of Hong Kong Island.

But when the aircraft reached exactly 250 feet over the water, the mercury switch in the package that the skiff man had placed in the plane's cargo hold, dumped, causing the ignition of ten pounds of weapons-grade C-4 explosive, shredding both Erwin and the airplane.

A pair of young German lesbians enjoying the sun and water on the infamous gay beach, Cheung Sha, on the southern coast of Lamma Island, happened to look up from where they were laying on beach towels sipping on the cold beers they had brought along in a cooler, later told authorities that the noisy floatplane had been approaching from the south. It was there one second, then there had been a blinding white flash, and then there was nothing, only small pieces of it falling into the water.

————

18 October 2007, Friday, 4:00 p.m. (HKT)
Olala Restaurant—Specialty, French Cuisine
#1 Electric Street—Wan Chai district
Hong Kong Island

The gang kingpin that the police were so desperately seeking in the body part caper was having a early dinner at the Olala, a French restaurant, on the first floor of the Hung Dak building when his cell phone rang. Finishing the sip of red wine he had been imbibing, he wiped his lips with a linen napkin before answering.

The one-sided conversation that ensued was short and sweet to the phone call's recipient. Calling was the skipper of the junk that was used to transport the body parts that the aircraft that flew out past the 12-mile limit, to a port not under the control of the Chinese communists. He had just reported that the last planned shipment out of Hong Kong had gone off without any glitches.

However the skipper said, he regretfully had to report that the aircraft that had been smuggling the illicit shipments for a year had mysteriously exploded in mid-flight after departing, totally destroying the aircraft and pilot.

The kingpin snapped the phone closed without saying goodbye and resumed eating his meal, chucking to himself that with the surgical suite operators dead, along with the naïve pilot that had smuggled the body parts out of Hong Kong gone to meet his maker, there was only one loose string that had to be tied before he would feel comfortable, free of discovery and prosecution. And he didn't intend to wait very long to eliminate that thorn from his side.

––––––

19 October 2007, Saturday, 11:05 p.m. (HKT)
Victoria Police Station
Old Bailey Street at Hollywood Road
Central district—Hong Kong Island

Patrolman 3rd grade Lau Lai walked out of the employee's exit of Hong Kong's Victoria Police station into the parking lot. He'd just changed into his civilian clothes, called civvies. He was mentally and physically beat—too tired to even stop for a drink before heading home. He'd reported to work as scheduled at 7 a.m. that morning, then been informed by his supervisor halfway through his shift that he was being held over to pull a 'double.'

The supervisor knew but didn't mention to Lau that his overtime was made necessary due to the unofficial practice by some of the older cops of suddenly coming down with the 'blue flu' when they heard there was a chance of big money to be made gambling on the horse races out at Happy Valley that night after hearing of the unusually wide point spread that was being reported on the Internet.

Lau had told the sergeant "Okay," and dragged his butt though a second eight-hour shift, answering calls that typically never were very interesting in the Central district. Lau sometimes regretted ever joining the tourist police although he had to admit it meant a little more money in his paycheck.

––––––

Businesses located in the Central district are mostly toney establishments that service the tourist trade. Hotels such as the Landmark, Mandarin Oriental, and New World Tower; tourist attractions like the Central Market, the shuttered Victoria Prison, Queen's Theatre, Swiss House, the Hopewell Center, the touristy clubs in Soho; and various government offices including the HKSAR Legislative Council Building located in Statue Square on Chater Road.

From 8 a.m. until just before midnight, the Central district is largely populated by foreign tourists. During those hours, half of the sworn officers assigned to the Central police station staff the tourist police contingent.

Assisting tourists for these trained and educated officers is considered good duty because you are generally free from the hazards of attempting to arrest desperate armed criminals in the commission of their various violent crimes.

Applicants for the position of the sought-after job of tourist policeman, which is set apart from regular constables by a red tab on the left chest and a unique shoulder patch, must fluently speak English and one other foreign language such as Japanese or German. They must be naturally polite which is an ingrained trait in most Chinese anyway, and are intensively trained in demonstrating a mindset that appears to favor the side of the tourist in minor altercations or disagreements with Hong Kong merchants.

———

Lau walked into the parking lot that had been formerly used by the adjacent prison, thumbing his remote door opener as he approached his car. The cops in Hong Kong had been warned by their supervisors to maintain increased situational awareness since the killing of the two cops, both of whom he knew casually and had partied with in the past.

Some of the younger cops his age, noting the age of the decedents, were already beginning to call in sick on the evening shifts, either out of fear or imagined self—preservation. Lau thought that was pretty funny especially because two cop killings in a police department of Hong Kong's size couldn't be classified as serial killings.

But Lau did note that despite the perceived increased threat, no more money had been allocated to replace the broken and burned out lamps in the freestanding light poles in the police station parking lots around the city.

The officer initially didn't see that all four tires on his car had been slashed. He'd just opened the driver's door and fallen into the well-worn seat before he sensed the car was sitting lower than usual. When he got out of the car and inspected his flattened tires, he split out a long series of oaths, a practice he normally didn't condone in his personal behavior.

Lau's mind was too tired to address the question of the motivation behind the vandalism, or to wonder who had committed the crime.

It was after 11 p.m. With his car out of operation until tomorrow he'd have to take the Mid-level escalator up to the Mosque Street apartment he shared with another cop. Tomorrow, in daylight, he would figure out how to get the tires replaced with some cheap recaps.

Lau walked back into the station and reported the vandalism to the desk sergeant. Which meant he received another lecture on maintaining his situation awareness until the cop killer was caught.

By the time the well-meaning supervisor had finished his admonishment, Lau had only a half hour until his alternative source of getting home shut down operation for the night. So he hurried out through the police station's front entrance and climbed the stairs up to the escalator station.

————

In 1993 the city fathers had built the 792-meter-long (2,600 foot) escalator between the Central Market and the residential area of the Mid-level district with the intent of reducing traffic congestion in the Central district.

The Escalator is actually a series of 20 escalators and three travelators, more-or-less horizontal people movers, all of which have entrance/exits to the surface streets the system crosses.

Even though the escalator system provides quick access to the toney bars and restaurants at its northern terminus near Soho, and the concrete canyons of the Mid-level district at it's southern terminus, all in all, as judged by its value to the entirety of Hong Kong citizens, it is pretty much a pink elephant.

Current day, the single-direction escalator heads down or northeast from 6:00 a.m. to 10:20 a.m. to transport people who live in Midlevel to work in Central, and then reverses and heads up, or southwest until Midnight.

This was particularly convenient for Patrolman Lau this evening as he lived at the far upper end of the escalator. But he had to hurry to get on it before the barricades went up and the system stopped running for the night.

————

Lau was boarding the escalator essentially in the middle of the system. He tried to enjoy the scenery and bright lights as it climbed over Staunton and Elgin streets, Caine Road, and the three short access streets that service Prince's Terrace.

When Lau reached the top, the end of the line, at Mosque Street and stepped off, city workers had already set the bright yellow-and-red barricades out and then driven off to do the same at each of the escalator's entrance/exits along the nearly half-mile route.

Sticking his hand deep in his jacket pockets to ward off the chill of the moist evening fog, he headed southeast on Mosque Street after casting a nervous glance at the darkened Mosque. The Muslim house of worship sat on a double lot just south of the escalator's upper terminus station. The mosque leaders had decided to turn off all lighting in the parking lot of the Mosque to deter the on-going vandalism that had plagued the house of worship since 9/11.

———

While it appears to tourists that the only thing Hong Konger's worship is money, religion plays a large part in the lives of its citizens. Most of the population is either Buddhist or Taoist. There are about 500,000 residents that profess to be Christian. Only 100,000 of Hong Kong residents claim to practice the Muslim religion.

Muslims being such a minority as compared to the other religions being practiced in the HKSAR is suspected to be one of the reasons that gangs of youths have systematically been defacing the city's Mosques.

The elders of this particular Mosque had adapted the out-of-sight, perhaps-out-of-mind, thinking. Since the automatic timers at the mosque began extinguishing all exterior lights at 11:00 p.m., vandalism had been reduced.

As he began the short walk to his apartment Lau heard a faint sound that reminded him of someone stumbling on concrete. Most of the sidewalks and parking lots in the Midlevel district were cracked and potholed. Their deplorable condition required attention to where you were stepping even in the daylight, let alone in the darkness on this moonless night.

Remembering his sergeant's warning to be alert to his surroundings, Lau stopped and carefully scanned the area around with his eyes as well as he could in the darkness. It was particularly difficult to see anything in the Mosque's parking lot due to the three-story height of the dark brick building beyond it.

He stood absolutely still and forced his ears to seek out sounds normally beyond a human's scope of audio capacity. There, he heard it again. Like a foot being moved to get a better purchase on a gravely surface. His mind shouted, *Get out of here, fool!*

But he waited realizing he would never be able to bluff a criminal in the future if he couldn't control his inner fears, here only a block from his own home, and in a familiar environment.

Perhaps it was a rat, Lau thought. Large wharf rats up to twelve inches in length and occasionally larger are plentiful in Hong Kong. But normally they are seen at much lower elevations close to the warehouses and the water that provide the *go-down* businesses with tenants.

Suddenly a flashlight lit up the darkness of the parking area. He could hear the steps of someone slowing walking across the gravely surface of the deteriorated parking lot towards him.

All of a sudden, exhilaration flooded Lau's mind and senses. Yes, he wordlessly yelled to himself. What a *Hau gui*, a Sea Turtle. It's just the Mosque's night watchman he'd seen a few times before that walked the perimeter of the building during the dusk-to-dawn hours.

All of the pent-up tension in his shoulders relaxed as he shielded his eyes from the glare of the flashlight that was focused on him. *I'll bet I scared the watchman as much as he scared me,* Lau thought humorously.

The watchman was now about 50 meters away and still walking towards me, Lau thought. *Apparently the guard was going to get a visual I.D. on me to fill up his incident log before returning to his rounds. Paperwork, always the paperwork,* Lau quipped to himself.

Following a barely discernable single *Phut* Lau didn't even hear, the first shot slammed into his chest to the right of his sternum, missing his heart but perforating arteries and a lung. The kinetic energy on his body drove Lau to his knees. The hydrostatic shock that followed the initial round pulsed through the tissues along the wound channel, rupturing the cells closest to the wound and causing blood to be force-fed to the arteries in his brain. The over-pressure behind the blood exploded capillaries in his brain, shorting out his sense of thought. In a single nanosecond patrolman Lau was deaf, dumb, and unconscious, all in a heartbeat.

The shooter realized that the first bullet hadn't hit the desired target. It hadn't been the kill shot the shooter had intended. The only weapon to which the shooter had access was intended solely for plinking targets at close range. Or close up and personal, like inside seven meters. Why did I shoot from over twenty meters away? The possibility that Lau might be armed even though it was against regulations spurred the shooter to go to a knee on the damp pavement and empty the remaining five rounds—*Phut-Phut-Phut-Phut-Phut*—in the pistol's magazine, at Lau.

Sensing rather than seeing that Lau was still moving the shooter frantically ejected the weapon's magazine, reached into a jacket pocket and pulled a handful of extra cartridges out, dropping one in haste as well as a small scrape a piece of a pink Please Call slip on which was marked with Lau's work schedule for October.

The shooter frenziedly thumbed the fresh cartridges into the metal magazine, its sharp edge completely shredding the thumb of one of the latex gloves the assassin wore.

Slamming the magazine back into the pistol with a heel of a palm, the shooter stood and continued a careful approach to where Lau lay withering in his own blood, heels drumming on the asphalt.

A larger gun, a .45 or .44 caliber, neither which the shooter had access to would have killed the cop instantly by completely obliterating his brain. However, the deficient in hydraulic shock posed by the smaller gun permitted a minor medical miracle that allowed Lau to briefly regain consciousness.

But as the man's consciousness returned so did pain and fear. It seemed to scorch his returning senses, causing Lau to scream and thrash around, causing the shooter alarm. The shooter knew this was a high-occupancy residential neighborhood of mostly Chinese bureaucrats and city employees struggling to stay ahead of poverty.

Some insomniac would soon become curious. And decide to stop watching late night television long enough to step out of their front door to take a look around to see what was making all the racket.

While this concern streaming through the shooter's mind, his victim's vision and hearing was returning. Lau found himself able to think once again, and even tried to speak. He began to cry out even though he fatalistically knew he was dying. Someone had shot him and perhaps it was the shape standing over him. Lau weakly reached out a bloody hand attempting to grab on to the shooter's pant leg.

This action infuriated the shooter so much that a large gob of spittle was spat onto the dying man's face and the pistol fired four more times, *Phut-Phut-Phut-Phut*, two at close range into the center of the man's forehead, and the remainder into his groin.

Now certain that Lau was dying the shooter turned and ran around to the rear of the Mosque where the stolen getaway car for the night stood waiting. Realizing there was no further need for the gun, the shooter threw it as far as possible into the darkness, betting that if the gun was found it would be by one of the Muslims who worshipped at this Mosque.

Considering the poor relations currently between the police and the Muslim community who were tired of being rousted everytime someone in Hong Kong committed an act that the police attributed to be of terrorist origin, the weapon probably would be buried or resold. In no case would a member of the Mosque's faithful turn it over to the cops.

In addition to the over-confidence the shooter brought to the killing field, the excessively long distance of the initial shot taken with a short-range weapon, and other careless mistakes, this assumption as to the gun's eventual demise was just another example of lack in judgment and due diligence the shooter would come to regret.

———

20 October 2007, Sunday, 1:30 a.m. (HKT)
Crime scene—Killing of a cop
132 Mosque Street
Midlevel district—Hong Kong Island

Lieutenant Du Ming had finally awakened me after using a credit card to slip my building's front door security lock, take the elevator to the penthouse floor, and pounding on my front door until he woke me from my slumber.

As I stood there aghast in my rumpled PJ's in my open front door, Ming pushed his way past me into the condo and said, "Get dressed, Boss. There has been another cop killing. The commissioner and Dispatch both tried to call you. All they received was a busy signal back from your line."

"When Dispatch demanded an emergency break-in on the line, the phone company told them there was no conversation in-progress. Then the commissioner had them contact me at the crime scene."

"The commissioner ordered me to send someone over here to see if you had also become a victim of this serial killer. Under our guidelines, this case officially became a serial murder case tonight when the sleaze increased his body count to three dead cops."

Ming took a deep breath, and continued, "I decided to come because I thought that perhaps with all the crap the commissioner's office is dumping on you, because the operators of the body part harvesting gang were already dead when Inspector Yin and I raided the funeral parlor, you might have gotten exasperated since that probably eliminated any chance of our solving the case, and said, fuck it, and just left the receiver off the hook."

I laughed, and said, "Don't think I didn't consider it, Ming," I admitted. "But I probably knocked the kitchen receiver off the hook by accident when I was fixing dinner. Give me a couple minutes to get dressed and I'll ride back to the crime scene with you."

———

When we arrived at the crime scene the criminalists had pretty much finished their processing. They hadn't come up empty-handed this time, or so the head CSI had assured me.

One of the rookie criminalists still in-training had wandered to the rear of the lot behind the Mosque to barf her guts out in private. This was the first time she had seen a body that was almost unrecognizable due to the mutilation from multiple gunfire wounds. She had been using her flashlight to find her way and noticed a pistol lying on the pavement.

The embarrassed rookie with barf on her CSI coveralls had put on her best game face and returned to the area delineated by the white crime scene tape and reported to her supervisor that she had stumbled across a pistol lying in the rear parking lot. The supervisor immediately followed procedure and the crime scene was enlarged to include the area where the gun had been discovered.

A preliminary dusting for prints revealed what could be a couple of unreadable smudges on the pistol's handle. The supervisor felt there was a chance that latent finger and thumbprints could be raised off the pistol's magazine, perhaps even off the cartridges still in the clip.

While it appeared that the shooter might have panicked, it was obvious that an attempt had been made to police up all the brass as had been done at the other two cop killings. However, due to haste or the fact that the parking lot lights were not lit, the shooter had overlooked one unfired cartridge that had been found lying about 50-meters closer to the Mosque.

The shoe scrapes and knee indentation in the dirt revealed that it was likely there that the shooter had laid in wait for the victim who by now had been identified as Tourist Constable Lau assigned to the Victoria police station on Old Bailey Street.

Du Ming had contacted the police station desk sergeant by cell phone and learned that Lau had pulled a double today. He had also reported to the desk sergeant before he left saying that he was going to have to ride the escalator up the hill to his apartment because someone had sliced the tires on his car. It had been parked in the employee's lot alongside the old decommissioned prison.

Considering the bloody outcome here on Mosque Street, there was not much question among the cops as to who had sliced the dead cop's car tires earlier that night, forcing him to take the obvious alternative method to get home.

The head criminalist assisting his evidence-gathering team in packing up their gear to go to yet another crime scene in the city mentioned to me that sputum had been found on the victim's face. Several samples of the sputum had been recovered using cotton cavity swabs then encapsulating them in sterile glass evidence tubes.

The body had been ambulanced to a hospital to be pronounced and would be transferred to the Medical Examiner's office about an hour later. There wasn't anything more that Ming and I could do at the scene. There were a few hours left until daylight so I asked him to drop me off at the crime lab. On the way I'd gave the crime lab head Inspector Xueguang Laoxi a ring at his home and requested his permission to assist in the forensics examination.

My reason for this unusual request was that while I had full confidence in Laoxi's lab, the fact is that with the current budget constraints most of the specialty departments of the lab are not staffed on the graveyard shift.

In a couple hours, the press was going to hear of the new killing from their crime beat reporters, and immediately pounce on David Tsang's back. He would pounce on the back of the police commissioner; who in turn would pounce on my back.

I wanted to have some answers before the feces began to roll downhill. Especially since with this third cop killing, we now were dealing with a serial killer. Media pressure could cost me my job as the case was still unsolved nearly three weeks after the first cop had been executed.

Laoxi had picked up the phone on the first ring. After I had explained the political considerations of this high-profile case to him, he readily agreed to give me full run of his lab. Before hanging up, presumably to return to sleep, he assured me he would immediately call the lab and so inform the night supervisor. I thanked the inspector for his accommodation and hung up.

I have continued to keep my certification current with the ASCLD, American Society of Crime Lab Directors, and as such, am frequently called on by the Hong Kong criminal courts as a certified forensic expert witness. Before I came to Hong Kong, I was fortunate to have been forensically trained by the NYPD and the FBI—who operate the two finest forensic labs in the world.

What I would discover in less than two hours would make me wish that I had left well enough alone and waited until the lab's day shift reported to work to process the prints.

13

20 October 2007, Sunday, 3:30 a.m. (HKT)
Hong Kong Police Crime Lab
Arsenal Street Police Headquarters
Wan Chai district—Hong Kong Island

Lieutenant Ming dropped me off at the crime lab and took himself to the homicide office a couple of hundred meters away to begin the endless stack of paperwork that is required every time a violent death is discovered in Hong Kong.

The crime lab's nightshift supervisor was standing waiting for me inside the bullet-resistant glass door at the lab's security entrance. The entrance is guarded 24/7 by two large armed fireplugs. They look more like hoods than rent-a-cops.

Following protocol the supervisor checked my identification even though we'd known each other for going on ten years, signed me officially into the lab, and issued me a picture I.D. that the guard force maintained there for the convenience of police department heads above the rank of inspector.

As we walked down the tiled floor to the lab's inner core the supervisor asked how he could "be of service at this wee morning hour?"

We discussed the evidence that the crime scene criminalists had just dropped off at the lab, collected from the Mosque Street shooting. He asked if this shooting was related to the other two unsolved cop executions that had occurred over the past two weeks?

I told him that if he would let me into the fingerprint lab perhaps I would have an answer to his question in a couple of hours. I was aware that due to budget cutbacks that the fingerprint lab was one of the several specialty analysis labs not staffed 24/7.

The night super punched his six-digit code into the inner security door, the code being changed daily, and we headed for the fingerprint lab when he casually mentioned to me that a partial print had been found at the scene of the second killing on Hollywood Road the weekend before.

Even though AFIS had rejected the print for comparison as being too incomplete—it could have been from a thumb, finger, palm, or elbow—I asked the scientist to please electronically transmit a copy of it to the fingerprint lab's computer.

Seeming as almost an afterthought before returning to the DNA lab where he spent most of his shift as it was one of the two specialty labs still staffed 24/7 due to the process flow time required for DNA sequencing, he asked what I wanted done with the sputum samples that had been collected earlier at the Mosque Street crime scene.

DNA sequencing routinely takes three weeks to process, even longer if the sample is so small or so degraded that the lab is forced to utilize mitochondrial DNA analysis.

I had less than three hours to come up with evidence that would tie a specific individual or individuals to the shooting, ideally, all three shootings. I would have to concentrate on raising usable prints off the unfired shell, the gun magazine and the unfired shells in that magazine, and the damp scrap of paper, all of which had been recovered at this morning's murder scene.

I suggested he get with Inspector Laoxi when he came in to work that morning to find out what his priority was on obtaining a DNA sequence from the sputum found on the face of patrolman Lau Lai.

On the way to the fingerprint lab I paused for a minute outside the hair and fiber lab. Like the DNA lab, it is also so busy it operates 24/7. It is a totally enclosed, strictly partitioned work area. Can't have air conditioning blowing the evidence media around, can we? The hair and fiber lab is broken up into several smaller labs and a common area.

The common room was stacked with boxes of evidence sent in from the various police stations throughout Hong Kong. They presumably contained swatches of tape that have sealed mouths or bound wrists; torn and stained clothing; or the bloody sheets of the bed recently occupied by the victim.

I noted a hair and fiber analyst at work through the lab's window. She had a pair of infant's pajamas hanging from a metal hanger over a table covered with white paper. Working under bright lights in the draft-free room, she was brushing the pajamas with a metal spatula, carefully working with the wale and across it, with the nap and against it. A sprinkling of dirt and sand disturbed by her motions fell down onto the white paper. With it falling through the still air more slowly than sand, but faster than lint, came a tightly coiled pubic hair.

Seeing a sudden look of satisfaction spring onto the woman's face, I mentally ventured a guess that she knew that piece of pubic hair, once processed for DNA, would one day put the nails in the coffin of another child predator.

The analyst must have felt my eyes on her. She spun around to direct her attention at where I was standing. Her look of satisfaction was replaced by one of irritation.

I knew why she was unhappy. I had trespassed on one of the few moments that make it all worthwhile for the dedicated criminalists who put up with the lousy pay and dreadful hours. When everything came together and she knew she was responsible for sending another child predator to Stanley Prison.

Where, if the citizens of Hong Kong were lucky, the scumbag would be hung. Hong Kong's basic law doesn't coddle criminals especially pedophiles and cop killers.

The analyst continued to maintain eye contact with me as if to say, "Move along—No spectators permitted." Feeling a little uncomfortable under her gaze I turned and continued down the hall to the fingerprint lab.

————

I was no stranger to the Hong Kong fingerprint analysis lab. It has always amused me that while the HKP fingerprint lab has windows contrary to established doctrine, the windows long ago had been covered with very effective blackout shades. Even on the sunniest day outside, the illumination in these series of small rooms can be manually reduced to the point that it is dark enough to permit the developing of film.

Flicking on the wall light switch revealed dozens of reference manuals and loose-leaf binders filled with established comparative data. One of the walls was dedicated to a long table bearing very expensive laboratory equipment. Centered on another wall is a shorter table occupied by a Krimesite imager that looks like a stubby telescope mounted on a tripod stand.

The night supervisor had left me three sealed and well-labeled plastic evidence envelopes, one the magazine for the discarded pistol that had been found a short distance from the killing field, another containing the fired cartridge, and the third bag, a damp scrap of pink paper. I couldn't wait to process them all for fingerprints.

Plucking a pair of white cotton examination gloves out of a box on the table, I was ready to begin. I've always found it thrilling when an examiner senses that he or she is closing in on a rabid killer.

Sticking the gun's cartridge magazine under the Krimesite microscope, it was easy to pick out a good latent thumb and what appeared to be an index finger print on it. Raising those would be a no-brainer so I returned the clip to its evidence envelope and momentarily set it aside.

My second best chance of raising a useable fingerprint was off the unfired cartridge. However, I would have to hold off testing it for later because it involved the use of chemicals that would alter the casing's coating and could conceivably set off the shell.

But I took the time to brush it with Magnadust anyway and placed it on the viewing platen in the Krimesite imager. Disappointingly, the results were *No Joy*, or in everyday terms, no image. Using conventional methods, excluding the pistol's magazine, I was unable to come with a single print based on ridge detail, not a single one, just smudges.

Prints found on an unfired cartridge at a crime scene are often challenged by the Defense anyway. Think about it. The prints could belong to anybody—from the manufacturer, to the packer who placed it in its box for retail sale, to the gun dealer who sold the ammunition, or even a handful of succeeding owners of the weapon or shells.

But I did have one more weapon in my arsenal to use before giving up on raising a print off the cartridge. Walking over to a locker, I removed a heavy black briefcase and set it on the floor, releasing two latches before gently lifting out a puissant lamp.

Carefully cradling the delicate device in both hands, I carried it over to a unoccupied spot on one of the tables and plugged it into one of the surge protector power strips that are provided for ease of use around the entire lab. This expensive lamp has limited uses, often misnamed as an imager, as it will only reveal an oily fingerprint if the shell has been handled in the past twenty-four hours.

I flipped on the strip's rocker switch and a bright high-intensity short-wave ultraviolet light flooded the Krimesite imager. My hopes sprung eternal as I used a pair of metal tongs to pick up the unfired cartridge from its evidence bag and held it up to the overhead light before placing it carefully inside the imager.

Donning a pair of orange-tinted protective goggles, I centered the shell under the imager's military-grade ocular lens. I opened the instrument's UV aperture all the way while slowly rotating the focus barrel and ring with my latex gloved right hand until the honeycomb-like viewing screen was visible.

Using my left hand I directed the UV light directly down on the cartridge, adjusting it minutely to one angle after another until I had selected the best overall angle. Then I carefully clamped the shell in-place.

Then the device took over the job of rotating the projectile, scanning for prints. I hoped the imaginer would pick up some prints so I didn't have to resort to destructive chemicals such as ninhydrin and cyanoacrylate. In the UV light, the cartridge was a ghostly greenish-white beneath the imager's lens.

Suddenly, the clear unmistakable print of thumb and index finger fluoresced from the rear of the frangible round. They would require high-intensity photographic processing before they could be run through the Hong Kong Police department's AFIS database to determine the print owner's name.

———

Glancing up at a clock on the wall, I noted it was already two minutes after 5:00 a.m. Only a couple of hours before the Media got wind of what I believed will prove to be the execution of a third young cop by an yet-unknown serial killer.

Next, I decided to check the damp scrap of paper for prints. Back at the Krimesite imager, I pulled on a clean set of white cotton gloves before picking the scrap of pink paper out of the sterile evidence envelope. I placed it on a large sheet of clean black paper and sat down on a stool, pulled a pair of safety goggles down over my eyes and a set of headphones over my ears to block out extraneous noise to aid in my concentration.

I removed an aerosol can of ninhydrin from a sealed finger print kit I'd taken from a cabinet in the lab. Removing the can's top I sprayed the pink scrap of paper moistening it, however but not too much as it already was slightly damp.

Though the spray contains no chlorofluorocarbons and is claimed to be environment-friendly, I have never found it to be especially human-friendly.

The mist bit my lungs, causing me to turn my head and cough to make certain I didn't contaminate the specimen.

Slipping the headphones off, I carried the chemical-smelling damp paper over to another workstation where a cold steam iron was plugged in and resting upright on top of a heat-resistant pad. I turned on the iron, which heated up quickly. I checked its operation by pushing the steam button to test it, and steam hissed out.

Placing the sheet of paper on a heat-resistant pad, I held the iron four inches above the paper and activated the steam function. Within seconds areas of the paper began to turn purple, and right away I can see purple marks from fingers, marks I knew weren't mine.

Because even rookie criminalists would rather die than be caught ungloved at a crime scene, I knew that when they had touched the scrap, retrieving it off the damp pavement, they never would have touched it with bare hands for any reason.

The first-responding cops at the crime scene never would have touched it because they know better. I was careful to not steam the paper where it had adhered to the damp parking lot surface on which it had been discovered.

Any contaminates the paper may have picked up off the surface of the parking lot were going to be nonporous and would not react to the ninhydrin.

Back at the Krimesite imager workstation, I sat down, put the headphones and safety goggles back on and slid the purple-spotted images on the paper under the lens of the imager scope. I flipped the imager on once again, then turned on the UV lamp and looked into the eyepiece at a field of bright green, smelling the unpleasant odor of the cooked chemical and paper.

My eyes immediately picked out the pale ridge detail of several fingerprints near the center of the piece of paper. I adjusted the focus, making the image as sharp as possible. The ridge detail showed several characteristics known in the forensics biz as 'points of comparison.' More than enough to process through the department's Automated Fingerprint Identification System.

The crime lab had already attempted to run the partial print from the second shooting through AFIS last week. They'd also done a handpull of the TenPrint cards of recent criminal arrests occurring in the past sixty days. They hadn't got any hits, probably due to the small size of the partial print.

In this case we had an actual print of the suspect to compare to other known prints in AFIS. It was like getting a Christmas present in July. This time I'd do a latent-to-latent search against the million of prints in the AFIS database.

If that didn't result in a hit, then I'd make certain the homicide detectives did a parallel hand search of the several dozen 'elimination' prints we'd already collected, just to touch all the bases.

Mounting a digital camera on top of the scope's eyepiece, I began to take photographs.

Greedily, although admittedly now overkill, I retrieved the magazine I'd set aside earlier and use basic fingerprint techniques-101 to raise and lift off a thumb and finger print. Now we had a total of three prints to compare against the partial print and the AFIS automated files.

Once I photographed the fingerprints lifted off the unfired cartridge, as well as the prints I'd just converted to a digital file from the scrap of pink paper, I called the lab's nightshift supervisor. He arrived within minutes.

We took the digital file containing the fingerprints I'd raised off the three sources to the AFIS room. It's kept under lock and key and is under closed circuit camera surveillance.

From this point on I would not touch the evidence further. I may be called as an expert witness when this case went to court. I needed to distance myself from the forensic evidence as far as possible in case I was summoned to testify. For that reason it was important that I project impartiality. Assuming that any one can be impartial in a serial killing of cops.

The AFIS computer contains millions of fingerprints including those of local criminals, city employees, students, and most everyone that has had contact with the criminal and civil bureaucracy in Hong Kong.

We were expecting to wait up to ten minutes for the system to run through all the permutations of the files it contains, but were shocked when in a less than four minutes a single card popped out of the slot announcing that the prints from all three sources of evidence are identical.

The night supervisor picked the card out of the retrieval slot, glanced at it, and showed it to me. I couldn't be more shocked if the card listed the Lord Jesus Christ, the Pope, or the head of any other religious order.

When I finally got my composure back, I looked over at the supervisor. I can tell he is also troubled but probably for a different reason. But he gave me his 'Stuff happens' shrug.

I asked him to run the prints recovered from the Mosque Street killing this morning against the partial print recovered from last weekend's second cop killing on Hollywood Road. In less than five minutes, a card kicked out saying that in AFIS's opinion, all the prints belong to the same individual.

The supervisor turned to me and said; "You have to leave the lab this minute, Chief Inspector. Otherwise you'll compromise the case when it comes in front of the Court. In hindsight, Inspector Laoxi should have never permitted you to run the prints yourself even though you are qualified to do so. You should have waited until a certified Lab employee came in to work in a couple hours and ran them for you."

He continued, "Now it is my duty to wake my boss again to inform him that we have a very nasty situation here. I don't look forward to that, sir!"

"You must immediately call the night desk at CAC, the Commission Against Corruption, and request that an agent be dispatched immediately to take possession of this evidence. If you are the one to notify the commission, it will go in your favor. Failure to do that will definitely mean your job. Now, do you have any questions?"

"Only one," I responded. "May I contact lieutenant Du Ming? He is acting head of my homicide squad while Inspector Ho Pham is on personal leave. May I inform him that we have a identified a hard subject in the cop executions and he can call his detectives off the case?"

"Chief Inspector, please don't take this to be a tasteless quip. Inspector Laoxi and myself are in serious enough trouble as it is with the brass, the Commission, and soon, the press. If you do what you ask, you will just be adding lieutenant Ming to the potential casualty list, understand?"

I sighed, and replied, "Thanks for being so up front with me on this. I know that I have inadvertently dragged all our bacon into the fire. I had no idea this individual was involved in these killings, or could even be involved in something like this."

"There has got to be a back story behind the motivation that drove the subject to commit these ruthless killings. But I guess until the Corruption Commission and the powers-that-be get through with documenting the case beyond a doubt and presenting it to the criminal courts, we'll won't learn the 'why.'"

I shook my head, and asked one further question, "May I use the lab's telephone to call the night desk of the CAC and inform them of our findings?"

The night lab supervisor replied, "Certainly, chief inspector. I'd strongly suggest you use our recorded line. You can access it as soon as I finished ruining what little remains of Inspector Laoxi's sleep for the night."

———

21 October 2007, Monday, 8:30 a.m. (HKT)
Crimes Against Persons Department
Arsenal Street Police Headquarters—Third floor
Wan Chai district—Hong Kong Island

My driver had just dropped me off at the office after what had been a terrible twenty-four hours since the identity of the serial cop killer had been revealed early Sunday morning at the crime lab.

Inspectors Yin and Ho were in their private offices. Despite the clamor of the phones and buzzing sound of the laser printer and the sound of the coffee pot perking, the department seemed eerily quiet as the proverbial church mouse.

Elizabeth, whose desk is located just outside my office door, was attempting to answer the flurry of in-coming phone calls, occasionally carrying the accumulating stack of pink Please Call slips to me a dozen at a time.

Besides saying a polite Good Morning to each other, neither one of us expanded the ritual greeting into a conversation. Normally showing up for work dressed to the nines, she hadn't even bothered to put on makeup this morning.

———

Sunday I had spent at home answering calls from the brass, the chief executive's staff, and the Media, all demanding my head and asking incredulously how I had permitted this to happen?

The 'this' they had reference to, was alternately:

(1) Why my people waited over twenty-four hours to hit the Queen's Street funeral parlor, once through the process of elimination, we had deduced it was the site of the illegal body shop harvesting operation?
(2) How in the world had three cops been executed and my people still hadn't made an arrest?

I knew that the identity of shooter wouldn't be released until the crime lab completed duplicating the specialized fingerprint analysis tests I had performed there early Sunday morning.

I knew by now the tests would have been completed and doubled checked by the Lab department head, Inspector Laoxi. No news was bad news in this case. Laoxi would have called me immediately if the results of the follow-on fingerprint analysis ordered by the CAC differed in the slightest detail from my own earlier tests.

Laoxi and I are friends. Knowing me personally he would instinctively know how upset I was now that I knew the identity of the shooter.

If the conclusions from their follow-behind tests matched mine in every detail, and there was no reason they wouldn't, the Commission wouldn't wait the several weeks required for the confirmation of the DNA sequencing before arresting the individual. Their justification for doing so was sound. The shooter had been identified by comparison of the fingerprints found at two of the three crime scenes.

They couldn't afford not to arrest the shooter. If the killer carried out a fourth assassination of a cop and the Media found out we had known the identify of the shooter in the early morning hours after the third execution, there would be a purge at the police department and the CAC that hadn't been equaled since Chairman Mao's cultural revolution in China in 1955.

The only positive note to my Sunday afternoon in between answering calls and attempting to slip in a nap was that Alicia called.

After she had finished complaining about my phone being busy, which I didn't even try to explain to her, she began to tell me how smart our son Augustus, Jr. was, attributing various advanced social skills and verbal responses to him that I found difficult to believe a 11-month-old child was capable of.

Alicia claimed Augustus, Jr. was already calling her mommy, and the maid, aunty, but appeared to be confused and was looking around his play room for a father figure to call daddy. Apparently, although she hadn't previously mentioned it, Alicia's father had recently died or she had been forced to put him into an Alzheimer's hospice home.

She began to tell me about how successful her father's practice had become since she took it over. Then, abruptly with no lead-in at all, she dropped the bomb on me.

"Augustus, when are you going to come up to visit your son and me here in Taiyunan? We talked about you coming up to spend the Christmas holidays. Jr. will have his first birthday on December 25th. I want our son to have a daddy and not a absentee father."

"I thought you visiting us up here would be a little like a trial run of our relationship to see if it can be every bit as wonderful as it once was. And more importantly, as least to me, is the opportunity to atone for my unfairness in not telling you about our son earlier."

"Well," I admitted, "I certainly am planning on visiting you and Augustus, Jr. over the holidays and was only waiting for you to ask. I can't get away right now because there is likely going to be a political explosion once the press finds out the identity of a killer that has been executing young cops here, three of them so far. And that I have known the shooter's name since about 5:00 a.m. this morning."

"I've been given a direct order by the Commission Against Corruption, one that can't even be countermanded by the police commissioner, that I am to stand mute on this case until they are certain enough with the identification to make an arrest."

"This is the reason the CAC was established in 1974. Like a super Internal Affairs squad that can arrest and prosecute any official, especially policemen, when they uncover evidence the commission believes to be probative of egregious conduct. This case is now their baby."

Shaking my head at the perceive unfairness of it all to the working cop that just was trying to clear homicides and solve major case crimes, I continued, "And if that wasn't enough to get the CAC and police brass on my butt, we also conducted a major raid on a illegal body part harvesting operation at a funeral parlor."

"Problem is some unknown party, probably the kingpin, had all of the suspects killed before we arrived. Leaving us with no one to question, let alone prosecute, after the bastards have waged war on the department, killing six cops and city employees."

"Oh, Augustus," she said. "Aren't you dramatizing it, a little bit? After all, I assume the death of the operators of the body part ring will at least temporarily drive it out of business. As to the cop executions, if higher authority tells you to stand mute, what choice do you have?"

"That's just it, Alicia. It isn't fair or logical, but it is reality here in Hong Kong. I am knowingly withholding information from my superiors; who are withholding it from David Tsang, the chief executive; who in turn is withholding information both from his folder-holders in Beijing, and the Hong Kong Media. Remember Tsang's predecessor Tung Chee-hwa was harassed by the press until he became so ill that he suffered a breakdown, in effect, driving him from power."

"Augustus, I don't know why you stay in that job. Over the ten years you have worked there, you constantly have to protect your back because you are a *gweilo* who has taken one of the very few well-paying jobs on the HKP which means a lot of jealous Chinese officers hate you. How long until the stress drives you to a nervous breakdown? Doesn't the possibility of suffering a stress-caused heart attack at age forty-seven give you concern?

"Yes, Alicia, it does. But Assistant Chief of Personnel Russell structured my employment contract so that I would not receive a pension from the HKP if I quit the job before I am eligible for retirement. That won't be until I have twenty years in, about 2017. I am convinced Russell is aware that I know enough about the skeletons he has in his closet here at the HKP to put him into Stanley Prison for the rest of his life."

"The only way he would release me from those employment contract obligations is if I was injured on the job, and after my injury more or less healed, I mysteriously would find that I could not pass the return-to-work physical. Even then, any settlement package they offered to pension me off for disability reasons would contain a clause that the package would be null and void unless I agreed to physically relocate my residence out of the HKSAR. This guy is scared of what I could do to him, politically and criminally, Alicia."

"If I was no longer under his thumb due to the termination of my employment with the department, he'd want me to leave Hong Kong, either willingly, or I likely would experience an unpleasant accident some night," I said.

"Russell's minion, chief inspector Deng, tried to have me killed back in 2005 and failed. Although my relationship with Russell has been stained since then, there have been no more attempts on my life. But that could change if I informed him I was quitting, and he panicked, knowing he would lose control of me and therefore of my discretion."

"Alicia, I am going to plan on coming to see you and Augustus Jr. at Christmas. Let's see how things go here with my employment. Especially after the Media learns I've withheld critical information from my superiors, indirectly from the chief executive, and them."

With sigh, I continued, "Perhaps the police commissioner will sacrifice me to save his own butt and our problem could be resolved without any unpleasantness. Only that I, at forty-seven, could find myself unemployable, depending on the quality of my subsequent exit interview and references."

We said good night, and hung up, and I went back to worrying about what Monday, today, would bring.

———

I had skipped lunch and worked all afternoon to finish turning out the hard copies of the various updates of our progress on the three cop killings. Not to mention the body part harvesting operation where we couldn't find anyone living to prosecute.

I was just finished inputting data into the department's Rapid Start case management system when I received a phone call that would literally change my life. After hanging up from that call, I leaned back in my chair and considered what I had just been offered by the caller.

The information the caller offered to provide might mean the difference between my team and I being fired for perceived ineptness over our failure to arrest anyone for the body part scam, or being receiving a verbal atta boy and keeping our jobs.

For the past several months I hadn't been overly concerned with the possibility of my maintaining my employment on the Hong Kong police department. But I felt I owed it to my staff to do whatever was required to make this mess turn out as advantageous as possible, relative to our performance as a group.

My concern whether I should attend the requested off-premise meeting resulted in my spending another half hour on the phone attempting to follow-up on the proposed one-on-one contact. The more people I talked to, the larger rat I could smell. So I called in Inspectors Chen Ho and Mimi Yin.

———

It was about 4:45 p.m. when I finished meeting with the inspectors. I was just walking out of my office to have Sergeant Zhou Ming take me to my condo to change clothes, eat dinner, and think through the scheduled meeting tonight when the two suits from the Commission Against Corruption brushed past us into our office, barely nodding to me. I knew they were here to make an arrest.

Although there was no way he could, Zhou somehow seemed to be aware of why the rat squad was entering our office. He intentionally bumped into one of CAC agents, almost knocking the man off his feet.

I used the flat of my hand to shove my Sergeant down the hall to the elevators, hoping the CAC agent would let the insult go.

———

Once we were in the Mercedes, I chewed out Zhou. But he kept his eyes straight ahead and concentrated on traffic until we reached my condo. After I got out, and closed the car door, he drove off still having not said a single word to me.

I would be taking a red top to the 11:00 p.m. meeting in the Mongkok district.

———

Naïve tourists, especially those who have never visited its mean streets, are often known to trumpet the colorful virtues of Mongkok.

Mongkok does have an outstanding bird market. The Chinese have long favored birds as pets. Local men strut around the streets airing their birds and feeding them food with chopsticks, often the same ones the men themselves use to eat. That is the reason some tourists come away with the feeling that the district of Mongkok is a safe, colorful and fascinating experience.

The district also has a domestic flower market with plants and blooms from as far away as the European continent and Hawaii. If you are looking for some specific type of flower, there are stalls and some smaller enclosed shops that feature multicolored arrangements of exotic blooms and potted plants, again from the world over.

However experienced Hong Kong police officers know Mongkok is no place to let your guard down. I know my white face was a shit magnet in that district. Regardless of race most police officers from headquarters never come to the Mongkok district unless they absolutely had to, couldn't delegate their presence to a subordinate, and then, only came in large numbers and almost never after nightfall.

When I had first been hired onto the Hong Kong Police force, my Chinese training officer made sure that was deeply burned into my memory. The district of Mongkok is one of the most populated and criminally overrun places on Mother Earth.

The people that live and work in the Mongkok district must have coined the homily 'Birds of a feather, flock together.' The population generally exhibits traits attributed to rattlesnakes, scorpions, and the huge tarantula spiders that thrive in some parts of the America's high-desert southwest. To say that Mongkok's population meets all the criteria of a criminal enterprise is a gross understatement.

If the Mongkok Chamber of Commerce has any boasts about their community it is that everyone is employed and rents are lower than dirt. What they never tell potential businesses that may be considering relocating to Mongkok was that the so-called citizens of this outlaw community had decades before banded together to protect each other. Protect each other from their next-door neighbors, who also were murderers, drug addicts, pedophiles, white slave runners, thieves, con artists, prostitutes, and other examples of the lowest scum on earth.

Close to seventy-five percent of the residents in Mongkok are illegal refugees from the People's Republic of China supplemented by dozens of American army deserters thrown in for spice from the Vietnam era. Those deserters could never return to America. In addition to the desertion charges, each has had multiple-murder charges hanging over their heads for the past thirty years. Capital murder has no stature of limitations.

Chinese refugees flooded Hong Kong by the hundreds of thousands when they fled Mainland China during Mao's Cultural Revolution. The population of the Mongkok district today is estimated to be over one million souls.

The Mongkok district, except for a rudimentary sewer system that surprisingly still works, had been unprepared for the massive influx of fleeing Chinese. With the exception of Japanese, who are hated by every person of Chinese progeny in the entire world, all manners of Asians had descended upon Hong Kong, most at least initially ending up in the Mongkok district.

The refugees include the Chiu Chow Chinese from Shantou to the south; Mongols from the far north; Shanghainese from the coast; Gurkhas from Nepal; and Sikhs from the northwestern frontier.

Fleeing deserters of one army or another have also settled in Hong Kong including Americans, French, and English. Each of them eventually settles in the lawless environs of Mongkok. In Mongkok they find they can disappear from the pursuit of their respective army's fugitive apprehension squads. And by being unafraid to dispense with what few morals they had left, they could at least earn a subsidence living.

The buildings of Mongkok, excluding the handful that are legal, house illegal enterprises. Sanitation and health codes are ignored. Literally hundreds of phony pharmacies have sprung-up that never require a prescription regardless of the drug. Counterfeit watches and knock-off brand name clothing manufacturers of all types, gun dealers, flagrantly-deviate whisky bars run by deserters, opium dens, and professional hit men, actually have storefronts from which they openly hawk their services.

Medical quacks perform operations in butcher shops and slaughterhouses after the businesses-of-record close for the day. Bootleg liquor flows by the tank car amongst the populace with no concern for age, addictions, or for those who eventually became blind from the poison or infected with fatal communicable diseases. A significant portion of the population is infected with STD's. A goodly portion of those, full-blown AIDS.

The only police presence in the district is the huge Mongkok police station on the corner of Prince Edward and Nathan Roads. Persons, including the corrupt police officers assigned there, if they are foolishly enough to depart through the front doors of the police station at any time of the day, are instantly swept away by the tides of human flotsam.

Filthy sewer-like streams of people flow down the sidewalks and into the roads, often completely blocking the entire width of a thoroughfare. Attempting to stop or extract ones self from the flow of the human river gets you trampled, slashed with dirty, disease-infected razors, or knifed. After this brutality, if you were still alive, or a possible candidate for mugging, you certainly would be thrown into one of the narrow, stinking, rat-infested, unlit alleys that double as open sewage troughs.

This never-ending river of human beings carried along by the masses filling the streets, blocking traffic, cutting through shops, climbing over cars, motorcycles and busses, can be compared to the dehumanizing act of being forced to defecate or masturbate in-public without the benefit of any privacy, hygienic facilities, or toilet paper.

That was the reason that all Hong Kong cops, regardless of physical size or the amount of firepower they carry, fear and hate the streets of the Mongkok district. And here I was headed right into the belly of the beast.

14

21 October 2007, Monday, 11:05 p.m. (HKT)
Rendezvous with Angry Dragon
An opium den
Mongkok district—The Kowloon Peninsula

As soon as I stepped out the back door of the opium den, I knew I had made a major mistake. A mistake that had a strong possibility of being fatal.

––––––

Angry Dragon had called me at work that afternoon. He seemed distressed and said it was critical that I meet with him that evening at 11:00 p.m. He named an obscure opium den in the Mongkok district where he claimed we wouldn't run into any Hong Kong cops. His assumption that I didn't want to be seen meeting with him was obscure, at least until the proverbial ceiling caved in. He promised he could guarantee that the operator of the opium den wouldn't betray our presence to the notorious Mongkok criminal element for a chance to make some fast cash.

If I accommodated his request for the meeting, he promised to turn over Interpol's entire file on the body part caper including the names of the Hong Kong parties behind the operation; the names of the Chinese funeral parlors that were active participants; the location of any other covert surgical suites; and last but not least, detailed facts on how the ring were smuggling the body parts out of Hong Kong.

I decided I couldn't pass up the opportunity to obtain the information he apparently possessed despite how skittish his selection of a meeting place made me.

The agent knew that after the set-up at the Five Ram funeral parlor that took two of my detective's lives; and the second Red Crescent van that had contained what turned out to be the booby-trapped body, subsequently taking two more lives, I would find it impossible to turn down his offer.

Angry Dragon claimed to know that the Hong Kong's chief executive had given me days, not weeks, to shutdown the black market scheme in Hong Kong and determine how the product was being smuggled out of the HKSAR.

After clearing the physical boundaries of Hong Kong and the People's Republic, the body parts could be reshipped anywhere. The four largest potential customers for illicit transplantable human parts like that were the United States, Europe, Japan, and affluent citizens in China.

As I had learned when circumstances had forced me to turn over a 'Plan-B' operation in 2006 to one of Angry Dragon's covert action teams, the Interpol agent gave new meaning to the term 'paranoid.'

Since June of 1997—the Chinese takeover of Hong Kong—the agent claimed that the PRC had moles in the Hong Kong police department, which of course I could have told him was absolutely true. The bottom line was that Angry Dragon refused to deal with anyone in the Hong Kong police hierarchy with the exception of myself.

In our brief telephone conversation this afternoon, he had warned me he would not make good on his offer to meet if I told anyone I was meeting him, brought anyone with me, or notified any of my superiors or co-workers of the meeting.

I had told him that since I no longer drove in Hong Kong, believing that only fools and professional drivers did it, I would need my driver Zhou Ming to chauffeur me to and from the meeting.

His paranoia was almost palpable over the phone as he responded that would be impossible. He said that if the HKP wanted what he was offering, I could take a cab to the meeting if I was unwilling or unable to drive. Angry Dragon then had repeated his promise to personally guarantee my safety at the meeting.

All I knew was that the powers-that-be were demanding my scalp unless the HKP shut down the illegal body part harvesting operation before any more cops were murdered trying to interdict it. Deciding I liked my scalp right where it was, I had no choice other than to agree to the meeting and his stipulations.

———

The red top had dropped me off a couple of blocks from the address the Interpol agent had given me that afternoon. At a few minutes before 11 p.m., it was as dark as a . . . well, you know, it was very dark.

To get to the meeting place I would have to walk one block south and two blocks east. At that hour of night, after the past nerve-racking days, I felt weary, exactly the way the structures I was walking by looked.

Lights were still on in a few of the shoddy structures but the only thing breathing I passed by was a stray dog who hadn't yet become part of some human's meal. Bursting green plastic garbage bags stacked at the curb along the length of the entire street. I wondered how and when they got picked up? To my knowledge, Mongkok didn't have a garbage collection department.

When I reached the address that I'd been given it turned out to be a small, one-story rundown building that had seen better days perhaps a century before. In front, there was a rickety-looking front porch. All the windows in the structure was dark, probably too filthy to permit almost any light to pass through in either direction.

There was no doorbell so I pounded on the door with my fist. The curtain in one of the windows was thrust aside and a pair of dark eyes peered out. The agent I knew as Angry Dragon opened the door, which proved to be the entry to one of Mongkok's dozens of illegal opium dens.

As soon as we shook hands and exchange pleasantries, he informed me that in the past half hour his people had seen a couple of the police department's Commission Against Corruption agents cruising the area in their radio antennae festooned, midnight blue Mercedes sedans.

Now that seemed odd to me. Why now, why tonight, what could they be looking for, if in fact they were actually there in the first place and this wasn't yet another example of the agent's paranoia. But he insisted that a change of location for the meeting was necessary to ensure our mutual security. As I was already in for a penny, I figured I had no option other than sticking my head out a little further, and go in for a pound.

He led me through the narrow aisle between the cots occupied by unkempt Chinese and Thai refugees who sell their souls once a day for a few puffs of tranquilizing dope. I'd learned years ago that the human ability to invent methods to destroy themselves was a bottomless pit.

Dodging a dangling arm here and a leg there, we reached the dilapidated rear door. Stepping aside he politely gestured me though the door before him.

As soon as I had crossed the threshold the thought *Big mistake, your idiot!* popped into my head, followed by a second thought, *I hope that I have an opportunity to berate myself for committing this rookie error at some later date.*

The light inside the room had been dim as in all opium dens. But as I pushed open the exit door and extended the toe of a loafer down to the asphalt of the pitch black alley, two mountains, namely Messieurs Hans and Gustav Hapwanegg, showed their primitive sides by stepping out of the darkness of the alley and putting a lot of body English into the swings of the blackjacks that impacted my skull.

———

When I woke up, a sweet smell of opiate lingered in the air. So I assumed we were still somewhere near the narcotic den.

There was a floor-to-ceiling mirror hung on the closest wall. That was unusual because most undereducated Chinese are afraid that mirrors and cameras will steal their soul.

Sitting about six feet from the mirror in a chair in the middle of the dim room was a guy with his hands tied behind the back of the chair, his legs to the chair legs, and a looped noose around his neck, the tail of which was attached to the rope around his wrists. Every time the two brothers hit the man, the noose tugged on his throat and the resultant pressure yanked his wrists up towards his shoulder blades.

The guy had blood running out of his hairline and down his face, and had a piece of duck tape was plastered across his mouth. I studied the unfortunate guy's reflection in the mirror carefully until I recognized that I was that guy.

My .50 caliber Israeli-made Desert Eagle, always bring your most impressive weapon to any secret meeting is my motto, was laying on a table just out of my reach even if my hands had been free. Alongside my gun was a vial of Sodium-Amytal powder.

One of the Aussie brothers was mixing up a cocktail by combining 500 milligrams of the powder with 20 milliliters of distilled water in a larger vial. *Just fucking wonderful* I thought.

The brother drew the mixture up into a hypodermic and then set the syringe back on the table. I knew enough about truth serum to know that if Angry Dragon planned on questioning me at length, he'd inject me in the arm or thigh muscle. If he wanted to get this unpleasantness over in a hurry, he'd inject it directly into my femoral artery where it would go to work immediately. But I didn't yet know whether the syringe they had prepared was for show, or go.

Angry Dragon stood legs askew in front of me with a superior look on his face. He apparently decided that since I was awake and known to be a sneaky bugger that Gustav should check to make certain the ropes that bound me were adequate.

The Aussie was quick and strong but displayed little knowledge of knot tying. He paced around me, yanking this piece of rope, jerking another, until they were so tight I knew I would lose my hands and feet to gangrene unless they were loosened or removed within fifteen minutes.

Figuring that there was a good chance that this was the end of my colorful if short life, I brazenly turned my head to look around what appeared to be an old kitchen.

There was a squat hole in the corner of the room that served as a bathroom for the occupants, and a pair of one-foot-square mesh windows set in the wall alongside the front door that were very grimy. As it was dark outside, I couldn't determine if any light filtered through them. Typically for ancient buildings in Mongkok, identical eighteen by sixty-inch plywood doors were set in the front and rear walls.

The door I could see to my rear in the reflection of the mirror seemed freer of cobwebs so that was probably the door they'd dragged me though after the Hapwanegg brothers had blackjacked me in the alley.

The Interpol agent sat on the edge of the sole remaining piece of furniture in the room, the table that held my weapon and the syringe. The scars on the agent's neck and face that I had glimpsed at the FBI academy in Quantico two years ago were red and irritated. Perhaps something that happened when his blood pressure became elevated due to agitation. Regardless, it gave his face a don't-fuck-with-me look.

Despite his angry look—I assumed that is the reason his handlers had given gave him the code name Angry Dragon—his eyes stared at me like I was a bug pinned to a board destined for a student's biology dissection. He apparently was extremely pissed about my department's refusal to stop digging into the body part scheme, which in his mind apparently had made this ugly scene necessary.

His dark eyes seemed bottomless. I thought I was looking though them into the evil depths of his mind. They were not the eyes of a mad man, or even a psycho. But rather those of a man who had been in complete control of lucrative operation until a stubborn ass like me choose to make it my department's business.

I believe he respected me somewhat from our prior association last year. But now he was curious of how I was going to handle dying, trussed up as I was like a Chinese fanged boar.

His appraisal of me apparently satisfied for the moment, he turned to the Aussie brothers telling them to make me wish I'd never stuck my nose in one of his operations. *Hell*, I thought, *he didn't need to turn those gorillas loose on me. I already sincerely regretted getting involved.*

Hans and Gustav were good at their jobs. Because we'd made fools of both brothers at the Five Ram funeral parlor crime scene, incarcerating them, holding them incommunicado for nearly twelve hours in one of our world-famous rat-infested holding cells, they gave my beating renewed effort, methodically starting with pounding my eyes closed, then proceeded south, ending up using a baseball bat on my knees.

Through the blood red haze and the overriding pain, the best I can recollect is that the beating was just getting interesting when there was an explosion. Both the room's doors blew off their hinges and into the room. Using the last bit of strength I possessed, I threw my body to the side which tipped the chair over and dumped me still bound onto the floor.

At the same instant the glass in the small room's front windows exploded out of their frames and showered me with sharp shards. Apparently using Safety Glass for windows was still a novelty in the Mongkok district. Smoke and 'flash bang' grenades followed through the now-empty window frames.

While trying to force my body to melt into the wooden floor I opened one of my swollen eyes to see a squad of men in dark pants, dark shirts, bulletproof armor, black helmets, carrying the silenced H&K MP-5 assault weapons of Hong Kong SWAT, poke the muzzles of their weapons through both open doorways.

I cringed as the silenced rounds *Phut-Phut-Phut* zinged over my body. The eardrum breaking *Kerbang-Kerbang-Kerbang* of the flash-bang grenades detonating was answered by the thunderous sounds *Kaboom-Kaboom-Kaboom* as the brother's Model 1911, Colt .45 Commanders returned fire.

The smoke soon became visually impregnable. Small fires had been started by the detonation of the flash-bang grenades. Individual whiffs of dust erupted from the clothing of the two Hapwanegg brothers as they were shredded by the fusillade of the SWAT team.

Suddenly the chair I was bound to was yanked onto its legs. My bonds were cut with wicked looking SWAT combat knife.

I noticed that Angry Dragon, whose name I would soon learn was Sinclair Leymon, was desperately attempting to bull his way past three SWAT shooters at the rear door.

Sinclair apparently figured that since the room had only two doors, and that shooters were coming through both of them, one door was pretty much as good as the other.

Angry Dragon was absorbing incoming lead from the SWAT shoulder weapons like a sponge. He'd get to his feet; fire at the shooters outside; take a handful of bullets; fall down; inspect his wounds; stand up, and begin the entire cycle again.

———

When the firing from both sides petered out the room grew as quiet as a church in prayer. Actually, that really wasn't the situation. It only sounded noiseless to me because I was temporarily stone deaf in both ears.

Miraculously, Sinclair Leymon was still alive but CTD, circling the drain, fast sliding down the slippery slope. With a great reserve of strength I doubt he knew he even possessed, he managed to pull himself up on one elbow and look over at me.

I was lying in my own blood, copiously hemorrhaging. The SWAT team medics had already hit me with an initial quarter grain of Morphine in each shoulder to take the edge off my blinding pain, and plugged two bags of blood expander into my veins.

The paramedics were cluttered about me like a gaggle of hens. Everyone's mouth was moving at once, no doubt making authoritative observations. They were frantically attempting to get a cervical collar on me, stop my bleeding, bandage my battered face, and apply splints to my broken fingers and shattered knees, all at the same time, before transporting me to the emergency room of the nearest hospital for trauma treatment in hopes of saving my miserable life.

Sinclair Leymon could only wheeze and croak. In addition to the bullets that had shattered his shoulders, punctured at least one of his lungs, severed his spine, and ruptured a nickel-sized hole in the right atrial camber of his heart, a bullet had also passed through his throat taking most of the voice box with it. But he managed to weakly whisper the words, "How? How did you know about the ambush? Please tell me."

I looked deep into his eyes which now were growing lifeless, empty of his trademark anger. It was obvious that he was aware he was dying. He'd be DOA long before he ever reached a hospital.

I glared at him and croaked in a couldn't-care-less voice, "No. No, Sinclair. You tell me where the cutting room is, who in Hong Kong either knew or took part in the operation, and how you got the parts out of the country, and maybe, just maybe, I'll tell you so you don't go to the grave without knowing what did you in."

As he lay there in his blood weighing what I had said, the medics were lifting me out of the chair that now was only suitable for fireplace kindling and placing me onto a collapsible aluminum gurney.

The medics had just lifted my stretcher, snapped its legs into place and began to roll it towards the front door when Leymon, now with streams of bright-red blood pouring out of his mouth, gasped, "Okay. But have to write it down—can't talk."

I motioned to the SWAT sergeant. He pulled out a spiral notebook out of a jump suit pocket and knelt down, holding the notebook for Sinclair as he attempted to write the information I'd demanded.

I admit I was blackmailing him. Hell, yes! I was demanding his answers before I would tell him how I had gotten on to him. And why I had violated our agreement by bringing SWAT and a dozen of my own detectives as backup to our supposed secret meeting. Since he was responsible for the deaths of our cops, I wouldn't lose a second of sleep over it.

It took the renegade Interpol agent less than a minute to write down everything I had demanded. The sergeant rose and carried the notebook over to me so I could read what he had written. After a minute I shakily nodded my head, concurring he had held up his side of the devil's agreement.

"OK, Sinclair, here it is. I tried to call you back to change the meeting location after you called me this afternoon. I no longer had the satellite phone you passed to me last year at Quantico. I compacted it."

"So I figured I'd call your case officer in Lyons (Lyons, France—Interpol headquarters) and attempt to get a number for you here locally so I could contact you."

"Well, Interpol HQ wouldn't let me talk to a case officer. "No security clearance" they said. I asked them to call HKP HQ to verify my credentials. When they called the Arsenal Street HKP headquarters back and verified I was who I said I was, they let me talk to your personnel director, a Ms. Gina Shultz."

Weakened now from my loss of blood, I tried to focus my concentration enough to provide the deathbed information I'd promised Leymon.

"Well, guess what, Sinclair? Personnel Director Shultz in a former life had been FBI Special Agent Shultz of the Baltimore office until she got herself involved in testifying for another woman agent in a sexual harassment case. Unfair but fact, that testimony ended Agent's Shultz's career with the FBI."

"At that time, Interpol was looking for trained intelligence agents and Shultz fit the bill exactly. But when she reported to your headquarters in

France she found that there were the same sexist primates running Interpol as she had worked with in the FBI."

"Interpol executives, uncomfortable with the thought of a feminist in the operations directorate, decided to shuttle Shultz into an administrative job in Personnel. But she soon decided she liked having control over for all those sexist male's personnel affairs. So she stayed in Personnel, worked regular hours, and presided over sexual harassment hearings at the agency. A lot of male agents were cashiered out due to her unrelenting efforts in support of female agents. To Shultz, it was a marriage made in heaven."

Seeing Leymon's head had dropped onto his bloody chest, I decided I'd better cut to the chase.

"I'll get to the point, Sinclair. Former FBI Agent Shultz told me that you and the brothers Hapwanegg here got your fingers caught in the till. The three of you were using your connections and custom's exemptions to traffic in drugs and weapons."

"On the morning that Interpol was planning to arrest you and the two Aussies, someone must have tipped you off."

"You and the Hapwanegg brothers disappeared without a trace. You somehow took your secure communication devices, identification, and code words with you, not to mention emptying the safe deposit boxes in the Paris branch of the Bank of France. The boxes in which the agency had foolishly permitted you to keep funds to pay bribes, emergency funds for equipment acquisition, paying for your contracted action teams, and other expenses. Shultz said she was told it amounted to nearly US$1,000,000 combined for the three of you."

Barely able to speak now as I was slipping down my own slippery slope into a deep drug-induced sleep, I muttered, "Even with all that money, looks like you partied yourselves poor. You setup the body part scheme that you initially learned about after reading news reports on it in the *New York Times*. Just to get money to live up to the standard of living you had grown used to . . ."

The SWAT sergeant put his hand on my shoulder, and said, "Chief Inspector, Mr. Leymon died about a minute ago. But I didn't want to upset you by breaking into the explanation I knew you felt morally obligated to give him, quid-pro-quo."

Then the sergeant said, "You're bleeding a lot." *What a god damn astute observation, dude!* Until he made that comment I had been unaware that in addition to the beating the Hapwanegg brothers had laid on me while

SWAT was getting their ducks in a row for the assault, I'd received other injuries when our people came through the door.

Glass splinters from the shattered windows that the flash-bang stun grenades had been tossed through somehow had found their way into my head, the corner of one eye, my face, chest and upper arms.

Blood was streaming from cuts in my scalp down my face. A quick self-appraisal revealed glass shards also were sticking out of my chest, arms, and the fleshy part of my legs, in addition to the blood seeping out of my shattered knees.

When I finally saw my injuries it was like someone had suddenly flipped a switch and pain began to flow. Even the pain from the superficial cuts was excruciating.

Fate was doing its dance with me, a two-step if I had to judge. I just hoped that it wasn't going to be my last dance.

15

01 March 2008, Thursday, 9:30 a.m. (HKT)
Woman's Mental Health Ward—Queen Mary Hospital
102 Pok Fu Lam Road
Pok Fu Lam district—Hong Kong Island

The orderlies assigned to transport the Shooter to the 12:00 noon mental competency hearing at the Magistrate's court on Old Bailey Street came for her at 9:30 a.m. Thursday morning.

At the request of her defense attorney, whose fee was being paid by her family back in Australia, the Court had ordered that she be committed to Queen Mary Hospital for a pre-trial mental evaluation. The evaluation would be required prior to commencement of her capital trial for three counts of First Degree Murder, with Forethought, the most serious charge possible in Hong Kong's New Basic Rule of Justice which had been adopted by the HKSAR Legislative Counsel on 01 June 1997.

Queen Mary Hospital is located in the shadow of Victoria Peak about five kilometers west of the HKP headquarters complex on Arsenal Road.

The Shooter had been held in an isolation cell at one of Hong Kong's nicer correctional facilities until a hospital bed opened up at Queen Mary on 01 January 2008. At that time she'd been transferred under guard to the mental health wing of the hospital.

She'd been institutionalized on the Women's Mental Health ward for the past sixty days while the doctors, analysts, and shrinks subjected her to endless sessions of evaluation. Their goal was to prove or disprove whether she had been in full control of her mental sense of right versus wrong when she had executed the three Hong Kong police officers in October of 2007.

The woman claimed the off-duty cops had gang raped her at her apartment on 22 October 2007 after they had all been out drinking at a nightclub in Stanley on Hong Kong Island.

Early on the morning on 22 October, the woman who soon would become the Shooter, had made an error in judgment by asking three cops up to her apartment for a nightcap after all four of them had been drinking excessively.

The young men had not been aware who the woman was or that she held a administrative position in an agency of the HKSAR. The woman on the other hand was aware that the three men were cops although she hadn't met them socially before that night.

At the woman's arraignment, her attorney told the Court that since she had known the men were cops, she'd not been concerned about asking them up to her apartment.

The reason the Shooter gave her attorney for not telling the men of her high-level administrative position was that she felt it might intimidate them. She confessed that she hadn't wanted to scare them away and miss the opportunity to get to know one of them that she found of interest, better.

———

Since she arrived on the Women's Ward of the mental health wing of the hospital, the Shooter had never missed an opportunity to appear positive in her thinking, polite, compliant, and often joked with the doctors, nurses and orderlies.

It was then that she told her doctors, who in turn told her attorney, that she had been infected with AIDS by one of the rapists. That fact was easily enough verified by subpoenaing the cop's personnel files including their most-recent medical evaluations, and the results of the woman's own blood work. The same personnel files the Shooter had accessed by illegally using the password of her boss to learn the names and work schedules of her assailants.

The attorney told her to not to get her hopes up because her charges alleged premeditation and therefore were very serious capital offenses. However, the fact that one of the men had known he was HIV-positive, a communicable disease only passed on through sexual activity, but still had made the conscious decision to become a willing participant in her rape anyway, might prove mitigating in her case. The hospital was now treating her with HIV cocktails although the medical personnel couldn't tell her whether the drugs would prolong her life.

A jury might be compassionate when weighing the question of mitigating circumstances when sentencing a woman who had killed her assailants after discovering they had knowingly infected her with a fatal disease.

———

Today was the shooter's second and final competency hearing with the Court where she would be apprised of the final recommendation of the hospital's mental health shrinks.

The facade she had maintained during her hospital confinement gave no hint to her caregivers that she didn't give a damn what sentence she received anyway. She intended to do whatever it took to avoid having to spend her final days caged like a rabid animal.

Based on the exemplary conduct she'd exhibited since arriving on the ward and her interaction with members of the staff that she'd gone out of her way to cultivate and attract, the orderlies decided this one time to ignore hospital rules. They decided not to follow the regulation that required handcuffing and leg-ironing of prisoners who were being transported between the hospital and the Courts.

The shooter had been permitted to wear one of her favorites, a yellow Chanel designer dress that one of the nurses had picked up earlier from her apartment. The patient was even permitted to use makeup that had been donated by the various female employees on the ward.

She was convinced that her 6 foot 2 inch body, enhanced by her best efforts in the application of her cosmetics, would not be wasted on the two unarmed orderlies who were responsible for getting her to Court. Nor on the Magistrate who was scheduled to rule on whether she had been sane when she had committed her offenses.

The two orderlies and the shooter walked out of the mental health facility and across the parking lot to a white Toyota sedan parked in a No-Parking zone. Due to the difference in height between herself and the orderlies, a full foot, persons who saw them walking to the car, the shooter in the middle, would be reminded of Mutt and Jeff.

The shooter's psychiatrist, recently divorced, had become fond of the young woman. He had insisted that the hospital's unmarked car, normally used almost exclusively for luminaries who had strayed across the line of propriety, be used to take her to Court that day. Those luminaries, because of their social status, were often permitted to spend their sentences for drunk driving at the hospital instead of a vermin-infected cell one at one of Hong Kong's thirteen correctional facilities.

The woman and the orderlies were out of sight of the hospital buildings, almost to the door of the car, when she faked a stumble and as would be expected, grabbed onto the arm of the closest orderly. She pretended to be shocked and rubbed her breasts into the helpful man's arm. Distracting the man with the crush of her breasts, she pivoted like her Karate instructor had taught her years ago, spun, kicked, and broke the collar bone arm of one man; then continued spinning with the speed of a cobra, and kicked the second orderly in the crotch.

With both men helpless on the pavement the woman had manically gone after them with her balled up fists killing them both in rapid succession with a blow to the throat, rupturing their windpipes.

The men died almost instantly. But in any case before they could sound the alarm. Being a big girl the woman she had no difficulty dragging the bodies behind a nearby dumpster. She methodically searched the two bodies, removing their wallets, cash and any loose change they had, in addition to the Toyota's keys and both their cell phones.

Then she individually boosted each of their bodies up, over the edge, and permitted them to drop into the green dumpster.

She got into the sedan. First she checked the glove box to see if what one of the nurses who had more than a therapeutic interest in her had mentioned in a moment of lust.

Shuffling through the paperwork she found there, the shooter was furious when she couldn't find the credit card the nurse had assured her was always kept in the car for emergencies. But then the woman pulled down the visor and down dropped the credit card.

Starting the car, she drove into a nearby parking lot. Then using a tool she found in the Toyota's trunk, she switched plates with a car of the same model and color. She figured the theft and plate exchange should give her almost eight hours before the person who owned the other car got off work. And, if the person were inattentive, perhaps he or she wouldn't even notice that their vehicle now bore the license plates of another car.

When the shooter was a 'no-show' at her scheduled noon hearing the Court could be expected to treat her case like any other FTA, failure to appear. At close of business a warrant for her arrest would be drawn up and circulated to the police.

The orderlies and car wouldn't be missed until nightfall. The Court was notorious for its deviation from hearing schedules. It wasn't unusual for a defendant to be scheduled to appear in front of the Court at noon but then be forced by a tyrannical self-important court clerk to sit on a grimy, uncomfortable wooden bench and cool his or her heels before eventually being given the opportunity to appear in front of the Magistrate.

First things first, the shooter thought. She had spent her nights while in the hospital coming up with the perfect plan. The staff hadn't even monitored her evening calls from the ward's pay phone. Again, she had been willing to buy the night shift nurses off with sex. Her escape should be a no-brainer just so she stuck to the plan.

She used both the orderly's cell phones to dial from memory the reservation numbers for six of Hong Kong's larger passenger airlines. She made a reservation for a family of three each time under her family name, eventual destination, Australia. The cops would no doubt check with the airlines and when they found six separate reservations for the same family, destination Australia, they'd go nuts trying to cover all those potential departing flights out of the Hong Kong International Airport.

All the shooter had to do now was unobtrusively drive out of the hospital parking lot and head south to Aberdeen Harbor. Two blocks away from Hong Kong's first McDonalds restaurant was the Aberdeen 24/7 private postal box facility where she had paid a year's rent in advance immediately following her first revenge killing, Johnny Yang.

Her Australian passport and $20,000 in U.S. currency mailed to that address by her stepfather using her family name before she had been adopted, was hidden in plain sight there. Guarded by nothing more that a combination lock on the exterior brass door of the box. She'd memorized the combination so she'd be in and out quickly, and wouldn't have to speak to anyone working there.

She planned to stop at a bargain clothes shop that catered to families that had lived on their junks in Aberdeen Harbour for generations. There she'd get rid of the noticeable Chanel dress, wipe all her makeup off, replace it with a little grime, and buy a set of black pajamas like the fisherman wore before cutting off every bit of her blond hair and covering her head with a black fisherman's skull cap.

Every bit of the clothing the lesbian nurse had brought her from her apartment to wear to Court would be left in the store's dressing room. Within minutes the thousand-dollar dress would no doubt disappear into some customer's handbag. The lucky woman wouldn't be able to believe her good fortune.

The shooter would then drive the stolen Toyota south down to the village of Wong Chuk Hang, abandon it, leaving the keys in the ignition, and catch a red top back to Aberdeen harbor. Then would come the easy part. Hiring a junk to take her to Po Toi, a small island south of Hong Kong.

When the junk dropped her off at the island she'd buy one of those disposable untraceable cell phones that were such the rage for criminals who needed to make covert phone contact without leading the cops to them or their call's recipients.

With a single untraceable phone call her stepfather would arrange transportation from Po Tai, via yacht to Taipei, Taiwan where he owned a reasonable number of the renegade country's ministers.

The ministers who her father had bought and paid for decades earlier would hide her and ensure her safety until the family's Gulfstream flew in to pickup her up for the return flight home to their 5,000-acre farm in the Outback of Australia.

All it would take is a little bit of luck. And she had always been blessed with exceptional luck.

EPILOGUE:

Chief Inspector Augustus Fox
Hong Kong Police Department

Seven weeks had passed since the 21 October 2007 attempt by Angry Dragon to kill Chief Inspector Fox. Winter has moved into Hong Kong with a vengeance bringing with it gale force winds, increased rainfall and lower temperatures.

Fox had recovered enough from his injuries to be discharged to home for rehabilitation. He was scheduled to begin physical therapy on 15 December. His debilitating wounds had required among other things total knee replacements including prosthetic carbon fiber kneecaps.

About the same time, Fox was officially informed by the Hong Kong police department and the police commissioner, represented by the department's lawyers and Assistant Chief of Personnel John Russell, of the department's findings relative to his eventual return to duty.

The letter, which was littered with officiousness, whereas and therefore's, stated that in the professional opinion of the department's chief surgeon, the gravity of Fox's injuries regardless of any successes he may achieve in future rehabilitative physical therapy, would prevent him continuing as an employee of the Hong Kong police department in *any* capacity.

The letter didn't come as a complete surprise to Fox. Nor the fact that Assistant Chief Russell had no doubt pulled rank on the department's lawyers to make sure he was the one who had delivered the career-ending document to the disabled chief inspector.

As Fox had predicted to Dr. Alicia Ho on 21 October about three hours prior to be ambushed by rogue Interpol agent Angry Dragon and subjected to a beating to end all beatings, Russell not only wanted him out of the department but also as far away from Hong Kong as possible. The reason behind Russell's decision was elementary. It was a matter of what Russell knew, that Fox knew.

Russell had been complicit in the torture/murder of Fox's at-the-time live-in lover. In addition, the Aussie was a mole of the People's Republic of China hiding under deep cover in the police department. Russell had given deceased Chief Inspector Deng marching orders to murder a number of HKSAR legislators. Included in that mandate was the 2005 attempt on Fox's life.

Fox's notice of 'Unacceptable For Continuing Employment' letter was accompanied by two structured offers of lump sum financial compensation, both conditional on Fox's not contesting his forced retirement.

The first offer stated that Fox's doctors had released him from the hospital as having his wounds reasonably healed. The doctors said Fox would be able to get around with the assistance of a cane, but without the need for devices such as a wheelchair or crutches.

It went on to say that based on the statements of his attending hospital physicians, the department was offering Fox a lump sum payment of US$200,000. The document further stated that the department felt no obligation to continue paying for any medical bills Fox might incur in the future.

The second offer differed from the first inasmuch as it acknowledged that Fox may have need of future medical attention for the wounds he had incurred in the line of duty. Therefore the lump sum figure would be increased to US$800,000 but was qualified with the stipulation that Fox must relocate out of the Hong Kong Special Administrative Region. The reasoning behind that stipulation the offer said, was that his continued presence in Hong Kong might be detrimental to the morale of the Hong Kong police department and its administration.

Fox had declined to make an immediate decision as to whether he would legally attempt to contest his forced retirement, or opt to accept one of the two lump sum retirement settlement agreements. He formally asked Russell for thirty days, until 15 January 2008, to either accept one of the buy-out offers or notify Russell that he intended to legally dispute the validity of the basis stated for the forced retirement.

Knowing Fox was not making an unreasonable request, Russell was aware that if he denied the request for thirty additional days to consider the offers it would be a no-brainer for the chief inspector to demand a civilian review board. They in turn were certain to rule in favor of a man who the

Hong Kong press was touting as a hero. Therefore, but with reluctance, Russell had agreed to Fox's request.

As soon as Russell had left his condo Fox had picked up the phone and called Dr. Alicia Ho at work in her Taiyunan office inquiring whether there was room in her home for a cashiered cop for the next month.

Breathlessly, Alicia had whispered some unladylike threats of what she would do to him if he didn't pack a bag immediately and catch a red top out to the Hong Kong International Airport. She told Fox to go to the China Air ticket desk on level 5. A first class ticket and 30-day tourist visa that she had previously arranged for in anticipation of they're spending Christmas together, would be waiting for him.

———

Fox had spent the entire month from when his plane touched down at Taiyunan airport the evening of 15 December 2007 until 14 January 2008 with Alicia getting reacquainted with her. Getting acquainted with their son who had celebrated his first birthday on Christmas day.

The chill of the Taiyunan winter didn't have any positive impact on Fox's recovery but he worked out everyday and Alicia helped him do exercises that promoted healing when she wasn't at her office.

On 14 January, Fox and Alicia with Augustus Jr. pulling on his pants leg, sat down and had a long discussion about their future together. He admitted he was worried because he was not yet able to walk any distance or do any physical labor.

Alicia had suggested that Fox temporarily take over the care of their son at her father's home, even though he had been a little uncomfortable when Alicia referred to his new job as being a 'house dad.'

Fox had brought the department's 'Unacceptable For Continued Employment' letter and the department's two offers of retirement compensation with him to Taiyunan a month earlier.

After he and Alicia had read them both over for about the hundredth time, Fox signed the second offer with a flourish as Alicia called FedEx for a pickup.

The letter indicating Fox's acceptance of the second offers was delivered in a FedEx global overnight envelope to a nervous Assistant Chief Russell the next morning in Hong Kong.

After reading it twice, the Aussie affixed his signature under Fox's and uttered a huge sigh of relief. Russell ordered his administrative assistant to drop everything she was doing to hand-carry a voucher request down to the Disbursement Department. It included hand-written orders from Russell to the director of that department to make certain a certified government check in the amount of US$800,000 was sent FedEx, overnight delivery, to arrive at Dr. Ho's Taiyunan residence no later than 10:30 a.m. HKT the following morning.

As soon as his administrative assistant walked out of the office on her way to Disbursements, Russell opened the bottom door of his desk, selected a unopened bottle of 100 proof Smirnoff Lemon-flavored vodka because it would be undetectable on his breath, and poured four finger's worth into his coffee cup which he chugged down, and immediately poured a second.

He was finally free of the *gweilo* that had plagued his sleep for the past several years.

———

Inspector Ho Pham, Homicide Squad
Hong Kong Police Department

Almost simultaneously after Angry Dragon's attack on Chief Inspector Fox had put him in Matilda Hospital for reconstructive surgery, Inspector Ho Pham returned to his desk. The reason he needed the personal time off had resolved itself.

As Asia is much less homophobic than the western world, no one made a big deal about the extended absence Ho had requested to bury and take care of the final affairs of his life partner.

Ho was prepared to return to his job as inspector of the homicide squad and let Lt. Du Ming, who has managed well in Ho's absence, return to running the day-to-day activities of the elite ten-detective squad.

However, the police surgeon had just informed the personnel chief that Fox would be off work for at least four months, and perhaps would never be physically able to return to lead his department.

Fox's department, Crimes Against Persons, employed 40 people including sworn detectives and administrative personnel. The department's performance over the past ten years had resulted in a case closure rate higher than any other law enforcement agency in Asia, let alone Hong Kong.

That department's clearance rate must continue to be stellar to maintain the currently positive approval ratings by which the police department, the police commissioner, and every one of his administrators and department heads was viewed by the citizens, the Media and most importantly, by the HKSAR Chief Executive, David 'Davis' Tsang's office.

The Crimes Against Persons department's past exemplary clearance rates were far too important to permit the office to just drift unguided by a stabilizing influence until the question of whether Chief Inspector Fox would return to duty was resolved.

However, Russell saw assignment of an interim boss to oversee the operations of the Fox's department to be far more complicated than the police commissioner perceived.

There still was a feeling in the police department hierarchy, as well as in the Media, that the criminals behind the killings of five cops and two Medical Examiner personnel should have been brought before the docket of the High Court on Old Bailey Street.

The HKSAR had wanted a show trial to demonstrate to its folder holder, the People's Republic of China, that Hong Kong is tough on crime and even tougher on scofflaws. The chief executive, the legislators, and the police brass, all had been deprived of the opportunity to preen and strut their stuff, and act extraordinarily executive, effective, and omniscient by having brought the evildoers to justice.

But Fox, abetted by inspectors Yin and Chen Ho, inexplicably had made the decision to delay the raid for over a day after they had learned the location of the body part harvesting operation. The decision to delay the raid had been had been made because, in Fox's words, "The detectives had been up for forty-eight hours straight; they were tired and worn out; and tired and worn out cops invariable get killed in armed confrontations."

But Russell reasoned that the cloud that hung over Fox, Yin and Chen Ho's head, at least in the police administration and the Media's collective minds didn't extended to Inspector Ho Pham who had been on personal leave at the time.

There was no way that anyone could include inspector Ho Pham in the criticism of how the timing of the raid of the Queens Road funeral parlor had been handled. No possibility of anyone assigning any blame to Ho Pham, because when the raid had finally been executed, detectives had found everyone at the location had been executed, presumably to keep them from talking and being prosecuted in a public trial.

That was the reason that almost immediately upon returning to his desk as homicide inspector, the police commissioner promoted 35-year-old Ho Pham to acting chief inspector of the Headquarters-Crimes Against Persons Department.

And that reasoning continued to be the commissioner's thinking months later when he made Ho Pham's promotion permanent after Fox had agreed to accept an financial settlement offer from the police department.

————

Assistant Chief John Russell (Personnel)
Hong Kong Police Department

John Russell was an Aussie ex-pat well past the age of fifty, a holdover from the days of the *raj*. When the People's Republic of China took over administration of Hong Kong in June of 1997, corrupt police officials sympathetic to the PRC warned the then-chief executive, Tung Chee-hwa, to retain Russell because the man knew where too many bodies were buried to even considering replacing him.

The PRC's decision to permit Tung Chee-hwa to allow the police commissioner to retain the services of Russell ended up setting the precedent whenever the question of personnel replacement on the law enforcement organization, then called the Royal Hong Kong Police, was discussed.

The commissioner and Tung Chee-Hwa were aware that Russell over the years had accepted money from the PRC to inform on Hong Kong police matters. Firing him would no doubt only result in the chief executive being ordered by the PRC to send the Hong Kong police commissioner a demand to reinstate Russell with full back pay.

In fact, that mind set is the reason that the organization, today called the Hong Kong police department, is still largely run and staffed as it was under the British. Its officers are proud to still be considered one of Asia's best police forces.

Russell, at well over 6 feet tall and 375 pounds with a ruddy Australian face, had over the years adopted the disgusting Chinese habit of spitting when ever and where ever he chose. Russell had been a closet drinker before Chief Inspector Fox retired, but with Fox's signed retirement agreement safe in his files, Russell had come to feel omnipotent, like he alone had power over his personal destiny.

Russell increased the rate and frequency of his drinking in his office, began to miss work, and invariably took extended lunch hours several days a week. The Commission Against Corruption reported to the police commissioner that Russell on several occasions had been observed having lunch with one or more of the Red Poles of Hong Kong's larger triads.

In the evenings the corrupt cop could be found in Wan Chai district at one of the strip clubs that never let high-ranking police officials pay for a drink.

It was at one of those clubs, one covertly owned by the 14K triad that Russell had been introduced by the club's general manager, to a beautiful young Chinese woman by the name of Jie Wei.

Jie Wei told Russell that she had just arrived from Beijing. She said while she was currently unemployed and almost out of money, she felt her prospects were excellent as her educational history included both Bachelors and Masters degrees, and her employment history included a position as senior administrative assistant working for the BOC, Bank of China.

The alcoholic Russell could not believe his good *joss*, luck, in meeting a gorgeous woman whose personal situation made her appear ripe for his plucking.

They had finished out the evening drinking the free cocktails the waitress continued to deliver to their table. Russell told the woman who he was and of his importance in Hong Kong.

While she had mulled that over, he'd asked her if he could take her back to his residence.

The woman had blushed and politely demurred, saying she was only 21 and still a virgin. And that she was saving herself to give to her husband someday.

Russell, once he told women who he was, had never before been turned down or refused. At least by the women he often met in Hong Kong's notorious strip clubs. That this woman had been brave enough to stand up to him, a high-ranking member of the police, enamored her to him. A normal man perhaps would have felt himself falling in love.

That night Russell continued to drink on the cuff at the club while his driver drove Jie Wei to the address she gave him, dropping her off in the driveway of the opulent Oriental Mandarin hotel.

Russell's driver had hurried off to pickup his boss who was waiting for him at the strip club, and thus didn't notice Jei Wei hail a taxi as soon as the limo was out of sight.

The couple had dinner together several times in the next seven days, once at the world famous China Club. Jei Wei acted very impressed and

Russell had thought, tonight is the night. But the woman begged off saying that while she was now willing to give her virtue to him, tonight she had a headache.

Russell by now was frustrated by the woman's refusal to give him sex like every other woman he encountered in his nightly forays to the Wan Chai clubs. He figured he'd make one more attempt to get through to the prize she protected so much.

Two nights later, Russell borrowed the yacht of a Chinese Taipan who the police some years ago had discovered having sex with two young boys. The man was more than willing to turn the boat over to Russell for the evening of lust with the understanding it would stay at anchor in its berth in the Royal Hong Kong Yacht Club.

Russell was already aboard the 175-foot yacht when Jei Wei arrived in a taxi for a promised evening of sexual opportunity. He had ordered a caterer to deliver the night's entrée to the yacht consisting of sautéed baby lobster served in melted butter. For libations there was a magnum of chilled Grey Goose gin in a sterling silver ice chest, along with pimento-stuffed olives, and in an identical chest, four chilled glasses.

That night had been going marvelously well Russell thought, up to the point where he got Jei Wei into bed. At that point, she refused to have sex with him unless he told her he loved her, would take care of her forever, and agreed to marry her the following week.

By that time Russell would have claimed he could fly and leap tall buildings in single bound in order to get into the woman's pants. So he had readily agreed to all of her stipulations.

When he had finally got her engaged in love making, something untold destroyed their night of bliss.

Unusual for a cop, Russell had never been able to stand the sight or the coppery smell of blood.

A few seconds after ejaculating in Jei Wei he had rolled off her, flipped the light on, and lit his usual after-sex cigar. Suddenly, he was shocked to find the high-thread-count silk sheets covered in blood, so much so he had dropped the lit cigar on his belly. He was revolted, sick to his stomach, and ran into the bathroom and threw up in the sink.

Leaving the door open he had continued to scream and threaten the woman for causing all the blood as he cleaned himself and attempted to use the toilet, but ended up splattering urine all around because in his anger he had forgotten to raise the lid.

Wrapping himself in a white over-size terry cloth towel he had returned to the bloody bed and slapped Jei Wei once, twice, and a third time. As she cried, she tried to explain that the blood merely was because this had been her 'first time.'

Russell had continued to yell at her hysterically to "Get dressed!" as he returned to the bathroom and continued in his attempts to scrub blood off his privates and his ample stomach.

Jei Wie continued to cry but afraid of the man's irrational anger, gathered up her things and walked to the stateroom door. She paused and wiped the tears out of her eyes before turning around and with a defeated look asked, "John, you never intended to marry me. You lied just to get me to give you my virginity, didn't you?"

Russell was astonished, laughed and answered her. "Of course I lied to you, Jei Wei. Did you really think I would give up my life of partying with a different woman every night to marry some whore who contaminated me with her blood, first time or not?"

He reached under the mattress to where, accustomed to being with prostitutes, he had hidden his wallet and gun when they had gotten undressed. He pulled a crisp US$100 bill out of the wallet, crumbled it up and threw it at her saying, "Walk down the gangplank and over to the Yacht club. They have a taxi stand. This should be enough cab fare to get you home, whore."

Jei Wie argued, "But John, your car and driver is parked in the lot below. Why can't you drop me off at home?"

Russell snapped back at her, "Because you have ruined my evening. You are a stupid woman, thinking I would ever marry you anyway. Now get out of here before I hit you again."

Jei Wei had took a deep breath and turned to walk out the door, effectively preventing Russell from seeing the look of absolute hate that contorted the delicate features of her beautiful face.

———

Two days later, Jei Wie had called Russell on his private line at work. She asked if there was someway she could make up her lack of cleanliness up to him?

She said she would do anything, any sexual act, to win his forgiveness. No, she no longer expected him to marry her. But she didn't want to leave such a sad state of affairs between them even though she understood that they were no longer going to be seeing each other.

"Please, John," she had begged. "Do this last thing for me. Have sex with me. I know you'll like me performing oral sex on you. And then I'll never bother you again."

———

That night they had met at a small hotel in the Suzy Wong district. Jei Wei had brought along a bottle of chilled Grey Goose gin, some stuffed olives and there were a couple chilled glasses in the room's refrigerator.

Russell's driver was ill so he had been forced to catch a red top cab to the fleabag hotel.

After consuming two drinks, Jei Wei had immediately got undressed and urged Russell on until he also disrobed. While he was hanging up his suit in the cheap room's closet, she made them two more drinks, blocking what her hands were doing with her naked body. Russell didn't see her slip two purple pills into his glass. Then she stirred both drinks well.

She carried both drinks over to where Russell was laying his back in the middle of the bed, and chugged hers. She offered to rub his entire body with a secret stimulating potion a girlfriend of hers had turned her on to, as soon as he finished his drink. Now erect and in lust, he readily tossed his drink down.

Less than ten minutes later, Jei Wei raised her head from where she had been working on Russell's limp penis. She pinched his scrotum between her thumb and index finger nails. Besides a light jump of his flaccid hips there was no response. Russell laid on the bed breathing deeply as if he was in a deep sleep.

Jei Wei dressed quickly making no attempt at being quiet. She knew the purple pills ensured Russell would be out for a good four hours.

Using a tissue Jei went around the small room wiping all the surfaces she might have touched in the forty-five minutes they had occupied the room. She pulled three objects out of her purse, a can of lighter fluid, a pair of latex gloves, and a book of matches before walking into the postage-stamp-sized bathroom to flush the used tissue.

She pulled on a pair of talcum-powdered gloves, snapping them to make certain they were tight against her skin. She removed Russell's wallet and gun from under his side of the mattress and slipped a gold Rolex President off his wrist, putting everything into her purse.

She folded the matchbook cover back behind the matches, and bent the head of one of the phosphorus-coated heads down so all she had to do was use her thumb to scrape the coarse striker surface to ignite it.

With purse now slung over her shoulder she walked over to room's exit door to make certain it would open easily and verified that the chain lock wasn't engaged.

She returned to the bed and spit on the unconscious man. Then using her left hand she poured the entire contents of the lighter fluid can over Russell's privates and tossed the can on the floor. Using her right hand, she employed her thumb to scratch the single bent match head against the striking surface.

When it flared up she turned the matchbook upside down until all the matches were on ablaze then dropped it on Russell's cock. Pulling the gloves off her hands and tossing them into the growing fire she hurried from the room being careful to make sure the door swung closed behind her, locking, without her having to touch the handle.

————

Jei Wei wasn't her name. She wasn't twenty-one, but fifteen years of age. And she was not the administrative assistant she'd told Russell. She was proud of the fact that she was a *paak yee mun*. A slang term meaning 'northern aunties.' Young, single, pretty Chinese female, grasping, scheming, on the take, and out to snare a husband. Like her *paak yee mun* 'sisters' she was fresh from the Chinese mainland and her native language was Mandarin Chinese.

She hadn't been a virgin since her father had first introduced her to sex and her new job in the family at age nine.

The blood that Russell had gotten so upset over was really pig's blood mixed with an anti-coagulant so it wouldn't clot. She'd bought it from a 'wedding night aids' vendor in the Mongkok district. It came in a knotted condom that she'd perforated with her fingernails under the guise of stimulating herself when they had been having sex several nights before.

Paak yee mun ladies routinely purchased the device to convince naïve men on their wedding night that they were still virgins.

Once she had left the hotel, she had taken a red top taxi to the main station for the KCR railroad. Once the train departed the station, she arrived safely at her family's home in Guangzhou in three hours, far out of reach of the Hong Kong police.

Elizabeth Stewart, Administrative Assistant
Crimes Against Persons Department
Hong Kong Police Department.

Fox's executive assistant had been arrested by CAC agents about 4:50 p.m., a few minutes after Fox had left his office on Monday, 21 October 2007.

When the agents first entered the office, Mini Yin and Chen Ho, discussing a case over the hp laserjet copy machine, hadn't noticed them. But then the two agents had identified themselves to Elizabeth, displaying their identification in one hand, while pulling their service weapons with the other.

Both agents had trained their weapons on Elizabeth who had been sitting at her desk enjoying a late afternoon cup of green tea. She had her hands folded primly as if she had been anticipating the two men's arrival.

The display of weapons by the agents was established police procedure when making a felony arrest. But it almost resulted in a potentially fatal firefight.

As soon as the two agents had pulled their guns on Elizabeth, the inspectors standing at the copy machine had caught a glimpse of the men's actions out of their peripheral vision. Mimi Yin and Chen Ho had dropped to the floor behind the bulky copier and trained their weapons on the two men who were unknown to them.

Both inspectors were shocked and confused. They hadn't been advised of the pending arrest because Chief Inspector Fox had been ordered to stand mute. Higher authority had prevented him from alerting anyone that Elizabeth would be arrested as soon as he left the office.

Just short of a firefight that would have no doubt would have taken several lives, Elizabeth took the initiative by standing up and turning to the inspectors, saying, "It's okay, Mini and Ho. I've been expecting them. It's the rat squad. You know, the Commission Against Corruption."

Without lowering her weapon Mini had come to her feet while Chen Ho continued to cover the agents. Inspector Yin walked forward until she could read the agent's identification and the warrant for Elizabeth's arrest one of them had slowly eased out of his jacket's inside pocket.

Elizabeth had walked out from behind her desk keeping her hands in sight and pivoted around for the agents to hook a set of handcuffs around her wrists, behind her back.

Upon seeing Elizabeth do that, both inspectors had holstered their weapons but continued to stand there in shock as if one of the agents had unzipped his fly and urinated on the floor.

Mimi Yin was the first to say something. "Why is Elizabeth being arrested? Please hold off on the arrest until Chief Inspector Fox can be called. What for the sake of Buddha is going on here?"

The senior agent turned to Mimi having also holstered his weapon and held his hands out in supplication. "Inspector Yin, all I know is that my Boss ordered me to serve this arrest warrant on Ms. Stewart here for the murders of police officers Johnny Yang, Chow Yung Su, and Lau Lai."

The agent continued, "My Boss told me that Chief Inspector Fox is aware of the arrest and has been ordered by the police commissioner not to alert Elizabeth, or to interfere in any manner. I suspect that when we were on our way in here and passed Fox in the hall, he was acting on a direct order from above to vacate the office."

Yin looked at Elizabeth and demanded, "Elizabeth, what is this all about? Why are these two guys claiming that you have murdered three cops? Why didn't you tell one of us, ask for our help? Say something!"

With a sigh, Elizabeth replied, "Because you couldn't have done anything, Mini. I did murder three cops, after they had murdered me. I was overconfident and careless at the last shooting. I got scared and ended up leaving some evidence at the scene. I imagine the crime lab easily raised my prints and maybe have even recovered my DNA off the body, because I remember spitting on Lau's body. Now just let these guys do their job, okay?"

Before she was led out the door, Elizabeth asked Mimi and Chen Ho to please clear out her desk. They were to send anything personal in it and her purse to her parent's home address in Australia. She'd obviously sensed that her arrest was imminent and had been prepared. She'd placed the address of her parents on a scarp of paper inside the purse with enough money to send everything FedEx.

She told Mimi that she had mailed her stepfather a letter last night explaining that she had done the killings and why. She'd expected to be arrested first thing that morning after a second casual lover in the crime lab had alerted her at home early that morning, saying that CAC agents were over there looking over bagged evidence that had her name on it.

———

Elizabeth had been arraigned in Magistrate court on Old Bailey Street the next morning, Tuesday, 22 October 2007. Her attorney managed to talk Elizabeth out of pleading guilty to the killings, believing the young woman could get a deal from the Courts if she could convince them she was criminally insane at the time of the shootings. That finding would permit her attorney to claim extenuating circumstances.

Yin, Ho, and Ming had been in attendance at Elizabeth's arraignment. Elizabeth had been surprised and disappointed that Fox hadn't come until Mini had slipped her court-appointed attorney a note. It said that Fox had been critically wounded in the takedown of the leader of the body part harvesting gang. He would be hospitalized for at least the next several months.

The Magistrate had set the date for the murder trial to begin on 01 March 2008. The judge strongly suggested to Elizabeth that she employ private defense counsel as she was facing a three murder charges, each with capital implications. Meaning, he explained, that there was the possibly of death sentence being handed down on any or all of the charges if the jury found her guilty.

He had also told Elizabeth that in his dealings with her in her official job function with the police department in the past, he'd always had the utmost respect for her. He said he could not believe she would have committed these horrendous crimes if she had been sane at the time.

Aware he was setting up the basis for a diminished capacity defense and not caring that he was doing so, he had committed Elizabeth to the first bed opening up in a mental health facility in Hong Kong for psychiatric evaluation. She would remain at the hospital until she came to trial in March of 2008.

––––––––

During Elizabeth's initial confinement at the mental health hospital, she had shared with her psychiatrists the gang rape she had experienced. She said she had been drinking heavily with a number of young off-duty cops at the Boathouse Restaurant Bar in Stanley on Hong Kong Island.

Shortly before 1:00 a.m. on Saturday 28 September 2007, three young cops she knew by first name only had offered her a ride home to her apartment in the Wan Chai district. The statement was not exactly factual. It had actually had been Elizabeth that had asked for the ride home.

When they arrived at her apartment it had been about 1:30 a.m. Elizabeth had politely asked them up for nightcap as repayment for saving her the cost of a taxi for the eight-mile ride home. The men had accepted.

When they got into her apartment, she had offered them all chilled Tsingao beers while she went into the bathroom to change from her party clothes into a pair of shorts and a tee shirt.

She returned and had been enjoying her beer when things had suddenly turned very, very ugly.

She had found herself physically pinned to the couch by one of the young men. Her clothes had been ripped from her body and they had forcibly raped her, one after another.

They had continued to assault her, and as they did, threatened her life if she ever mentioned what had happened to anyone. They told her that she knew they could get at her anytime because they were cops. She feared for her life, as she knew their threat was not only possible but also probable.

After the men had finally left, she'd stumbled to her sleeping area. She was furious, determined that no one got away with raping her against her will. So using the rudimentary knowledge of forensics she had picked up around work, she'd gathered together the makings of a crude rape kit.

She wiped herself down with cotton Q-tips to gather semen as she had heard that nurses do in the hospital, putting those in a clean zip-lock bag and writing on it with a Sharpie, the location from which the sample had been taken, the date and time, and her initials.

Then she felt around her vagina with her fingers attempting to locate any sore spots or lacerations, which she attempted to photograph. Next she pared the underside of her nails to obtain scrapings of the men's epithelial cells.

At that point Elizabeth had only intended to take the homemade rape kit to her friend in the Crime Lab and ask her to covertly check the semen and finger nail scrapings she had collected for DNA, and anything else that would make her case stronger when she confronted the men, as she planned on demanding a formal departmental conduct hearing on the egregious rape and assault.

Her plan fell apart when she called the lab and found that her friend was on vacation in France and wouldn't return to the lab for three weeks.

Three weeks, Elizabeth reasoned, would be too long. If she didn't have the samples analyzed immediately the specimens would degrade. If the samples were allowed to degrade, DNA could not be obtained. It would weaken her case, and the men could hire a sharp defense attorney and claim the sex had been consensual.

After she given it more thought, Elizabeth's confused mind rationalized that she might be able to get some money out of the three men. After she had the money that the families of the three men would pay to ensure her silence, she would claim to have changed her mind and publicly expose the men in the press as rapists.

When Elizabeth had reported to work on Monday, 30 September 2007 she still hadn't made up her mind on a plan. But she knew it couldn't hurt for her to find out everything she could on the three cops although it would require abusing her authorized use of her boss's password.

First thing that she had done, when at an opportune moment she found her boss and the inspectors in a closed door meetings, was to run a search of the Hong Kong police personnel database using only the first name she knew for any of the men. Then she had created a search parameter bracketing male cops between 21 and 30 years of age.

When the computer had told her it had a selection matching the search parameters ready for her to review, she had clicked on each until she came across the full names of all three men. Then she had compared those names against the police academy graduation pictures.

Inside forty-five minutes she had name, rank, department ID number, current assignment, department history and their work schedules for the next month.

She looked around the office until she discovered some files that were overdue from being returned to the Records department on the second floor.

Before heading that direction she had forged Fox's signature on a records request for the three cops, marking it CONFIDENTIAL—CASE RELATED ensuring the removal of three files wouldn't be officially logged into the personnel file tracking system.

————

Later that day she'd had poked her head in her boss's office and told him that she was going to records to return some files for the inspectors. Then she planned on taking a break in the first basement cafeteria before returning to the office. Fox had just absently mindedly waved his hand and didn't look up as she quietly closed his door.

She remembered to grab her purse, 'for the cafeteria' remember, and the past due files before heading for Records with her forged file request.

When she walked into the Records Department the front desk had been a madhouse as always. She picked the cutest male clerk and walked over using the hip swing she had worked on for years as a teenager. When she got to his window the clerk looked up with a look on his face that her knew was him thinking, *How did I get this lucky?*

With a seductive look on her face that she knew from years of experience said "Please fuck me" she had slipped the overdue files across the marble counter surface to the clerk making certain her fingers brushed the back of his hand.

Then she handed over the forged file request, telling the blushing clerk that the chief inspector said he only would need them for about thirty minutes. As the young man turned and nearly stumbled over a co-worker in his haste to get into the achieves to retrieve the three files for her, Elizabeth enjoyed a private grin and once again thanked her birth mother and father for the genes that had made her a gorgeous woman.

The clerk had returned with the three personnel files in less than five minutes time. Elizabeth took them in her hands, pressing them to her chest, making certain the bulky files pushed her breasts forward and up. Before turned away, she assured him she'd hand-carry them back as soon as the chief inspector finished with them. And of course, she'd returned them personally to his window.

Elizabeth had walked out of the Records Department and located the closest Ladies room. There were a couple of women standing at the mirror primping their hair when she located one. As soon as they had left, she slipped into a toilet stall, closing its door and locking it behind her.

Then, still pressing the files against her breasts, she had used her right hand to pull her skirt up and her panty hose down before sitting down on the toilet seat.

She pulled a small notebook from her purse and began to flip through the files noting the particulars, checking the last page in the file to make certain none of the rapists had somehow convinced a supervisor to give them a concealed weapons permit that would have allowed them to carry a gun off-duty.

She had decided that she'd better empty her bladder in case someone had come in and was standing around listening, waiting for an unoccupied stall. She had just opened the third and last file and began to pee when she came across a medical report from a civilian doctor addressed to the department medical officer.

When she read what the report said she was so shocked that she began to stand up unconsciously in mid-stream and ended up peeing all over her the panty hose that were gathered at her ankles.

She cursed men in general, cursed the cop whose personnel folder would have fallen off her lap if she hadn't had her left hand on it, and cursed her pantyhose.

What had upset the tough Aussie woman so badly was the civilian physician's statement in the report that said that a series of clinical tests had confirmed conclusively that this individual had advanced HIV that possibly had already morphed into AIDS. The private physician had recommended to the HKP department's medical officer that the officer be relieved from all contact with the public, forthwith, as in immediately.

This infected bastard and the other two had effectively killed her, ending her life. It was then that Elizabeth had decided to kill all the cops that had raped her.

She had removed her sopping pantyhose and used toilet tissue to dry herself. Them she had dug around in her purse until she found a near empty bottle of Nasty Girl spray-on perfume, and applied it liberally to her clothing. Wrapping her ruined pantyhose in toilet tissue, she flushed it, pulled down her skirt and stooped to wipe off the tops of her leather pumps.

When she had opened the stall door she was thankful that there was no one currently in the restroom.

Making an effort to strut her stuff as she walked back to the Records office, thinking how deliciously shocked everyone would be if they knew she was naked under her skirt, she tossed the three files into the night deposit slot certain they would be returned to their proper location by the following morning.

———

The next morning she again abused her databank password privileges to look up the work schedule of one of her casual sexual partners, a woman, to find out what shift she was working in the evidence room that week.

Finding the woman was working the day shift that week, Elizabeth made a mental note to herself to bring a large shoulder bag with her to work the following day.

About 10:00 a.m. the next morning, normally the slow time for the evidence locker since most of the detectives had already picked up their evidence for Court, she rode the executive elevators down to the 2nd basement. Approaching the counter she had been thankful to find her lover sitting on her sizable ass, cracking her knuckles.

Elizabeth had suggested a quick tryst. In response her lover had promptly opened the locked gate, allowing her to slip through. A half hour later Elizabeth walked out of the cage touching up her lipstick with a Ruger .22-caliber Model Standard target pistol with a 4.75 inch polygonal barrel and a box of 100 rim fire cartridges shoved deep in her purse under some tissues.

The only thought going through Elizabeth's insane mind at that moment had been, *Let the killing begin*!

———

Elizabeth had decided that she wasn't willing to take the chance that the Court would exonerate her for the murders. On 01 March 2008, as she was being transported to what would have been her final competency hearing at Old Bailey, she had overpowered and killed the orderlies who had been escorting her.

She had taken their wallets, cell phones, and the car, a white Toyota sedan of which there likely are 500,000 copies in Hong Kong alone. To the authorities knowledge, Elizabeth had never been seen in Hong Kong again.

Investigators felt that by some means she'd managed to work her way back to Australia. As with most every place in the world today, it only takes money to lubricate the local authorities and the fleeing felon figuratively becomes invisible. And Elizabeth's wealthy parents had plenty of that.

Angry Dragon
A.K.A. Sinclair Leymon

The death of former Interpol agent code-named Angry Dragon temporarily closed down the illegal body part harvesting operation in Hong Kong. However, the practice continues today in more than 50% of the supposedly civilized countries in the world.

Before his death, Leymon had revealed to Chief Inspector Augustus Fox that people under his orders had eliminated the link that transported the processed body parts between Hong Kong and a Chinese junk that loitered just beyond the twelve-mile limit.

In his last official action before Interpol had found him out, Leymon had stumbled across Cary Erwin, an ex-Australian Air force pilot, an ex-pat who had fled Sydney in front of a felony Transportation of Heroin indictment some five years previously.

When Leymon first met Ervin, the Aussie was nearly penniless and down on his luck, and like so many other fugitive ex-pats living in Mongkok, attempting to sell counterfeit Methamphetamine to gullible tourists. While normally a colorless volatile liquid, in powder form it is used primarily as a central nervous system stimulant.

Leymon always had kept an eye out for professionals who were down on their luck. With a little detoxification and ego priming they could become valuable to him in one of his many off-the-books criminal schemes.

Ervin had been drinking for so long that it eventually had required shock therapy to get him back into a reasonable facsimile of a sober pilot. After that, he only dabbled in liquor and left mind-altering drugs completely alone.

Using his contacts in Hong Kong, Angry Dragon arranged for Erwin's pilot's license to be reinstated. Then he extorted a used Beaver seaplane from a drug dealer facing indictment in Singapore with the understanding that the man's legal problems would go away.

When the drug dealer's attorney told him that somehow the prosecution's evidence had disappeared, the defendant was so ecstatic that he even paid for the old Beaver to be overhauled, repainted, and re-registered under a phony aircraft number that Leymon had provided.

Leymon had arranged for the aircraft, burdened with an asset-secured collateral loan from the Bank of China, to be delivered to Erwin in Hong Kong.

Leymon had permitted Erwin to start up a small aerial sightseeing business in Hong Kong that specialized in taking tourists on flights over the China Sea Islands, which are located due south of Hong Kong.

Erwin's only obligation to Leymon—the airplane and business even was in Erwin's name—was to make one flight daily out to a specified fishing junk with a cargo of refrigerated ice chests. Unknown to Erwin, the chests contained the smuggled body parts that Angry Dragon's gang had harvested that day at the Queens Road funeral parlor. Erwin had been warned to keep him mouth shut about things that didn't concern him.

The afternoon of 17 October 2007, a Thursday, Chief Inspector Fox had left a phone message on Leymon's answering machine advising him of the impending Hong Kong police raid on the funeral parlor early the next morning.

Angry Dragon had been forced to move fast and with extreme prejudice.

First, he sent a kill team from a Chinese triad in Macau to the funeral parlor to execute the medical employees who performed the illegal removal of body parts from corpses.

Fortunately, the funeral parlor's body part 'take' that day had already removed by an criminal associate whose knowledge of the operation was restricted to picking up the ice chests and transporting them to the docks.

There under the cover of darkness, another associate, unknown to the first, covertly loaded the refrigerated chests filled with the perishable body parts onto Erwin's plane that was tied up after nightfall at the seaplane dock at Fenwick pier.

Leymon, being too greedy to just abandon Thursday's body part haul that had already been picked up, contacted the fishing junk and arranged with its captain to have a altitude-activated bomb slipped onto Erwin's plane during his morning's delivery to the junk.

Cary Erwin, former crack Australian Air Force pilot and his Beaver, were currently feeding the fishes at the bottom of the deep-water channel between Lantau and Lamma islands, south of Hong Kong.

Leymon in a deathbed-type statement had told Fox the identity of the mysterious mechanic who had been wearing a regulation police coverall when he removed the counterfeit Red Crescent van from the police impound yard.

Leymon revealed that the mechanic had been a transgender former cop who had been cashiered when he was caught stealing feminine hygiene products out of the ladies-only restrooms at the Victoria police station.

Detectives would later learn that the former cop had been killed on the orders of Angry Dragon to prevent the police from arresting him, and forcing the transgender thief to roll over on the next person up in the gang hierarchy. And so on, until eventually the cops would have learned the Interpol agent's identity.

GLOSSARY

AH BUN: Cantonese. Filipina maid, of which there are literally hundreds in Hong Kong.

BAD JOSS: Cantonese for Bad luck.

BAIDU: Cantonese for Acting chief executive.

BANGSHOU: Cantonese for Assistant.

BEIJING: China's capital city. Sometimes still referred to as P king.

BOA: Bank of China.

BOLO: International police procedural for, Be on the lookout.

BOOC: Beijing Olympic Organizing Committee.

BOOHOWDOY: Cantonese for an Entry-level triad soldier.

CACOPHONY: Languages spoken in Hong Kong include Minnahhua, Cantonese, Mandarin, Putonhua, Vietnamese, Korean, and English.

CCP: Central Communist Party (China).

CGO: Hong Kong's Centralized Government Offices, located at #11 Icehouse Street.

CHENG: Cantonese for Please. (An invitation.)

CHINESE MINORITY RACES: Ethnic Moguls, Manchu's, Tibetans, and Highurs.

COD: Cause of Death.

CODIS: Computerized method of comparing known DNA files. Combined DNA Index System. Renamed National DNA Index System by FBI in 1988.

CULTURAL REVOLUTION: Began in 1954, and left fifty million Chinese dead.

CYANOACRYLATE: Superglue fumes in an enclosed container that can reveal fingerprints that are nearly invisible to the naked eye.

DAI TAU LUK YEE: Cantonese. Sikh and Punjabi Pakistani guards for business. The Hong Kong term meaning 'big heads and green jackets,' a reference to the turbans and the color of their uniforms.

DATA BASES, FINGERPRINT: Ten Print, Palm Print, Latent and Partial Print.

DNA: [D(eoxyribo)N(ucleic)A(cid).

DOH JEH: Cantonese for Thank you. (For gift).

ELECTRIC POWER: Hong Kong is a voracious user of oil-fired electric power.

EXCHANGE RATE: About one USD for every HK 7.80.

EXEMPLAR: In Forensics, an exact copy, such as a positive casting of a shoe tread; fingerprint cards; a positive impression of the bite of a set of teeth.

EXPAT: Expatriate. A non-Asian foreigner working or living in Hong Kong.

FALUN GONG: Dissadent religious group in China.

FANN GWOI: Cantonese. Literally, Foreign devil, non-Asian.

FAN-TAN: Chinese gambling game.

FENG SHUI: Mandarin for 'Wind Water.' A primarily Asian belief in the placement of objects, things, and buildings, oriented in such a way as to encourage good luck, and repel bad. Cantonese equivalent is 'Fung Shui.'

FLIGHT-OR-FIGHT: When confronted by a dangerous situation, you get sweaty palms and your body introduces more adrenaline into your blood stream. Your breathing and heart rates increase and your muscles get ready to either run away or face the danger.

GAN: Cantonese for the obscenity, Fuck.

GAOL: Hold over English term used in Hong Kong for Jail, or prison.

GAY HO NEI YAU SUM: Cantonese for Fine, thank you.

GO-DOWN: A warehouse.

GWEILO: Cantonese. Foreigner; long-nose barbarian, Caucasian.

GWEIPOU: Cantonese. Literally, ghost woman. A Caucasian. Most likely an expat.

HAI: Cantonese for Yes. Also, SHIH.

HAI GUI: Cantonese for Sea turtle.

HAN: Chinese racial majority. Consists of Fujianese, Cantonese, Mandarin, and Taiwanese.

HKSAR: Hong Kong Special Administrative Region.

HO HO: Cantonese for Good.

HOL LAK NGOH YIU: Cantonese for Well, I must go now.

HONGSE: Cantonese. The color red.

IAFIS: FBI's Integrated Automatic Fingerprint Identification System.

IAOGAIDUI: Cantonese. The People's Republic of China's prison system.

INDICES, FINGERPRINT: Loops, ridge counts, islands, ulnar loops, deltas, bifurcations, whorls, and tented arches.

INSTANT INMATE SINCERITY: Defined as a means by which to identify a ex-con.

JOI GEN: Cantonese for See you.

JOSS: Cantonese for Fate.

JO SUN: Cantonese for Good Morning. Also JO SAHN.

LEGCO: Legislative Council.

LOABAN: Cantonese for Boss, or Supervisor.

MACAU: Located forty-five miles due west of Hong Kong. Accessible from Hong Kong via hydrofoils, or (much slower) ferries.

ME: Medical Examiner.

MEI DAN MGOI: Cantonese for The check, please.

MEIGUO: Cantonese for Money.

MIDDLE KINGDOM: The term used by Chinese in reference to their culture and existence.

M'GOY: Cantonese for Thank you or Please, depending on usage.

MITOCHONDRIAL DNA: An involved, costly process used mostly on bones, hair shafts, and extremely small highly degraded DNA samples of all types. Process can take thirty to ninety days to complete. A preliminary DNA profile of blood or tissue by a cheaper, if less exacting method can be accomplished in seven to seventeen days in a 24/7 forensic specialty lab.

MM HAI: Cantonese for No. Also POO SHIH.

MOOK: A triad member, scumbag, criminal, degenerate, military deserter.

M'SAI M'GOY: Cantonese for You are welcome.

MSAR: Macau Special Administrative Region.

NEI HA MA: Cantonese for How are you?

NEI HUI BIN DÓ A: Cantonese for Where are you going?

NE HO LAN: Cantonese for You are beautiful.

OCKHAM'S RAZOR: A principle stated by William of Ockham in the mid-1200's, that loosely translated from the Latin (Pluralitas Non Est Ponenda Sine Necessitate) is 'Do not make things unnecessarily complicated without necessity.'

PAAK KWU: Cantonese. Literally, northern aunties. Young, pretty, single Chinese females, openly dismissed as grasping, being on the make, and out to snare a husband.

PCR: Polymerase Chain Reaction. A modern method of DNA profiling. STR—Short Tandem Repeats, further enhances it. Which can be used on bloodstain samples as small as a dot on this typed page.

PLA: People's Liberation Army (China).

PLUTO: Usually seen as 'Plutoed.' New word in 2006. The act of being demoted.

PM: Post-mortem. A forensic autopsy.

POLITBURO: The chief political and executive committee of a Communist party.

POPULATION: Estimates of China's population vary between 1.23B and 2.0 B.

PRC: People's Republic of China.

PROBATIVE: Qualifying as evidence. Serving to test or prove. Furnished as proof.

RAPID START: A management tool adopted by the Federal Bureau Of Investigation that permits interchanging of personnel assigned to a particular case, without the necessity of the individual having to go through a learning curve to acquire the history of the case. Rapid Start lays out the pertinent facts on a case, chronologically, and requires that the designated primary agent on a case, or his or her designee, maintain and update the Rapid Start case file every twenty-four hours, or less, if appropriate. A newly assigned agent need only pull up the case file on his secure computer to familiarize himself on the sequence of events and facts, from case inception to current day, which permits the agent to be productive from day one, if not hour one. Easy to implement, a superior management tool that would be of benefit all law enforcement and investigative agencies.

RED POLE: The disciplinary officer, also 2nd-in-command of a triad.

SAI YAN: Cantonese. Literally, a Western person.

SAR: A special administrative region of the People's Republic of China.

SHENZHOU: Cantonese. Literally, means Divine Wind.

SMOG: Photography buffs visiting Hong Kong often complain that their attempts at taking photos in the SAR result in a quality less than they anticipated, primarily because rolling mills and other heavy industry are totally coal-fired in the PRC and New Territories. And if that doesn't explain particulates in the air, add in the fact that Hong Kong manufactures all its electricity by using oil-fired generators.

STAR FERRY: Inexpensive way to travel between Hong Kong (Island) and the Kowloon (Peninsula). Late 1990s, passage was one US dime; now thirty cents.

STR: Short Tandem Repeat. DNA Method that along with PCR replaced RFLP.

SUCCINYLACHOLINE: An injectable poison, a favorite of triad killers in Hong Kong and San Francisco. It takes six milligrams of the drug to kill a victim. The poison completely metabolizes in the body, even after the body's organs and systems have ceased working. The drug's presence in a dead body is impossible to detect after death by traditional port-mortem toxicology scans. Traditional first-aid is a waste of time. The post-mortem results only show that the victims died of a massive heart attack.

SUN YEE MUN: Cantonese. Literally, a new immigrant from the PRC. Only 150 Chinese are permitted to emigrate from China to Hong Kong each day, or a total of 54,750 per year.

TAIPAN: Extremely high-ranking official or citizen in Hong Kong, perhaps a industrialist, a large business owner, or a bank president.

TIANANMEN SQUARE: Open square in the center of Pēking (Beijing); one of the largest public squares in the world

TING: Cantonese for Wait.

TOD: Forensic and police procedural term for Time of Death.

TONG: Societies of Chinese who have common interests. Merchant Associations.

TRAVELING ROAD SHOW: A term for the FBI's invaluable program of providing training to local police departments across the country. Typically, the FBI's training agents go to a central point in the jurisdiction, and the police officers from the local departments travel to that location on a daily basis, saving their departments the attending student's travel and lodging expenses.

TRIAD: Chinese criminal associations. In Hong Kong, 14K triad is most predominant.

WAI: Cantonese for Hello (telephone).

WOO: Cantonese for Fog.

XIONG: Cantonese for Breasts.

YANG: Sunny side of the mountain.

YIN: Side of the mountain in shadows.

YINDAO: Cantonese for Female genitals.

YINJING: Cantonese for Male genitals.

ZAIJIAN: Cantonese for Goodbye; also JOY GEN, depending on intended usage.

REFERENCES AND SOURCES

ASCLD: American Society of Crime Lab Directors.

Biometrics: Personal Identification in a Networked Society; Burge, M., and Burger, W.

Black, David Et. Al., Triad Takeover: A terrifying Account of the Spread of Triad Crime.

Carroll, Brian P, Major Case Management, FBI Law Enforcement Bulletin.

Cottrell, Robert. The End of Hong Kong, 1993.

Crime Scene Investigation, Goddard, K., Reston Publishing Co, Reston, VA.

DNA Crime Labs: The Paul Coverdell National Forensic Sciences Improvement Act.

DNA Profiling and DNA Fingerprinting, Epplen, Jorg T.

Forensic Medicine, Dr. Tedeschi.

Forensic Science, Dr. H. J. Wall.

Forensic Science: An Introduction to Criminalistics, De Froest, P., McGraw Hill Press.

Finckenaeur, James O., Chinese Transnational Organized Crime: The Fuk Ching.

Harrison's Principles of Internal Medicine. A medical reference book.

HKSAR, Deputy Secretary for Security 1: Miss S.H. Cheung.

HKSAR, Permanent Head of Security: Mr. S. Yong, JP.

HKSAR, Secretary of Security: Mr. A. Lee, IDSM, JP, Head of Security Bureau.

HKSAR, Deputy Secretary of Security 2: Mrs. J. Clok, JP.

Hong Kong Police Force. Wikipedia, redirected from the Hong Kong Police.

LexisNexis: For-fee search service of legal precedent, court findings, media coverage.

Modern Law Enforcement and Police Science, Williams, E.W., C.C. Thomas.

NIBIN: National Integrated Ballistics Information Network.

Pharmacological Basis for Therapeutics. Goodman & Gilman. Pharmacology Text. *Practical Homicide Investigation: Tactics, Procedures, and Forensics*, Geberth, V.J.

Rapid Start: The Case Management Tool, Jefferson County Sheriffs Office.

The former FBI Agents Association.

The FBI Law Enforcement Bulletin.

The Use of Statistics in Forensic Science, Stoney, D.A., Ellis Horwood, Chichester, U.K.

U.S. CIA Factbook—China. U.S. Central Intelligence Agency.

U.S. CIA Factbook—Hong Kong. U.S. Central Intelligence Agency.

BACKGROUNDER:
HISTORY—HONG KONG POLICE FORCE

Source: Wikipedia-Redirected from the Hong Kong Police.

Overview

*T*he Hong Kong police force has distinguished itself as one of the oldest yet most modern police forces in the world. Formed in 1842 with a total strength of 35, the force evolved from an extremely broad-based role (with responsibilities that included firefighting, prisons, and immigration) to that of a traditional police service, with only law enforcement responsibilities.

As of 31 December 2006, the Force had a manpower strength of 30,551; 86.9 percent of officers being men and 13.1 percent, women. The HKP also has a civilian staff of 5,540 members.

The Hong Kong Auxiliary Police Force was originally formed in 1914 as a reserve to assist in times of natural disaster or civil emergency. As of 31 December 2006, 4,324 volunteer citizens supported the regular force in performing crowd control duties at public events and festivals. The responsibility for providing assistance during times of emergency often is assigned to the volunteers.

Police in Hong Kong operate within the traditional constabulary concept of preserving life and property, preventing and detecting crime, and keeping the peace with a strong emphasis on enlisting community support. In times of emergency, the force has paramilitary capability.

Structure

A Commissioner of Police, Mr. Lee Ming Kwai, commands the Hong Kong Police Force. Reporting to the commissioner are two deputy commissioners, Mr. Tang King Shing and Mr. Fung Siu Yuen. One deputy Commissioner supervises all operational matters. The other is responsible for the direction and coordination of the management of the Force, including personnel, training and management services.

The Force is broken down into seven regional commands that are responsible for twenty-six districts and six railroad lines/trams. The Regional Commands report to a Director of Operations (SACP), and the Districts to a District Commander (DC).

Ranks in order of importance are:

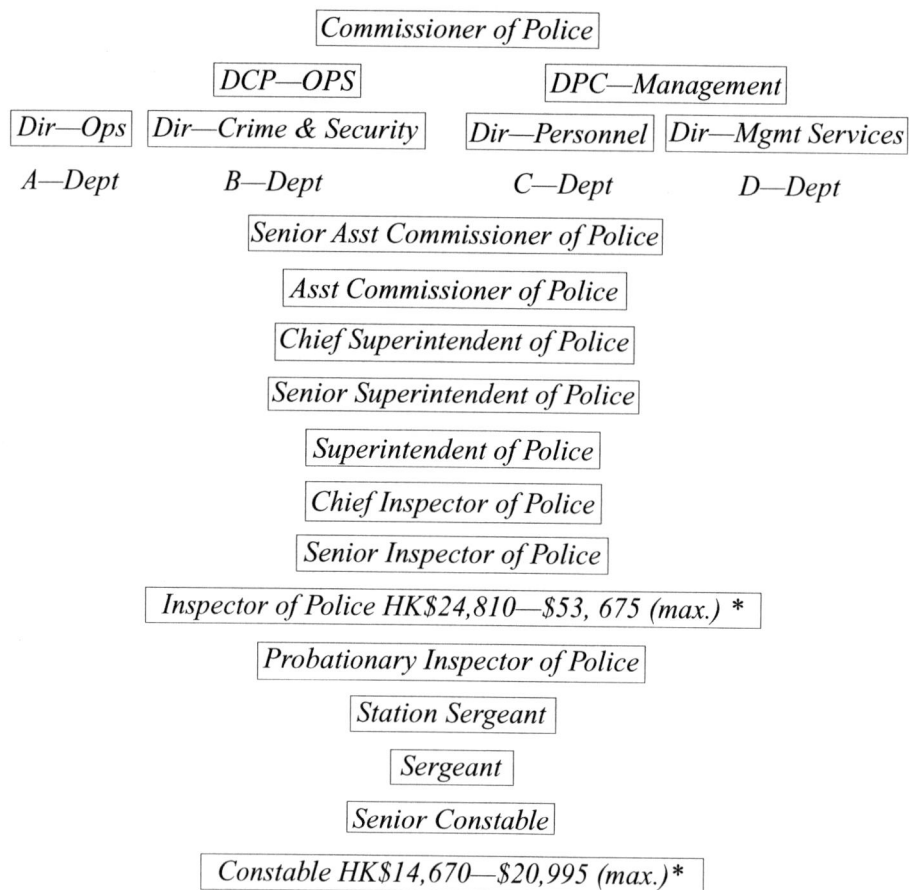

BACKGROUNDER:
OVERVIEW—TRIADS

———

FAC: What are triads?

*T*riads are the Asian equivalent of the Italian Mafia; however, they are greater in numbers and are more powerful, controlling much of the world heroin trade.

FAC: What is their history?

Before turning to criminal enterprises, the triads actually began as a resistance movement to the Manchu emperors. The Manchu were from a country north of China (Manchuria) and were seen as foreign rulers who ruled China's northern capital (Pēking) by force, and established their dynasty in 1674.

In the thirteenth year of the second Manchu emperor (King His), a monastery of fighting monks (Siu Lam) was recruited by the emperor to defeat a rebellion in Fukien. This monastery received some imperial power as a reward. Due to court jealousies, the Fukien Buddhist monks were then themselves seen as a threat, and an army was sent to suppress them.

Eighteen monks escaped, five of them each founded their own secret society dedicated to overthrowing the Manchu (also known as the Ching) Dynasty, and restoring the previous Chinese Ming Dynasty, which was seen as a golden age for China. Their motto became "Crush the Ch'ing, establish the Ming."

The family name of the Ming emperors was "Hung" and their color was red, so both Hung and Red are associated with Chinese secret societies. The societies call themselves the "Hung Mun." Secret codes were developed to frustrate the emperor's spies.

However, this secrecy and subsequent martial arts training eventually led to the associations being used for criminal purposes instead of political ones. During this period many Hung Mun were seen as protectors of the people against a repressive and sometimes vicious regime of the emperor.

The secret societies played roles in several rebellions against the Manchu's. Notably the White Lotus Society rebellion in Szechuan, Hupeh and Shansi in the mid-1790's; the "Cudgels" uprising in Kwangsi province, 1847 to 1850; and Hung Hsiu Chuans's Kwangsi-based rebellion 1981-1865. Hung called himself Christ's brother, and the rebellion (called T'ai Ping) was crushed with the aid of the Western Powers.

The Boxer rebellion in Peking in 1896-1900 involved the White Lotus Society, as well as other triads called the "Big Swords" and the "Red fists."

Sun Yat Sen, the founder of republican China, and interestingly enough probably one of China's most famous and well-thought-of statesmen, was allied with the Hsing Chung triad society in his 1906 rebellion. Meanwhile, the Western Powers and Japan virtually raped China, enforcing opium drug sales by war, stealing gold and heritage antiques, and demanding huge compensation for any affront.

The Manchu's (the Ch'ing) were overthrown in 1911, but there were no Mings left to restore. Sun Yat Sen's successor was warlord Yuan Shik Kai who worked with the triads in corruption.

A known killer and criminal member of the Shang Hai Green Gang, Chiang Kai Shek, headed the Nationalist government set up in 1927 in Nanking. The triads took over the government of southern China, and fought the communists, later under Mao Tse Tung, for total control. The Western Powers used this "Green Tang" organized crime group to suppress any labor unrest and to kill communists.

When the Japanese invaded most major Chinese cities in World War Two, the triads offered to work for them instead. In Hong Kong, the triads ran criminal enterprises for the Japanese. The Japanese united the gangs under an association called the "Hing Ah Flourishing Organization." The gangsters were used to police the residents of Hong Kong and to suppress any anti-Japanese activity. The gangs were paid through a Japanese front company, called Lee Yuen Company.

Following World War Two, the target of the West and the Triads became the Communists, once again. Chiang Kai Shek's nationalist government campaigned to increase triad membership. In Southern China this campaign was under Nationalist Army Lieutenant general, Lot Siu Wong, who had his HQ at number 14, Po Wah Road, Canton. This is where the name of the "14K" triad is thought to have originated. It was estimated that in 1947, there were 300,000 triad members in Hong Kong alone.

By 1949, when Mao Tse Tung's communists reemerged as the victors, some triad nationalists relocated to Hong Kong, Macao, Thailand, San Francisco, Vancouver, and Perth Australia. The remnants of Chiang Kai Shek's KMT (Kuomointang) South China army was forced into the Burmese highlands, where they became pivotal to smuggling drugs to the West, via Thailand, under Khun Sa. The communists suppressed triads on the mainland, executing and imprisoning many. Mao's Prime Minister, Chou En Lai, banned cultivation and use of opium in 1950.

In 1956, there was a major riot in Kowloon, which was exploited by triads from Taiwan. Emergency (Detection Orders) Regulations were passed by the colonial government and 10,000 suspected members were arrested. Triads then went into a semi-dormant period.

The Cultural Revolution in Mainland China, which began in 1954 and resulted in the deaths of fifty million Chinese, was one of several factors, which caused massive emigration and social problems, including resurgence of triad criminal activity, much of it centering around Hong Kong, but extending to several continents.

Today, the 14-K triad is the most powerful criminal syndicate in the world, controlling much of the world's drug trade, and having branches in every major city. With the return of Hong Kong to Mainland China, more and more triads flee Hong Kong every year, seeking their fortune in such profitable areas such as the U.S., Canada and Western Europe.

Source: The Author, Angry Dragon.

BACKGROUNDER:
OVERVIEW—TONGS AND TONG WARS

FAC: What are Tongs and how did Tongs get set up in the U.S.?

*W*ith *the first wave of Chinese immigrants that came to America in the 1800's, many Chinatowns sprung up along the U.S. west and east coasts, and in various mining towns throughout the west. These Chinatowns acted as Chinese communities with everything from barbershops to restaurants.*

Eventually, these Chinatowns developed various Merchant Associations, which acted as local "political parties" for the community, hosting various cultural/social town events for the community. However, with the establishment of the Chinese Exclusion Act, many of these "benevolent" merchant associations soon began to focus their attention on providing vices to the Chinese population including gambling, prostitution, and opium.

With Washington's issuance of the Chinese exclusion Act, the Chinese miners were prohibited from bringing over their wives. This effectively created a "bachelor" society within the Chinese American community with many Chinese turning to the vices the Merchant Associations (Tongs) provided.

Eventually the Merchant Associations soon began to rival each other for control of the vices. The two most powerful merchant associations were the Hip Sing Tong and the On Leong Tong.

As expected, this ultimately led to the Merchant Associations going to all out war with each other, known in history as the Tong wars. Fights broke out in almost every major Chinatown across the U.S. from the mid-1800's up through to the 1970's. In fact, it is from the tong wars that various Chinatowns obtained their reputations as being neighborhoods full of violence, opium, and just general hedonism.

Eventually, the competition between the Tongs began to dissipate and the out-and-out wars, ceased. Many of the tongs, however, retained their criminal ways, and even today continue to engage in extortion, murder, gambling, prostitution, smuggling illegal Chinese immigrants into the U.S., and of course, supplying heroin, a.k.a. China White, from the Golden Triangle.

BACKGROUNDER:
OVERVIEW—TONG HIERARCHY

*O*ne *of the structural characteristics that make Chinese organized crime different from other forms is the relationship between some of the street gangs and certain adult organizations. The merchants associations are called Tongs and are often affiliated with Asian street gangs as their muscle.*

For example, in New York, the street gang, Fuk Ching, is affiliated with the Fukien American Association, a merchant association. The Fukien American Association, as with other Tongs and their relationships with gangs, provide the Fuk Ching with a physical place to gather and hang out. They allow the gang to operate on their (the Tong's) territory, thus legitimizing them with the Chinese community. The Tong also provides criminal opportunities (such as protecting gambling operations), as well as supplying money and guns.

*Tong-affiliated gangs, like the Fuk Ching, have an ah kung (Grandfather) or shuk foo (uncle) who is their tong leader. The top gang position is the dai dai lo (big **big** brother). Communications between the tong and the gang occurs principally between these two individuals.*

Below the dai dai lo, in descending order are the dai lo(s) or big brothers, the yee lo/saam lo (clique leaders), and on the bottom rung, the mai jai or little horses. This evolved as a name for the tong-aligned criminal gang's foot soldiers that originally had been called boohowdoy. Which is Cantonese for hatchet boy because they preferred a hatchet or cleaver as their weapon of choice.

There are a variety of norms and rules that govern the gangs. These include respecting the ah kung, beating up members of other gangs discovered on your gang's turf, following orders of the dai lo and not betraying the gang. Violators are punished, often severely, through physical assault or being killed.

BACKGROUNDER:
OVERVIEW—BASIC FORENSIC SCIENCE

*T*he *first real-life forensic scientist was Mr. Hans Gross in 1893.*

The first documented history of forensic science being used to solve crimes was in 1923 by an LAPD employee, a Mr. August Volmer.

Before Forensic science could develop into what it is today, science in general had to reach a certain level of maturity, and acceptance by the general public.

The basic cannon behind modern forensic science investigation is called the Locard's Exchange principle. "Every contact you make with another person, place or object, results in an exchange of physical materials."

Forensic sciences involved in the practices of solving crimes, or the ruling out of suspects, today, include:

A. *Pathology: Study of disease of the body.*
B. *Toxicology: Study of drugs and poisons.*
C. *Serology: Study of Blood.*

Factors that have advanced forensic science include:

A. *Invention of the microscope.*
B. *Development and refining of photography.*
C. *Understanding of ballistic trajectories.*
D. *Discovery of blood typing and DNA Analysis.*

Initial three steps required before establishing a Forensic Science Crime lab:

   A. *Establish and equip a trained evidence collection unit.*
   B. *Establish and equip a trained photography unit.*
   C. *Establish an absolute-chain-of-evidence control by designating a restricted access evidence storage facility.*

Typical procedures conducted in a Crime Lab:

   A. *Fingerprint analysis.*
   B. *Toolmark and impression analysis.*
   C. *Blood analysis.*
   D. *DNA analysis.*
   E. *Trace evidence evaluation.*
   F. *Ballistic evaluation.*

Typical Job titles:
   A. *Criminalists: Deals with physical evidence.*
      1. *Crime Scene Investigator.*
      2. *Latent Print Examiner.*
      3. *Firearms Examiner.*
      4. *Tool-mark Examiner.*
      5. *Document Examiner.*
      6. *Trace Evidence Examiner.*

   B. *Forensic Investigator: Legally owns the body. Determines cause of death.*
      1. *Pathologist: MD with specialty training in Pathology.*
      2. *Anthropologist: Studies remains to determine cause and time of death.*
      3. *Odentologist: Matches dental patterns.*
      4. *Entomogist: Study of insects to determine time of death.*
      5. *Forensic Psychiatrist: Conducts psychological autopsies.*
      6. *Serologist: Determine the presence or absence of antigens in blood, semen and salvia.*
      7. *Toxicologist: Determine what drugs and poisons are present.*
      8. *Botanist: Examines plant residues found on bodies or suspects.*

Typical Criminalist turnout kit:
  A. *Crime-scene tape to demarcate and secure the scene.*
  B. *Camera and film to photograph the scene and evidence.*
  C. *Sketchpad and pens for scene sketches.*
  D. *Disposable protective clothing, masks, and gloves.*
  E. *Flashlight.*
  F. *Alternative light sources such as laser, ultraviolet, and infrared lighting for exposing certain types of evidence.*
  G. *Magnifying glass for finding trace evidence.*
  H. *Tweezers and cotton cavity swabs for collecting hair, fiber, and fluid evidence.*
  I. *Plastic and paper evidence bags and glass tubes to collect and transport evidence.*
  J. *Fingerprint supplies, which include ink, print cards, lifting tape, and various dusting powders and exposing reagents like Luminol/Fluorescein.*
  K. *Casting kit for making casts of tires, footwear, and tool-mark impressions.*
  L. *Serology kit for collecting blood and other body fluids.*
  M. *Entomology kit for collecting and preserving insect evidence.*
  N. *Hazmat kit for handling hazardous materials.*
  O. *Sexual assault kit for collecting evidence in rape or assault cases.*

Essential equipment in Crime lab:
  A. *Standard laboratory-grade microscopes.*
  B. *Comparison microscope.*
  C. *Microspectrophotometry (for identifying color variations).*
  D. *Polarized light microscope and Ultraviolet Spectroscope.*
  E. *Scanning electron microscope (SEM).*
  F. *Stereomicroscope.*
  G. *Vapor Trace Analyzer.*
  H. *Gas chromatograph-mass spectrometer (GC-MS).*
  I. *Thin-layer chromatograph.*

ABOUT THE AUTHOR

---

*G*eorge H. Stollwerck is the author of seven acclaimed police procedural thrillers, and seven boots-on-the-ground travelogues on modern Asia. He is a commercially rated aircraft and helicopter pilot and recently retired from a career with a major international airline. His career has also included aircraft engineering, public school administration, administrative law enforcement, and coordination of his airline's operating plans in the L.A. Basin during the 1984 Summer Olympics.

During his career the author has traveled extensively throughout Asia, specifically Hong Kong, the People's Republic of China, Thailand, Singapore, Korea, Malaysia, and other international destinations.

Mr. Stollwerck spends his time between residences in Washington State and Lake Havasu City on the Colorado River, and currently is working on his eighth novel.

Should you have questions or comments please feel free to direct them to the author at ghstoll@rraz.net. No attachments, requests for endorsements or story ideas, please. Your email will be responded to as time permits.

Thank you for your continued interest in my writing.

George H. Stollwerck